I have spread my dreams under your feet;
Tread softly because you tread on my dreams.

WILLIAM BUTLER YEATS

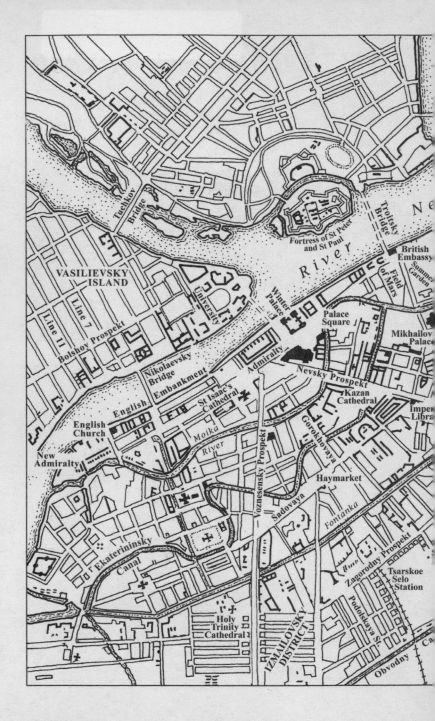

# Andrew Williams

After studying English at Oxford University, Andrew Williams worked as a senior producer for the BBC's *Panorama* and *Newsnight* programmes, then wrote and directed history documentaries. He is the author of two bestselling non-fiction books: *The Battle of the Atlantic* and *D-Day to Berlin*. His acclaimed first novel, *The Interrogator*, is also published by John Murray.

## Praise for *To Kill a Tsar*

'A dense, meaty affair which pulls off the trick of gripping the reader and bringing a complicated, alien world to life' *Guardian*

'An appealing blend of *Doctor Zhivago*, Conrad's *Under Western Eyes* and Boris Akunin's 19th-century crime fiction. His ability to bring a past world to life matches Furst's' *Sunday Times*

'Elegantly serpentine plotting and finely etched characters confirm Williams's place in the front rank of the new English thriller writers' *Daily Mail*

'Bravura story-telling . . . Andrew Williams is the real thing: a writer who can marry popular genres to the sophisticated treatments of political arguments' *Independent*

'A very accomplished novel which can be enjoyed as a gripping and moving thriller. Yet it is more than that, for it invites us to reflect on questions of morality, and on that age-old question of when, if ever, violent means may be held to justify worthy ends; whether, indeed, such ends can ever be achieved if the means are inescapably criminal' *Scotsman*

# TO KILL A TSAR

**ANDREW WILLIAMS**

JOHN MURRAY

First published in Great Britain in 2010 by John Murray (Publishers)
An Hachette UK Company

First published in paperback in 2011

2

© Andrew Williams 2010

Map drawn by Martin Collins

A CIP catalogue record for this title is
available from the British Library

ISBN 978-0-7195-2411-0
Ebook ISBN 978-1-84854-346-1

Typeset in New Caledonia by Palimpsest Book Production Limited,
Falkirk, Stirlingshire

Printed and bound by Clays Ltd, St Ives plc

John Murray policy is to use papers that are natural, renewable and
recyclable products and made from wood grown in sustainable forests.
The logging and manufacturing processes are expected to conform to the
environmental regulations of the country of origin.

John Murray (Publishers)
338 Euston Road
London NW1 3BH

www.johnmurray.co.uk

For Lachlan and Finn

# ST PETERSBURG, c. 1880

Alexander Bridge

Shpalernaya Street

House of Preliminary Detention

Liteiny Prospekt

Tavrichesky Garden

Smolny Cathedral

Smolny Institute for Noble Young Ladies

Slonovaya Street

Nikolaevsky Hospital

PESKI DISTRICT

Malaya Italyanskaya

Anichkov Bridge

...nka Lane

Nikolaevsky Station

Church of Our Lady of Vladimir

Church of St Boris and St Gleb

Nevsky Prospekt

Alexander Nevsky Monastery

...ky ...round

N

0    1    2

miles

# 1879

... [the] requirements of the constitution consisted: first, in the promise to devote all one's mental and spiritual strength to revolutionary work, to forget for its sake all ties of kinship, and all personal sympathies, love and friendships: second, to give one's life if necessary, taking no thought of anything else, and sparing no one and nothing ... these demands were great, but they were easily fulfilled by one fired with the revolutionary spirit, with that intense emotion which knows neither obstacles nor impediments, but goes forward, looking neither backward nor to the right nor to the left ...

**Vera Figner on the constitution she upheld as a member of the executive committee of The People's Will**

# 1

I ce is scraped from the carriageway in readiness, but it is still treacherous and the tsar must tread with care.

At eight o'clock the guard at the commandant's entrance to the Winter Palace came smartly to attention and the doors swung open for the Emperor and Autocrat of All the Russias. A tall man with the bearing of a soldier, Alexander II was in his sixtieth year, handsome still, with thick mutton chop whiskers and an extravagant moustache shot with grey, a high forehead and large soft brown eyes that lent his face an air of vulnerability. His appearance was greeted by a murmur of excitement from the small crowd of the curious and the devout waiting in the square. On this iron grey St Petersburg morning, the islands on the opposite bank of the Neva were almost lost in a low April mist, and tiny drops of rain beaded the tsar's fur-lined military coat and white peaked cap. As was his custom, he walked alone but for the captain of his personal guard who followed at several paces. Head bent a little, his hands clasped behind his back, a brisk ten minutes to clear his thoughts before the meetings with ministers and ambassadors that would fill the day.

From the north-east corner of the square he made his way into Millionnaya Street and on past the giant grey granite Atlantes supporting the entrance to the New Hermitage Gallery his father had built for the royal collection. Then to the Winter Canal and the frozen Moika River, its banks lined with the

3

yellow and pink and green baroque palaces of the aristocracy. A carriage rattled along the badly rutted road, sloshing dirty melt water across the pavement and the tsar's cavalry boots. At the Pevchesky Bridge, he turned and the square lay open before him again, the stone heart of imperial Russia: to his right the Winter Palace, and to his left the vast yellow and white crescent-shaped building occupied by the General Staff of his army. A score or more of his people stood at the corner of this building, stamping their feet, blowing vapour into balled hands, waiting for a glimpse of their 'Little Father'. From this group, a tall young man in a long black uniform coat and cap with cockade stepped forward and walked towards the tsar. His features were half hidden by the upturned collar of his coat and a thick moustache. He stopped beneath one of the new electric street lamps at the edge of the square and, as the tsar approached along the pavement, gave a stiff salute. Something in his demeanour, in his wide unblinking eyes, caught and held the tsar's gaze and brought to his mind a childhood memory of a bear he had seen cornered by hunting dogs. He walked past but after a few steps this uneasy thought made him turn to look again.

In the young man's hand was a revolver. Struggling to balance it. Struggling to aim. Barely more than an arm's length away. A flash. Crack. Flakes of yellow plaster splintered from the wall on to his shoulder. Crouching, spinning, the tsar began to run, weaving like a hare, to the left then to the right, and as he did so time wound down until it was without meaning. Shouts and screams reached him as a muffled echo at the end of a long tunnel. He could hear distinctly only the pounding of his heart and again the sharp crack, crack of the revolver. It was as if there were only the two of them in the square: Alexander, the Emperor of Russia, stumbling towards his palace, and a young man with a gun in his trembling hand. He was conscious of the short shaky breaths of the assassin and the scuffing of his boots

4

on the setts behind him. Crack. A shot passed through his flapping greatcoat and he swerved to the left again. On and on the madman came with his arm outstretched. Another crack, and a bullet struck the ground a few feet in front of him. Was this an end to joy, an end to love? Breathless with fear, lost in this tunnel. For what purpose? Who could hate him so much?

Then someone was at his side, a hand to his elbow, and time seemed to turn again.

'Your Majesty—'

Shaking like a leaf in an autumn gale.

'I . . . I am all right.'

It was just a few seconds. That was all. Slowly, the tsar turned to look over his shoulder. His pursuer was on the ground, curled into a tight ball, kicked and punched by the police. The revolver lay close by. Something obscene. Cossack guards were running from the palace and a calèche was drawing to a halt a few yards from him. An old woman, tightly wrapped in black rags, had fallen to her knees and was rocking a prayer of thanks. She clutched at his coat as he brushed past.

'Thank God! Thank God!' And she crossed herself again and again.

As he stepped into the carriage there were angry shouts. The tsar turned to see the assassin dragged senseless to his feet. He did not notice the young woman with dark brown hair who was walking away from the gathering crowd. No one paid her any attention. She walked with a straight back and a short purposeful stride. Her clothes were faded and a little old-fashioned but she wore them well. At the edge of the square she stopped for just a moment to pull an olive green woollen shawl over her head and across her nose and mouth. Her face was hidden but for her eyes, and they were pale grey-blue like the sky on a summer afternoon or the colour of water through clean ice.

At the end of the Nevsky Prospekt she took a cab. Her driver

5

guided his horse with great care, for the city's main thorough-fare was bustling with trams and carriages, merchants to the Gostiny Dvor trading arcade, uniformed civil servants to their ministries. The droshky came to a halt just before the Anichkov Bridge. The young woman paid the driver with a five kopek coin, then walked across the bridge towards the pink and white palace on the opposite bank of the Fontanka River. At the first turning to the right beyond it she paused to look back along Nevsky, then, lifting her skirt a little to lengthen her stride, she hurried into the lane. Sacks of wood were being unloaded from a wagon, and she passed an old man pulling a barrel organ, its mechanism tinkling in protest. A small boy in a red shirt was playing on a step with a kitten and a yard keeper scraped hard ridges of ice from the pavement in front of his building. Before a handsome blue and white mansion, she glanced up and down the lane then stepped forward to ring the door bell.

The dvornik, who was paid to fetch and carry for the building, showed her up to an apartment on the second floor. The door was opened by a short, plump man in his late twenties, well groomed in a sober suit and tie. He had a round fleshy face, a neat beard and black hair swept back from a high forehead.

The dvornik gave a little bow: 'A lady to see you, Alexander Dmitrievich. She won't give her name.'

Alexander Dmitrievich Mikhailov must have recognised his visitor, though he could see only her eyes, because he stepped aside at once to let her into the apartment. Three more young men were sitting at a table in front of the drawing-room window. She collapsed onto a chair beside them.

'The tsar lives.' She paused to let her words resonate, then said, 'He fired five times but by some miracle . . .'

'Five times.'

'. . . and they have taken him. He's alive and they have taken him.' Her voice cracked a little with emotion.

Then a flurry of questions. Quietly, calmly she told them of what she had seen, of the tsar stumbling towards his palace, of shots fired at almost point blank range.

'Will he speak to the police?'

'He will say nothing.'

For almost an hour they talked of what happened in the square. What filthy luck. Was it the gun or simply fear that caused him to miss? Only when they had examined every detail did Alexander Mikhailov remember to offer her some refreshment. Mikhailov served tea from the brass samovar bubbling in the corner of the room. Fine Indian tea. He made it in a silver teapot and poured it into glasses delicately decorated with gold leaf. Settling back at the table, he was reaching for his own when there was a hammering at the door.

'The police!' he hissed at her. 'You were followed!'

Jumping to his feet, he reached into the drawer of the desk behind him and took out a revolver. His comrades were too shocked to move.

Then from the stair they heard the voice of the dvornik: 'News, Your Honour! News!'

He was wheezing on the step, his little eyes bright with excitement, clutching at his straggly beard.

'Murder! They tried to murder His Majesty. This morning in the square. A madman. There are soldiers everywhere.'

When the door had closed Mikhailov turned to her. 'Go. Go now.'

Gendarmes were stopping the horse-drawn trams in the Zagorodny Prospekt and emptying their passengers on to the pavements. A security barrier had been placed at the edge of the Semenovsky Parade Ground and she joined the crush of people edging slowly towards it. Red-coated Cossacks trotted down the prospekt from the direction of the station, their swords at the ready. There was an air of collective hysteria as if the city was preparing to repel a foreign army. She could see it in the faces of the people about her, the peasant clutching the ragged bundle of food he was hoping to sell in the Haymarket, a priest in a long black robe muttering a prayer, the old lady with frightened children at her skirts.

Opposite the railway station, the bells of the new cathedral were chiming frantically as if to summon divine retribution. At the barrier, a harassed-looking lieutenant in the green and gold of the Semenovsky Regiment was inspecting papers.

'And why aren't you in your classroom this morning, Miss Kovalenko?'

'I was visiting a sick friend in the city.'

The young lieutenant examined her face carefully then smiled, captivated for a moment perhaps by her eyes: 'All right, let Anna Petrovna pass.'

And slipping through the barrier and past the soldiers on the pavement, she hurried into the ticket hall of the station.


In the House of Preliminary Detention across the city, the would-be assassin was stretched full length on a prison pallet, eyes closed, his breathing a little laboured, a rough grey blanket pulled to the chin. There was an angry graze on his left cheek and some bruising about his eyes but nothing that could account for the pain that was drawing his lips tightly from his teeth in an ugly grimace. A prison guard stood against the bare brick wall close by, and, at the door, two men in the dark green double-breasted uniform jackets and white trousers of the Ministry of Justice. On the left breast of the shorter man the twinkling gold star of the Order of St Vladimir and at his neck its red enamel cross.

'He says he's a socialist revolutionary and an atheist.' The city prosecutor's voice was thick with contempt. 'A proud enemy of the government and the emperor.'

In his twelve years at the ministry Count Vyacheslav von

Plehve had acquired a reputation as the state's most brilliant and ruthless young lawyer.

'His name is Alexander Soloviev,' he continued. 'And this will amuse you, Dobrshinsky: he was a law student. Yes – a law student.'

The count's companion was of lower rank, a Class 6 civil servant, his name familiar to only a few, but those who knew of Anton Frankzevich Dobrshinsky's work as a criminal investigator spoke of him with respect – if not with warmth.

'Will he cooperate?'

'As you can see, he's not in a fit state to be questioned properly.' Von Plehve turned away from the prisoner to beat on the door with a chubby fist: 'All right.'

It swung open at once and both men stepped out on to the first floor of the wing. The prison was built on the new American model, with cells opening on to a concertina of wrought-iron landings and steps about a central five-storey hall. A vast whitewashed, echoing place that in the four years since it had opened had held political prisoners from every corner of the empire.

The count took Dobrshinsky by the elbow and began to steer him gently along the wing. 'He tried to kill himself. Cyanide. They managed to remove the phial. He's sick but he'll live. His Majesty has let it be known he's going to ride through the city in an open carriage to show himself to his people. He's convinced God has saved him . . .' He stopped for a moment and put his hand on Dobrshinsky's arm, '. . . but this is just the beginning. Believe me. Soloviev was not alone.'

Dobrshinsky nodded slowly. He was a tall man in his early thirties, thin with a pinched face and sallow skin, small dark brown eyes and an unfashionably modest moustache. There was something watchful, a little vulpine in his manner.

'. . . it's already been agreed.' Von Plehve turned to make eye contact. 'You will take charge of the investigation. It's simple enough to state: find who's behind this.'

Dobrshinsky frowned and pursed his lips.

'Of course,' said the count, 'I know what you're thinking. Yes, it's like fighting a Hydra. But there will be new security measures.'

'As Your Worship wishes.'

'My dear fellow, it's not my wish. It's the wish of the emperor's council.'

The barred gate at the end of the wing swung open and the guards stepped aside to let them pass. The count's carriage was waiting at the bottom of the prison steps. In the far distance, the sun's rays were breaking through cloud, bathing the blue and white baroque facade and domes of the Smolny Cathedral in a rich golden light.

'Perhaps the Almighty did come to the aid of His Majesty,' said the count as he settled on the seat of the open carriage. 'But will he next time?' He paused then leant forward earnestly, his left hand gripping the door: 'Who are these terrorists, Dobrshinsky? Who are they? What kind of fanatic tries to murder his emperor then kill himself?'

A snap of the driver's whip, and his carriage pulled away from the pavement. Dobrshinsky watched it turn right in front of the munitions factory on to the Liteiny Prospekt and disappear from view. What kind of fanatic? He felt sure he knew: a new kind who would stop at nothing, a terrorist who was prepared to take his own life and the innocent lives of others. The count was right: Soloviev was not alone. Somewhere in this city of almost a million souls there were others intent on murder in the name of freedom and progress. In time they would be hunted down, but how much time did he have?

# 2

It was only a short cab ride from Dr Frederick Hadfield's apartment to his uncle's house, and an even shorter journey by boat, but neither could be hired for love nor money. The morning after the attempt on the tsar's life the city was paralysed by police patrols. From the end of the street he could see the gendarmes stopping traffic on the bridges across the Neva. He had been woken by shouted orders and the clatter of their boots and weapons in the street. The city's university and many of its best academies were a short distance from his home and, as every Class 14 clerk in the police department knew, places of learning were full of dangerous radicals. Students and intellectuals and foreigners had lived in Vasilievsky Island's numbered streets or lines since the days of Peter the Great. Hadfield considered himself to be fortunate to have joined them at a reasonable rent in one of the smarter lines at the eastern end of the island. Line 7 was bohemian but not enough to frighten his wealthier patients or excite the opprobrium of his family.

His uncle's large town house was on the south bank of the Neva, almost directly opposite the end of his line. It had been home to four generations of the Glen family; Hadfield's mother was born in a bedroom on the second floor. Older and less fashionable than the houses at the other end of the English Embankment, it was still one of the most desirable addresses in the city. Anglo-Russians had lived on the embankment for more than a hundred and fifty years. The Cazalets were at Number 6, Clarke the grain merchant at 38, the Warres at 44, and the physician to three tsars, Sir James Wylie, had once lived at Number 74, his old blue and white mansion one of the most prominent on the river. Hadfield claimed Wylie as family on his father's side, and his mother's people were still pillars of this little community. There were two types of Englishmen in St Petersburg: the old families who spoke the language and lived and worked among the Russians all their lives, and the new families who mixed only with their own kind. Embankment families belonged to the former.

On the Nikolaevsky Bridge, Hadfield managed to hail a droshky, only for it to be stopped by blue-coated gendarmes before it had travelled a hundred yards. The young officer in charge eyed him suspiciously and demanded proof of his identity. Hadfield's Russian was good but he was young, a foreigner and flamboyantly dressed for a city where almost all the best doctors were sober-suited Germans. Beneath his heavy black coat with its fur collar he was wearing a brown tweed suit with a high-buttoned waistcoat and a raffish blue Ascot tie in an extravagant soft bow. He was twenty-seven years old, tall – a little over six feet – with fine, regular features, warm hazel eyes, a neat closely cropped beard and light auburn hair – the gendarme officer would have described it as 'radical' shoulder length – and instead of sweeping it back carefully it flopped across his forehead in an unruly fringe. His younger female patients considered him handsome, the older ladies charming, but it was a charm that was lost on the gendarmes. Hadfield need only have mentioned his uncle's name and he would have been allowed to pass without question, but in the weeks since his return to the city he had been careful not to exploit his connection. It was ten minutes before the officer in charge was satisfied enough with Hadfield's papers to let the cab pass.

At the end of the bridge the driver turned right on to the embankment and a moment later pulled up in front of the yellow and white building that served discreetly as the English Church. Hadfield paid the driver and walked on a little further.

Five doors down from the church stood Baron Stieglitz's recently refurbished mansion – the grandest at the west end of the embankment – and in its long shadow, Number 70 – General Glen's home.

A footman in an old-fashioned uniform coat answered the door. Alexei Petrov had served the general in the army and then the family for more than thirty years.

'Your Honour.' He bowed his grey head respectfully.

'Are you well, Alexei?'

'Yes, Your Honour. And your mother, is she well?'

'Yes. Thank you. Quite well.'

The old man led Hadfield up the white marble stair with its fine wrought iron filigreed banister to the first floor and knocked politely on the polished mahogany doors. They opened at once, throwing the startled servant off balance.

'Frederick!'

Alexandra Glen ran forward to kiss her cousin on the cheek: 'Why are you so late? Father was very grumpy.' She pouted at him flirtatiously.

'I'm sorry. I had to walk.' He smiled at her.

'You should have walked a little quicker.'

She took him by the hand and led him into the drawing room. His Aunt Mary was sitting ramrod straight on a plum velvet sofa beneath a picture of the Holy Family, severe in a black woollen dress, her grey hair gathered tightly in a bun. She greeted him with a warm smile and stretched her hands out to him. He held them for a moment and bent to kiss her cheeks.

'How lovely to see you, Frederick,' she said in Russian. 'And you look so well. I'm afraid you've missed your uncle. He was called to his ministry. This terrible business . . .'

'Has something . . .'

'Frederick! Are you the only man in the empire who hasn't heard of the attempt on the life of His Majesty?'

13

'I was almost arrested for the crime a few minutes ago, Aunt.'

Alexandra laughed and pushed his arm playfully: 'I told you, Mother, Frederick is a dangerous revolutionary. He was a student in Switzerland – Father says that's where all the worst ones live. There – I've found you out, Freddie!'

'Really, darling, that isn't funny,' said his aunt. 'Frederick?' She inclined her head to indicate he should sit beside her.

Mary Glen was in her early fifties, small and plain with a long oval face and thin lips unkindly scored by age. On first impression it would have been easy to take her for a dour Scottish minister's wife but she was a bright, good humoured woman with an infectious laugh and a Presbyterian contempt for airs and graces. General Glen had met and married her on a visit to Fife thirty years before and he had chosen wisely. From the first she had thrown herself into her husband's life, spoke faultless Russian and to the family made a point of speaking nothing else. Her daughter Alexandra was an only child, eighteen now and as petite and pretty as her mother was plain, with the fine features of the Glen family, green eyes and auburn hair. Hadfield was very fond of both of them, the more so because his warmth was so openly reciprocated.

'Your uncle says there are to be new security measures. Military governors, something close to martial law.' Mary Glen shook her head. 'We're all going to be inconvenienced because one or two madmen want to kill the emperor. What on earth are they hoping to achieve?'

Hadfield frowned and dropped his head a little in a polite show of incomprehension.

'But tell us of your visit to the south,' she continued after a moment. 'We were so frightened something would happen to you.'

'As you see,' he said, stretching his arms wide, 'I'm in rude health.'

Hadfield had returned to Russia only a few months before

and on an impulse answered a national call for doctors to prevent the spread of an old contagion. No one in the capital believed the reports from Astrakhan at first. Was it possible that such a thing could happen in a time of progress? But Hadfield had seen it with his own eyes. Hundreds of men, women and children dying of plague, and more had been driven from their villages by the army in a desperate effort to prevent the spread of the disease. There in his uncle's drawing room, beneath a glittering chandelier, the walls papered in red silk damask, the furniture rich velvet, he spoke of what he had seen, of fires at dusk, smoke spiralling in thin columns against an indigo sky as homes and barns were put to the torch.

'And now there is talk of famine in the south. It is quite medieval.'

Mary Glen leant forward to touch his hand sympathetically.

'Oh, Freddie, it's awful.' Alexandra's voice shook a little with emotion. 'And they say a man has died of plague in Petersburg. Could it really happen here?'

'Of course not, dear,' said her mother briskly, 'we live in a modern city.'

Then there was talk of Hadfield's mother in London. Perhaps she could be persuaded to visit her old home? Sarah Somerville had left St Petersburg eighteen years ago with a new husband and her son and never returned. Frederick had been eleven when his father died of consumption and twelve when his mother married again. His stepfather was an engineer and entrepreneur, successfully exploiting the new fashion for electric lighting in public buildings and country houses. James Somerville was too wrapped up in his work to take any interest in his stepson and, after the first years of their marriage, he showed precious little more in his wife. Frederick's mother had channelled her loneliness and frustration into her son's upbringing. They spoke only Russian to each other, and during the long vacations at Cambridge he had visited his uncle, and twice more as a student at the University of Zurich. There had never been any question of him doing anything but follow his father into the medical profession, and his mother was delighted when, after two unhappy years in London, he had announced he was returning to the city of his birth. Hadfield was still finding his feet, but thanks in no small part to his uncle's patronage he had been offered a good post at the Nikolaevsky Hospital.

'You will come to dinner? Your uncle must hear of your work in Astrakhan.'

'Yes. Thank you.' He could hardly refuse.

'You should tell him everything. He may be able to help in some way.'

Hadfield was touched by his aunt's concern, but sceptical nonetheless. The general would listen to an account of the hardship his nephew witnessed with a polite show of concern. It would then be followed by a hectoring defence of the government of which he was a member. Hadfield had learnt to avoid conversation that might loosely be described as 'political' in his uncle's house.

Hadfield spent the afternoon on the wards at the Nikolaevsky, then at five he took a droshky back to his apartment to change. Frock coat, top hat, patent leather shoes and his father's silk waistcoat, for his uncle would expect nothing less formal even when only the family was to dine.

It was a cheerless dining room in dark stained oak, and on either side of the large carved mantel hung very ordinary Belgian tapestries of a nobleman and his entourage hunting with dogs. Two new gas chandeliers in the Russian style were shedding indiscriminate pools of dirty yellow light, the dining table caught in the gloom between. Heavy baronial chairs of oak and red Moroccan leather with a shield and crest carefully painted on the scroll at the top were set around the walls. General Charles Glen was the first in his family who had felt the need

16

to bear arms. He was sitting now at the head of the table, his large hands gripping the chair as if squeezing life from a serpent: 'Can you imagine a man like that responsible for shaping the minds of the young?' he snorted in disbelief. 'Can you?'

'Can I what, General?' asked his wife at the other end of the dining table.

'Can you imagine this man – Soloviev . . . you know, he was a teacher for a time?'

A footman stepped forward to serve the general a consommé from a brash silver tureen.

'The trial is a formality, of course, the fellow will be hanged.'

Hadfield was sitting on his uncle's right, with his cousin across the table from him. Behind her and between the windows opposite there was a full length martial portrait of the first General Glen, who had left Scotland to serve the Empress Catherine. The artist had caught him in middle age, his long red hair and cavalry moustache tinged with grey, his face a little fleshy. His grandson – the third General Glen – was sixty-five and entirely grey, but in all other respects the resemblance was striking: the same dark blue eyes and regular features, the same china white skin and Cupid's bow mouth and the same nakedly belligerent spirit.

'This year there's been an attempt on the life of General Drenteln, the murder of Prince Kropotkin in Kharkov – countless smaller outrages – and it's only April. A clever chap from the Justice Ministry has been given the task of tracking these nihilists down. The time has come to crack down hard. What do you say, Frederick?'

Hadfield dabbed at his lips with his napkin while he tried to frame a diplomatic answer. This was the sort of question he hoped to avoid.

'Please, Father, that is quite enough talk of murder. Your soup is going cold.'

17

Hadfield glanced across at Alexandra and she gave him a knowing smile.

'I've had enough,' said the general with a wave of his hand.

The footmen cleared away the dishes then served a baked pike cooked *à la Russe* with potatoes and sour cream. For a time the conversation was of a general nature with talk of the theatre and the new production of *Roxana* at the Mariinsky. A well known prince had lost a great deal of money at cards; there were rumours of a new electric tram for the city, and Sophie Gordon, the heiress to a small fortune in manufacturing, was to have her dearest wish: she was betrothed to a noble at last, a poor count with an estate near Tula. And the general had visited the new British ambassador and his wife.

'Lord Dufferin is a man of great experience and integrity. Prince Gortchakov and I were with him when he was presented at court. He made a very favourable impression on His Majesty.'

'You know, you must introduce Frederick, my dear,' said his wife.

'Yes, Father, you must!' Alexandra leant forward to touch her father's sleeve. 'The ambassador won't want a German doctor.'

'And Frederick is wonderfully well qualified,' said his aunt, turning to smile at him. 'Cambridge, London, Zurich . . .'

The general picked up his wine glass and contemplated its contents. 'I think Frederick would do well not to mention his time in Zurich.'

He took a sip from the glass, then, placing it carefully back, turned his head to stare at his nephew. Hadfield was at a loss to know what to say. His aunt came to his rescue.

'Not everyone who studies in Switzerland becomes a revolutionary, dear.'

'They all find shelter there,' said her husband hotly. 'Herzen, Bakunin, Kropotkin, and that madman, Nechaev – and now the young woman who tried to murder the governor general of the city – free to come and go as they please.'

'I am sure Frederick didn't move in those circles.'

His aunt's unspoken 'Did you?' hung in the air. For a few seconds there was an embarrassed silence at the table.

'No. No.' Hadfield was conscious he sounded flustered. 'No. I was too busy. Too busy enjoying myself to care about politics.'

The general gave a short conspiratorial laugh then leant forward a little and touched his hand: 'But it's not politics, Frederick. As Prince Metternich said, "Freedom cannot exist without order." These people want to plunge us into anarchy. They want to force a revolution on us. Who do they speak for? Nobody.'

'I haven't been in Russia long enough to say,' Hadfield ventured, 'but I know there are reasonable people who would like to see peaceful change and some form of democracy.'

'Well, I can't understand why so many of them come from very good families,' complained his aunt.

The general smiled patronisingly at his wife then turned back to his nephew: 'Only order and firm government will hold this country together. This is not Great Britain. The emperor and the Church are the only authority the people recognise here. Change, yes, but gradual change.' He leant a little closer and said with hard emphasis, as if throwing down a challenge: 'Take it from me. It's the only way.'

'I am not sure there is time for gradual change, sir.' Hadfield's voice was quiet, his words measured in the hope that a placatory tone would disguise the unbridgeable gap between them. 'The educated read of what is happening in other countries – the freedom of the press, representation of the people – and they want the same basic rights here in Russia. '

At the words 'basic rights' the general stiffened, his breathing became strained and he took on a dangerously high colour. It was perhaps fortunate for the state that he did not have a chance to press his nephew further. At the other end of the table his wife raised her hand.

'I think we've heard quite enough politics,' she said in English, as if to give a sharper edge to the steel in her voice.

There was no further talk of anarchy and the conversation settled into a comfortable drawing-room rut for the rest of the evening. A little before midnight Hadfield was able to excuse himself and retrieve his top hat and cloak from the sleepy Alexei. He stood on the pavement outside, breathing deeply to purge his mind and body of his uncle's stale complacency. It was a clear night but warm for April with a promise of spring and the melting of the ice on the Neva. Across the river the lights were burning in the House of the Academics at the bottom of Line 7. The great Jakobi – a pioneer of electric motors and wire telegraphy – had lived and worked there, the botanist Famintsyn too, and it was still home to many of the university's finest academics, a place where people strove to change the world for the better and celebrated progress in science and medicine – and politics. As he began to walk back along the English Embankment, Hadfield could not help reflecting again that he was fortunate to live on the opposite bank. A good deal more than the width of the river seemed to separate the island from the embankment.

On the Nikolaevsky Bridge he was stopped by the same bored troop of gendarmes and obliged to present his passport again. This time his evening dress, top hat and cloak proved of more value than his papers in distinguishing him as a gentleman to be trusted. The gendarmes clearly believed a desperate revolutionary would never wear such finery.

It was some time before Hadfield could rouse the dvornik who serviced his rooms.

'Did Your Honour forget his keys?' he asked, swaying drunkenly on the doorstep. Hadfield slipped him a few kopeks.

'Thank you, Your Honour. A boy delivered a letter for you

this evening.' He shuffled along the corridor to his room and came back clutching an envelope between grubby fingers.

Hadfield took the envelope and followed the dvornik up the stairs to his first-floor apartment. The small chandelier in the drawing room spluttered and a circle of light began to creep across the polished parquet and Astrakhan rugs. It was a sparsely furnished room – he had not had the time to purchase more – but there were a few fine English pieces from his uncle's home: a bureau, a serpentine-fronted sideboard and a round mahogany dining table with brass feet. A dark oil of his father looking rather humourless hung over the fire, and to the right of the mantel a finer pastel of his mother as a young woman.

'Can I do anything more for Your Honour?'

'No. That's all.'

Hadfield waited until he heard the heavy clunk of the apartment door and then, taking a paper knife from the bureau, he deftly slit the envelope open and took out a single small sheet. Written in a fine hand was the following:

*Fontanka 86 on Sunday 8th April, 3.00 p.m. Come alone. Be careful.*
  *Vera.*

He folded it back into the envelope, opened a drawer and placed it inside. Then, taking a small brass key from his medical bag, he locked the front of the bureau.

So, Vera had returned to Petersburg.

# 3

The twisted mass of the body lay on the rug, head thrown back, mouth wide open. One knee was pulled up to his chest, the other bent awkwardly away, as if frozen in urgent movement. His hands were tied behind his back. The woollen threads of the rug were stained black and matted, and even by the light of the single candle Dobrshinsky could see the gaping wound at his throat.

'Open the drapes,' he said irritably.

One of the gendarmes stepped over to the window and dragged the heavy curtains back. The shabby little hotel room filled with sunlight and the comforting noise of life as it continued to be lived on the Nevsky Prospekt below. The ugly neck wound drew the eyes of all in the room. The throes of the dying man had forced the vicious cut open, peeling skin from his throat, exposing pink muscle and the cartilaginous rings of the windpipe.

'His name is Bronstein. He was working for us,' said the gendarme officer at Dobrshinsky's elbow. Nothing in Major Vladimir Alexandrovich Barclay's voice suggested he felt the slightest remorse or compassion for the dead man.

'An informer?' Dobrshinsky turned to look at Barclay.

'Yes. A Hebrew.' The major wrinkled his face in a show of contempt he expected all in the room to share. 'We caught him agitating at a Moscow factory and he agreed to work for us rather than go to prison. Pity. He was useful.'

'Who found the body?'

'The hotel owner's son.'

Four young men in their twenties – one of them Bronstein – had taken rooms in the Neva at the beginning of the week. Barclay knew from the informer that the leader of the group was a student called Popov, the son of a well-to-do civil servant; the other two were factory workers from Moscow. Bronstein had reported to his contact that Popov was to meet an important socialist to talk about the formation of a new party dedicated to terrorist action.

'But as you see,' said Barclay, 'someone must have discovered he was working for us.'

Dobrshinsky stared at him, an intense appraising gaze that would have cowed many, but Barclay returned it without flinching. A competent officer, a man of careful method, Dobrshinsky thought, just the sort of fellow he could use. The Third Section was supposed to be an elite branch of the police, all-powerful, all-seeing, with special responsibility for suppressing political subversion in the empire. Its head was the Chief of the Corps of Gendarmes and he answered to the emperor in person. But the last incumbent had been stabbed to death in the street on the way to the section's headquarters and his successor, General Drenteln, had only weeks before escaped the same fate by the skin of his teeth. If the section was unable to protect its own chief, Dobrshinsky thought, what hope for emperor and empire?

'All right, shall we look at him, Major?'

There was a startled look on Bronstein's thin white face, as if his death was impossible to imagine, his brown eyes wide, his mouth a little open. His goatee beard was thick with blood, and so were his trousers and peasant shirt.

'There's something attached to his chest,' said Barclay, squatting beside the body. 'A piece of card.'

He reached across to unpin it and was obliged to steady himself by placing a hand on the rug. 'Damn it, I've got the Jew's blood on me.'

He got to his feet and handed the card to Dobrshinsky. 'In case there was any doubt . . .'

Written on the card in capitals was:

*N.V. BRONSTEIN, TRAITOR, SPY, CONDEMNED*
*AND EXECUTED BY RUSSIAN SOCIALIST*
*REVOLUTIONARIES. THOSE WHO FOLLOW*
*BRONSTEIN'S EXAMPLE WILL SHARE HIS FATE.*
*DEATH TO ALL JUDAS BETRAYERS!*

As he gazed into Bronstein's dull eyes Dobrshinsky reflected that it was hard to feel sorry for a dead Judas, even if he was your own. He turned away to examine the room. It was small, just a single bed, three plain wooden chairs, a table covered in a grubby checked cloth and a large unvarnished wardrobe of pine. As Bronstein had thrashed despairingly for air he had speckled the furniture and walls with his blood. But the murderer had severed the windpipe, not the jugular, so there was less than might have been expected. Bronstein had almost certainly drowned in his own blood and he had been dead for at least twenty-four hours. One of the chairs lay on its side at the bottom of the bed and the sticky pool on the boards beside it suggested it was there the murderer had cut his victim's throat.

'Go through his pockets,' said Barclay, nodding to one of the gendarmes at the door, 'and the rest of you – turn this place upside down. Clothes, papers, anything, I want to see it all.'

He led Dobrshinsky into the dingy corridor: 'Do you smoke, Your Honour?'

'No.'

Taking a Sobranie from his cigarette case, Barclay rolled it gently between his fingers, squeezing the packed tobacco down into the black paper. He was a curious-looking man, in his late forties, short and a little overweight, with a ruddy clean-shaven face, heavy but perfectly arched eyebrows and thinning brown hair. He had spent ten years in the Gendarme Corps but still looked uncomfortable in its sky blue uniform, as if by some quirk of fate a man born to manage a bank had been miscast as a military policeman. He would be trustworthy in either capacity, Dobrshinsky thought, thorough and energetic and, when necessary, ruthless.

The bedroom door opened behind them and a gendarme sergeant stepped into the corridor and saluted. 'We found this under the mattress, sir.'

Barclay took the small scrap of paper. Scrawled on it in pencil were six names: *Kviatkovsky, Goldenberg, Presnyakov, Morozov, Mikhailov, Kovalenko.*

'Bronstein,' said Barclay, handing the note to Dobrshinsky, 'I recognise the hand. He must have hidden it.'

'And the names?'

The policeman rubbed his chin thoughtfully with his chubby fingers. 'Goldenberg is wanted for the murder of the governor general of Kharkov – and Presnyakov . . . Presnyakov has been living in exile for the last two years, after he murdered one of our agents.'

'Perhaps Presnyakov is back in the city,' said Dobrshinsky. 'He may be involved in the new party Bronstein spoke of.' He stood gazing at the names for a few more seconds then slipped the paper into his waistcoat pocket. 'You will be hearing from me soon,' he said, and nodding to Barclay he began walking down the hotel corridor in the direction of the staircase. The gendarme officer watched his bent shoulders for a moment and the image of a fox on hind legs flashed through his mind. Like the fox in the old folk tale, he thought, who seemed so mild and inoffensive but stole the fisherman's food and appropriated the warmest corner of his home.

In the bedroom, his men were beginning to prise the

floorboards from the joists. Bronstein's body still lay crumpled on the rug.

From the opposite bank of the Fontanka river it looked like a nobleman's mansion, and even those who passed beneath the delicate wrought iron canopy that hung over the pavement in front of its entrance were hard pressed to detect any clue as to its true purpose. And yet Fontanka 16 was one of the best known and – for all its elegance – least loved buildings in the city. Dobrshinsky had been given a large room on the second floor, with windows overlooking the river. The head of the Third Section of His Majesty's Chancellery and Chief of the Corps of Gendarmes, General Drenteln was on the opposite side of the grand staircase, close enough to make his presence felt but a comfortable corridor away from the day-to-day business of his section. At first the general had resented the appointment of a special investigator from the Justice Ministry to his headquarters, but after only a few days it was evident to all in the building that he had gratefully accepted the excuse Dobrshinsky offered to delegate most of his work. And the special investigator did not blame him for taking the opportunity: who wouldn't have done the same? It was a delicious irony that a force feared more than Baba Yaga herself and invested in the public imagination with some of the same supernatural powers was in reality so close to collapse. In a country renowned for the corruption and incompetence of its institutions, the secret police had distinguished itself by its inefficiency. The task of clearing this stable was now Dobrshinsky's, and when there was time to reflect upon it he found himself close to laughing aloud. Protect the emperor and bring the nihilists to justice, and in the course of your work breathe new life into the Third Section – that, in so many words, was how von Plehve had put it to him. Failure would bring disgrace, of course. So General Drenteln was doing what any

26

old soldier would do when faced with overwhelming odds – retreating with as much of his honour as he could salvage. It was Dobrshinsky's lot to lead *Les Enfants Perdus*.

The clerks in the outer office jumped to their feet as he stepped through the door.

'I want the files on these names now,' he said, handing a clerk the scrap of paper.

Within the hour Agent Fedorov from Investigations was standing at the edge of his desk with the little the Third Section registry held on the men. Barclay was right, all of them but one were listed as 'illegals' wanted by the police, dangerous men capable of murder – capable of regicide. Kviatkovsky and Goldenberg had been seen last in Kiev, Presnyakov was thought to be living abroad – until now – and Morozov's whereabouts were unknown. It was the fifth man, Mikhailov, who interested the special investigator the most: Alexander Dmitrievich Mikhailov. From a family of gentry, he was in his early twenties, educated in Petersburg, active in the student demonstrations in '75 and reportedly the leader of a small cell of revolutionaries who styled themselves 'Death or Freedom'. Clever and elusive, there was circumstantial evidence implicating him in the planning of the murder of the last Third Section chief the year before. There was no mention of a 'Kovalenko' in the section's files, but clearly he was a member of the same group.

'And we have this too.' A single sheet of paper was trembling in Fedorov's hand. 'It's from an informer.'

Dobrshinsky took the paper and glanced down at it quickly. The source was the man now lying in a crimson pool on the bedroom floor of a third-rate hotel on Nevsky. Bronstein had reported to his contact that Mikhailov had visited the Neva two days ago. He had taken Popov aside and spoken to him in a confidential whisper, and for a time Bronstein had been afraid that his role as an informer had been discovered. He had only just managed to quell a desperate urge to run from the room.

But Mikhailov had been civil to him when he left, quite the gentleman – although such things were not meant to be of importance to socialists – and this had allayed his fears. Later, Popov had told them all that Mikhailov was an important revolutionary with 'progressive' views on 'the struggle' for freedom. Bronstein had taken this to mean he was an advocate of terror. One of the other men in the hotel room said he knew their visitor to be a friend of the man who attacked the tsar in Palace Square. Popov had flown into a rage at this, railing about the need for better security and for everyone to hold their tongues. And again, Bronstein had been frightened that the remark and the anger were directed at him in particular.

He had been right to be afraid, Dobrshinsky thought. His throat had been cut only hours after seeing his police contact for the last time.

'I want descriptions, personal details, everything we have on these men circulated to police and gendarme stations,' he said, looking up at the little agent. 'Speak to their families, watch known associates. I want our agents to talk to their informers. These men will be living under false names and with false papers. Our people need copies of any photographs we have. I'm particularly interested in Alexander Mikhailov.'

'Yes, Your Honour.' Fedorov turned to leave. But as he was reaching for the door Dobrshinsky spoke again.

'I want you to find another office on this floor – empty one if you have to. An officer will be joining me to help with this investigation.'

'May I ask who, Your Honour?'

'Major Barclay of the Corps of Gendarmes. Although . . .' Dobrshinsky gave the agent a dry smile, '. . . the Major does not yet know of his good fortune.'

# 4

Winter slipped away in the night. The city woke to the jangle of cathedral bells that second Sunday in April to find the Neva flowing freely after months choked with ice. By midday its banks were lined with Petersburgers enjoying the sunshine and the spectacle of the governor's barge as it made its stately way upriver to the Winter Palace, a flotilla of smaller craft in its wake. In the splendour of the Great Antechamber, the tsar and court were waiting as the clergy prepared a little wooden chapel on the embankment for the traditional blessing of the river's slate-grey waters. There was still a carnival atmosphere three hours later as Frederick Hadfield's droshky began pushing slowly through the crowd spilling on to the road before the Admiralty. Caught by the change in the weather, his driver was sweating profusely in a padded kaftan, exuding a vintage odour of stable shit, foul enough to offend even the horse. With relief they turned on to the Fontanka Embankment at last, and at the Chernyshev Bridge he jogged the smelly Ivan's elbow. The cab rattled to a halt, he paid then waited at the edge of the pavement as it pulled away.

The three- and four-storey mansions on either side of the Fontanka were not as imposing as those a little further up the river; many had been sold by the great families that once owned them and divided into apartments for army officers, lawyers, Class 6 civil servants and below, and after years of neglect they were in desperate need of a coat of paint. Number 86 was on the opposite bank, a pink and white house in the Russian classical style with an elegant blind colonnade of four pillars in the middle of its facade. Hadfield had found an excuse to saunter past earlier in the week – to check the address, he told himself – but once there, he had begun to make a mental note of the embankment, to search for men loitering in doorways or at windows, to scrutinise the faces of passers-by. After only a short time he had given up, forced to acknowledge he had no idea what he was looking for and that an anxious imagination was capable of turning every builder and bargeman into a police informer.

Number 86 looked a brighter shade of pink in the sunshine but in all other respects quite as it had before. Did it matter? He was visiting it at the invitation of his friend Vera: a tight ball in the pit of his stomach told him it did matter. A scruffy dvornik was loafing at the door of a neighbouring mansion with his pipe in hand, but he eyed Hadfield with no more than mild curiosity. Beyond him four well-dressed children and their governess were throwing crusts to a flotilla of swans. A fine brougham with a coat of arms painted on its shiny blue door clattered past. It was Sunday quiet and Hadfield had the uncomfortable feeling that the only person behaving furtively was himself. He leaned forward to flick imaginary dust from his trousers, then, rising quickly, he walked across the road to the end of the bridge and between its great stone pavilions to the opposite bank.

After glancing up and down the street again, he stepped forward to the door of Number 86 and gave the bell a decisive tug. It was opened by a footman in a faded green velvet uniform, a gangly youth of no more than eighteen with a long pimply face. He ushered Hadfield inside at once. The entrance hall and the marble stairs that led from it were elegantly proportioned but shabby, the yellow and white painted walls stained with damp, the burgundy runner threadbare. With a graceless sweep of his hand, the footman indicated to Hadfield he should follow him to the first floor.

'Who lives in the house?'

The footman sneezed then wiped his nose on his sleeve. The iron filigree of the banister was thick with dust.

'My mistress, Yuliya Sergeyovna Volkonskaya, Your Honour.'

An aristocratic name – Hadfield remembered from his school books that a Volkonsky had commanded Russian forces at the battle of Austerlitz – this member of the family must have fallen on hard times. A full-length portrait of a soldier in the white uniform of the Life Guards dominated the landing. A polished mahogany door to the right of the picture was ajar and voices were gusting through it. The footman walked across the landing and opened it without ceremony. The sudden movement must have startled those close to the door because faces turned to Hadfield and for a few seconds there was a wary hush. But a young man in tweed with a rakish soft blue tie and shoulder-length hair was most unlikely to have arrived with a troop of gendarmes and conversation resumed with something close to a collective sigh.

A smartly dressed woman in her fifties glided across the carpet to greet him. 'Have we met before?' Her voice was high pitched and imperious.

'Doctor Frederick Hadfield, madame.'

'Vera Nikolaevna's English friend?'

'Yes.'

Yuliya Sergeyovna offered him her hand but not her name, presuming with the assurance of her class that he would know it already. She was short and gamine, her face startlingly thin – her sallow skin hung in folds from her cheekbones – a high forehead, bottle-black hair pinned and parted in the centre and small restless hands. She was wearing a fine emerald green skirt with fashionable pleated frills and ruching and a matching jacket: clothes she might choose for a tea salon at the imperial court.

The drawing room was large and rectangular in shape, dimly

31

lit by gas sconces, and the blinds were pulled down conspiratorially over the windows at the far end. There were perhaps forty people chatting in small groups, drinking tea and smoking, some standing, some perched uncomfortably on gilded French sofas and fauteuils. Most were men in their twenties, dressed informally in short jackets, some with open-necked shirts. Lounging at the large marble fireplace, a group of students in the high collared uniforms the authorities required all who studied at the university to wear. From infancy to dotage, it seemed to Hadfield, there was a uniform for every age, every occupation in the empire. He had mentioned it to one of his colleagues at the hospital who told him with a resigned shrug that the country hung from a thread of braid because a Russian only knew his place if he was in uniform. Doctors were the exception to this rule and Hadfield considered it fortunate the only uniform he was obliged to wear was a hospital coat.

Madame Volkonskaya led him through the gathering to the opposite end of the room where three young women were bent together in close conversation, their faces in silhouette against the dim light of a window: 'Vera, dear . . . your English friend . . .'

Instinctively they stepped away from each other like children caught sharing a guilty secret.

'You're late, Frederick,' Vera said, holding out her hand to him, small and cold to the touch, 'I'd almost given up on you.'

It was four years since they had met last but her manner was as cool and matter-of-fact as if she had seen him only that morning and had been waiting a little impatiently to go to one of the lectures they used to attend in Zurich.

'How are you, Verochka?'

'Quite well. As you can see,' and her hands fluttered gracefully down her black dress. More than well, he thought, she was even more beautiful than he remembered her: chestnut-brown hair tied in a bun, finely cut features, almond-shaped eyes and full lips that turned down a little disdainfully at the corners. A small intimidating frown played constantly between her dark eyebrows. It was a severe beauty. Poor Alexei Filippov: Vera's husband was a provincial lawyer with decidedly conservative views. It was the most unlikely of marriages. Hadfield had watched Filippov trailing around Zurich in Vera's wake, pink with embarrassment and irritation as the eyes of a hundred adoring students followed her hungrily about the medical faculty.

'And Alexei?' Hadfield asked. 'Is your husband with you?'

'We're no longer together,' she said coolly.

'Oh. I'm sorry.'

'Don't be. It was the right thing to do. I'm Vera Figner again.'

Madame Volkonskaya began to twitter nervously about freedom from domestic drudgery and the importance of educating young women. Her views were muddled and it seemed to Hadfield she was paying no more than lip service to the rights of women out of polite deference to Vera. After a few uncomfortable minutes she made an excuse and slipped away.

'Yuliya Sergeyovna is a sentimental supporter,' said Vera in a low voice. 'One of her uncles took part in the Decembrist revolt and was executed by Nicholas. She's really a liberal.' She pursed her lips in a show of disapproval that made her look even more beautiful.

'Frederick used to join our discussion group in Zurich,' she said, turning to her companions. 'He spoke to us about his time at Cambridge University and of his friend Professor Maurice's ideas about Christianity and socialism. But he's read Marx too.'

'Are you a believer, Dr Hadfield?'

'This is my younger sister, Evgenia,' said Vera, introducing the questioner.

Evgenia had her sister's fine features and chestnut hair but her face was a little fuller, and, if not as classically beautiful, it was less severe. Hadfield had enjoyed the company of another of the Figner sisters in Zurich: Lydia had studied medicine too and rented rooms with Vera and her unfortunate husband. He had been closer to Lydia than her older, more formidable sibling. She was not as pretty, but warmer, with a bold sense of fun, quite careless of society's good opinion. They had been lovers for a time. The memory of it made him feel uncomfortable.

'A believer? Only in Christ's teachings.'

'Frederick does not accept the need for revolutionary methods,' said Vera acerbically.

'Terror? No. That sort of talk was fashionable in Switzerland. Some of our comrades were intoxicated with the idea that a revolutionary should be free to murder and steal on our behalf to bring about a more civilised society. Dangerous romantics, and very naive too.'

'You've spent too long away from Russia, Doctor,' said Evgenia sharply. 'Our experience has taught us to view things differently.'

'A lot has changed since I saw you last,' said Vera. 'Things are worse here.' And she told Hadfield of the months she and Evgenia had spent 'among the people', working in the villages and hamlets of Samara.

'You know, I was twenty-five years old and I'd never spoken to a common person before, not properly. We travelled the countryside visiting what the peasants call their "stopping huts". Within minutes there would be thirty or forty patients – sores, wounds, skin diseases, incurable catarrhs of the intestines and syphilis. Filthy, unhygienic – in some places the pigs lived better.'

The Figners had held political classes to persuade the peasants the tsar was not their champion but their oppressor. Only a revolution could bring a more equal society, better health and education to Russia.

'But what is the point in trying to convince people whose only concern is survival that they should protest, resist – they were completely crushed, Frederick.'

34

In the end, Vera and Evgenia were forced to flee. All over the country young radicals were being rounded up and charged with political crimes. Most were guilty of no more than calling for an end to despotism.

'It was hopeless. We were going to change nothing, it was the same story everywhere – protests broken up, arrests, persecutions . . . but it was at this time . . .' Vera's voice tailed off as if she were in two minds about saying more. Then, after looking carefully about: 'Alexander Soloviev came to visit us to talk to us about his plans . . .'

A frisson of anxiety tingled down Hadfield's spine. Vera leaned closer: 'Are you afraid?'

'Only for you – and your sisters.'

She gave a short humourless laugh: 'Don't be.' Then, lowering her voice until it was barely more than a whisper: 'We'd already agreed there should be a direct campaign of violence against landlords and the police but it was impossible to recruit people to carry it out. Alexander Soloviev felt the death of the tsar – one man – would purify the atmosphere, that it would help persuade the intelligentsia of the need for a campaign among the masses.'

'Purify? Oh, please,' said Hadfield. 'Tell me you weren't foolish enough to be part of it.'

'Alexander is a martyr.' Evgenia's voice was shaking with barely repressed fury and she made no effort to lower it. 'He is the kindest man I know. He knew he would be taken.'

The murmur of voices seemed to die away and heads turned towards them.

'He has given his life for the people.' Reaching for her lace handkerchief, Evgenia pressed it in a trembling hand to her mouth. The drawing room was quiet enough to hear the chink of cups being married to saucers.

'The tragedy is that he missed.' An unusually high-pitched voice broke the silence. 'I wouldn't have.'

There was a gasp of surprise. The steely determination in the would-be assassin's voice left no one in doubt he spoke in deadly earnest. Hadfield turned to find him standing in front of the fire only a few feet away. He was a singular-looking man: Jewish – Hadfield was sure of that – in his early twenties, short and slight, with a thin face, wispy red hair and a small goatee beard. He was wearing a belted chemise of red cotton.

'I applaud his courage, of course.' The would-be assassin stared at Hadfield defiantly as if daring him to make some sort of riposte. After a few awkward seconds, one of the students at the chimney piece came to his rescue.

'What purpose would it serve – the death of one man?' he demanded. 'Is that going to win freedom for the people? Of course it isn't.'

'An active attack on the government – a blow to the centre,' the would-be assassin countered forcefully.

Vera Figner leant forward to whisper: 'Goldenberg. Grigory Goldenberg from Kiev.'

Incensed that anyone should seek to justify the assassination of the emperor in her house, Madame Volkonskaya weighed boldly into the debate: 'He freed the serfs from bondage – the Tsar Liberator, the people love him!'

'He is the persecutor of the people,' Goldenberg countered hotly.

'He is badly advised by those around him . . . he, he . . .' So great was their hostess's indignation she was unable to speak for a moment. In desperation, she cast about her drawing room for an ally and her gaze settled on Hadfield. Too late he realised her intention and looked away – to no avail. 'Doctor, what do you say as an Englishman?'

All eyes turned to him again.

'I believe in democracy and education, good healthcare, a fairer distribution of wealth,' he said, after a moment's thought, 'but I think terror will set back the cause of reform by frightening liberal opinion – just as it's done in Ireland.'

There was a gentle murmur of assent in the room and, emboldened a little, Hadfield added: 'And I am a doctor, Madame Volkonskaya, it is my duty to save life not take it.'

'You're afraid! Afraid.' The young woman's voice was dripping with scorn. She was standing behind a sofa opposite. 'What do you know of the suffering of our people?'

Again, gasps of surprise. Hadfield flushed hot with anger: 'I have spent . . .'

She cut across him. 'You talk of change but you aren't prepared to do anything to bring it about!' Her blue eyes flashed angrily about the room as if her challenge were to them all. 'Alexander Soloviev loves the people and has sacrificed himself for them. But you cannot understand, you are a foreigner . . .' And she turned away from him in a show of disgust.

Hadfield stood there for a moment, dumbfounded, as the debate washed round him like the tide about a rock. He felt humiliated, and his cheeks were burning with self-conscious indignation. He watched his persecutor bend to speak to a well-dressed man with lazy eyes who was sitting on the sofa. They must have spoken of him because she looked up to catch his steady gaze upon her. She frowned and looked away again but not before he registered the startling lightness of her eyes, their profound sunshine blue, and he sensed great energy and purpose. Five feet four or five, he thought, petite, dark brown hair tied back without care, very white skin, a small round face with full pink lips and an elegant neck. She was wearing a worn, ill-fitting black dress that had clearly been made for a much larger woman.

'Don't take it to heart.' Vera Figner followed his gaze. 'Anna is very close to Alexander Soloviev. This is an unhappy and worrying time.'

'Do you know her well?'

'A little. She's a friend of Lydia's.'

Hadfield frowned: was that why she had exhibited contempt so publicly for a man she had never met? Her name was Anna Petrovna Kovalenko and she was from a village in the eastern Ukraine, Vera told him, the illegitimate daughter of a landowner and one of his serfs. 'She has done wonderful things in Kharkov, organising workers into a union. They respect and like her. We all do.'

Well-to-do socialists were always dewy-eyed about comrades who were sons or daughters of the soil, in Hadfield's experience, so he was inclined to take this endorsement with a pinch of salt. And yet more than resentment drew his gaze back to her; dark and restless, those remarkable eyes – she was intriguing, and, yes, he had to admit it, attractive in an unconventional way. Perhaps he was just as sentimental about peasants as Vera.

'The time spent in the country educating the people achieved nothing . . .' Goldenberg had taken command once more and was holding forth in a thin little voice. '. . . only by striking directly at the machinery of oppression – provincial governors, ministers, the Third Section, the tsar . . . the time has come for action – a new phase in the struggle . . .'

There were a few nods of approval but for the most part the room listened to his call to revolutionary arms in cool silence. Liberals or popular revolutionaries like me, Hadfield thought, passionate about democracy and the need for change but opposed to terror. He caught a glimpse between heads of their hostess slipping through the doors at the end of the drawing room. It was too bloody and uncompromising for Madame Volkonskaya, not at all the sort of political salon she would have wished for. He wanted to escape from the smoky gloom and plotting too, and to feel the wind off the Neva on his face, hear the bells of the old Russia ringing out around the city.

He glanced across at Anna Petrovna again. She had bobbed

38

down to exchange words with the man on the sofa who was gazing calmly at Hadfield, his plump hands clasped about his crossed leg.

'Alexander Mikhailov is one of us,' said Vera. 'Very clear thinking . . .'

'Why did you invite me here, Verochka?' Hadfield asked, turning to look her in the eye.

'You were with us in Switzerland.' Then, after a pause, 'We both want Russia, the world, to be different.'

'But your views on how to go about it have changed.'

'The people cannot wait any more. The whole nation will have gone to seed before the liberals get anything done. History needs a push.'

He did not reply. The gathering was breaking into conversational groups again. Their hostess returned with an anxious hand to her face. Anna Kovalenko had drawn Goldenberg aside and it was clear from her angry gestures they were engaged in an ill-tempered exchange. Hadfield began to make his excuses, but as he was reaching for Vera's hand she said abruptly:

'Lydia meant something to you, didn't she?' There was a steeliness in her manner, in the set of her jaw, and she held on firmly to his hand when propriety required him to withdraw it.

'Yes, of course. Lydia was a very good friend to me,' he said slowly. 'Is she in St Petersburg?'

'St Petersburg?' Vera gave a bitter little laugh. 'Lydia was arrested for distributing propaganda. Imprisoned. Exiled. She's been sent to eastern Siberia.'

Hadfield turned his head away. Lydia with the soft brown eyes and teasing smile. He felt a lump the size of a fist in his throat. For a short time they had meant so much to each other. He had not seen or heard from her for three years but her last angry words troubled him still. He knew he had caused her great pain.

'I'm sorry, Verochka.'

Vera Figner was gazing at him intently. She had not released his hand.

'There is no freedom to protest peacefully here, Frederick. No alternative to terror. You'll see.'

Old Penkin was a wily bird. He knew to keep his eyes open. He knew when there was a rouble or two to be earned for a little information. They had been coming and going all afternoon. He had watched them from the street and then from a chair at his gate. One of them had even asked him directions to Number 86. A young gentleman in a fine black fur-lined coat had stood gazing at the Volkonsky place only feet from him. Foreign-looking. Penkin had made a mental note of them all. He was the yard-keeper at the Kozlov house opposite, had been for fifteen years, and he knew all about Yuliya Sergeyovna Volkonskaya and her friends. He had spoken to Constable Rostislov about them before.

'Fairy tales,' the policeman had said at first. 'Fairy tales, old man. Bugger off. You're not getting vodka money from me.'

That was before a madman tried to kill the tsar. Since then Constable Rostislov had been falling over himself to pay for the dvornik's scraps. Of course, no one liked an informer. Penkin hated informers himself. But who would begrudge an old man a little extra money after fifteen years of fetching and carrying in all weathers for kopeks? On the quiet, that was the thing, just a word in the constable's ear.

'Hey, Tan'ka,' he called through the kitchen door, 'I must go out for a while.'

The maid rolled her eyes: 'Don't expect me to lie for you, old man. And don't come back drunk.'

Penkin scowled at her: 'Shut up, you trollop. I've got business. Important business.'

'I know your sort of business,' she replied with a harsh laugh.

'Shut your mouth.' He wanted to take his hand to her. He

offered her money instead. 'Two kopeks for you if you tell them I'm out on house business.'

'Five.'

'Done.'

The local police station was only a short walk away on Gorokho-vaya Street. Penkin was careful to be sure no one saw him enter. As fortune would have it, Constable Vasili Rostislov was on duty and at the station. They sat in a large office full of empty desks and bookcases stacked high with police files. Penkin could not read but he could count. He knew it was important to count.

'They began arriving at a little before three o'clock. Her footman told me she was inviting politicals, so I knew to be looking out for them.'

'Names?' the constable asked.

'No. But I can tell you what they looked like. You can ask Yuliya Sergeyovna for the names, if you want them.'

Rostislov pulled open a drawer and took out a notebook and small leather folder of photographs. He opened it and began placing pictures on the desk in front of the dvornik. 'All right. Only the truth now. If you lie I'll find out and you'll regret it.'

Penkin began to move the pictures round the desktop with a dirty finger, picking them up, peering at them, scratching his nose thoughtfully, shifting on his chair. Students – men and women – nicely dressed, expensive, some in uniform and some in frock coats and ties. What did they have to worry about? Nothing. There were two he was sure he recognised, and he handed them back to the policeman. Rostislov stared at him: 'Have you been drinking?'

'No,' said the dvornik sulkily.

'Are you sure about these two?'

'Yes.'

'This one?'

Penkin nodded.

'Wait here. Don't touch anything.' The policeman pushed his chair away from the desk and crossed the office to a door in the opposite corner. He opened it and Penkin caught a glimpse of a brightly lit room with clerks bent over desks before it swung to behind him. The time slipped by and the dvornik began to grow impatient. He had been away from the Kozlov house for almost half an hour. The maid could not be trusted to make a decent job of lying for him – not for five kopeks. At last the door opened again.

'You're coming with me,' Constable Rostislov said, lifting his uniform coat from a peg.

'But I have to be back. They'll miss me.'

The policeman laughed. He was clearly in great good humour.

'Too bad. We're going to Fontanka 16.'

# 5

The earnest faces and desperate talk left a dull grey impression on Frederick Hadfield's mind for days and he resolved to be busy if another invitation was delivered to his door. He thought of Lydia Figner often and found himself consumed by feelings of guilt about the careless way he had ended their affair. As the days passed and he heard nothing more from her sisters, he began to wonder if they had just dismissed him as a hopeless case, beyond redemption, another fuzzy liberal without the vision or courage necessary for their great socialist project. For the most part, he was happy to be considered so, even if it was impossible to entirely ignore the truth of Vera's parting shot: there is no freedom in Russia. With a stroke of his pen the tsar had made the army master of life and liberty in his empire. Men and women suspected of 'subversive tendencies' could be brought before a court martial and either imprisoned or banished without any recourse to an appeal.

From time to time he would cross the Neva by the pontoon bridge at the eastern tip of Vasilievsky and stare across the water at the grim stone face of the St Peter and St Paul Fortress. The enemies the state simply wished to forget were held in the cellars of the Alexeevsky Ravelin until cold and hunger carried them away. Would the Figners die in this Russian Bastille? And he would imagine Vera shivering in the darkness, her white face still defiant, an unspoken 'Didn't I say so' in the damp air between them.

But Hadfield was too busy on the wards of the Nikolaevsky and with a growing list of private patients to brood for long on the fate of the Figners or the country's future. With the help of his aunt, he began to establish his reputation as a physician in embankment society, in particular with Anglo-Russian women of mature years, of whom there were a goodly number. So much nicer than those German doctors was the general view, and so well qualified. Some remembered his father with affection, and one old lady had 'the honour' to have been examined by his great-uncle, Sir James; 'You are so like him, dear,' she had said, with a tear of memory in her eye. And it had been suggested to him more than once that the emperor would one day favour the great-nephew of such a loyal servant of the House of Romanov with a royal appointment. Hadfield was grateful but a little embarrassed by the attention and looked forward to his afternoons at the Nikolaevsky with those who could not afford to pay for his services and would never dream of inviting him to dinner.

On the last Sunday in April, the dvornik huffed and puffed up the stairs to his apartment with a note from the British embassy. It was from one of the consuls, an old friend of his father's: the ambassador's wife had taken to her bed with a fever and he would be grateful if Dr Hadfield could spare the time to attend upon her. A victoria was waiting at the door for an answer, the surly coachman tapping his whip impatiently against its iron frame.

The embassy and its residence were at the seat of imperial power on the embankment before the Field of Mars where the emperor reviewed the royal regiments, within hailing distance of his palace. A fine eighteenth-century mansion, it had belonged to the first Alexander's tutor and councillor, and the tsar-conqueror had often danced in its famous White Ballroom. With less ceremony, Hadfield was shown up the bright marble staircase, through the embassy's formal rooms and into the private quarters in the east wing.

The Countess of Dufferin was suffering from no more than

a severe head cold and an acute attack of anxiety. But Hadfield was charming and concerned and left her with just the sort of large brown bottle she was expecting and would have been disappointed not to receive. A generous dose of honey and lemon to be taken on a silver spoon. By the following day she was much improved and fulsome in her praise for 'my doctor' and his 'miracle' cure.

Hadfield visited her twice more and, as her spirits improved, he found her to be engaging, with a keen interest in her new home. Lady Dufferin was not handsome: she had an angular face with a heavy brow, small dark eyes and loose curled hair, difficult to tame, judging by the number of pins and bands used to hold it in place. But the impression was of a lively woman with a wry, self-deprecating sense of humour. A little guarded – no doubt in keeping with her position – she had none of the aristocratic hauteur he had encountered in some of his patients in London. She questioned Hadfield closely about his work and expressed an interest in visiting the Nikolaevsky. The ambassador would accompany her, she said, the Earl of Dufferin wished to be familiar with all aspects of Russian life.

'And your uncle, General Glen . . . Of course, he has made us very welcome, but I fear I may have offended him. I understand the general goes to church every day during Passion Week. Do you go to church that often, Doctor?'

'Not as often as I should and not as often as my uncle would like,' Hadfield said with a little shake of the head.

He had grown a thick diplomatic skin – the loss of his father, the strange 'Russian boy' at an English boarding school, the studied patience of medical practice – these had shaped a personality naturally inclined to please, but had also taught him a comfortable degree of detachment. An admirer of Darwin and Huxley, he was an agnostic, a firm believer in natural selection and the descent of man, but he was careful not to express these views in what his mother liked to describe as 'polite company'. For her sake he had accompanied the Glen family to the English church on Easter Sunday.

'Your uncle is a man of forthright opinions. He was concerned that Dufferin and I had only been to the English church once at Easter.'

Hadfield's face must have betrayed the irritation he felt, for Lady Dufferin lifted her eyes to his and her patient smile became a conspiratorial one: 'Well, the general recommended you. In practitioners, at least, his judgement is not to be faulted.'

The following day the embassy coachman delivered a warm note from the ambassador requesting the pleasure of Dr Hadfield's company at the opera.

His father's diamond studs, top hat, tails and black leather shoes from Jermyn Street – later he would smile at the rich irony of meeting her at the theatre in the company of a countess.

The Dufferin party was seated in the grand tier to the right of the imperial suite in a box designated suitable for grand dukes and ambassadors. The Mikhailovsky was glittering silver in the brilliant light cast by the new electric sconces the management had installed at great expense.

Her Ladyship had invited what she called a 'select band of six'; Hadfield, the first and second secretaries at the embassy, and *The Times*'s man in St Petersburg, Mr George Dobson. It was a lively group, and the ambassador clearly believed he was among friends, presuming on a doctor's discretion and the self-interest of a newspaper correspondent. He regaled them with a humorous anecdote told to him by the prime minister, Lord Beaconsfield, then there was talk of the war between Russia and Turkey and the seeds of discontent sown throughout the empire by the incompetent handling of the campaign.

'Do you know, Doctor,' said Lady Dufferin, turning to Hadfield, 'a terrorist tried to kill the chief of the secret police—'

'The Third Section—' her husband corrected her from the seat beside her.

'. . . just around the corner from our house? Two shots were fired into his carriage. They missed, but now they're threatening to murder his daughter. And Mr Dobson says a girl walked into a party in Moscow last week and shot a man. That's correct, isn't it, Mr Dobson?' Lady Dufferin leant back to catch the eye of the correspondent.

'Yes, Your Ladyship. They say the victim was ordered to shoot the emperor but fled from Petersburg to avoid doing so and that the girl was sent to punish him.'

'Well, what do you think of that?' Lady Dufferin asked in a voice that left no doubt as to her own strong opinion on the matter.

Hadfield was relieved when the conversation turned to the ambassador's first official visit to the Winter Palace. Leaning forward a little, he could see the only empty seats in the house were in the imperial suite. That Meyerbeer's *The Prophet* was not to royal taste was hardly surprising, for it had been a great favourite in revolutionary circles in Switzerland where it was held to be a salutary tale of tyranny and religious hypocrisy.

'. . . I don't like it at all,' said Lady Dufferin. 'The electricity spoils the effect of the chandeliers. The balcony's in darkness. And here,' with a graceful flourish of her gloved hand she indicated the boxes on the opposite side of the grand tier, 'the lamps are too bright. Look, the lights flicker and change colour. It just isn't as gay as gas. But what an extraordinary modern age we live in.'

Yes, yes, what a modern age. Hadfield nodded as if hanging on her every word, but his attention was fixed on the gloom near the back of the stalls. Later, he would wonder what had drawn him to her of the many hundreds seated below: Anna Kovalenko, his persecutor at the political salon, Anna with the strikingly beautiful blue eyes. Perhaps it was because even at such a distance he could sense she was restless and ill at ease. Evgenia Figner and Madame Volkonskaya were sitting to her right; to her left, the vociferous and blood-thirsty Goldenberg. The imperial suite with its huge orange velvet and gold fringed drapes was almost directly above them. Fortunate then that the chairs inside it were empty, Hadfield thought with a wry smile, or the evening might have been spoilt.

'Have you seen someone you know, Doctor?' asked Lady Dufferin. 'A patient?'

'An acquaintance – a friend of my cousin's,' Hadfield replied, leaning back in his seat.

The Anabaptists plotted and the wicked count carried off fair Bertha to his castle and for a while he was lost in the rhythm and grace of the music. But after a time, maddeningly, Hadfield's gaze drifted from the stage to the orchestra pit and across the gentlemen in their tail coats and white ties, the ladies in taffeta and pearls, to the little band at the back of the stalls. What would they think of him if they knew he was in a tidy velvet box with a countess and the gentlemen of the British embassy? But did it matter what they thought? He had the troubling sense that his life was losing some of its shape. He had felt something of the same the week before, when he had rushed from a dirty crowded ward at the Nikolaevsky Hospital to a scented boudoir on the English Embankment to treat the wife of an iron master who was suffering from nothing more than a severe case of indigestion. From the grand tier he could imagine his shadow in the stalls below – the doctor who argued with passion for better public health, for a fairer distribution of wealth, the doctor who walked a humbler but principled path with comrades who thought the same.

At the end of Act Two the mezzo soprano took her curtain call, the electric lights flickered and burst into life and the door of the box was opened by a waiter with a tray of tinkling glasses.

Hadfield made his excuses: 'So tiresome . . . friend of my cousin . . . really feel obliged . . .' Lady Dufferin was all gracious understanding. From the stairs, he searched the shining pink faces in the foyer below but he could not see Evgenia Figner or her companions, and so with the single-minded purpose of a doctor summoned to a medical emergency, he began to shoulder his way through the scented press, deaf to the fluttering chorus of disapproval. Madame Volkonskaya was the first to see him and she gave a little shake of her handkerchief in welcome: 'Doctor.'

The women had wandered to the front of the stalls and were standing at the rail beneath the proscenium arch, gazing into the orchestra pit. Goldenberg was nowhere to be seen.

'How fortunate that we should find you here, Doctor.' Madame Volkonskaya offered him her hand and he held it for a moment, then, turning to the younger women, he gave a stiff little bow.

'I don't think you've been,' Evgenia paused, 'formally introduced.' She placed provocative stress on the word 'formally'. 'Anna Kovalenko – Doctor Frederick Hadfield. Anna remembers you well, Doctor' – this with a mischievous little smile.

Anna had coloured a little, but her jaw was firmly set and there was an unmistakable look of defiance in her blue eyes. 'Doctor.' She was not wearing gloves and the hand she offered Hadfield was small and cold to the touch.

'Are you enjoying the opera, Doctor?' asked Madame Volkonskaya. She did not wait for an answer: the mezzo soprano was quite wonderful, didn't he agree, the handsome tenor singing the part of John of Leyden too. Wasn't it an inspiring work – so many valuable lessons? On she twittered like a lark.

'I know Vera will be sorry to have missed you,' said Evgenia, cutting across her.

'Vera was so fond of opera. Is she still in the city?'

'She's visiting our family in Kazan . . .' Evgenia hesitated. 'My mother . . .' The uncomfortable frown hovering between her dark eyebrows suggested to Hadfield this was a half truth at best. Anna came to her rescue.

'Which hospital do you work at?' The question was fired with a peremptoriness that made him start.

'The Nikolaevsky, Miss Kovalenko. And I have some patients of my own.'

'Patients who can afford to pay.'

'Yes,' he said, drawing the word out into a challenge. He was not going to be bullied into feeling guilty.

'The Nikolaevsky is a military hospital, isn't it?' Again it sounded like a criticism.

'But it doesn't treat only soldiers.'

'You said at Madame Volkonskaya's salon you believed in working among the people, winning their trust, and that you thought that was the only way to make them listen to us.'

'I do believe that.'

'There is a clinic for the poor not far from your hospital, in the Peski district. Evgenia and I do what we can there on Sundays. We need a doctor. Will you help us?' She leant forward a little, her eyes shining with fervour. Hadfield could feel the colour rising in his face.

'What a wonderful idea! Do say yes, Doctor,' Madame Volkonskaya gushed. 'I am sure you're right. If we help them, they will learn from us. That is the only way to bring about reform.'

How foolishly sentimental Madame Volkonskaya made his views sound, he thought, patronising too. Anna was still looking at him intently with those piercing blue eyes, and his heart beat a little faster.

'Well, Doctor, will you help us?'

'Of course, yes.'

A small satisfied smile was playing on Anna's lips and she looked away at last, the spell broken. The theatre bell began to ring for the third act, the musicians drifted back to their seats in the pit, the auditorium began to fill with the excited hum of anticipation.

Sitting in the darkness behind Lady Dufferin, Hadfield wondered what on earth possessed him to agree. He was being drawn into association with people who – for all their philanthropy – believed killing and maiming could fashion a civilised society. Perhaps they were at the Mikhailovsky to plan just such an outrage, taking note of discreet corners beneath the imperial suite, while on the stage the basses thundered the unthinking dogmas of Meyerbeer's Anabaptists. The light catching the pearls around the neck of the ambassador's wife, the scent of pomade from the hair of her young gentlemen, crisp white cuffs and polished black shoes, and the thick orange velvet covering of the balcony rail; he took pleasure in these details like a scientist examining a slide beneath a microscope, for they were the comforts of the world in which he lived most of his life. But how much keener his appreciation if there was the risk of losing them – a small chance, granted – but enough to give life more edge. In Russia, guilt by association might secure even a well-connected doctor several years in a katorga in Siberia. Excitement, then, and no small satisfaction, in Sunday work the student doctor of his Zurich days would have respected.

The stirring last chords, a polite second's silence then a crescendo of applause as the heavy curtains swept back to reveal the first of the principals. With moist eyes, Lady Dufferin turned to her party then back to the stage, her gloved hand gripping the edge of the balcony. Hadfield leant forward a little to peer over the countess's, shoulder, and through the dark forest of hands he could see there were four empty seats. He felt a pang of disappointment: dowdy clothes, her neat little figure, her softly spoken accented Russian, her strange physicality, the frown that hovered between her dark brows – a little too closely set for classical beauty – her arrogant

51

defiance and yet a certain reticence, and those searing blue eyes – those and more. He was intrigued and pleased, pleased he was now obliged to spend the following Sunday at Miss Kovalenko's clinic.

# 6

Major Vladimir Barclay did not see the executioner kick the steps away but he heard the gasp of thousands like the sighing wind on the winter steppe. The charged silence that followed was broken only by the priest's prayers and the lazy creaking of the scaffold. Alexander Soloviev was twitching at the end of the rope. This was what they wanted, the young merchants and the old ladies wrapped in black, the frock-coated civil servants, these were the precious seconds they had waited an hour or more to witness. Kicking and shaking and slowly turning as life was choked from him before their eyes.

What a spectacle! Turning his back on the scaffold, Barclay began pushing through the crowd towards the line of carriages in front of the Semenovsky Barracks. It was not that he felt sympathy for Soloviev – it was only what he deserved – but the business was managed so badly. The hangman was a drunken criminal who emptied a bottle of vodka down his throat before he fumbled through his task.

Barclay's driver had abandoned his post for a favourable view of the execution and was now lost in the crush of spectators. After a few minutes he came puffing up, red-faced, peaked cap in hand, which he swept before the major as he bowed contritely.

'Fontanka 16 and smart about it,' Barclay snapped.

But the entertainment was well and truly over, the crowd drifting away, and for all the driver's easy cursing, the brandishing of his whip, the carriage crept on to Zagorodny at no more than a walking pace. A file of soldiers was marching along the prospekt to the lazy beat of a drum and the driver was obliged to join the carriages trundling in its wake.

Barclay had spent twenty years in uniform with the army and then the Gendarme Corps. Secret policeman, guardian of the state, he sometimes wondered if his name and background had directed his choice of role, as if he had felt it necessary to prove his loyalty to the empire. The Barclays had made their money in the timber trade; worse still, they were 'foreigners' of Scottish descent. Collegiate Councillor Dobrshinsky was the same. He was a member of the hereditary nobility from Kiev, but his family was Polish – they were 'foreigners' too. After observing his new superior for a week, Barclay was inclined to the view that this was almost the only thing they had in common. Dobrshinsky was single and unattached, a curious state of affairs for a thirty-five-year-old gentleman who, if not handsome, was quite prosperous enough to be eligible. Of course, there were many senior government servants who preferred the society of the *demi-monde* but no one Barclay had spoken to suspected the collegiate councillor of an exotic private life. He was bookish, an academic by disposition and a lawyer by training, distant, even a little cool with colleagues, and yet he enjoyed a formidable reputation as an interrogator, not of the bullying sort but as a student of the mind, a follower of Professor Wundt and the German school.

Barclay was flattered Dobrshinsky had singled him out to join the special investigation, although a good deal of his enthusiasm was dissipating as the size of the task they faced became apparent. Dobrshinsky had explained in his quiet measured way that it was their duty to protect His Imperial Majesty, and if that meant arresting every radical in the empire then that was precisely what they were going to do. With good intelligence that would not be necessary; well placed informers, more agents and better trained, a complete shake-up of the Third Section. Failure was unthinkable, the consequences immeasurable.

The special investigation team at Fontanka 16 had begun to creep across the first floor. A score of agents was assigned to the inquiry, clerks, copyists, an archivist and even a dedicated telegrapher with one of the new Baudot transmitters. The Third Section had seen nothing quite like it since the days of Tsar Nicholas. From dawn until long after dusk, clerks scurrying from room to room with telegrams and reports from gendarme stations across the empire, plain-clothes officers taking witness statements or questioning known radicals, street superintendents flicking through photographs in an effort to identify 'illegals' in their districts, and at the heart of this frantic activity, the special investigator himself. Dobrshinsky was at a blackboard with an agent when Barclay stepped inside the main inquiry room. There was an unnatural hush; the officers bent low over their desks like schoolboys before their teacher. Cheap furniture had been crammed into the office to meet the needs of the investigation and the agents sat in a phalanx of desks pressed together in the middle of the room. Along one of the walls, three large sash windows with a view over the Fontanka; against the rest, wooden filing cabinets, bookcases, blackboards and tables.

'Vladimir Alexandrovich, how timely,' said Dobrshinsky with an expression Barclay took for a smile. 'We have something of great interest at last, please . . .' and he indicated with a look and a brisk sweep of the hand that the gendarme officer should follow him into his office. 'And you too, Kletochnikov,' he said, addressing the agent at his side.

'A good show?' Dobrshinsky asked as he settled behind his perfectly ordered and polished mahogany desk.

'A large crowd, Your Honour.'

'No need for formality,' said Dobrshinsky, offering them both the leather library chairs opposite. 'It was a pointless waste. In time, I might have won Soloviev's confidence. Justice has not served us well in this case, a little too blind and impatient, I fear. But we have something . . .'

He reached into his drawer and pulled out a red leather-bound file, opened it and spread his hands on the desk in front of him in a gesture of satisfaction.

'Yes, thank goodness we have something. Two valuable pieces of intelligence, the first, a report taken from a yard keeper on the Fontanka Embankment a short distance from here. The second, well, that is why Agent Nikolai Vasilievich is here.'

Kletochnikov coloured a little with embarrassment and glanced down at his hands twisting in his lap. Well, well, a secret policeman who blushes; Barclay suppressed the temptation to smile. The poor fellow seemed very young, no more than thirty, slight, round-shouldered, with a thin intelligent face and spectacles.

'The dvornik was questioned by a local constable and he gave a remarkably good description of what was almost certainly an illegal gathering at a mansion opposite. It's owned by a . . .' Dobrshinsky glanced down at the file, 'a Madame Volkonskaya, a sentimental old aristocrat, a champagne revolutionary.'

It was a Sunday afternoon, which was why the yard keeper was sober, he explained. The old man puffed on his pipe and watched the comings and goings at Number 86 with keen interest and with a surprising eye for detail.

'Students, some respectably dressed young women, a young man in tweed with an exotic blue tie, but of more importance, these two.' Dobrshinsky took two small photographs from the file and slid them across the desk to Barclay.

'The one on the right is Mikhailov – rather an old photograph, and on the left, the Jew, Goldenberg. The dvornik had no difficulty in identifying him. Mikhailov arrived and left with a young woman, petite, dark.' Dobrshinsky paused, lifting his elbows to the desk, hands together as if in prayer, intense concentration written on his face. 'Her description seems to match one we have of a woman seen leaving the square after the attempt on His Majesty's life.'

'Do you want me to arrest Madame Volkonskaya?' Barclay asked.

'Leave her – for now. Keep the house under surveillance. Have her followed. I don't expect Mikhailov tells her anything, but he may risk using Number 86 for another gathering. She's probably giving him money. I think it's fair to assume Mikhailov and Goldenberg are still in the city. And now, if you please . . .' Dobrshinsky nodded to the young agent perched anxiously at the edge of his chair.

'Yes, Your Honour.' Kletochnikov looked unsure quite what was expected of him.

'Tell Major Barclay what the city police have told you.'

'It's Popov, Your Honour, the student revolutionary implicated in the death of the informer – Bronstein. He's been seen among the men at the Baird Works.'

One of the foundry hands had tipped off the local police, Kletochnikov explained. Popov and the Muscovite labourers with whom he shared the room at the Neva were organising political meetings in the homes of sympathisers, distributing propaganda, agitating for a secret trade union, and the socialist gospel they preached was attracting new recruits, although the city police could not be sure how many.

'So, as you see, another opportunity,' said Dobrshinsky, impatiently pushing back his chair and rising to his feet. 'Which is well and good because General Drenteln and the Justice Ministry are impatient for results. Soloviev was a nobody. It's the men who gave him his gun and sent him out that we want.'

He turned to gaze out of the window on to the Fontanka, and for a moment the silence in the room was broken only by the noise of a carriage clattering along the embankment below and the heavy tick of the French clock on the mantelpiece.

'Popov may be close to Mikhailov – Bronstein saw them together,' Dobrshinsky said, turning to face them again. 'Let's find out where he lives then pick him up. He's a nobody but he may take us one step closer to the six on the hotel list. '

With a nod and casual wave of the hand, the collegiate councillor drew the meeting to a close. He slipped back behind his desk and was pulling a file across it when, almost as an afterthought and without lifting his head he said, 'Oh, Vladimir Alexandrovich?'

'Your Honour?' Barclay was halfway to the door.

'Would you like my clock?'

'I don't understand, Your Honour?'

'What don't you understand? Would you like my clock?' he asked again with an enigmatic smile. 'It is an excellent clock. It never seems to wind down or stop.'

'Thank you, Your Honour, I have one of my own.'

## 7

It was with more than a little trepidation that Frederick Hadfield stepped from the droshky on to the pavement at the foot of St Boris and St Gleb's. Pressing five kopeks into the cabby's hand, he plucked his father's battered medical bag from the seat and turned towards the shell of the new church rising from a forest of scaffolding on the bank of the Neva before him. Three towers in the Byzantine style were almost complete, but construction of the central dome had barely begun. The low wharf buildings and the school adjoining the site were painted in pink dust and probably had been for every one of the ten years since the foundation stone was cemented into place. The city's wealthier inhabitants were not inclined to reach very deeply into their pockets to pay for a church they would never visit. The Peski district had an unsavoury reputation for crime and drunkenness, and gangs of youths roamed its badly lit, rubbish-strewn streets at night, unchecked by the police. Behind the peeling facades of its old rooming houses, the poor lived from hand to mouth in cramped and unsanitary conditions. A warren of dark corridors and flats, with many families forced to share a single noisy insalubrious room, privacy a thickness of tattered curtain. The district was home to a class of society the city government tried to pretend it owed no obligation to – shop assistants, factory workers and their families, apprentices, students, the jobless and destitute. The poorest of all lived in ramshackle wooden buildings – some no more than huts but others of two or three storeys – thrown up on unclaimed ground between the mansion blocks. Hadfield had never needed to visit

Peski although the Nikolaevsky Hospital was at the edge of the district and some of his patients were drawn from its streets. But a foolishly sentimental thought and an ambush at the opera placed him under an obligation to spend the day of rest in this most unappealing part of the city. *The Times*'s man, George Dobson, had inquired as to his mental health then accused him of being a dangerous radical.

'How on earth did you get roped into it? When I write your obituary,' he joked over lunch, 'I will be sure to inform our readers that choosing to venture into Peski on a Sunday was not the selfless act they might think but a disgracefully vain one.'

They had dined well together and for too long at one of the city's best restaurants and Hadfield was an hour later than promised at the church. He was to wait in front of the dusty scaffolding at the west end where he would be met and taken to the clinic. Swinging his medical bag a little to draw attention to his profession, he wandered to and fro in its shadow, scrutinising the faces of passers-by for a flicker of recognition. He was on the point of giving up when a boy of about ten, in a traditional belted shirt and with a shock of unkempt red hair, ran out of an alley at full pelt and across the square towards him.

'Doctor?' he asked breathlessly, his head bobbing in an awkward show of deference. 'This way, please.'

'You've been sent by Miss Kovalenko?'

'To take you to the clinic,' he said, wiping his nose with a dirty hand. 'You're late.'

It was all Hadfield could do to keep pace as the boy set off at a trot across the square. On into the dingy alley he had burst from with its galleried timber houses and shop fronts clinging to the mansion blocks like growths, damp and rutted underfoot, the air thick with the stench of rotting vegetable matter and effluent. On past a tavern, a drunk lying face down on the cobbles, the beery carousing of many rising from the cellar below. Right then left then right again, twisting and turning, laundry dripping from the balconies above, an old man in rags hobbling along with his stick, street urchins with bare feet playing with a simple wooden top in the filth, and a young woman with greasy hair, her face empty of expression. After fifteen minutes' hard walking the boy stopped at the door of a long two-storey building rather older in style than the rest of the street and, judging from what was left of the plaster, once a blue-grey colour. Chunks of render had fallen from the wall, exposing the naked pink brick behind, and there were rusty bars before the windows, opaque with grime and bird shit. The boy's fist was raised to the door but it opened before he could knock to reveal a babushka with three small children. Beyond them, a gloomy hall with at least twenty people standing against the walls or sitting on low benches, their faces turned towards Hadfield and the light.

'They're waiting for you,' the boy said, pushing roughly past the old lady. A young man rose from a bench and rapped on a door at the far end. A moment later, Anna Kovalenko was striding across the floor to meet him, the sharp purposeful click of her heels echoing through the hall. She was wearing a white pinafore over her skirt and blouse and her hair was pulled back in a severe bun. The deep frown he remembered so well from their first meeting at the political salon creased her brow and he felt ashamed he had lingered long over coffee and a cigar when sick people were waiting to see him.

'Doctor Hadfield,' she held out her little hand to greet him, 'thank you for coming.'

'I'm so sorry I'm late. I . . .'

But before he could make an excuse she dismissed it with a wave: 'Can we begin?'

Evgenia Figner was waiting in the treatment room. She restricted her disapproval to a sharp look and small shake of

61

the head. The room was rectangular in shape, lit by two sash windows in the short wall opposite the door. A narrow white table stood in the centre with enamel bowls, scissors, strips of cotton cloth and medicine bottles on its scratched and pitted surface. A white bucket for medical waste had been placed on the rough boards beneath it. In one corner of the room a Russian stove, and along the wall a low table for patients' clothes and belongings.

'Is there anything else you need?' The note of apology in Anna's voice to explain there was nothing else.

'No.' He opened his medical bag and took out his coat: 'All right, let's begin.'

The first of the procession: the elderly and the very young, a pregnant woman with severe abdominal pain, a young bargeman with a knife wound to a forearm, a Tajik with infected gums. Burns, cuts, suppurating boils, and the sicknesses of poverty – rickets, malnutrition and a man with the telltale skin lesions of pellagra. Some patients he could refer to Anna and Evgenia for cleaning and bandaging, but most he was obliged to treat himself. At a little before five o'clock, he saw a boy of six with the acute onset of flaccid paralysis in his right arm. His face was pinched, the skin pulled tightly over his cheekbones, and he looked at Hadfield with careless eyes.

'Where's this boy's mother?'

'In the waiting room with her other children,' Anna replied.

'I think he has poliomyelitis. Ask everyone to leave the treatment room and bring her in. And I should look at her other children.'

It was Anna who spoke to the boy's mother using the simple language of the village. The woman was dressed in a grubby purple and white striped dress, her full dark face framed by a red scarf, buxom, no more than twenty-five years of age, new to the city. Her boy was very sick, Anna explained, stroking the woman's face tenderly with the back of her hand. He should be kept from other children, even his little sisters, clinging to their mother, their faces buried in the folds of her dress.

'Do you have something to make him better?' the woman asked, turning to Hadfield. 'You're a doctor, aren't you?' Her lips and chin were twitching with barely suppressed emotion.

'Do you have a room where the boy can sleep on his own?' Hadfield asked.

She shook her head and looked away, but not before Hadfield could see she was biting her lip in an effort to hold back the tears. Anna touched his elbow and took a confidential step closer: 'There are several families in one room. She shares a corner with her sister and her sister's children.'

'And the father?'

'She hasn't seen him for months.'

What could he do? The contagion would have to run its course. It might leave the boy a cripple for life or carry him away, but with nursing and good food there was a chance too of a full recovery. Lifting his medical bag on to the stool beside him, he took out a slip of paper and a pen and wrote a short note.

'Take the boy to the Nikolaevsky Hospital tonight. Will she find it?' he asked Anna.

'I will send someone with her.'

Turning to the boy's mother again: 'Ask for one of my assistants, Anton Pavel, and give him this,' and he handed her the note. 'He will take care of your son. Be sure to ask for Anton.'

They worked on into the gloom of evening, the smoky light from the oil sconces casting Gothic shadows upon the walls. By seven it was clear there would not be time for the many still waiting patiently on the hard benches in the hall and he sent Evgenia to take some simple notes to identify the priority cases. Anna worked beside him in the treatment room and he was impressed by her dexterity; she was an able nurse, sensitive and quick to learn. As he was reaching for scissors to cut a dressing, he touched her cold hand and she looked up at him with a twinkling smile that left him trying to remember the task he was supposed to perform. They were treating their last patient of the day – a man in his twenties with the first bloody signs of consumption – when there was a loud knock at the door, and without waiting for a summons, Grigory Goldenberg walked into the treatment room.

It was more than an unwelcome intrusion. Hadfield felt as if a cold wind had swept in with him, lowering the temperature in the room. Goldenberg was at the clinic to treat no one. He was there to talk of revolution, dressed theatrically for the part in the belted red chemise and high black boots he had worn at the political salon. But Anna was not in the least surprised to see him and offered him her cheek and a warm smile in greeting.

'We haven't been formally introduced, Doctor,' said Goldenberg, offering his hand. 'Such valuable work.'

'Thank you. We've almost finished,' he said, turning to soap his hands in the bowl of water Anna had brought him.

'Then join us for some tea.'

'Yes, Doctor, you must,' said Evgenia from the door.

Hadfield turned to reach for a cloth and glanced over at Anna but her back was turned to him, her head bent over a box of dressings.

'Perhaps just for a few minutes,' he said.

The samovar was set at the edge of a rough table in a long low-vaulted room that looked and smelt like a refectory. Evgenia explained that the building was a poor school but the church had given permission for it to be used as a clinic on Sunday afternoons. What would the priests say if they knew why these 'good women' were administrating to the corporeal needs of their flock, Hadfield wondered. But perhaps that was unduly cynical. Goldenberg's presence was acting as a dark prism, distorting his perception of the work they were doing.

'No milk, I'm afraid,' said Goldenberg. He filled a tarnished pewter pot with water from the samovar, poured a glass and pushed it towards Hadfield. 'We drink tea the Russian way.'

'And so do I,' said Hadfield, settling at the edge of a bench.

'Would you like something to eat, Doctor?' Evgenia asked.

'Thank you, but I'm not hungry.'

'Grigory?' Reaching down to her bag, Evgenia removed the remains of a loaf and some sausage and slid them across the table to Goldenberg, who set about them with gusto.

'Do you intend to make St Petersburg your home, Doctor?' Goldenberg asked between mouthfuls.

'I think of it as home already. I was born here.'

'Dr Hadfield was a close friend of my sisters in Switzerland,' said Evgenia.

'Lydia?' Goldenberg gave a little shake of the head, showering wet crumbs on the table. 'Poor Lydia.'

'I must go,' Hadfield replied and he swung his legs over the bench to rise.

'So soon? Have a little more tea,' said Evgenia.

'My medical bag is in the treatment room.'

'I'll fetch it,' said Anna.

'No, no, that's perfectly all right, I know my way.'

The battered old Gladstone was just where Hadfield had left it on a shelf above the dispensary. He picked it up and made his way back along the dim corridor towards the refectory. The door was ajar and as he approached it he could hear Goldenberg's high-pitched voice.

'I've been following him all week – to and from his office . . .'

On an impulse Hadfield did something he would have condemned as ungentlemanly in others: he waited and listened and watched at the door.

'It would be foolish to attempt it from a moving cab –

65

not after the last time,' Goldenberg continued. The women exchanged a worried glance.

'I don't think we should speak of it now,' said Anna.

'He's guarded, of course: four gendarmes and the driver.' Goldenberg ignored her. 'But it would be possible from the pavement outside Fontanka 16 or close to his home.'

'Let's wait until Alexander's here,' he heard Anna say with steel in her voice.

'What – oh, the doctor . . .' Goldenberg tailed off.

Taking this as his cue, Hadfield pushed open the door and stepped inside. For a few seconds there was an embarrassed silence in which they were careful not to make eye contact with each other. It was Anna who eventually broke it: 'Let me take you to the church, Doctor. You can pick up a cab there.'

'Thank you, but I can find my own way.'

Anna was insistent, rising to her feet: 'The streets are badly lit and it would be easy to lose your way.'

Snatching her coat from the table, she made for the door, plainly anxious to guide him from the building as quickly as possible.

Walking beside her in the dark street, Hadfield was deeply troubled by what he had heard, and he knew from the charged silence that she was conscious of it.

'Are you involved in this?' he asked at last.

She flinched, startled by his directness: 'What did you hear?'

'Enough.'

They were at the corner of a street immediately opposite a small church, a cluster of golden domes, the patriarchal cross silhouetted against the faint gaslight of the city. From a lane a little further on, angry drunken voices drifted closer.

'I've known Grigory a long time, Doctor,' she said, and even in shadow he could see the furrow between her dark eyebrows.

'He has a wild imagination. Yes, we talk of the need for action to bring about the revolution, but . . .'

Her words tailed away as the drunken argument spilled from the lane on to the street. They waited, looking everywhere but at each other, while three peasants, to judge from their clothes, staggered past and into a yard.

'It's idle talk – that's all. Who would trust Grigory to carry out such a . . .' she hesitated, 'delicate, such a delicate task?'

'Murder?'

'No. No,' and she recoiled a little, hurt by the suggestion, 'an attack on the system of oppression.'

'Ah. Yes.'

'Grigory is a talker, that's all. Please believe me. There are no plans for any sort of . . .' she hesitated again, 'political action. I will talk to Grigory, warn him he must be careful what he says.'

She took a step forward, her head at his shoulder, her white face tilted up to him, and his heart beat so fast he was sure she would hear it pounding.

'You won't speak of this to anyone, will you?'

'No.'

'Please forget it. Foolishness, that's all.' She paused and retreated a step, satisfied. 'I'm glad we're going to be friends.'

It was only five minutes more to the square in front of St Boris and St Gleb's. There was not a soul to be seen and little prospect of a cab. She offered to wait with him and he wanted to accept for the pleasure of her company, but he brushed the thought aside as ungallant. 'I know my way from here. I'll take a cab on the embankment. But how will you get back to the school? You can't walk alone.'

She was capable of looking after herself and knew the district well, she said, but thanked him for his concern with a summer smile that set his heart fluttering like the wings of a butterfly.

'And will you help us again?'

'Yes. I will help you.'

Yes, he would visit the clinic the following Sunday and perhaps the Sunday after that. But not for the poor of Peski or from the same woolly operatic urge to 'do something' that had led him to agree in the first place. No. It was curiosity, the shadow of her smile, the scent of her hair as she bent close over the treatment table, and the effortless grace with which she moved.

Not for a moment, for a second, was he taken in by the gossamer thin veil she had attempted to weave about Goldenberg's words. Yes, he was vain and boastful and insecure, so much was obvious, but he was dangerous too. There was a certain self-righteous vanity in all who felt they had a right to kill in cold blood in the furtherance of their cause. Hadfield had met men and women who for all the talk of freedom were motivated by something more prosaic – self-regard or money or sexual desire, or by a simple need to belong – and they would play their part in the revolution too – if it came.


'Ah, Anna, you're back. And how is the good doctor? I was just telling our comrades the story of St Boris and St Gleb's Church.'

Alexander Mikhailov had a soft, cultivated voice and a good-humoured if slippery smile. He was perched at the edge of a long refectory table, Goldenberg and Evgenia sitting on the bench at his feet, and a young man with bad skin and lank greasy hair – a student, to judge from his shabby uniform coat – was standing behind him.

'The city's bakers are paying for the church as a thanks offering for the miraculous deliverance of the tsar from the hands of the revolutionary who took a shot at him ten years ago,' said Mikhailov, shaking his head in a show of incredulity. 'They would have looked pretty silly if poor Alexander Soloviev had aimed a little straighter.'

'You should have let me do it,' said Goldenberg, petulantly. 'I can shoot straight.'

Mikhailov turned lazily to him, his face empty of expression: 'Well, it's taken the bakers ten years to get this far with the church. Perhaps someone will make a decent fist of it before they finish and disappoint them yet.'

Slipping from the bench, he smoothed the tails of his frock coat and turned to Anna: 'We must speak.'

From the refectory, he led her down the corridor and out into the courtyard at the rear. The carriage gates were closed and looked as if they had been for years. On the other three sides, the windows of the building were roughly boarded like a derelict prison. But for a thin shaft of light spilling from the open door across the cracked and weedy flags, the yard was dark, oppressively so. Mikhailov stood at the door with the light at his back, his shadow falling theatrically across her. A showman with a love of conspiracy and the shade, but in the months Anna had worked alongside him she had learnt to recognise that he was the sharpest, the best informed and most security conscious member of their little band. Ruthless, a truly dedi- cated and energetic revolutionary, he was cut from Bakunin's classic mould: everything that promoted the success of the movement was moral, everything that hindered it immoral.

'The English doctor, can he be trusted?'

'Vera Figner says so.'

'And you?'

'I think so too.'

'Is it worth the risk?'

Anna paused to collect her thoughts, sweeping a loose strand of hair back in a single graceful movement. 'Yes, it is worth the risk. He can be useful.'

'But our work is more important than the patients at the clinic.'

'Of course, yes, I know. I'm not a fool. I mean he is very well connected. His uncle is General Glen . . .'

'The financial controller?'

'Yes.'

'Well, that is a different matter, yes.' Mikhailov was impressed. 'But is he with us?'

'He's not against us. I think he can be persuaded . . .' She paused, as if in two minds whether to say more.

'Well?'

'He likes me.'

Mikhailov chuckled and took a step forward to place a hot plump hand on her upper arm. 'We all like you, Anna.'

She shook it free at once, grateful that the darkness was covering the colour she could feel in her face. 'He may be useful, that's all.'

'Yes, he may.' There was nothing in Mikhailov's voice to suggest he felt any embarrassment. 'Just be careful.'

'Of course. It's not me you need to speak to.'

'Oh?'

And she told him of Goldenberg's plan to kill the head of the Third Section. 'The doctor must have overheard him. I tried to convince him it was just silliness, but he isn't an idiot.'

Mikhailov turned away from her and stepped back to the open door, his head bent, pulling distractedly at his thick beard.

'All the more reason to be careful,' he said at last. 'I will speak to Grigory. The time isn't right for another attempt.'

They made their way back along the corridor but at the refectory door Anna stopped and, without turning to look at him, said, 'Did you hear of Alexander?' Her voice shook a little with emotion.

'He showed great courage on the scaffold.'

'You were there?'

'No. But Popov was there.'

'Popov?'

'The student I brought with me tonight.'

Turning the handle sharply, she pushed the door open and walked purposefully into the refectory. They all knew the risk they were taking. Time mourning her friend was time that should be spent fighting for the revolution he gave his life for. What was it Mikhailov had said to them all on the eve of the attempt? 'We can do anything if we are not afraid of death.' Alexander Soloviev had not been afraid.

Goldenberg and Evgenia Figner had been joined at the table by Morozov and Kviatkovsky, Presnyakov and other familiar faces.

'Thank you for coming, comrades,' said Mikhailov, pouring himself a glass of tea. 'We are running a risk, meeting so soon after Alexander's death, but I have some important news. A conference has been called to discuss our ideas for a new party.'

It would be held at a city in the south-west, he told them, invitations delivered by hand to socialist groups all over Russia. 'This is our chance to argue the case for our campaign. The people want us to lead them and they need something to fight for.' To prepare for the conference, they must visit supporters and raise money. It would have to be done in complete secrecy.

'And that brings me to the spy, Bronstein.' Mikhailov placed his glass on the table and clasped his hands together like a priest in prayer. 'Madame Volkonskaya's house is being watched. No one should go there or try to contact her. Our friend Popov,' and he nodded towards the unprepossessing figure lurking at the fringe of the circle, 'has been making contacts with the workers at the Baird Foundry but he is being watched by another informer. You seem to attract them like flies to dung, don't you, Popov? Tomorrow he will leave the city. And you, Grigory,' he said, turning to Goldenberg, 'you must leave too.'

Goldenberg's face fell. 'Why me? How can you be sure they're looking for me? I don't . . .'

Mikhailov cut him short. 'You know better than to ask.' No one in the group doubted that Mikhailov knew of what he spoke. Time and again he had presented them with startling intelligence, like a magician pulling a rabbit from a hat. His sources were jealously guarded, and the group was obliged to take what he told them on trust. Knowledge is power, he had told them, when speaking of their struggle, and his unique access to it placed him first among equals.

The conversation turned to the formation of workers' groups, new cells in the army and navy, and of Mikhailov's plans for a printing press. At a little before ten o'clock the meeting broke up and they began to slip into the night in ones and twos.

'Did you instruct Popov to – to deal with Bronstein?' Anna asked when she was alone again with Mikhailov. They were standing at the front door waiting for the yard keeper to return and lock the school.

'Why do you ask?'

She paused to consider her words carefully. 'Is it right that one person can take the decision to kill in the name of the group?' she said at last.

'Don't you trust me?'

'That isn't the point.'

'Anna. Think.' And for once his soft at-your-service voice was sharp with impatience. 'You know perfectly well that in such cases there isn't time for a motion and a vote.'

Mikhailov was right, she knew that, and yet she felt uneasy. It must – as always – have been written in her face.

'Is there more?' he asked, his small brown eyes hunting for hers. 'Is there something you aren't telling me? Perhaps this English doctor?'

'Don't be foolish.'

But the clever little smile had returned to Mikhailov's face. 'Let's hope he is a servant to the movement. We'll know soon enough, won't we?'

'Yes.' Her voice was a little husky, barely more than a whisper: 'Yes, we will.'

# 8

It was clear from his restless movement that the yard keeper did not relish the opportunity he had been presented with to serve his tsar.

'Calm down, man, for God's sake.'

Major Barclay had no time for his squeamishness. What was his name? Barclay had forgotten. These smelly gatekeepers all looked the same with their padded jackets and shaggy beards. They were side by side beneath the carriage arch of a large terracotta-coloured mansion block, the soft early sun blinking over the roof of the building opposite. Five minutes to the signal. His men were in place. Both ends of the 3rd Izmailovsky Regiment Street and the open courtyards in the district sealed. Two entrances to the apartment block. The front covered from the building on the opposite side of the street, and the back by a dozen gendarmes in the doorways and shadows of an especially gloomy little yard. If he had any sense, Popov would have reconnoitred a number of escape routes, but Barclay was confident he had covered all the possibilities. He glanced at his pocket watch: 'All right, it's five, let's get him.'

Grasping the dvornik's upper arm, he led him none too gently into the street then almost immediately right through the open doorway of the mansion block. He knocked lightly at the first apartment he came to and Kletochnikov opened the door. In the room behind him another agent – Postnikov – dressed as a labourer in a peaked cap and short woollen coat.

'Check your weapons again,' said Barclay, drawing his own Smith and Wesson: six good .44 Russian cartridges in the cylinder. Then turning to the dvornik: 'It's up to you now.' The man was shaking like a leaf. 'Come on, you were in the army, weren't you?' Barclay placed a firm hand on his shoulder. 'He isn't expecting us. Remember, stand aside as soon as he opens the door. Have you got the letter?'

Rummaging inside his padded jacket, the yard keeper pulled out an envelope and offered it in a trembling hand to Barclay.

'No, no. Dmitry, isn't it? Dmitry, you give it to Popov.' He tried to keep the frustration from his voice.

Anxious to get the business over with, the silly Ivan began thundering up to the first landing at a pace unknown to his breed.

'Wait!' Barclay hissed. 'Wait there.' He turned to Kletochnikov. 'You first.' He nodded to the stairs. 'I'll follow in thirty seconds. Go.'

He watched the two men make their way as quietly as policemen can up the broad stone steps to the second landing. Then, leaning close to the dvornik's ear, he whispered fiercely: 'Try again. And don't let me down.'

Shoulders hunched, the yard keeper set off up the dark stairs with Barclay at his back. There were six heavy green doors on the third landing. Barclay's men were on either side of the one at the top of the stairs. Kletochnikov wiped his arm across his forehead nervously and his revolver thumped against the door frame. Barclay shot him a withering look. Was the fool deliberately trying to alert the student?

'Call him,' he whispered, pushing the dvornik towards the door. For what seemed an age, he stood there blinking on the step. Barclay was about to step forward when the man finally raised his fist and hammered on the door. The echo bounced up and down the stairs. Barclay pressed himself to the wall behind Kletochnikov.

'Call him,' he mouthed.

'Your Honour. A letter.'

Barclay waved his fist at the wall to indicate he should knock again. But before the dvornik could do so, they heard the turning of the lock on the inner door.

'What is it, Dmitry?' There was no mistaking the wariness in Popov's voice.

'A letter. An urgent letter.'

Just the degree of obsequiousness one expected from a yard keeper: Dmitry was warming to his role.

The reply came from the thickness of a door away: 'Push the letter under.'

'I can't.'

'Is there anyone with you?'

'No.'

'I don't believe you.'

'Suit yourself,' the dvornik grumbled. For sure, he was earning his rouble now. 'I'll take it away then, shall I?'

No reply.

'Well?' Dmitry asked.

'Leave it there,' came the muffled response.

'As you wish.'

The yard keeper bent to place the letter at the foot of the door, then, rising, turned with pleading eyes to Barclay who nodded approvingly and gestured to the staircase. The relief was transparent in the dvornik's face, even beneath his thick beard. But cleverer than he looks, Barclay thought, as he listened to his steady tread – at least he had remembered to take his time.

The echo of his footsteps began to die away and Barclay could sense the revolutionary a few feet from him, his ear pressed to the door. He was acutely conscious of the sound of his own short shaky breaths and of Kletochnikov's beside him. Was Popov a patient man? It was only a matter of time before one of the other tenants caught them there or a careless movement gave them away. Pressed against the wall like an animal waiting to pounce, his heart thumping in his chest, Barclay had no sense of how long they had been standing there but his arm was aching with the strain of holding the heavy revolver up in readiness. On the opposite side of the door, little Postnikov was squatting with his head against the wall, his gun beneath his chin, the letter at his feet.

Barclay could hear the groaning of the floorboards behind the door as the student shifted his weight in the hall. Then the rattle of a key pushed into the lock. Kletochnikov raised his weapon. The door swung open and Popov was standing there with a terrified expression on his face, in his right hand a revolver. For a fraction of a second he was caught between fight and flight, pushing at the door and at the same time raising his weapon to fire. But Postnikov's shoulder was against it: 'Drop it!'

Then the deafening crash of a shot fired at close range. Kletochnikov lunged at the student's outstretched arm but missed and struck his head against the edge of the door.

'I'll shoot!' Popov shouted, stepping back into the apartment.

Another shot rang out, reverberating up and down the staircase. A woman in an apartment on the landing below began to scream. At the foot of the door, Agent Postnikov was groaning pathetically, plucking at the right leg of his trousers as blood flowed across the stone in a widening circle. Barclay could hear the boots of the gendarmes racing up the stairs towards them.

'Come out with your hands above your head,' he shouted through the half open door. 'Don't be foolish. Come out and we can talk.'

There were half a dozen men shoulder to shoulder on the landing now, rifles at the ready.

'See to him,' he said, pointing to the prostrate agent. Fat lot of use the rifles would be in a small apartment.

Barclay was angry. A bad plan. An agent wounded. Damn it, he was not going to let Popov get away with destroying evidence too. There was nowhere for the bastard to go. He pushed at the outer door and it swung open a little further. Beyond it, a small dark hall and beyond this, three doors off a corridor, the nearest the student's bed-sitting room.

'Follow me,' he hissed to Kletochnikov. The agent was pressing a bloody handkerchief to the cut on his brow. 'Come on, man, he's a student, not a Leshy.'

He pushed at the inner door. Its stiff hinges squeaked noisily. The corridor was no bigger than the width of a man's outstretched arms and a bullet fired blind through a door might very well find a mark somewhere. Barclay pressed the flat of his hand against the wall to warn Kletochnikov he should step away from the firing line. Then, taking a position to the left of the first door, he squatted on his haunches and reached for the handle.

'I'll shoot anyone who comes through that door!' Popov shouted, fear ringing in his voice, but determination too. A second later, a shot rang out, deafening in the narrow corridor. Splinters flew from the edge of the door as the bullet ricocheted against it and out on to the landing. Behind Barclay, Kletochnikov was breathing very hard, blood from the wound on his brow trickling unchecked down both cheeks. Barclay clicked his fingers sharply to capture his attention, then shook his revolver angrily at the agent: concentrate, stand ready. Popov's careless shot had helped clear his mind and in the time it took for the echo to die away he knew what he must do.

'Lay down your weapon. I'm coming in,' he shouted and, bending low, he turned the handle of the door. It was neither locked nor bolted. Shards of wood splintered above his arm as another shot rang round the little hall. Go now as Popov's arm is shaking, his ears still ringing. Go while he is surprised and afraid of the sound of his own weapon. Go. And Barclay launched himself at the door, stumbling low into the room, dazzlingly bright with sunlight. Confused, he cracked his knee

77

on a piece of furniture and fell heavily on to his shoulder. Where was Kletochnikov?

He could see the silhouette of Popov against the window, only four or five feet from him, his weapon at arm's length. The shot would be almost point blank.

'Drop it,' Barclay shouted. 'Drop it.'

The gun was trembling in Popov's hand, the low sun kicking off the barrel. Barclay could not distinguish the expression on his face but he could see the student's finger curled about the trigger.

'Drop it,' he shouted again. 'You're under arrest.' Where was that bastard Kletochnikov? Fire then, damn you. Fire.

But Popov gave a small high-pitched whimper like a child and staggered back against the wall. With a rigid jerk like a marionette, he lifted the gun to his own head. It hovered at his temple for a fraction of a second then 'crack'. Blood erupted from the side of his head, plastering window and walls, his lifeless body crumpling to the boards with a sickeningly final thud.

'Are you all right, sir?'

Someone was holding Barclay's arm but he paid no attention. His gaze was fixed on the window, the sun shining through a coagulated mass of pink and white brain matter sliding slowly down the dirty glass. The spark of life lost in one foolish moment. An impulse. But he owed his own life to that impulse. An accident of time, place, circumstance, and on a different day it would be his tissue the gendarmes would scrape from the corners of the room.

He let Kletochnikov help him to his feet. His knees were shaking. The gendarmes had crowded into the room to gaze at the body of the student.

'Go on, get out until I call you,' he shouted. Surely they had seen a dead man before? 'Not you, Kletochnikov. I want you to see if he's got anything on him.'

The agent began pulling gingerly at the dead man's jacket, while Barclay shuffled about the room in search of anything that might be a clue. The student must have been preparing to leave his flat that day, his personal belongings were packed into a small suitcase he had left at the door. In spite of the earliness of the hour, Popov was dressed and had eaten – the remains of a stale loaf and a glass of tea were on a table close to the window. The bed was stripped, the blankets neatly folded at the bottom of it. Barclay picked up the case – it was surprisingly heavy – and threw it on to the bed. Books. The usual texts; Marx, Chernyshevsky, Bakunin, a novel by Dickens and some threadbare and rather dirty clothes.

'Anything?' he asked, turning to Kletochnikov.

'Only this ticket,' he replied, rising stiffly to his feet. 'Today's train to Moscow, and another for Voronezh. Some money. A photograph.'

'Let me see?'

It was of a woman in her late forties or early fifties, elegant, conservatively dressed, her figure a little matronly, perhaps Popov's mother, but in any case not a terrorist. But then who could be sure these days?

'Have you checked his boots and hat?'

Kletochnikov turned back to the body and began pulling clumsily at the dead man's boots. The student's navy blue cap had been thrown to the floor by the force of the bullet bursting from the side of his head and was sticky with blood and flecks of tissue. Barclay ripped at the cotton lining and it came away with ease. Nothing. No prisoner, no papers. It was a fiasco. For a few unpleasant seconds his thoughts turned to the interview with Dobrshinsky that would follow later in the day. Picking one of Popov's shirts from the bed, he wiped the blood from his hands. Kletochnikov was still grunting over the student's legs, making very heavy weather of a simple task.

In his effort to prise boot from foot, the agent had dragged the body from the window, leaving a crimson trail across the boards. Barclay's eyes were drawn to a slash of sunlight flickering across the floor close to the student's shattered head. The wood was scorched black.

'Leave it, will you.'

There was a brutal thump as Kletochnikov dropped a booted foot.

'Help me roll him over.'

Beneath the student's body was a crushed heap of damp ashes and fragments of charred paper. Crouching beside it, Barclay took a pencil from his coat and stirred the pile for something worth salvaging. Popov had done a good job. There were only five pieces with anything he could decipher. Handwritten on the largest strip were a number of dates and the names of cities in the south – Kiev, Kharkov, Voronezh. The student was about to set out on his travels. There were two small fragments from an internal passport, almost certainly Popov's own. A wanted man, he would have travelled on forged documents, although Kletochnikov had found none on his body. But it was the last two fragments that proved the most intriguing. They were from the same distinctive light blue letter paper and written, Barclay noted, in a cultured hand. Mikhailov's? He would be able to establish that beyond doubt because a handwriting specimen collected from the revolutionary's family was sitting in the top drawer of his desk at Fontanka 16.

*Kovalenko will meet you at the station at precisely . . .*
The time was lost . . . *money and instructions for you.*
*Destroy all your papers then leave at once, and under*
*no circumstances return to your apartment. It is being*
*watched. We will deal with . . .*

'. . . with the informer,' Barclay muttered.

'Your Honour?'

'Find the dvornik and ask him when Popov last received a letter. Take a description of whoever delivered it.'

So the student knew he was under surveillance. Mikhailov had warned him. How on earth did he find out? And Kovalenko – that was one of the six names on Bronstein's list. Who was he? And the names of cities – contacts or meetings? Questions. Questions Barclay would have put to the fool at his feet if he had not blown the little brain he was blessed with about his shabby room.

'All right,' he shouted irritably to the gendarmes. 'You can come in now.'

He would have them take the place apart, but he was quite certain they would find nothing more. At least the student had spared the empire the expense and trouble of a trial for murder. Sadly, the collegiate councillor was unlikely to take quite such a generous view of the morning's events.

# 9

Hadfield remembered why the address was familiar over a breakfast of coffee and warm rolls. Fontanka 16. Foolish to forget. The Third Section of the tsar's private chancellery. Goldenberg was watching a secret policeman or officer of the Gendarme Corps. Who? He worried at it like a dog with a bone. The answer came to him as he was brushing his jacket. Someone had attempted to take the life of the head of the Third Section. Hadfield had heard mention of it at the opera a few weeks before. A revolutionary fired two shots through the window of General Drenteln's carriage and narrowly missed with both. Goldenberg was watching the general, no doubt with a view to making a better fist of it next time. But if that was the case, what on earth should he do about it? He was pondering this question before his dressing mirror when there was a sharp knock at the door of the apartment. Sergei, the dvornik, was on the step with an armful of birch logs for the fire, at his back three serving women in peasant smocks with stiff brushes attached to the soles of their boots.

'The floor, Your Honour,' he said, reaching awkwardly for his cap. 'You said it would be convenient?'

Hadfield let them pass, then retreated to his bedroom to finish ministering to collar and tie. Gruff instructions and the squeak of furniture on the move reached him through the door and when, a moment later, he stepped back into the drawing room, it was to find the women gliding across his parquet like patineurs in an ice waltz. By the time he returned from the hospital the floor in every room would be polished to glassy perfection.

A little after eight o'clock the cab rattled to a halt before the main entrance to the Nikolaevsky. Hadfield was so caught up in his thoughts that the driver was obliged to jump from his seat and stand at the front wheel with his dirty palm open for the fare. What was there to decide? Hadfield asked himself as he counted out the kopeks. That he should go to the police was quite unthinkable. A few careless words and he would condemn not only Goldenberg to years in a Siberian camp but Anna and Evgenia too.

'Very generous, Your Honour.'

The broad smile on the cabby's face suggested Hadfield should have concentrated harder on the fare. He knew it would be wiser to have nothing to do with the clinic in Peski. Inevitably, he would be drawn into further contact with Goldenberg or men very like him. Resolve to have no more dealings with her while it is in your power to do so, he thought. Resolve now, here in this hospital on this bright morning.

'Good morning, Your Honour.' It was the old porter who kept order at the main door, cap in hand like a peasant on rent day. The long benches in the entrance hall were already crowded with soldiers and their families waiting to see a doctor. Nurses in stiff white pinafores and scarves bustled about them taking names and regiments and the symptoms of their complaints. The Nikolaevsky had opened as a military hospital in the reign of the tsar's father and grown steadily ever since, its imposing yellow and white frontage creeping year by year down Slonovaya Street. In the few months Hadfield had spent there he had formed the impression that it was well run, clean and surprisingly progressive. Most of his patients were on the general wards, but his departmental superior was familiar with a paper he had written on public health and the pathology of diseases, and he had been asked to carry out a discreet review of general practices in parts of the hospital. It was his duty that day to visit the department for the treatment of mental diseases for the first time. The Nikolaevsky was an unforgiving place and although he asked for directions more than once he was still wandering its maze of broad white corridors half an hour later. Finally losing patience, he pressganged a porter into service as a guide. From the main buildings, he was led along a path through a rough garden to the hospital's boiler house. Two low workmen's huts had been built against its high wall, their roofs of rusty iron, their rough timber walls weathered and bare but for a few sloughs of green paint, their windows partly boarded.

The porter pointed to the door of the first hut.

'That's Department 10? Are you sure?'

'Yes.'

Hadfield knew a little of its reputation from a Russian colleague who had threatened him in jest with exile to Siberia or worse – Department 10. Knocking at the first hut, he was greeted by an oath then the scraping of a key in the lock. The door was opened by a ruddy-faced man in his early sixties with the broken veins and bloodshot eyes of a heavy drinker. He was wearing a faded green army uniform, the jacket stained with food and unbuttoned to the waist. He took Hadfield in at a glance.

'Ryabovsky, Your Honour. Fyodor Ivanovich.' He made a low insincere bow. 'Warder, porter, nurse and general dogsbody.'

There was an insolence in his manner that made Hadfield's hackles rise. 'Where are the patients?' he snapped.

Ryabovsky turned to the inner door behind him and unlocked it with a key that was hanging from the chain on his belt. Even before it was fully open, Hadfield was revolted by the over-powering smell of stale urine. Reaching for his handkerchief, he stood in the doorway, his eyes slowly adjusting to the gloom. By the light of a single oil lamp he could see the hut was laid out as a ward, but in place of beds the floor was strewn with rough straw mattresses. And it was heaving with bodies, young men for the most part, military coats fastened over dirty hospital

84

gowns. The plank walls were caked in soot and smoke hung thick about the hut, although the two primitive stoves that were the only source of heat were unlit.

'Who are these men?' he asked, turning again to Ryabovksy.

'The war with Turkey. They're sick in the head.'

'Why don't these men have proper beds?' It was a sordid unsanitary scene that brought to his mind an engraving of the hospital at Scutari twenty-five years before.

Ryabovsky gave a careless shrug: 'Perhaps no one knows what to do with them, Your Honour.'

Frightened faces, empty faces, hollow faces, half-dressed, bare chilblained feet, some with dirty bandages or undressed bed sores, some curled tightly into whimpering balls like children, others defiant. Hadfield stepped among them, stopping to examine those with symptoms of a condition he was qualified to treat, but most were beyond his help. Perhaps they were lucky not to have been shot. He had read enough of these strange war injuries to know there was precious little sympathy in the army for casualties like these. He knew what Anna and Evgenia would say: 'Fool! See how the tsar treats his most loyal servants.'

'And is it the same in the other hut?'

'A few less, Your Honour.'

'This is a disgrace!' Hadfield spat the words at Ryabovsky.

But the old man merely shrugged again.

Hadfield was still shaking with rage five minutes later as he stood among the brambles in the boiler-house garden, the June sun warming his back. Cross with the army for neglecting the men, and with the hospital authorities, but cross most of all with his medical colleagues for making a joke of such a place. But he knew too that if he confronted them they would give him a very Russian shrug of resignation. 'How can you be surprised?' they would ask. 'Such places exist in Russia. What would you have us do?'

The superintendent's suite was on a bright first-floor corridor above the main entrance. It was the one place in the hospital that did not smell of ammonia or boiled cabbage but of floor polish and gentleman's cologne. Military clerks in immaculate green uniforms glided from panelled room to panelled room through perfectly weighted mahogany doors that swung silently to behind them. It was as remote from the day to day business of the hospital as his uncle's ministry.

'Have you an appointment?' the superintendent's secretary asked. 'As you can see, Doctor, there are others waiting.' He turned to indicate two uniformed public servants and an elderly man in a frock coat whom Hadfield had seen in the corridors of the hospital and knew to be a surgeon.

'It is a matter of great urgency,' Hadfield replied calmly. 'One that affects the reputation of the hospital.'

The secretary frowned. 'May I suggest you go through the usual channels, Doctor, and speak to your head of department?' This was clearly meant to be his final word on the matter. Turning to the surgeon, he opened his leather-bound file and was on the point of handing him an official-looking letter when Hadfield gripped him firmly by his upper arm.

'I really think you should speak to him,' he said, tugging him to one side. 'Believe me, you'll regret it if you don't.'

'Why will I regret it, Doctor?'

'You know, of course, that my uncle, General Glen, is a good friend of the superintendent's?'

He had promised himself he would never use his uncle's name for advantage but he had to admit to a quiet satisfaction as the supercilious expression on the secretary's face changed in the blink of an eye.

'Of course, of course. I understand.' The secretary's words pattered like gentle rain.

'And did reason prevail?' Dobson asked.

Exhausted, Hadfield had collapsed into one of the leather

smoking chairs in the correspondent's office at a little after six o'clock that evening. He was still angry, but satisfied too that a day of frantic activity, of threats, flattery and cajoling, promised to make a difference to the lives of seventy very sick men.

'Not reason. Nepotism and naked self-interest. And you know, George,' he said, as Dobson pressed a glass into his hand, 'I was surprised by my own mendacity.'

Dobson laughed. 'You're an educated man, Hadfield. You used the weapons available to you for the benefit of those men. Besides, there is nothing you can teach a public servant in Russia about lying he doesn't already know. '

'But where does one draw the line?' Hadfield had spoken to the superintendent of public scandal, of a friend on the *St Petersburg Gazette* who was pursuing a story on the treatment of casualties in the recent war. He had mentioned a confidential visit his uncle was hoping to make to the hospital with other members of the government. And he had told the bucolic old superintendent that the general had told him a prominent member of the royal family had expressed his concern.

'I even mentioned the foreign press and my friend on *The Times*.'

'You snake,' said Dobson with a short barking laugh. He took a cigarette from a silver box on his desk, lit it then flopped into the armchair opposite Hadfield. 'And what is going to happen to Department 10?'

The superintendent had promised beds and nursing care, that he would gradually transfer the men to the body of the hospital and contact their families. 'And those who do not recover will be moved to an asylum – although I suppose that will be like jumping from the frying pan into the fire.'

'But you've done what you can,' Dobson replied, leaning forward with the wine bottle to fill Hadfield's glass. 'And risked a good deal to do so.'

'Not really.'

'Well, what about good relations with General Glen? It would be unwise to rub him up the wrong way. You will forgive me for saying so, I hope, but your uncle is not a man to cross.'

It was rumoured the general was pursuing newspapers that had the temerity to criticise his stewardship of the empire's finances and that the censor was on the point of stepping in to suppress further adverse comment. 'At least the general has helped you do a good turn, even if he is threatening to put the rest of us out of our jobs,' he said with a cheerful twinkle.

It was entirely typical of Dobson to find humour and the kernel of something positive in even the grimmest of situations. In a relatively short time, he and Hadfield had become friends. They were much the same age, Englishmen who considered Russia to be home, they shared a passion for the language and a fascination with the people and their customs. Dobson had taught himself Russian, then persuaded *The Times* to accredit him as a war correspondent, and had reported with distinction on the recent conflict with Turkey. His father owned a small cotton mill in one of the new manufacturing towns in the Midlands. Less fortunate in his education than Hadfield, he had more than made up for his shortcomings by becoming a ruthless autodidact. He was a little on the plump side, but his flabby good-humoured face and high forehead leant him a certain ageless quality. One of the second secretaries at the embassy had likened him cruelly to Mr Pickwick. But anyone who took Dobson for a gull was a poor judge of character. He was not only resourceful but determined, with a reputation at the embassy for clinging to a story like a ferret to a rabbit. In politics, he was a new town liberal, in favour of universal suffrage for men but not for women, an admirer of Mr Gladstone and a passionate supporter of a free press. In his column for *The Times*, he was a discreet critic of Russia's despotic government but had no time for 'nihilists' or 'socialist revolutionaries'. As they sat in the correspondent's comfortable study, surrounded by piles of Russian newspapers, books and maps, and his prints of Petersburg, Hadfield wondered what his friend would say if he knew the sort of people he had been consorting with at the clinic. A little heady after two glasses of wine on an empty stomach, he was almost tempted to confide in him, but Dobson would speak sharply to him of the risk he was running, would advise having nothing further to do with Anna and the Figners and might even suggest reporting Goldenberg to the police: in the end he chose to keep his counsel.

'Let me ask you again, Dobson, where does one draw the line beyond which the means cannot be justified by the ends?'

Easing his heavy frame from the chair, the correspondent reached across the desk for another cigarette, lit it and inhaled a long thoughtful stream of smoke: 'Are you suggesting one is obliged to draw a different line in Russia?'

'Yes, I suppose I am.'

'Of course one has to be guided by conscience . . .' Dobson paused to flick a little ash from his cigarette, 'but perhaps we can be forgiven for taking a few more liberties with the truth in this country. It would be quite impossible to change anything for the better otherwise.'

When Hadfield visited Department 10 the following day, things had already changed markedly for the better. Most of the men had been moved to other wards, but those that remained were in beds, the floors were clean, the rooms well lit and workmen were fitting glass to the windows. Warder Ryabovsky had been replaced by two large and efficient-looking middle-aged women in blue uniforms who were dispensing Hadfield's prescription of potassium bromide and morphine to the patients. Some of the men were sitting on benches in the sunshine, watching a work gang cutting back the brambles and burdock in the garden. The story of the 'English doctor's' triumph was already known throughout the hospital and military doctors he had never met stopped him in the corridors to offer their congratulations. He took particular care to ensure a favourable report reached his uncle by visiting his aunt and cousin during the day when the general was at his ministry. 'But he will want to hear all about it,' his aunt said, holding his hand between hers. 'How on earth did you manage to persuade the hospital?' In reply, Hadfield was fulsome in his praise for the superintendent – 'a most reasonable and caring man'.

His aunt pressed him to join the family for a carriage ride into the countryside on the Sunday, but he made his excuses. Although he had resolved more than once not to go to the clinic, he went to some lengths to be sure he had no other commitments. He was still debating the wisdom of his promise to Anna in the droshky that afternoon as it rattled and swayed across the Nikolaevsky Bridge, and even while he stood in the fine summer rain before St Boris and St Gleb's, waiting for his guide. The boy with red hair who had met him on his first visit was his silent companion again. After twenty minutes weaving through the streets of the district, they reached the clinic at last to find a crowd gathered about the entrance. His guide drew him by the sleeve round the throng to where Anna was standing a little apart. She glanced up at him as he approached, then away without a word, the intense frown that never left her for long troubling her brow. A frosty sort of welcome, Hadfield thought, and particularly galling after a week in which she had often been in his thoughts. He stared at her for a moment, hoping she would register the frustration in his face, but her attention was fixed on the circle of men. Turning to follow her gaze, he caught a glimpse of what he took to be a man kneeling, crumpled forward at their feet, and he pushed forward, parting the shoulders of the men in front of him: 'I'm a doctor.' The circle began to close, heads straining to see what the gentleman was doing. A woman was shouting at them to step back and as he sank beside the slumped figure he was conscious of Anna standing above him.

'Can you hear me?' he asked, and he shook the man gently.

But it took only a few seconds for Hadfield to realise he was never going to hear anything in this world again. By a quirk of fate the man had collapsed to his knees as if in prayer. Too late for that, Hadfield thought, lifting his head to look into his lifeless brown eyes. Early forties, grizzled beard, florid face, his mouth a little open, revealing black and broken teeth, a dribble of blood at the corner. A broad man reduced in death to a malodorous ball.

'No one wants to touch him,' said Anna in a low voice.

Hadfield looked up to find her bending close. 'Do you know who he is?'

'They say he's a drunk, a vagrant,' she said hesitantly. 'He's been seen loitering in the district, sleeping rough.'

'Well, why on earth doesn't someone move him or call the police?' He realised at once that this was a foolish question to ask.

'It's bad luck.'

There was a murmur of assent from those close by.

'For God's sake! Do you believe that?'

'Of course not,' said Anna. The colour rising in her neck and cheeks suggested this was a half truth.

'We can't leave him here for people to step over. You and you,' said Hadfield, pointing at two men in the crowd, 'help me, will you?'

It took an hour of bullying and coaxing in equal measure before they were able to persuade willing souls to help them move the body into the school. And in that hour a waiting room packed with the sick and anxious began to empty.

'It's him,' said Anna when they were alone, and she nodded

at the corpse on the table before them. 'It's bad luck to be in the same building.'

'Superstitious nonsense. I'm going to look at him. He wasn't struck down by a devil.'

'Does it matter what he died of?'

The wariness in her voice surprised him: 'Well, for one thing it's important to know if it was something infectious. You can leave this to me if you like?'

'No,' she said firmly.

'Here . . .' He tossed her a surgical mask.

It took only a few minutes for Hadfield to be sure they were in no danger of catching a disease. Beneath the dead man's jacket, his shirt was stained with a ragged circle of congealed blood. A thin blade had been driven into his heart.

'Murdered,' Hadfield muttered, 'and by someone who knew what he was doing.' He turned to look at Anna: 'Are you all right?'

Her gaze was fixed on the seeping wound in the vagrant's chest. He watched her lift a trembling hand to her lips where it hovered uncertainly. She looked pale, her eyes large and glittering, the pupils dilated.

'You look as if you've seen a ghost.' He touched her elbow gently. 'Do you recognise him?'

She turned quickly, suddenly aware of his hand on her arm. 'No. No.'

'Are you sure?'

'I've never seen him before.'

'I'm sorry. It was crass of me to ask you to help . . .'

'No, it's quite all right,' she said. 'I am used to the dead.' She was her brisk matter-of-fact self again.

There were precious few patients left to see, and within an hour the waiting room was empty but for the school dvornik dozing on a bench, his shoulders wedged into the angle between two walls.

'Did the crowd know our man was murdered?' Hadfield asked as he slipped back into his jacket.

'Yes,' she said simply. 'The waiting room will be full again next week.'

They covered the body with a dirty blanket and left it in the surgery for the priests. Tearing a leaf of paper from his journal, Hadfield began writing a note. 'I'm going to tell them he was murdered. I'll leave my address. I don't expect the police will bother to contact me but they may want . . .'

'No.' She took an urgent step towards him and snatched at the paper.

'What on earth—'

She stood over him tugging at the top edge of the note, but he had it firmly anchored to the table with his fist and after a few seconds she let go.

'Let me have it!' Her jaw was set, the colour high in her cheeks, that same deep, stubborn frown on her face. 'Please.'

'Certainly not,' he said quietly. 'Not until you explain yourself, Miss Kovalenko.'

She took a deep breath and turned reluctantly away. 'Isn't it obvious?'

'Not to me.'

'The police would want to know what a smart foreign doctor was doing in Peski on a Sunday afternoon. And they would want to know who was with you,' she said. 'Leave it to the dvornik. He will say he found the body outside.'

'I see. But why didn't you say so? Why throw a tantrum?'

'Wasn't it ladylike?' she said with something close to a sneer in her voice.

'It was ill-mannered.'

Her shoulders seemed to drop a little, and she closed her eyes, the anger and tension draining from her: 'Yes, perhaps. You won't leave your name?'

'No. If it's so important, no, I won't.' He picked up the

paper, ripped it in half and offered her the pieces: 'Here.'

Anna took them without making eye contact and tore them in half again: 'I'll speak to the dvornik.'

Hadfield waited beside the body. He was astonished by her outburst. After a few minutes she returned and began clearing away the things they had used for the surgery in silence, at pains to avoid his gaze. She was clearly a little embarrassed and would probably have welcomed an excuse to soften the atmosphere that lingered in the room like the smell of formaldehyde. But Hadfield was content to watch her, enjoying her discomfort.

'I will take you to the church,' she said, turning to look at him at last.

'Thank you.'

Standing awkwardly at the school door, Hadfield could not suppress an acute sense of disappointment and frustration. This was not how the day was supposed to be, and he fought to extinguish the ember of resentment that was still glowing inside. Anna was in conversation with the dvornik who was leaning against the door jamb, a sullen look on his face. Hadfield cleared his throat and was on the point of addressing her when she turned sharply to look at him: 'Do you have a few kopeks you can give him?'

'Of course. Twenty?' He gave them to the dvornik, who counted them laboriously then held out his greasy palm for more.

'That's enough,' said Anna sharply, but the grizzled old yard keeper stood there unmoved, his hand held flat like a Russian Buddha.

'Oh, for God's sake, take this!' Hadfield handed him twenty kopeks more. 'Satisfied?'

The dvornik gave a broad toothless grin.

'The old devil!' Anna said as the door closed behind him. 'What did I buy?'

'The right story, of course. He found the body. We weren't here.'

'Ah.'

'This way.' She set off down the street at a brisk pace, passing from sunlight into the shadow of the four-storey lodging house opposite. From every open window, from the doorways and the yards on that hot summer Sunday, the restless sound of humanity packed cheek-by-jowl into single rooms and corners. He watched her stride purposefully on as if careless whether he followed or not: past a little group of children, barefoot, in rags, racing sticks across a puddle of dirty water, and on a little further to where three immodestly-dressed young women were gossiping in a doorway – one of whom directed a remark at Anna then burst into a peal of raucous tipsy laughter. He caught up with her at the end of the street.

'Miss Kovalenko, if you have no other appointments, can I persuade you to walk with me a little?'

She turned to him with a shy smile, her blue eyes twinkling like sunshine on ice. 'Yes, you can persuade me.'

From St Boris and St Gleb's, they ambled north along the bank of the Neva, and Hadfield told her of his first meeting with the Figners, of their time together in Zurich and of the unhappy years he had spent in London since. 'It was always my ambition to return to St Petersburg.'

'To leave your home?'

'St Petersburg is my home.'

'And General Glen is your uncle?'

He smiled at the disingenuously casual way the question was slipped into their conversation. 'Yes. Of course, we don't see eye to eye on many things but he has been very kind to me.'

'Does he know about your time in Switzerland, your views?' she asked.

'I try not to talk politics.'

'Do you go to grand parties with him?'

'Sometimes.'

'What are they like?'

'What are they like?' He turned to look at her to be sure she wasn't teasing. 'Actually, rather dull.'

But Anna was not to be deflected and pressed him to describe a ball he had attended, from the sparkling crystal to the servants and the dance card, and – in so far as he was able – the dresses of the society ladies. And although he failed to do justice to the opulence of the occasion in his rather clinical descriptions, she seemed captivated by the picture he painted for her.

'But ask the Figners! I'm sure they've been to fashionable parties and could tell you much more about dresses than I can,' he said.

She pretended to look shocked. 'What on earth would they think of me?' she asked, and her shoulders shook a little with silent laughter.

In the gardens of the Smolny, they settled on a bench close to the School for Noble Girls and he asked her of her family and her home. Her father had been an army officer and a gentleman with an estate near Kharkov, her mother one of his servants. As a small child she had lived with an old babushka in the village, and on winter nights had sat at the stove and listened to folk tales in the Ukrainian language and stories of Cossack heroes. With the emancipation of the serfs, Colonel Kovalenko had used his influence to register Anna as a member of the meschanstvo – the lower middle class – and sent her to the local gymnasium. She was never close to her father, she said, even as a young girl the thought that her mother was no more than a chattel who could be sold to another member of the gentry was intolerable. At school she had been teased and bullied because she was illegitimate, and even her father's servants spoke of her as 'the bastard' behind his back. One summer her father had hired a student who had been exiled for his part in the Polish Revolt to tutor her, and he had spoken of his own country's struggle for freedom. 'Then someone gave me a copy of Kondraty Ryleev's poem "Nalivaiko". Do you know it?' she asked. 'It had a great effect on me. It's the story of a Ukrainian uprising, of the struggle for justice and freedom: "There is no reconciliation, there are no conditions / Between the tyrant and the slave; / It is not ink which is needed, but blood, We must act with the sword." There – what do you think of that?' Anna's eyes were shining and she was twisting her small hands in her lap.

'Yes, I . . .' He was groping for something that might do justice to her feelings.

'And you know Ryleev gave his own life for freedom!' Her voice was shaking with emotion. 'He was executed by Tsar Nicholas. Freedom and revolt always walk arm in arm with suffering and death. That is what history teaches us.'

She turned away, but not before he saw her brush a tear from her cheek. They sat there in silence for a minute or more as well-dressed, comfortable Petersburg ambled past, promenading couples, children in straw hats and lace with ruby and plum coloured bows and sashes, merchants in light summer suits, a nanny with the latest English perambulator, a peaceful, ordered, somnolent scene as remote from the revolution and sacrifice that filled Anna's thoughts as it was possible to be. Before he could speak to her again, the bells of the Smolny Cathedral began to chime for the evening service and roused by their restless rhythm, she rose quickly to her feet. 'I must go.'

It was apparent from her face that there was little point in attempting to persuade her to change her mind. As they strolled slowly through the garden towards the road, he asked her about the children she taught at the school in Alexandrovskaya and the life she lived in the village.

'Do you think I'm a sentimental revolutionary?' she asked. 'It's different for you. I'm used to a simpler life than you and Vera.'

'And the gentleman I saw you with at Madame Volkonskaya's?'

'Who do you mean?'

'The man sitting on the couch.'

'Alexander? He's a friend.'

The wariness in her voice and the colour that rose to her cheeks suggested more.

Hadfield hesitated, trying to find a propitious way to say what he wanted to say. '*C'est ton fiancé, n'est-ce pas? Cet homme, tu vas l'épouser. C'est evident.*'

Anna stared at him for a moment. 'Are you trying to humiliate me, Doctor?' she asked in Russian.

'Of course not,' he said, taken aback. 'What on earth makes you think that?'

'You are making fun of me,' she said coldly. And she turned her back on him and began walking briskly towards the cab stand in front of the cathedral.

'Miss Kovalenko, I don't understand . . .'

Her step did not falter for an instant. She had clearly made up her mind to have nothing more to do with him that day.

'Wait . . .' He began to hurry after her.

Their little pantomime was attracting smiles and the comment of cabbies on the opposite side of the square, and a smartly dressed elderly gentleman in a top hat shook his head in disapproval as Hadfield hurried past. As he fell into step with her, Anna quickened her pace.

He reached for her arm: 'Please. Look, I'm sorry but . . .'

'Don't touch me,' she said, shaking herself free. 'I didn't have the privilege of an education like yours but I understand our people!' She turned away from him with a disdainful toss of the head.

'So you don't speak French,' he shouted after her. 'Is that it?' She had turned away from the cab stand, conscious of the glances they were attracting from the drivers. 'This is ridiculous. Please stop.'

And she did stop, turning angrily to him. 'You are drawing attention to us.'

'I'm sorry, I didn't know you couldn't speak French,' he said in exasperation. 'It means nothing. I just thought perhaps that Alexander was your fiancé.'

'What business is it of yours anyway?' she snapped at him. 'Now let me go.'

'I'm sorry,' he said. 'I had no right to ask. And I'm sorry this afternoon has ended so badly.' He was confused, a tangle of feelings, aching with regret and anger. 'Let me see you to a cab.'

Her face softened a little with the suggestion of a smile. 'No, I'm quite all right, thank you. And you should know he is not my fiancé. He's a good comrade. He will never be my fiancé . . .' For a few seconds she stood there avoiding his gaze, biting her bottom lip uncertainly, and then she continued. 'I am not interested in such relationships . . .' Something in his expression must have suggested he did not take this remark as seriously as she would have liked because she took an urgent step closer, fixing him with an intense blue stare. 'Believe me, Doctor. Revolutionaries should not marry or have families.'

Hadfield pulled a sceptical face: 'Aren't socialists just like everybody else?'

'No. I've given my life to the struggle – like Kondraty Ryleev and many others . . .'

'And what of love?'

'I will not change my mind, and . . .' she hesitated and looked away again, the colour rising to her cheeks, 'and you should know . . .' She did not finish the sentence but stood there avoiding his gaze. The seconds passed, a minute, and worshippers began to trickle from the west door of the cathedral onto the pavement, old ladies hobbling home with their black shawls pulled tightly about them even on a summer evening.

'What should I know?'

Anna turned to look at him and he was taken aback by the intense expression on her face – not of anger this time, or defiance or resentment, but a deep trembling sadness close to pain.

'You should know I'm married.'

# 10

The cause of such confusion and not a little heartache was lurking in a doorway a short distance from the Church of the Assumption. Alexander Mikhailov's gaze was fixed on the shadows beneath the splintered awning of a modest two-storey building. A low drinking den, like so many others in the Haymarket district, it was doing steady trade even on the Lord's Day. Patrons were obliged to step over the prostrate form of an elderly peasant who had staggered no further than the door before collapsing in a stupor. No one seemed in the least concerned and Mikhailov wondered if the landlord was leaving the drunk on the step as barely living proof of the purity of his vodka. A couple of young women in gaudy rags were accosting all who came and went. That the broad fellow in workman's clothes who had been following him for almost an hour should try to conceal himself close to frumps plying their trade was nothing short of pitiful. Still, it was a simple enough task to lose one police spy, the sort of challenge he enjoyed, but perhaps there were others.

Without looking left or right Mikhailov began picking his way round the empty market stalls and piles of rubbish, putrid and thick with flies, to the opposite side of the square. On most days of the week the market was bustling with peasants and merchants; this was the 'belly' of St Petersburg, with every manner of object and animal for sale, women and children too. Respectable folk only chose to visit the district on business, although Mikhailov had heard stories of literary pilgrims in search of Raskolnikov's attic. And only the day before he had seen Dostoevsky in the street with a posse of admirers.

From the square, he walked at a steady pace to the Ekaterininsky Canal then along its embankment into the city. A little beyond Gorokhovaya Street he turned right into a gloomy courtyard and strolled nonchalantly across it to a door on the opposite side. It was open as he knew it would be. Up the bare wooden stair, across the landing and down again to the main entrance, where he paused for a moment to listen for his pursuer. Thump, thump on the bare boards behind him, and for the first time Mikhailov's heart beat a little faster. Not one but two men. Too bold to be just informers. Slipping out of the front, he crossed quickly to a decaying four-storey apartment block a little way up the street and turned without hesitating through a wicket gate hanging loosely from its hinges. An old lady was sitting on a stool in the yard behind, two small children playing in the dust at her feet. He nodded politely to her as he made his way towards a door at the corner of the building opposite. Behind him, the creak of the gate and the scuffing of courtyard stones as his pursuers hurried towards him. No time to look. He reached into his jacket pocket, took out a key and unlocked the door. A shout and the clatter of boots as they broke into a run. Glancing back he could see they were close: two plain-clothes policemen. Time only to turn the key in the lock before the sound of a shoulder crashing against the door.

'Open up!' The beating of fists. He waited a moment, collecting his thoughts, his right hand on his pounding chest. It would be only minutes before the banging and shouting on the other side of the door roused the dvornik or one of the tenants. He must move quickly.

Mikhailov was a thorough man and he had gone to great lengths over many months to ensure his comrades would continue to benefit from his very particular skills. He found the servant's corridor without difficulty and began weaving his way along it to the front of the building. An old lady in a black dress and goatskin slippers was struggling up the steps of the entrance hall with a bag of laundry. Mikhailov brushed past her and on into the street. Turning right, he walked as quickly as he could along the pavement without drawing attention to himself, crossing to the other side just beyond the railings of the Assignation Bank. A few yards further on he stopped outside a handsome yellow and white classical mansion, glanced left and right then retreated a step into the road to examine the windows on the first floor. At the bottom of the one on the extreme right there was a small blue diagonal strip of paper: it was safe to call.

Tarakanov was waiting for him on the first floor landing, an anxious expression on his chubby face.

'I saw you in the street,' he said. 'Come in, come in quickly.'

Councillor Tarakanov was as timid as a hare. The small circle who knew of his role in the movement had given him the code name 'Bucephalus', after Alexander the Great's highly strung horse. Time in his company passed slowly, but *in extremis* there was no safer place in Petersburg. He was the most trusted of the movement's 'Ukrivateli' – concealers – for he was the last person the authorities would suspect of revolutionary sympathies. Short, fat, fastidious, he was also a councillor at the Ministry of Interior and a social snob.

'Did anyone see you at the door?' he asked, stepping over to the window.

'Of course not,' replied Mikhailov.

'You know the lodger downstairs, a nosy old crone with great staring eyes, she's a milliner, I think, she always looks at me strangely when I meet her. She's a spy, I am sure of it.'

Mikhailov rolled his eyes by way of a reply.

'You don't know the risk I am taking,' said Tarakanov petulantly.

'I do, I do, believe me. You're a good chap. And I won't be here long, now come away from the window before someone sees you.'

But Mikhailov's pursuers had given up the chase. Collegiate Councillor Dobrshinsky was listening to their report in the investigation office at Fontanka 16, a map of the city open in front of him. The other agents were bent low over their desks in an effort to avoid catching his eye.

'He knew his way through the building, Your Honour.' Agent Myshkin shifted his weight to the other foot, his hands clasped awkwardly in front of him. His companion – Zadytsev – looked just as uncomfortable.

'He must have known he could lock the door and slip out to the lane at the front.'

'Show me.'

Dobrshinsky followed the agent's finger as he traced the route they had taken from the Haymarket. When he had finished the collegiate councillor sat back and stared at them coldly.

'You made yourselves conspicuous,' he said at last. 'What use are you to the investigation if you can't follow a suspect without giving yourselves away?'

'He kept stopping, Your Honour . . . He knew what he was doing.'

'That's enough,' said Dobrshinsky. 'I don't want excuses. Redeem yourselves. I want you to question every porter and yard keeper in the area.' He tapped the map with his fingers. 'Take the local gendarmes with you. And begin with the house where he gave you the slip. I want to know who is helping Mikhailov.'

'Now, Your Honour?' asked Myshkin tentatively.

'Yes. Now. At once,' said Dobrshinsky, rising abruptly from the desk. 'What are you waiting for?'

He watched them scuttle out of the office, then turned to

one of the clerks. 'Do we have the report on the dead informer?'

The clerk opened a file on his desk, took out a single sheet of paper and handed it to him.

'It took only a few seconds for Dobrshinsky to glance through the report. Just the bare bones. Body in a Peski street. Stab wound to the chest. A vagrant by the name of Viktor who used to keep his eyes and ears open for kopeks. He had given them the student Popov. The dvornik at a local school had found the vagrant's body on the doorstep. Murdered before he had a chance to give them anything more.

'Why are we always left with a corpse?' he muttered under his breath.

Alexander Mikhailov knew it was wise not to presume too often or for too long on Bucephalus's hospitality. Besides, there was an appointment he had to keep. And so, after an hour spent sipping tea in the comfort and security of the councillor's drawing room, he made his way by a back stair to a door that opened on to the courtyard behind the mansion. It was nearly eight o'clock, and to avoid being recognised in the empty Sunday streets he hailed a cab with a canopy and directed its driver to take him across the Fontanka. The short journey took Mikhailov along the embankment past the Third Section's headquarters and he could not resist leaning forward to glance at it as the cab swept past. He was the sort of revolutionary popular writers like Dostoevsky branded a 'fanatic' because he dedicated his life to the cause but he was not anxious to be hauled down the steps into the basement cells at Number 16. Stay one step ahead of your enemies, he told his comrades – and with the help of the man he called 'the Director' he would do.

The cab driver turned right off Fontanka into one of the handsome little streets opposite the Summer Garden. Mikhailov paid without a word and with just enough of a tip to be unmemorable. He appeared for all the world, if the world was watching, an unassuming young gentleman, modestly dressed in a light brown summer suit, perhaps a civil servant returning home after a day in the country. He walked at an unhurried pace, saluting a young couple who made way for him to pass on the pavement. At the bottom he stopped and, pretending to check the time, cast a look back down the street. Satisfied, he turned right on to Solianoy Lane and strolled down to the handsome little red and white church on the corner.

The last public service of the day had ended some time ago but the air was heavy with the sweet smell of incense. The church was empty but for an old lady nodding and clicking her rosary beads before the icon of St Panteleimon. Mikhailov paid for a votive candle, lit it and pressed it into one of the iron banks before the iconstasis, then, hands clasped, he muttered a meaningless prayer to a god he did not believe in any more. The flickering light of the candles seemed to breathe life into the grim painted faces of the patriarchs gazing down on him from the pillars and walls. Revolutionaries too, he thought with a smile, recalling the English doctor's description of Christ as a 'socialist'. Memories of childhood, his mother holding his hand, the rumble of the cantor, the silver framed icon held aloft by the priest, shimmering in the candlelight – he could feel the pull of that old religious order still. What was it Karl Marx had called it? – *das Opium des Volkes* – but not in a disparaging way. Ordinary people were not going to give up their belief in God and heaven until the world changed for the better and it was no longer necessary to turn to faith for the comfort of hope and forgetting.

'Please God, where is the Director?' he whispered under his breath. For how long was he going to have to keep up this pretence of piety? His sacrilegious prayer was answered, for he heard a footstep and was conscious of someone at his shoulder.

The 'Director' stepped forward and pressed his own candle into the stand then crossed himself several times.

'You're late, Alexander,' he said at last. 'I was worried.'

'A little trouble,' Mikhailov replied. 'Nothing that need concern you.'

He led the way to a bench half hidden behind a curtain and in deep shadow at the back of the church. The man who slumped round-shouldered beside him was in his late twenties, thin and rather pasty. He had a long solemn face and a badly trimmed beard, a beetle brow and large brown intelligent eyes, enormous when glimpsed through the lenses of his spectacles. His clothes and general demeanour suggested an industrious but downtrodden junior clerk. 'The body of the spy was found in the street outside the school in Peski,' he said. 'A report has been made by the local station.'

'Do you know how he found Popov?'

The Director shrugged: 'A chance to make a little money for vodka. He'd worked for the police for a while. Saw Popov at the Baird Works and followed him. But there's something else . . .' He edged a little closer. 'Dobrshinsky's going to bring in a woman called Volkonskaya for questioning.'

Mikhailov frowned thoughtfully: 'She doesn't know a great deal. Some names . . .'

'You, Goldenberg, Morozov, Kviatkovsky . . . here are the people they are most interested in . . .' The man reached into his pocket and handed him a small square of paper.

Mikhailov glanced down the list of names: 'Who is this Madame Romanko?'

'Kharkov has sent her records through – early twenties, brown hair, blue eyes, attractive – meets the description of the woman seen leaving the Volkonsky mansion in your company. Don't you know her? They suspect she may have been in the square with Soloviev when he missed.'

For a moment Mikhailov stared at the paper, then turned to his companion with a small smile: 'Thank you, Nikolai. Thank you again.'

They spoke for a few minutes more only, the Director casting anxious glances around the church. Mikhailov told him of the conference that was to be held at Voronezh and of the new alliance he hoped to forge there: 'But you, my friend, must stay here in Petersburg. It's most important.'

The Director nodded.

'And Dobrshinsky?'

'He's not popular. But he's clever. He's brought in new people – the major from the Gendarme Corps who was there when Popov shot himself.'

'And your position – is it secure?'

'Oh yes,' said the Director with a little laugh. 'Quite secure. I'm a good conservative. And the bits you feed me go down well.'

'Good,' said Mikhailov, getting to his feet. 'And now I must go. Next time we must meet somewhere different. I'll send word the usual way.' Turning his back on his companion, he walked over to the bank of flickering candles and stood with his hands together waiting for the clunk of the closing door.

The city's clocks were striking nine when Mikhailov stepped into the street once more. It was a 'white' Petersburg night when the sun hovers low on the horizon but does not set and the delicate pink and blue of early evening meets the dawn. A fresh breeze was blowing off the river and the city breathed easy again after the heat of the day. The streets about Nevsky were alive still with prosperous couples promenading in their summer finery, groups of inebriated students weaving noisily up and down the pavements, streetwalkers with an eye to Sunday business and the constant rattle and squeak of the horse-drawn trams and carriages. Mikhailov slipped in and out of the crowd unnoticed until he reached the cab rank in front of the Imperial Public Library. No matter the lateness of the hour, there was a task he wished to perform. It was going to put him to no small amount of trouble but it was quite impossible to ignore.

It was half past ten by the time he stepped on to the narrow wooden platform at the village of Alexandrovskaya. The school-room and adjoining house were set back a little from the main street, just five minutes from the station. Mikhailov walked slowly down the dusty lane, glancing left and right as if searching for a house. A sick-looking dog trotted hopefully towards him but there was no sign of its master or any other living soul, only the flicker of candlelight in windows and the distant rattle of a nightjar. The modest three-room schoolhouse was built of wood in the traditional manner and looked very like the rest of the village, if better cared for, with a coat of fresh green paint and a neat little garden, a honeysuckle twisting up the wall. From the lane he could see the smoky yellow glow of an oil lamp in the window. Anna was awake.

'Who is it?' she asked at the door.

'It's me. Alexander.'

'Why are you here?' But before he could answer, the door opened abruptly and she stood away from it to let him pass quickly inside: 'Are they chasing you?'

'I have important news.'

'What's happened?' Her voice was taut with anxiety.

'It's all right. Don't worry.' He settled himself on her couch. 'First, is there any tea?'

She stood staring at him. She must have been preparing to go to bed because the top of her white cotton blouse was hanging open, her hair loose about her shoulders, her feet bare.

'The water's still hot,' she said reluctantly.

Mikhailov watched as she busied herself with the tea, admiring the curve of her bottom and thighs as she bent to light the samovar flame. Yes, other men would find Anna attractive, not a fashionable beauty, her nose a little broad, her brow a little dark and heavy, but handsome nonetheless, with a neat figure and striking blue eyes. Above all, there was lively but graceful purpose in her every gesture and movement that even a man who did not share her view of the world might recognise and admire.

'You've put the picture on the wall, I see,' he said.

'Yes, do you like it there?' she asked, without turning to face him. Her voice was calmer. It was a little watercolour of folk dancing he had given her, young Ukrainian men in traditional Cossack dress, twisting wildly to fiddle and flute. It was hanging close to the stove along with a cheap icon of the Virgin that the priest had left for her when she took the position. It was a simply furnished room with a few functional sticks of furniture, an old wooden table and four kitchen chairs, a basic range for cooking and heat, and drawn across the windows, smoke stained cotton curtains. The only piece that would be at home in a bourgeois drawing room was the couch Anna had bought for herself.

'Well?' she asked, a little coolly.

He held his breath for a moment as she leant forward to give him the glass of tea. Her eyes were darker blue in the dim lamplight. He watched her over the top of his glass as she turned to sit at the table.

'I've been to see a friend I call "the Director". It's a joke we share. A code name, I suppose. His job is to guide the move-ment. I found him a year or so ago and helped him to his . . .' he paused for a moment, searching for a discreet euphemism, 'a special position.'

He sipped at his tea before continuing: 'The Director says Madame Volkonskaya will be arrested and questioned. She will give them some names, of course . . . no, sit down, please.'

Anna was half out of her chair: 'Have you spoken to Vera and Evgenia?'

'They've left for Voronezh. They're safe for now. And you must go too. First thing tomorrow.'

'But I don't think Madame Volkonskaya knows my name.'

'My dear Anna,' he said. He placed the glass on the floor at his feet then leant back with his arms folded across his chest and stared at her.

'Well?' She lifted her right hand to her lips nervously. 'Why have you come?'

'The most extraordinary coincidence. The police are looking for a mysterious woman with brilliant blue eyes, a fine figure, brown hair. Someone who seems to know me, someone very like you, but who goes by the name of Madame Romanko.'

'Oh?' said Anna, rising quickly to her feet. She turned her back on him and went over to the samovar, but not before he had noticed with amusement the colour rising in her neck and cheeks. After a few seconds' silence she turned back to the table, careful to avoid his eye.

'You know, I like you, Anna.'

She looked up at him and gave him an uncertain smile, her shoulders narrowing insecurely.

'You and I are dedicated to the revolution, to sacrifice . . .' Mikhailov eased himself on to the edge of the couch. 'And we share that burden . . .'

'Yes.'

He slowly got to his feet and walked over to the window, lifting the smoky curtain to one side to stare into the blue summer night. Then turning abruptly to face her again: 'Are you married?'

'That's my concern.' Her voice rang with cool defiance, but her face was pink with indignation and embarrassment.

'Have you left him?'

She paused to consider whether she should answer, then reluctantly: 'He left me two years ago.'

'Anna,' he said breathily, taking a step towards her.

'Please,' she said, her hand hovering above her lap as if hoping to push what she knew to be coming away. 'Please.'

'I've fallen in love with you.' He edged closer to the table: 'No, sit please, don't move.' He held his hand close as if to restrain her.

'Please, Alexander, we're comrades . . .'

'Marriage is nothing. A prison. But love – we can help each other. Comrades, yes, and lovers,' and he bent down a little and touched her arm.

She shrank from him. 'I don't love you . . . this, this is damaging the revolution. There is no place for . . .'

Mikhailov bent swiftly, reaching for her cheek with trembling fingers, so close, the smell of her, her breasts beneath the cotton blouse: 'I love you . . .' His voice was barely more than a whisper. And he touched her hair, the back of her head, trying to draw her closer, but she pulled herself free.

'No!' She jumped to her feet, her chair crashing to the floor. 'We're comrades!' she said angrily from the other side of the table. 'Comrades, that's all. I think you should go.'

Mikhailov's face felt hot. He was struggling to hold his temper. He never lost his temper. Who did she think he was? He turned away from her and threw himself down on to the couch. 'Is it the Englishman?'

'No!' she said indignantly. 'No. It's you.' She was still standing at the table, arms wrapped anxiously around herself. 'Go, please.'

'This English doctor can't be trusted. He isn't one of us, you know that?' Mikhailov said coldly.

'It's nothing to do with him. Now go. Please.'

'Tell him not to come to the clinic. It's too dangerous.'

'Look, I'm sorry, I've hurt you, but . . .'

'Don't be ridiculous! You haven't hurt me. I only care about what is best for our cause, best for the people. And you should think of that too.'

'I do,' she said quietly.

Silent seconds ticked by as they stared at each other. The

walls of the room seemed to press upon them in the flickering light of the lamp like the sides of a box. In the end, it was Anna who looked away and down at the table.

'Before you go,' she said coolly, 'I want to remind you that we agreed the doctor could be of use to us. He has connections. We agreed that. And he has already proved his worth. There was a body in the street today . . .'

'I know,' said Mikhailov. 'The Director told me.'

'The Director? But why did he think the death of a beggar in Peski worth mentioning?' There was an intense frown on her face.

'Because he was a police informer.'

'Dr Hadfield was sure he was murdered by someone who knew what they were doing. Did you kill him?'

'This is getting us nowhere,' he said coldly. 'The security of the movement is my concern.' Getting quickly to his feet, he stepped up to the table and, placing his chubby hands upon it, he leant across until he was only an arm's length from her: 'Leave first thing tomorrow. I will see you in Voronezh. And think about what I've said. In the next few weeks we will make brave decisions that will change this country for ever. You will play your part, I know.' He stared at her for a silent few seconds, his face hard with certainty. Anna did not flinch. Turning at last, he snatched his hat from the table and walked to the door, only glancing back as he opened it to where she stood in the shadow. It closed with a quiet click and she was alone.

# 11

For a time, news of Madame Volkonskaya's arrest helped set the seal on further contact with the clinic and the women who worked there. In the days that followed her detention a sharp knock on the door or raised voices in the street sent a chill down Frederick Hadfield's spine and he would wait with bated breath for the police to burst into the room.

But life went on as always, his hospital duties consuming more of his time, his list of well-to-do patients longer by the day. He had been treated with new respect at the Nikolaevsky since the closure of Department 10. Colleagues were grateful for the opportunity to share their problems with him, even when he was manifestly unqualified to solve them. And it proved to be a welcome distraction, a chance to make new friends and cement relations with old ones. A week passed, then two, and fear of arrest and the pain it would cause his family slipped away to be replaced by a dull ache that pressed heavier on his spirit. At empty moments of the day and at night, he was unable to free himself from thoughts of Anna, her small rough hands, the frown lines on her brow, the ice blue sparkle of her eyes, the timbre of her voice and their awkward parting. Of course, it had been foolish to press her about her friendship with this 'Alexander' and downright impertinent to wring from her the admission that she was married. It was apparent from the embarrassed silence that had followed the revelation that she deeply regretted it and was in no mood to confide more. A hasty and confused goodbye, and a feeling on his part at least that their paths were unlikely to cross again. But he had a duty to the clinic. If he dropped his Sunday commitment it would be evident to Anna he was more interested in her than his patients and that was something he did not want to admit, even to himself.

So on a hot July Sunday Hadfield took a cab to the dusty square in front of St Boris and St Gleb's once more. Gazing through the tangle of scaffolding, it seemed to him that not a brick had been added to the church in the month since his last visit. The filthy streets were oppressive with the stench of human waste familiar to those tied by poverty or duty to the city in summer. In the waiting room of the clinic, the dvornik was patrolling the crowded benches as before, grumbling officiously about the noise and the mess the children were making of his floor. 'Can I help you?' A well built middle-aged woman in a starched white headscarf and pinafore bustled up to him.

'Dr Hadfield. I work here sometimes.'

'Oh?' She looked puzzled. 'I wasn't told you were coming.'

'Is Miss Kovalenko here?'

'No.' Miss Kovalenko was not at the clinic. Miss Kovalenko was visiting her mother near Kharkov. Miss Kovalenko's mother was very ill. No one was sure when she would return or if she was intending to do so.

'And Miss Figner?' he asked. 'Is she also visiting her sick mother?'

The nurse coloured a little. 'I don't know a Miss Figner, Doctor.'

No one knew more or would say. Hadfield had met none of the four women on duty at the clinic before but they knew of him, and he felt obliged to stay. Trudging back to the square at the end of the day, he felt relief, even satisfaction, that he had managed to clear the benches. It had helped to take the edge off the disappointment of knowing Anna was not at his side. Perhaps the attraction, the strange connection he felt between them, would break and she would drift away until it was impossible to imagine the curve of her hips or the line of her face or the precise blue of her eyes.

This dull thought was with him through the week, and the following Sunday he made his way to the clinic again. The same four women were there but they had heard no word from Anna. And as he ministered to his patients' cuts and infections, the diseases of hunger and neglect, he reflected that while it was often simple to treat the body, the mind was almost always a lost cause.

The Glen family were at their dacha near a spa town on the Gulf of Riga, where the general was taking the waters to ease his arthritis. Hadfield had declined an invitation to join them. Lady Dufferin had left for England and was not expected to return to St Petersburg before the autumn. In her absence, the third secretary at the embassy had taken on the role of master of revels to alleviate the boredom and isolation of those left in the city. Hadfield found himself pressed into a 'diplomatic theatrical', a new piece called *La Belle de Venise* written in French and Russian. Dobson was taking a part, too, and for a week or so they dined together then rehearsed rather drunkenly in the correspondent's apartment. Neither of them made an effort with their lines until it became clear Lord Dufferin was taking the occasion rather more seriously and had invited a number of ambassadors and senior government figures to the performance.

'Damn it, enough of this nonsense!' said Dobson, throwing his script on to the couch. Both men were dressed for dinner after an expensive evening at the Palkin, although the correspondent had discarded his frock coat 'the better to perform'. 'What possessed Hamilton to choose this drivel? And why do I have to play the butler?'

'Because you're an inky hack, George,' Hadfield replied with a tipsy grin. He was slumped in a leather armchair in front of the journalist's desk, with a glass of brandy in one hand and his lines in the other.

'You snob, Hadfield. Your egalitarian principles are skin deep, aren't they?'

'Grub street reporters are in a class of their own.'

Dobson grunted and turned to pluck the brandy bottle from a silver drinks tray balanced on a table beside the fire.

'You know, I have it on good authority that Count von Plehve will be at the embassy,' he said, flopping on to the couch. 'It will be worth playing a fool if I can inveigle myself into his circle.'

'Von Plehve?'

'Don't you read the papers? He's the chief prosecutor,' said Dobson. 'Tipped to be a government minister in time. And absolutely the man to tell me more about this new nihilist group.'

'Is there one?'

Lifting a plump thigh on to the couch, the correspondent shuffled round to face Hadfield, his eyes sparkling with interest. 'Narodnaya Volya. "The People's Will". An army friend introduced me to a comrade of his called Barclay, a major in the gendarmes, who told me there was a gathering of revolutionaries in Voronezh last month and the militants – I thought they were all militant but it appears not – the militants have united behind a new banner – "The People's Will". Barclay says the police are expecting more outrages. Damn thing is – I can't print a word of it.' Dobson shook his head angrily. 'The bloody censor. When they decide the time is ripe everybody will get it – the Russians, the Germans, even that lazy hack from the *Daily Telegraph*.'

'What is the point of cultivating this von Plehve if you can't print what he says?'

Dobson gave an almost Russian shrug. 'You never know.'

But the next time Hadfield saw the correspondent he was – to judge from the stream of invective he launched at the wardrobe master – feeling less philosophical about life's vicissitudes.

'For God's sake, man, haven't you got something that fits?'

The dresser from the Mikhailovsky Theatre was struggling with the butler's buttons. The drinks tray was close by and Hadfield gestured to it.

'A stiff nip to help with first and last night nerves? Remember your Count von Plehve is in the audience.'

'Ha bloody ha, Hadfield.'

The performance was managed with just enough aplomb, and the audience entered into the spirit by applauding buffoonery whether it was intended or not. 'Wonderfully British,' the ambassador declared in his vote of thanks. The loudest applause was reserved for the young master of revels, Lord Frederick Hamilton, who had played the part of the fierce grey-haired 'Countess Gorgonzola' with great panache.

A light supper was then served in the splendour of the embassy's White Hall, where Tsar Alexander I had danced the quadrille before meeting his generals to plan the defeat of La Grande Armée. A masterpiece of the Russian baroque in white and gold, fit for the visit of the heir to Byzantium, the tall pier glasses reflected an exuberant plaster tableau of 'Plenty'.

'Magnificent,' said Dobson, gazing at the life-size carvings of Pan's followers above the frieze. 'I doubt there is anything to touch it in England.'

'And a fine view to the Peter and Paul Fortress too,' said Hadfield, waving his champagne glass at the windows.

'What a joy you are to be with, old boy. You should have left your socialist baggage at the door. Look,' he said, nudging Hadfield lightly with his elbow, 'there's that wily old bird Gortchakov.'

The grey head of the Russian foreign minister was bent in conversation a few feet from them, peering at the ambassador over his spectacles like an indulgent father. He wore a broad blue sash across his chest and diamond stars on his coat, the glittering honours of twenty years' service in the courts of Europe.

'A shocking flirt, you know,' Hadfield whispered. 'He likes to know if a new ambassador has a pretty wife. If the answer's no, then he says the ambassador will fail at court because he's already lost the most important argument.'

'Goodness, patients tell their physicians everything, don't they,' said Dobson with a cynical little shake of the head. 'And does he think Lady Dufferin pretty or is your source silent on the subject?'

'She's the wife of the British ambassador. Of course he thinks she's pretty. Don't you?'

Dobson laughed: 'You're wasted in the medical profession.'

'Quite right. A born actor,' said Hamilton, stepping up to them with a broad smile. 'It went swimmingly, don't you think?'

'You looked very comfortable in that dress, Your Lordship,' Dobson replied.

Hamilton inclined his head graciously. The young third secretary was a little effeminate, tall, curly-haired, strikingly handsome and amiable enough, if rather too full of his family connections.

'A jolly good turnout,' he declared, with an extravagant flourish to the room. 'French, German and Italian ambassadors, Baron de Budberg, and over there,' he nodded discreetly at an elderly gentleman sitting serenely by the window, 'Prince Davidov – he was educated in Edinburgh. He knew Walter Scott. A little deaf.'

The *crème de la crème* of summer society drifting with the practised ease of profession and class about the hall. Ladies in black satin dresses and diamonds, the men in a glittering array of court uniforms and frock coats, the murmur of diplomatic French, the clink of champagne flutes and the comfort of a small string orchestra: counts, princes, grand dukes and barons, a timeless display of wealth and privilege. As the third secretary rattled through the names of more guests, Hadfield wondered why a doctor, the son of a doctor, had been invited.

It became clear enough minutes later when Lord Dufferin touched his arm. 'There's someone I would like you to meet, Hadfield,' he said, and led him across the ballroom to where a man with the gold Star of the Order of St Vladimir at his breast was confidently holding forth to a lady.

'Your Highness, here is the gentleman I was speaking of,' said Dufferin with a little bow. 'My wife is adamant he's the best young doctor in the city.' And turning to Hadfield: 'The Princess of Oldenburg and Count von Plehve.'

Hadfield bent low over the gloved hand the princess offered him then gave a stiff bow to the count.

'Lord Dufferin tells me you're a nephew of General Glen's,' the princess said with a patronising little smile. She was rather a plain woman of middle years, but there was a rich confidence in her manner, her poise, the way she held her head, that a man might find fascinating, even attractive. She was dressed in a fashionable Parisian gown boldly cut off the shoulders.

'Of course the count knows your uncle too,' she said, turning to von Plehve. The chief prosecutor inclined his head a little by way of affirmation, scrutinising Hadfield carefully.

'The count was just telling me of these madmen . . .'

'And mad women, Eugénie Maximiliovna . . .'

'Yes, mad women too,' said the princess with a little laugh. 'Poor Madame Volkonskaya, what will become of her?'

The count stroked his moustache thoughtfully with his forefinger. 'Women are such dangerous creatures, Eugénie Maximiliovna. So much more dangerous than men, don't you agree, Your Excellency?'

'I do,' replied Dufferin with a polite smile.

'Actually, we're looking for one woman in particular,' von

Plehve continued. 'A revolutionary called "Romanko" who a witness places in Palace Square when the attempt was made on His Majesty's life. An associate of a fellow called Mikhailov.'

Von Plehve told them a little of Alexander Mikhailov, of his privileged background, and that he had given agents the slip only a few weeks before. 'We know he attended a gathering of nihilists in Voronezh in June and that he was one of those who championed a campaign of terror.'

'This new group,' said the princess, 'what do they call themselves?'

'"The People's Will".'

'You are so fortunate, Lord Dufferin,' the princess said, 'that you don't have people like this in your country.'

'We have our Irish Republicans.'

'And what is your opinion, Doctor?' von Plehve asked, turning to fix Hadfield with his curiously intense stare.

'My opinion of what, sir?'

'Of our revolutionaries.'

'I've learnt as a doctor to avoid controversy,' Hadfield said smoothly. 'My opinion might have a detrimental effect on a patient's blood pressure, which would be unforgivable – not to mention unprofitable.'

'Ha! There you are, Count! Admirably discreet,' said Dufferin, raising his glass to Hadfield.

'Admirable, I'm sure,' von Plehve replied with a taut smile. 'But can you trust a man who refuses his opinion?'

'You can trust me to give you a frank opinion of your health, Count.'

'Don't persecute the doctor,' said the princess, shaking her finger at von Plehve. 'I for one applaud his discretion.'

The count smiled and gave a magnanimous little bow.

'What do these people want, Count?' the princess asked.

'The People's Will? They want to put the government of our country in the hands of illiterate muzhiks.' Von Plehve paused to consider his next words carefully, a frown creasing his high forehead. 'If our intelligence is correct, some ruthless fanatics have joined the group – men like Mikhailov – and others.' Then with a brightness that seemed a little forced: 'But we have good people working on this case, rest assured, we'll find them.'

Glancing up at the windows of the candlelit ballroom an hour later, Hadfield smiled to himself. A friend to ambassadors and princesses, as discreet as the pure white plaster figures gazing down upon one more perfectly ordered scene in which they belong and yet remain apart. The disquiet he had felt when the count had so pointedly asked for his opinion was gone, and he was conscious of a certain satisfaction at straddling two mutually hostile worlds.

Dobson had wanted to know everything von Plehve had said. 'You're fortunate in your family connections,' he grumbled.

Hadfield had told him of the chief prosecutor's fears, of Mikhailov and his associates, and of the new party – The People's Will – confident his friend would be discreet. But there were pieces of the conversation and thoughts he kept to himself. As he walked along the embankment towards Palace Square they swirled through his mind like the dark waters of the Neva. Where was the woman he knew as Miss Anna Kovalenko?

# 12

Anna had visited the cottage a dozen times before, but the winter days were drawing in and by five o'clock the rough path from the cemetery was almost lost in the spectral blue light that lingers after sunset. Walk towards the silhouette of the church tower – it was plain enough to her left – cross the track, then follow the monastery wall away from the village. It was the path the day labourers at the Moscow factories were accustomed to taking home. Half an hour and they would begin emptying from the trains at the local station. She needed to be quick: a young woman struggling with a heavy bag at twilight would arouse interest, even a little suspicion. Anna had lived most of her life in a village and understood that anything remotely out of the ordinary was a cause for comment in a small community – and Preobrazhenskoe was more tightly knit and warier of outsiders than most. It was a poor quarter on the southern edge of Moscow, and for many years a refuge from persecution for Old Believers who scraped a living from small allotments, growing fruit and vegetables to sell in the city markets. They did not welcome strangers. Alexander Mikhailov had given strict orders that movement to and from the cottage should be kept to a minimum. Nothing should be said or done to antagonise their neighbours. Some of Anna's comrades dismissed the Old Believers as fools and laughed at their strange ways: who in his right mind would account it a sin for a man to shave? But Anna had a grudging respect for the sincerity and

123

dignity with which they clung to their faith and their traditional forms of worship. Surely there would be a place for Old Believers in the Russia the new party was fighting for, freedom from persecution, from prescription? For all that, she was as careful to avoid contact with them as the others. Mikhailov knew he could trust her. Most of the members of the new party had no idea how to make themselves anonymous in a village like Preobrazhenskoe.

At the corner of the monastery wall she stopped to catch her breath, placing the white canvas sack carefully on the ground at her feet. An old man, his grey beard tucked into a belted shirt, was plodding along the track, a wooden hoe in one hand and a bag of vegetables in the other. He glanced sideways at her but walked on without a word or gesture. Beyond the wall, a thick belt of waste ground, a patchwork of small market gardens and spoil heaps, and at intervals, the outline of a tumbledown house, a faint light flickering in the window. The little one-storey cottage the party had bought was at its edge, just a stone's throw from the main railway track to Kursk and all points south. With no small effort, Anna swung the sack back on to her shoulder and set off again, head bent low over the path of beaten earth. She stumbled on for five minutes, her dress catching on a tangle of brambles, concentrating hard on where she placed her feet, glancing up only to be sure of the dim light at the window of the first house. So anxious was she not to lose the path, she did not hear their footfalls or see the men approach until they were only a few yards from her. As they loomed out of the darkness, the sack almost slipped through her fingers and she gave a little gasp of surprise.

'Did we make you jump, love?'

Three men. Young men. Railwaymen or tinkers. Their faces lost beneath peaked workmen's caps.

'You surprised me, yes,' she said as calmly as she was able.

'Where are you going? Here, we'll help you with that.' The man nearest to her held out his hand. He was broad, his beard too short for an Old Believer, a thigh-length jacket and boots, and as he bent closer she could smell beer on his breath.

'Pretty . . .' one of his companions muttered.

'My friend likes you, love,' the first man said. His hand was still open in front of her.

'Then he won't mind stepping out of my way, will he?' This time there was steel in her voice. She was angry. Who were these men to accost a woman at night?

'I'm sure he would be happy to do more for you than that,' replied the first man, turning for approval to his companions who were sniggering like smutty children.

'Let me pass!' She took a step forward.

'Now, now. We're only being friendly.'

They were not going to let her go. What did they want? Was it just the bag? Her heart was pounding but her mind was crystal clear.

'My husband and his friends are in that house there,' she said, retreating a step. 'Hey, Mishka! Thieves! Thieves!'

Her voice split the still night like a knife to the belly of a beast. It was a scream to wake the conscience of a dead man. The first man lunged at her. Swinging the sack from her shoulder, she struck him on the side of the head, throwing him off balance and heavily to one knee. The sack was at her feet now and the second man grabbed at it, pushing her away. But he was smaller and struggled to lift it with one hand.

'Here,' she screamed again. 'Thieves! Murderers!'

'Shut up or I'll finish you.'

'Murderers!' And she kicked out blindly at the first man rising to his feet. Angry, she was so angry, grinding her teeth with anger.

Then from somewhere a man's voice: 'Hey, what's happening there?'

She glanced up to see a lantern swinging towards them. 'Thieves!'

In desperation, one of them tugged at the sack, lifting it from the ground to hoist it on to his back. She threw herself on him with her fists, bending to sink her teeth deep into his hand. A cry of pain and the sack slipped from him. But someone had her by the hair and was dragging her down. Then she was struck hard in the face, knuckles jarring her cheekbone. She fell backwards, her head bursting with white light. She curled instinctively into a ball. The sack was close at hand, and she reached out to grasp it by the neck. But one of the men kicked out at her viciously, catching her just below the ribs, and she slipped into darkness, heaving for air, conscious of nothing but the pain in her face and side. Then anger and fear kindled inside her again.

'No, no!' And with a stubborn act of will, she opened her eyes and clutched the sack tighter and with both hands, tensing in readiness for the next blow. But it did not come. They had gone. She pulled the sack towards her and lay in the long grass beside it, trembling with shock, a film of cold perspiration prickling her skin. Her cheek was throbbing and as she lifted her head, the shadowy world within her circumference began to spin.

'Hey, is anyone there? Where are you?' Someone was pushing quickly through the grass towards her.

'Here.' How pathetic her voice sounded. 'Here.'

The ring of light from a lantern and a bent silhouette above her. Her rescuer crossed himself, and she could tell from the two fingers he used to perform his blessing that he was an Old Believer.

'Are you all right?' he asked, sinking to his haunches and lifting the lantern close to her face.

It took another supreme act of will just to lift one foot in front of the other; every jarring step sent a frisson of pain through her body. She had no choice but to let him carry the sack. Her Good Samaritan was called Vladimir and his home was close to the railway track, a stone's throw from the newcomers' cottage. She did not need to tell him where she was going, he led her there without question.

It was a poor wooden place, like most of the others in the village, close enough to the track for the trains to rattle the windows. The party had paid a thousand roubles, and Lev Hartmann, whose parents were workers and who knew how to behave like one, had been chosen to live there with a comrade posing as his wife. And it was Sophia Perovskaya who opened the door to Anna and, after only a glance, threw her arms about her. 'What's happened to you, Annushka?'

Before Anna could speak, her guide stepped into the light from the door and dropped the sack at her feet.

'Thank you, Father,' Anna muttered. 'Thank you.' But Vladimir had vanished without a word.

'Does she have it?' A strange apparition of the man Anna knew to be Lev Hartmann had come to the door. He was caked from head to foot in mud. 'Is this it?' he asked, snatching up the sack.

'For goodness sake, get back inside,' Sophia said, shooing him like a goose back into the house, 'someone could see you like that.' She led Anna by the hand into the living room and made her sit at the table. 'Was it the police?'

Anna gave a little shake of the head. She was exhausted, and now she was among friends the courage began to seep from her.

Sophia poured a little warm water from the samovar into a bowl and placed it on the table with a fine linen cloth and some soap. 'Let me.'

'Thank you,' Anna whispered, struggling with the tide of emotion welling inside. Sophia Perovskaya stroked her cheek lightly with the back of her hand then dabbed the corner of the cloth in the water and began gently, so gently, wiping the mud from her face. Anna was full of gratitude for the warmth and tenderness in her friend's blue eyes and round innocent face. This woman is my family, she thought, and she reached for Sophia's free hand, a fellowship of people committed to the highest ideals: me – the illegitimate daughter of a landlord and serf – and Sophia Lvovna Perovskaya, from one of the noblest families in the empire.

'Why are you smiling?' Sophia asked.

'I was thanking a god I don't believe in for your kindness, Sonechka, and for our comradeship.'

Sophia Perovskaya gave her hand a little squeeze: 'Yes. But now you must tell me what happened?'

Painfully, hesitantly, Anna gave a brief account of the attack and her rescue. And as she spoke her friend smoothed cool arnica ointment on her bruised cheek and hands. So delicate, so gentle, what a strange childlike creature she is, Anna thought. Diminutive, petite, with flaxen braids and fine features, Perovskaya was twenty-five but often taken for ten years younger. In her simple country smock she looked very like a peasant girl.

'The executive committee of the party owes you its thanks,' she said, bending forward to kiss Anna's cheek. 'It's a small miracle you weren't blown to pieces.'

'But there isn't very much, is there?' said Hartmann. He had lifted a box from the sack and placed it on the table near them. Prising it open with a chisel, he took from it a short brown cylinder of dynamite – eight inches long and one and a half in diameter – twirling it between his fingers.

'Alexander is looking for more dynamite,' Anna replied.

Hartmann nodded.

'How far is the tunnel?'

He gave a non-committal shrug and turned, his hand on the knob of the door to the adjoining room: 'Grishka is in there with Aronchik. But it's my turn again, I think.'

'It's too slow,' said Sophia Perovskaya when he had gone. 'We're still twenty yards short.'

'Is Grigory Goldenberg with you?'

'He's in the fields spreading the earth from the tunnel. But men like Grigory are not used to this sort of work – that's why we're behind.'

There had been one problem after another, Sophia explained. The party's intellectuals were breaking under the strain of real labour. First they had driven the tunnel up against the base of a telegraph pole, then heavy rain had brought the gallery roof down, leaving a crater in the ground close to the path used by the gendarme patrols. And when the tunnel finally reached the railway embankment they had been forced to use a drill to cut their way through stone. It was claustrophobic, back-breaking labour, the tunnel no wider than a man's shoulders. The digger wielding the spade at the face carried a dose of poison in case he was buried alive.

'But we've all taken a vow not to be taken alive.' On a bench beneath one of the windows there was a large bottle of nitro-glycerine; on the table within easy reach, Sophia Perovskaya's pistol. 'If the gendarmes burst in upon us I'm to fire a bullet into the bottle,' she said. There would be enough explosive to blow the three-roomed house and all its occupants to kingdom come – and some of the gendarmes too.

'But now you must sleep a while, Annushka. You can't go back tonight. You can sleep in my bed,' said Sophia, pouring vodka into a glass tumbler. 'Here, drink this.'

'I'm fine, Sonechka, really,' said Anna, getting slowly to her feet. She stood in front of her friend, swaying like a tipsy peasant, her right leg trembling in protest.

'Sit down!' said Sophia Perovskaya with the cool firmness of one used to being obeyed. For all her smallness of stature, her childlike face, she was an 'illegal' who had escaped from custody and was near the top of the police's wanted list, a dedicated and resourceful revolutionary, cut from the same fine cloth as Mikhailov. Anna took the glass she offered her. But when at last she was led to bed in the adjoining room, sleep was out of the question, her mind racing in spite of the crushing tiredness she felt.

In the three months since the birth of 'The People's Will' Anna had travelled thousands of miles on its behalf. Station waiting rooms, telegraph offices, a different house, a different bed almost every night, an agent and courier of its executive committee, for ever vigilant, for ever on the move. This was her new life. She had sworn an oath that bound her to the party, a pledge to reject family, love and friendship, to renounce personal hopes and desires for the people and, if necessary, to sacrifice her life for a revolution in Russia. She was glad of the certainty of knowing this was her future. Freedom and the love of comrades fired with the same revolutionary spirit were worth dying for. She had already turned her back on the prison of a loveless marriage with a good-for-nothing husband old enough to be her father, a drunkard who treated her like one of his chattels. The promises they had made to each other in the new party were profounder than her wedding vows, for in them lived the shared ideal of liberty.

And yet, and yet . . . as the days and miles slipped by – rattling down a seemingly endless piece of track with her thoughts – she could not entirely bury the memory of an English doctor who had looked at her with warmth and longing. She rolled their last words over and over in her mind and was sorry for the way they parted, sorry too that she had made no effort to explain that her father had given her away in marriage when she was only seventeen, like one of his serfs. And there were times when she let her imagination wander with pleasure to take comfort in the knowledge that she was desired as a woman should be.

As she lay there in Sophia Perovskaya's narrow bed, she could hear the murmur of voices in the room next door. They must have closed the tunnel for the night. Most of the Moscow cell was living in the nearby city, travelling to and from the cottage as discreetly as possible at dawn and dusk. Anna had taken a room in a cheap guesthouse close to Kursk Station under an assumed name and with papers that had been prepared for her by the party.

The door opened and Sophia crept in with a candle. 'Are you sleeping?' she whispered softly.

'No. I can't.'

'I will fetch you some soup.'

'I will get up, Sonechka. I want to be with friends.'

There were five men round the table. Hartmann and two other comrades were bent over bowls of steaming broth, their clothes and hair stiff with mud. Goldenberg was sipping a glass of tea, and there, with his back to the door, was Alexander Mikhailov. He turned to look at her as she entered. 'Anna, please,' he said, and, half rising to his feet, offered her his chair. But Sophia Perovskaya had already pulled one to the table.

'Are you all right? Sophia has told us what happened to you.' Mikhailov's voice was businesslike. 'That's a nasty bruise.'

Anna blushed a little and lifted a hand to her cheek. 'I'm fine.'

'I've been telling the others: our comrades in Alexandrovsk are almost ready. The explosive cylinders are in place and they have all they need to detonate them. But we can take dynamite from Odessa. The attempt there is off. The tsar's train will leave from Simferopol instead.'

Anna felt Sophia Perovskaya's tiny hand on her shoulder as she placed the bowl of vegetable broth in front of her.

'We still have two chances to catch him but we need to work quickly now,' said Mikhailov coolly. 'We don't have much time – three weeks at the most. The tsar will return to Petersburg before the end of the month. We'll receive word when his train leaves the Crimea.'

For a few seconds there was silence at the table. After weeks of toiling in a tunnel no wider than a coffin, the day, the hour, was approaching when they would make their attempt on the emperor's life. It was the party's first objective. They had passed a formal death sentence: the tsar must be killed to free the nation. Only then would it be possible to hand supreme power to the people.

'But we need more dynamite . . .' Mikhailov said at last. He was looking pointedly at Goldenberg. 'You must visit Vera Figner in Odessa and bring back all you can.'

'But I'm needed here!' Goldenberg insisted.

'This is more important,' said Sophia Perovskaya. 'You must go first thing tomorrow.'

'Why can't Annushka go?' he asked.

'Of course she can't!' snapped Sophia.

'I can,' said Anna, putting down her spoon. 'I'll go.'

'No!' The bowls and glasses jumped as Sophia slammed her tiny fist on the table. 'Look at her. Alexander—'

Mikhailov shrugged. 'Perhaps two people would be better.'

How calculating he is, Anna thought. He had only suggested Goldenberg because she would offer to go too. Dearly though she cared for him, Grigory was not to be trusted with a task of this importance. She would make the arrangements and Grigory would carry the case of dynamite. They must leave at once – leave before dawn.

# 13

There was a queue at the telegraph reception where an elderly Jew was struggling to make himself understood to the clerk. Vera Figner was losing her temper, her foot tapping impatiently on the tiled floor, click, click, click, and every few seconds her eyes turned to the large post office clock on the opposite wall of the hall. She edged her way to the counter at last and the clerk slipped a telegram beneath the grille. She turned away with the ribbon of paper between her fingers, concern and excitement written in the fine lines of her face.

'Well?' Anna asked.

'Here,' and Vera pressed the message into her outstretched hand. 'He's ready to leave the Crimea.'

The telegram was in simple code: 'PRICE OF FLOUR TWO ROUBLES. STOP. OUR PRICE FOUR. STOP.'

'Fourth coach of the second train,' whispered Vera, with a discreet shake of the head. 'Let's go now. It will be a miracle if we aren't arrested. Can you imagine a more obvious code? You know the telegraphers are under orders to look out for strangely worded messages.'

She led Anna from the Central Post Office on to the busy street and hailed a cab. 'There's a train in half an hour. You must go at once.'

Anna had arrived in Odessa the day before. Vera's cell had worked hard on its own plan for an attack, only to discover the tsar would not be travelling through the city after all. It had left them feeling flat and a little resentful that they had no further part to play, but it had been agreed that Goldenberg would leave with their supply of dynamite on an earlier train and meet Anna when she received word from the Crimea.

As the cab began to turn before the station, Vera leant closer: 'Good luck, Annushka, good luck.' Her voice shook with emotion. 'Please be careful. The gendarmes have stepped up their patrols.'

'Do you think they know something?'

Vera Figner gave a little shrug: 'I don't know, but be careful.' And she bent to brush Anna's cheek lightly with her lips.

Vera was right. A squad of gendarmes was questioning travellers and checking papers on the concourse and Anna was obliged to show hers with the rest. A plume of steam and soot was rising from the mouth of the station and she had barely settled into her seat in third class when, with a hiss and a jolt and a clanking of couplings, the train began to pull away from the platform. Her carriage was crowded with a rich slice of southern Russia: peasants with poultry; a Greek shopkeeper and his family, his small children screaming for the attention of their mother; Jews, Armenians, even a young Muslim man from the Crimea in a bright red Tatar cap. Anna found herself pressed against a middle-aged clerk in a stained and threadbare frock coat who fell asleep almost at once. Opposite her was an old soldier with a thick grey beard and small inquisitive eyes. He gave her a lascivious toothless grin when she caught him scrutinising her and he refused to look away. For a while she followed the comings and goings in the carriage – the officious ticket collector and tipsy vodka seller, the children peeping cheekily through their fingers at strangers – and she listened patiently to the everyday troubles of her neighbours. But the late sun glinting yellow in the glass made her blink and slowly she succumbed to the weariness of the passive traveller, drifting away to the rattle of the train. It was an uneasy sleep, broken at each station along the line by the slamming of doors, the guard's whistle and the traffic of new passengers up and down the carriage. For hours she floated in that restless demi-world between sleep and consciousness in which dreams are shaped by memories and the images that form and dissipate are familiar. In one, the tsar was waving from his carriage, his long fingers beautifully manicured, a gentle look in his eyes, and he was beckoning to her, 'Come, come,' offering her the seat beside him. But she knew he was going to die, that it was too late, that he must die and that if she sat with him she would die too. But would he be suspicious if she refused? Was it her duty to take the seat and die for the people? She wanted to live. What would the others say? No, she must die for them. And she could see the face of the English doctor gazing at her, his hazel eyes full of pain, and she wanted to kiss him and feel his arms wrapped tightly round her. But he turned his back on her and kept walking, and she was furious for showing she cared.

She woke with a start as the train juddered to a halt, her mouth dry, her neck stiff. It was dark and her neighbours were still dozing, blankets pulled up to their chins. She examined her dim reflection in the window, discreetly tidying loose strands of hair. She felt dirty and cold and would have given almost anything for a bath and a comfortable bed. Elizavetgrad was only a little further and it was there she had arranged to rendezvous with Goldenberg and a portmanteau of dynamite. With the bag on the rack above them, she would have to be on her mettle for the rest of the journey. The old soldier opposite was awake and eyeing her intently. She ignored him and gazed out into the November night as the train began to gather speed, wisps of steam whisking past the window like spirits at a witch's dance. And soon she could see the yellow twinkle of Elizavetgrad and the train began to slow. The plump clerk beside her, who had grunted and snuffled in his sleep for most of the journey, stirred as if an unseen hand was shaking him roughly to give notice the city was only minutes away. Placing his hands on his knees, he hoisted himself groggily to his feet and reached up for his trunk. Most of the passengers were preparing to leave the carriage. It would make it easier for her to pass unnoticed on the platform.

From the edge of the platform, Captain Alexander Zabirov could hear the rails singing and knew the train was only minutes from the station. He glanced at the waiting-room door then a little way beyond it to where he knew his men were waiting in the darkness beneath the canopy for his signal.

'You're sure he's in there, Turchin?' he said, turning to the sergeant at his side.

'Quite sure, sir. He's not going far with that trunk.'

'Very good.'

It was Turchin who had noticed the Jew struggling along the platform with a heavy portmanteau. A small man with wispy red hair and a goatee beard, dressed in an old student coat, he had stepped off the Odessa train at a little before six o'clock that evening and taken refuge at once from the bitter chill. Ordinarily, Turchin would have presumed he was on his way to a university in Moscow or Kiev, but he had been briefed every day for a fortnight to be on the lookout for nihilist conspirators at the station. Names and descriptions and even a few photographs had been sent by the Third Section to every gendarmerie in the empire: almost at the top of the list was the man pressed into a corner of the waiting room. Turchin had not been able to remember his name but he knew he was wanted for murder and he was too long in the tooth to risk tackling him alone.

'Where is the next train to, Sergeant?' asked Captain Zabirov.

'Kiev, sir.'

'He may take this one. He's from Kiev.'

Word of the approaching train must have reached the waiting room because the door opened and people began drifting out and along the platform.

'He'll be armed,' Zabirov muttered to himself. Then to the sergeant: 'All right, let's take a look.'

They moved towards the waiting room, but after only a few steps they saw their man through the lighted window. He bent down and a moment later a battered leather trunk appeared in the half open doorway. He was pushing it with his foot. How fortunate that he is going to have his hands full carrying his luggage, the captain thought with a wry smile. He touched the sergeant's sleeve and whispered: 'Stop. We'll let him drag that thing to us.'

The end of the platform was almost lost in a hissing cloud as the train rumbled into the station. As the steam began to clear Anna leant closer to the window in the hope of catching a glimpse of Goldenberg's diminutive figure.

'You got someone meeting you?' It was the nosy veteran with his twinkling little eyes. His voice was husky with age and he spoke with a hard 'e' that suggested he had spent a good deal of time in the Caucasus.

'Yes.'

'A friend?'

'Yes. A friend.'

'You from these parts?'

'No.'

'Here, let me carry your bag.' He reached down for the small leather suitcase at her feet.

'No. No, thank you,' she said firmly, leaning down quickly to lift it from the carriage floor. Turning to join the queue for the door, she could sense his hard inquisitive eyes boring into her back.

The train drew to a halt, the carriage door opened and the Greek shopkeeper in front of her began coaxing his sleepy-looking children down the steps on to the platform. In the dim yellow gaslight, friends and family waited, warmly wrapped against the cold of the November night, their faces lost in clouds of freezing vapour.

As she edged closer to the door Anna was surprised to see their attention was fixed not on the travellers decanting from the carriages but on the smoking head of the train. There was a murmur of excitement and one of the porters climbed on his trolley for a view over the press. Seconds later a gendarme and one of his men pushed carelessly past.

'Bit of trouble.' It was the voice of the old soldier.

Ignoring him, Anna stepped off the train and began to shuffle through the throng towards the commotion. She caught words and snatches of conversation between those tall enough to see what was happening: the gendarmes had arrested someone. There had been a struggle. Who was he? A thief or a murderer?

She had to be sure. The attention of those waiting on the platform began to turn to the friends they were meeting from the train. The entertainment was over and the porters were in search of custom again, the train guards shutting carriage doors for departure, the travellers gathering their bags and drifting towards the station hall. As the platform cleared she saw a squad of gendarmes in their sky-blue coats at the door of a waiting room. Close by, the steaming black engine, its driver and the fireman smoking and chatting on the platform, intrigued by the little scene unfolding before them. The shrill blast of a whistle, then another, and they hauled themselves back into the cab. A moment later there was a whoosh of steam and soot and the driving rods began to turn.

It was madness. She was taking too much of a risk. If they had taken him it was too late. No purpose would be served by a second sacrifice. As the train began to pick up speed, she turned away, preparing to retrace her steps to the station hall with the last of the passengers. The guard's van cleared the platform edge and rumbled into the night. A moment later she heard shouted commands and, glancing over her shoulder, she could see the waiting-room door was open, the gendarmes standing in close order to receive the prisoner. A second later it was beyond doubt: almost lost between two burly military policemen, half marched, half dragged – Grigory Davidovich Goldenberg.

She forced herself to stop and stare as everyone about her was doing. He would be escorted past her and she would look at him and hope that he might draw strength from her love and trust. A careless glance, a foolish word or gesture, and he would give her away, but she wanted him to know that she trusted him implicitly.

'I thought I saw you here.'

Anna turned angrily. The old soldier from the train had sidled up like the serpent in the garden. 'Why don't you leave me alone?'

He shrugged non-committally: 'Filthy Jew.' And she saw his sharp little eyes turn to Goldenberg. 'Probably one of those terrorists.'

The gendarmes' boots crunched on the packed cinder surface of the platform in time, as if to demonstrate their power to grind men like Goldenberg into submission. His head was bent, his hair falling about his face, and she could see by the yellow station light that he must have put up a fight because his coat was torn in two places and dirty. She would offer him comfort if he saw her, offer with her eyes the love and reassurance he always sought. As they approached, she stared intently at his bent head, willing him, silently begging him, to look up.

And he did look up, with frightened eyes. But only as he was on the point of passing did he find her. He gave her a fleeting smile of recognition before turning his head away. Behind him, two gendarmes were carrying the portmanteau between them.

'He smiled at you, didn't he? I saw him smile.'

Anna turned quickly to look at the old soldier at her side. He was smiling at her too but it was not a pleasant smile.

'I don't know who he was smiling at,' she snapped. 'Perhaps he was smiling at you. Now why don't you leave me alone?' And without waiting for a reply, she began walking briskly towards the station hall.

'It was you!' he shouted after her. 'Is he the friend you were meeting?'

What was wrong with him? He was still shouting after her. She cursed herself for taking foolish risks when the party was in need of the intelligence in her possession. As she entered the station hall, she turned to look back; the old soldier was hobbling after her.

'There's no reward for catching me, old man, if that's what you're thinking,' she muttered under her breath. A choice: leave the station and take refuge in the town or face it out? There was a train to Moscow in twenty minutes and she had to catch it. Across the ticket hall she could see two gendarmes lolling in a very unmilitary fashion against the wall, casting lazy glances at the travellers gathered about the stove in the gloomy waiting room opposite. Instinct told her they were the sort who prefer things to be simple and do not ask many questions, and she trusted her instinct. She began scurrying noisily towards them. In the middle of the ticket hall she seemed to trip and her case clattered to the tiled floor, drawing the eyes of all on the concourse. With a little cry, she snatched it up again and ran breathlessly on, almost cannoning into the gendarme sergeant who had taken a step forward to meet her: 'Hey, miss, is the devil at your heels?'

'An old devil!'

'Calm yourself, please,' he said. 'What is it?' The sergeant was in his mid-forties, a little overweight, with bloodshot eyes and a florid complexion.

She dropped her suitcase and fumbled in her coat pocket for a handkerchief. 'An old man. He's mad. He's followed me from Odessa. He says he loves me,' she said, snivelling into her handkerchief.

The sergeant chuckled: 'Well, at least he's got good taste. Is that him?' And he laughed again. 'An old soldier, well, that explains it.'

Anna burst into tears: 'But—'

'There, there. I'll speak to him.'

It was quite apparent from the expression on his face, even at thirty yards, that the old man was surprised and disappointed to find Anna in the company of a gendarme.

'Here he comes,' said the sergeant, 'the light of battle in his eyes. What's your name, miss?'

'Anna Petrovna. A schoolteacher. I was visiting a sick friend in Odessa and am on my way to Moscow.' Her voice trembled a little.

'You have beautiful eyes, Anna Petrovna. Doesn't she?' The sergeant turned to the private at his side who was too callow to think of a chivalrous response. By now, the old soldier had made his long journey across the hall and was wheezing consumptively before them, too breathless to spit out his story. Anna shrank from him as if from a leper.

'You should know better than to chase pretty young teachers at your age, old man,' said the sergeant, wagging his finger at him. 'You've had your day. Leave it to younger men.'

The old soldier managed to gasp a few words: 'The Jew . . . the prisoner smiled, smiled at her . . .'

'Ha. I bet you smiled at her too,' said the sergeant good-humouredly. 'I can't stop smiling at Anna Petrovna.'

'She was going to meet him, I tell you!'

The sergeant was taken aback by the ring of conviction in

his voice: 'What does he mean?' he asked, looking down at Anna.

'I have no idea,' she replied, reaching for her handkerchief again. 'He won't leave me alone.'

'She knows. She was going to meet the Jew! The terrorist. He smiled at her.'

'Is that a crime?' she shouted angrily. 'Can I help it if a Jew smiles at me? Why would I be meeting a Jew?' The vehemence of her attack shook the old man and she saw a flicker of doubt in his beady little eyes.

'Shame on you, old man.' The sergeant was losing his patience. 'Go home and leave Anna Petrovna alone.'

'I tell you . . .' he spluttered. 'At least ask her where she's going, Sergeant . . .'

'I know where she's going,' the sergeant said irritably. 'Now get lost before you feel my boot up your backside.'

'I served His Majesty for thirty years . . .'

'I don't care if you served the Frog Prince. Go home before I arrest you for wasting my time.'

The old man turned disconsolately away, pulling his green uniform coat tight about him for comfort, cursing under his breath.

'Thank you,' said Anna. 'He was so persistent, and this crazy story about the Jew . . .'

'At your service, Anna Petrovna, and be sure to remember Sergeant Alexander Dmitrievich in your prayers.'

'I have a brother called Alexander Dmitrievich,' she said with a demure little smile. How Alexander Mikhailov would laugh if he could hear her. 'I will be sure to remember your kindness, Sergeant. God bless you.'

The waiting room was icy and no one was inclined to give up their place by the stove. For a while Anna was warmed by the recollection of her own audacity. What was more unthinkable in Elizavetgrad, she wondered, to be a Russian revolutionary or a Jew? Sometimes it was necessary to say and do disgusting things in the name of the people, to lie, to slander, to be someone hateful. They were preparing to blow the tsar and his family to pieces. None of them would take pleasure in carrying out the death sentence on Alexander Romanov, but it was necessary. And she owed it to Grigory.

'Please,' she said, edging her small frame between two large babushkas who were sitting as close to the heat from the stove as was humanly possible. The rough telegram paper was still in her pocket. Scrunching it in her little hand, she opened the fire door with the sleeve of her coat and threw the ball of paper into the flames. Fourth coach. Second train. She would be in Moscow by the morning.

# 14

They had argued for some time over who should have the honour. In the end they decided that to avoid the suspicions of the neighbours Lev Hartmann and Sophia Perovskaya would connect the wires. Anna was to observe the explosion from a clump of bushes a little way from the track. In the first hours after her return to Moscow the question of who would detonate the mine seemed academic. Surely when word of Goldenberg's arrest and the dynamite haul reached St Petersburg the Third Section would put two and two together and stop the imperial train? The atmosphere was tense and gloomy as Anna had known it would be when she tramped across the snowy wasteland to the cottage with her news. The burden of Grigory Goldenberg's arrest had weighed heavier on her shoulders than a sack of dynamite.

'Will he speak?' Sophia Perovskaya had asked her. 'You know him better than me, Annushka.'

Anna did not know what to say. Until tested, who could be sure they had the inner resources to withstand isolation, interrogation, torture? They had talked for many hours about what they should do and resolved to press on regardless, working day and night to complete the tunnel. The gallery kept flooding and they were forced to bail, a tight human chain along its length from the face to the cellar. At the end of each shift the work teams collapsed, exhausted and muddy, on to the pallets that were scattered about the house. Anna and Sophia forced them to eat and brought them warm water to bathe. Nerves were frayed, and it took the quiet determination of both women to drive the tunnel the last few yards to the track. Alexander Mikhailov had sent a cryptic few lines from the city, urging them to finish the work by the evening of November the 17th and promising to visit the cottage as soon as he was able. But his silence worried them all. Sophia Perovskaya learnt in casual conversation with one of their neighbours that the gendarmes had stepped up patrols along the railway and were carrying out house to house searches. On the evening of the 16th there was a loud banging on the door. Perovskaya snatched her pistol from the table and stepped closer to the bottle of nitro-glycerine.

Shivering on the doorstep was a drunken neighbour who had taken such a skinful he was unable to find his way home. Hartmann took him by the arm and led him through a heavy snowfall to his cottage, where he received a hot reception from his wife.

They finished the tunnel on the afternoon of the 17th and sat around the samovar with their own exhausted thoughts. Alexander Mikhailov joined them at dusk, brushing the snow from his beard and black fur-lined coat, his cheeks boyish pink with the cold.

'Well?' he asked, slapping his gloves on the table.

'It's done,' Sophia Perovskaya replied.

'And the mine?'

'In place.'

'Good,' and he beamed at them all like an avuncular older brother. His gaze rested on Anna: 'And you? I'm sorry about Grigory. They won't break him. He's strong.'

'Yes.'

'First a toast.' Mikhailov reached down to the bag at his feet and lifted out a bottle of vodka. 'Glasses, please.'

And there was more: fresh bread, smoked fish and caviar, cold meats and cheeses and three bottles of Georgian wine.

'To our work,' said Mikhailov, lifting his glass to the men and women patiently waiting on his word. 'The tsar has left the Crimea.'

Silence at the table. Mikhailov raised his glass again, making eye contact and saluting all of them in turn. After weeks of toil and anxiety the moment was almost upon them.

'How can you be sure?' Hartmann asked at last.

'I've received word from "the Director". The imperial train will pass through Alexandrovsk tomorrow.'

'And the others are ready there?'

'Yes.'

Hartmann raised his glass of vodka to return the toast: 'To the Director, whoever he is,' and he drained it and poured himself another.

'The security police are arresting progressives in every town between the Crimea and St Petersburg as a precaution,' Mikhailov continued. 'But the route is the same.'

'And Grigory? Do you know what they've done with him?' Anna asked.

'He is still in Odessa. The head of the Third Section has been told of his arrest and of the dynamite. Security is tight but they haven't cancelled the train.'


That night the cottage was still for the first time in weeks, the tunnel sealed, the candles extinguished, but sleep was harder than ever to come by. Anna lay at Sophia's side, conscious of her warmth and the scent of her hair. A kaleidoscope of images played through her tired mind: the plough at the front of the imperial train forging on through a suffocating wilderness of white, its plume of steam against the night sky, and the tsar at his polished table with gleaming silver, the rich red velvet of his liveried servants. Then a blinding yellow flash and the empire turned upside down.

'It's for the greater good, you know,' whispered Sophia beside her. 'Only if he dies can we hope for freedom. I wasn't sure at first . . .' She turned on her side and felt with her tiny hand for Anna's cheek and stroked it tenderly, so delicate, so child-like and yet so strong.

'But I am sure now. He must die. We are doing a noble thing, Annushka, a noble thing.'

'Yes,' she said quietly. 'Yes, I am sure we are.'

The following day Alexander Mikhailov – a plump raven in his black coat – was on the doorstep again and it was clear from his face as he kicked the snow from his boots that he was the bringer of bad tidings. There was fresh word from the Director; the imperial train had arrived safely in Kharkov.

'It passed through Alexandrovsk. Something must have gone wrong,' he said, warming his hands round a glass of tea. 'There's been no report of an explosion. Zhelyabov and the others may have been arrested. That leaves us, the Moscow cell. The Director says the train will reach us on the evening of the 19th – tomorrow.'

There was nothing they could do but wait and listen to the steady ticking of the simple kitchen clock. Mikhailov decided to wait with them. The security police were crawling over the Moscow stations like beetles on a dung heap: 'And they've issued a book of photographs – of wanted revolutionaries – I think I'm on page two,' he said, with a chuckle. 'Sophia, you are in there too. I'm afraid none of the rest of you make it. But don't worry, I'm sure you will after tomorrow.'

That night they held a little party, with Mikhailov the master of ceremonies: 'To celebrate our liberty and the first giant step in the revolution.' Hartmann played the accordion and they sang Russian folk songs and danced in the flickering candlelight.

'Dance with me, Anna.' Mikhailov grabbed her by the hand and pulled her to her feet. 'The mazurka, Lev!'

He whirled her about the rough floor with aristocratic panache and she was too intoxicated by the dance and the excitement of what tomorrow would bring to care that he was squeezing her waist tightly and pressing her a little too close.

'Huzzah, huzzah!' they all cheered.

'What a couple we make,' he whispered.

And later, when she slipped out to clear her head, he followed her and offered her his fine fur-lined coat. She shook her head, but he insisted on placing it about her shoulders. As she stood in the sober night air listening to his talk of revolution and the people, one sad thought held her: nothing would be the same after tomorrow.

'And have you thought of what I said?' he asked her. 'We would be comrades, loving comrades, serving the party.' He reached out to put his arm about her shoulders.

'No! No.' She took a sharp step away. 'Nothing will be the same. Nothing. How can you ask?'

'What are you talking about?'

'Tomorrow. After tomorrow.'

'Don't be ridiculous. As long as we're free . . .'

He seemed to want to say more but she had turned to the door and was on the point of stepping inside.

'Please. We're comrades,' she said, glancing back at him. 'That's all. That's all we'll ever be.'

Mikhailov left before sunrise without a word to her. The others followed, slipping from the cottage one by one until only the detonation party was left sitting at the table. For the most part, they sat in silence. Anna tried to occupy herself by darning a hole in the elbow of her coat but she made a poor job of it. Every hour on the hour, Lev Hartmann climbed down to the cellar to check the water level in the tunnel and the detonation wire. He was to fire the mine from the window overlooking the railway embankment the moment he saw Sophia's signal. At intervals, the floor of the cottage would tremble as a train rattled along the track and they would jump to their feet even though they knew not to expect the imperial train before nightfall.

They sat and ate a little bread and cold meat together at dusk. They had no appetite, but it would be many hours before they would have another opportunity. When it was over, they were to rendezvous at the corner of the monastery wall, where one of their comrades would be waiting with a horse and cart to take them to Moscow.

At eight o'clock Anna reached for her coat: time at last to take her place. Thank God, she thought, it will be over soon. Her head ached and her chest was tight with anxiety, and she could see the others were feeling the strain too. Sophia's face was as stiff as a painted doll's and Lev Hartmann had been biting his nails most of the day. As she hugged him goodbye, she noticed a pulse jumping in his neck.

The clump of bushes she had chosen for an observation post was little more than a stone's throw from the track. Cocooning herself in her coat and blankets, she settled down to wait, glad to be free of the cottage walls at last. Second train, fourth carriage. The first would be carrying court officials and the emperor's retinue; the target would follow soon after. It was a bright night with the snow reflecting the light from a sprinkling of winter stars and a white sickle moon. She would see the plume of smoke from the south first, and she knew Sophia would be watching carefully for the same. It was below freezing. Two pairs of woollen socks and she had stuffed her fur-lined boots with newspaper, but it was not enough to preserve the feeling in her feet. If the train was delayed she might be at her post most of the night, but she felt calmer on her own and in the open. From time to time, she jumped up and walked around in a tight circle, stamping her feet, slapping her hands against her sides, confident that she was hidden from view. She took comfort from the candle burning for her in the cottage window and once the door opened and she saw Sophia's diminutive silhouette against the light.

After two hours she had sunk into something close to a stupor, her mind and body numb with cold. But at a little before ten o'clock she caught a glimpse of a small grey cloud on the dark horizon. It disappeared for a few seconds then reappeared a little closer, and her heart leapt into her mouth. There was no mistaking it now: a pillar of smoke and steam rising from an engine. It was the first train at last and it was gusting towards her, four, five, six seconds and she could see a snake of ten carriages. It disappeared into another cutting, but only for a moment. Closer and closer, just as she had imagined it, the snow plough at the front with the plume of smoke trailing back along the train. And as the ground began to tremble beneath her feet she wondered if it was really possible to dislodge such a force. On to the railway embankment it rumbled, past the little cottage and over the tunnel they had excavated over so many difficult weeks. The driver's face was lit by the demonic orange glow of the firebox. Blazoned on the side, the symbol of oppression – the black eagle of the Romanovs. The curtains were drawn in the carriages but she could see soldiers on the plates between and more in the guards' van at the rear. Then with a whoosh of steam it was gone, powdery snow swirling in its wake, and Anna was shaking with excitement for surely the tsar was only minutes away. Minutes.

She could imagine those two pieces of wire trembling in Hartmann's rough hands. A small electrical impulse that would change Russia for ever. The tension was unbearable. She felt nauseous and struggled to check a desperate urge to jump up and pace up and down. She must be calm. The moment for action was almost upon them. The only way to free the people. Free Russia. She wanted to shout and jump and run to release the agony of waiting, and, pulling off her gloves, she dug the nails of her right hand into the back of her left, pinching herself, distracted for a moment by the pain. She could not say how long she waited, with every minute an hour, staring into a darkness broken only by pinpricks of light. Once, she was sure she saw something grey on the short horizon and sank back further into the thicket only to realise she had been tricked by her fevered imagination. And slowly the fear began to creep into her mind that the imperial train had been stopped and the sacrifices and hopes had all been in vain. So when at last she saw what might be a spiral of steam – lost for a few seconds then found – she would not accept it was the train until its shadow was quite unmistakable. And with certainty came a cold stillness. As if in a trance, she watched it draw closer and listened to the rails singing close by. Through a junction, across the river and, as it approached the long embankment, its klaxon split the night with a bellow like a wounded buffalo that chilled her to the marrow. Sh-sh-sh. On it came, the two-headed eagle just visible now on the carriages. Courtiers and guards, the kitchen, the dining car and the fourth carriage was the tsar's saloon. Around the last corner. Seconds from the cottage. The yellow lamp at the front of the engine like a giant's eye searching the track. The sh-sh-sh filling her mind. Thirty yards, twenty yards. Unblinking and breathless. And the engine rumbling over the gallery packed with dynamite. Now. Now. Do it now. And she bent her head, pressing her hands to her ears. One second, two seconds, three . . .

The white blast sucked the air from her chest and left her confused and completely deaf. For a few seconds she stared senselessly at the dense cloud of acrid smoke hanging over the track. Slowly she became aware of a distant whooshing like an Arctic wind. The engine had ground to a halt close by and the driver was releasing steam from the boiler. Where was the cottage? It was as if she were viewing everything through the bottom of a bottle. Dazed soldiers jumped from the train and half ran, half fell down the embankment into the snowy field below. As the smoke began to drift she could see the train twisting off the track with the ragged silhouette of a carriage on its side. A splinter of rail rose at a right angle to the embankment, and beneath it the raw earth rim of the smoking crater. It was as if a hand had scooped the train from the track like a toy then dropped it carelessly back. And she felt a warm rush of pride. They had done it! The tsar was dead. No one in the fourth carriage could possibly have survived the explosion. Debris spotted the snow beyond the embankment as far as she could see. Railwaymen and soldiers were still stumbling from the train and a small group was gathering at the lip of the crater. Rising to her feet, she eased her way back through the thicket and away from the hissing engine. Before long they would find the remains of the gallery and follow the trench back to the cottage. Her comrades would be waiting anxiously to hear what she had seen: what news she could bring them! What joyful news. The tyrant was dead.

# 15

Not content with ringing the new electric bell, the clerk from the Justice Ministry was banging his fist on the door and making enough noise to wake not only Dobrshinsky's respectable neighbours in Furshtatskaya Street but the devil himself. The bleary-eyed porter opened it in his nightshirt. Certainly, His Honour was at home but, like every good Christian, in his bed at such an hour. The clerk was insistent: he was required to deliver his message at once. It was a matter of the utmost importance.

The long case clock in the hall was chiming half past three as the young man was shown into the special investigator's study. Anton Dobrshinsky was standing at his desk in a flamboyant Chinese blue silk dressing gown which would have surprised those familiar with his sober public persona. He had just struck a match and was on the point of lighting a cigarette.

The clerk stepped forward at once with the letter: 'Compliments of His Worship Count von Plehve.'

Dobrshinsky examined the handwriting on the envelope for a second, then picked up a paperknife and with a single easy motion slit it open. Five polite but deliberately vague lines that left him in no doubt the count had received serious intelligence:

*My Dear Anton Frankzevich,*

*I am sorry for the lateness of the hour, only a matter of the greatest importance to the Fatherland would lead me to request a meeting. I have sent a carriage with instructions to bring you to my home. My dear fellow, please make haste, there is much of a confidential nature that we must speak of at the earliest opportunity.*

*Yours truly,*

*Vyacheslav Konstantinovich von Plehve.*

An attack? Dobrshinsky wondered. This new terrorist organisation, the arrest of the Jew with a suitcase of dynamite: he had warned the head of the Third Section there would be an attempt on a member of the imperial family or the government. The dogs had been barking a warning in the streets.

'I'll be down shortly,' he said, slipping the letter back in the envelope.

It was only a matter of a few minutes' drive through the empty streets to von Plehve's home on the Moika Embankment. The count greeted Dobrshinsky in the hall and, with the face of an undertaker, led him to his study.

'My dear fellow, terrible news,' he said as the polished mahogany doors closed behind them. 'It concerns His Majesty . . .'

Dobrshinsky looked at him impassively for a moment then said: 'I warned General Drenteln the imperial train was in danger.'

'How did you know?' demanded von Plehve.

'The gendarmes arrested a Jew called Goldenberg at Elizavetgrad Station eight days ago. He was carrying a large quantity of dynamite.'

'You mean this could have been prevented?' The count gestured angrily towards one of the English armchairs in front of his desk. 'The Emperor's Council will want to know why the train wasn't stopped.'

He slumped heavily into the chair opposite Dobrshinsky and with his elbows on the arms, placed his fingers to his lips and stared coldly over them at the special investigator: 'The second attempt on the tsar's life this year. It will be me who has to answer for this.'

That was not, strictly speaking, true. Dobrshinsky knew the names of half a dozen ministers and more senior civil servants who would be asked to account for a failure in security before the count – the head of the Third Section, General Drenteln, for one.

'It would be helpful if Your Worship told me what has happened.'

'As you've clearly surmised, the emperor has not been hurt,' said the count dryly. 'But the imperial baggage train was derailed by an explosion outside Moscow this evening. The order of the trains was changed, the emperor's was to have been the second train but at the last minute it was agreed he would travel before the baggage.' The count rose again and walked over to the fire to ring the bell to the right of the mantelpiece. 'A piece of remarkably good fortune – His Majesty has probably declared it another miracle – you see, the bomb went off beneath the fourth carriage. The emperor's saloon was the fourth on the imperial train. If he hadn't insisted on switching the order of the trains he would be dead. And . . .' the count lowered his heavy frame back into the armchair, 'and you and I would be eking out a living in a provincial city. Thankfully no one was hurt, but the royal supply of jam was a casualty.'

There was a knock at the study door and a servant entered with a delicate china tea service which he placed on a table by the fire.

'They're very well informed,' said Dobrshinsky with a frown. 'The terrorists?'

'It's possible they were watching the imperial train in the Crimea . . .'

'But you think there's more?' said the count, accepting the cup offered by his footman.

'I am afraid I do.'

First the dead informer, Bronstein, in the hotel. Then the student who had blown his brains out to avoid arrest. Someone must have tipped him off because he had destroyed his papers and was on the point of leaving Petersburg. And the local police informer in Peski too – the vagabond – he had been stabbed outside a church school on a Sunday. 'You see, Count, every time we try to place someone in this new party, they are murdered. Every time we try to make an arrest, the bird has just flown. Our promising leads come to nothing?'

'But you've arrested this fellow with the dynamite,' von Plehve pointed out sceptically.

Dobrshinsky's face stiffened a little. Was the chief prosecutor implying he was making excuses? 'It was pure luck. Goldenberg was dragging a bag of dynamite along a station platform. Even the local gendarmes were able to identify him as a suspicious character.'

'I see.'

For a minute, neither of them spoke but sipped their tea and stared at the crackling fire.

'Just to be clear,' von Plehve said at last, 'you think someone is giving this "People's Will" intelligence – they have a spy somewhere?'

'Perhaps,' Dobrshinsky replied cautiously. 'Some of them come from noble families. They have influential friends.'

'This woman, Sophia Perovskaya?'

'And others. The Volkonskaya woman has given us a few names and descriptions, although she was trusted with very little.'

'The foreigner she mentioned, have you been able to identify him?'

'Not yet. She thinks he's German or perhaps English.'

'A plot to destabilise the country?' Something in the tone of this question suggested the count's subtle mind had fastened on an interesting new possibility. 'It might be useful to brief our newspapers. They could suggest something of the sort.'

'I am more interested in the Jew, Goldenberg,' replied Dobrshinsky. 'We suspect him of being involved in the murder of the governor of Kharkov.'

Von Plehve put his cup back on his saucer. 'I am sure you will do all you need to do to extract the truth from him.'

Ah, spoken like a true Russian, Dobrshinsky thought, and he could not help a sardonic little smile.

'Does that offend you?'

'Not in the slightest, but it won't be necessary. I have my own methods.'

Von Plehve grunted. 'That's up to you. I don't care how you break him. Just be sure you do.'

# 16

> . . . We are convinced that our agents and our party will not
> be discouraged by this failure . . . They will go forward with
> new faith in their strength and in the ultimate success of
> their cause . . .

'No comfort for the authorities there,' said Dobson with a short
laugh. He was standing in front of the fire in his study, a dog-
eared leaflet in his hand. It was a bleak Petersburg evening,
dark at five o'clock, a wind from Siberia driving all but a few
from the streets, snow rattling at the window.

'These political zealots love their Bible, don't they, with their
talk of "faith" and "sacrifice", "forgiveness" and "martyrdom".
Listen to this:

> If Alexander were to recognise the evil he has done to Russia,
> if he were to hand over his power to a General Assembly
> chosen by the free vote of the people, then we for our part
> would leave him in peace and forgive his past misdeeds . . .

Here . . .' Dobson leant forward to offer the pamphlet to
Hadfield, who was sprawling in a leather armchair, his stockinged
feet thawing at the fire.

'And you know the maddening thing is the story was broken
by a Hun, one of the German correspondents in Moscow,' he
added with a shake of the head. 'Of course the censor tried to
suppress the news here. The Germans were able to read about
the attempt on the tsar's life before his own subjects. What a
country this is.'

Hadfield did not lift his eyes from the pamphlet: '... *implacable war.*'

'What?' Dobson asked. 'Yes. They want to wage "implacable war". Old Testament rather than New, I grant you.'

'Where did you find it?' Hadfield asked, lifting the paper from his lap.

'Oh, you can pick them up in the street, but my new friend Major Barclay gave it to me. Cost me a dozen oysters at the Europe Hotel.'

The leaflet was dated 22 November – three days after the explosion, a statement by the executive committee of The People's Will.

'Impressive, don't you think? This party's shaken the empire after only a few months – and it has a printing press so it can boast about it too,' said Dobson.

'Are you a zealot if you advocate one man one vote?'

'In Russia? Of course. But they don't stop there: they're in love with violence and secrecy and martyrdom ...' Dobson paused to shake his head a little in disapproval. 'Actually, they're incurable romantics.'

'That's your diagnosis? Do you know any members of this party?'

Dobson grunted. 'Do you? You're being cussed now, old boy. Do I look like someone who wants to spend the rest of his life in Siberia?'

'Sorry – I thought it was the job of a correspondent to represent both sides of an argument. Or are you content with Mr Dostoevsky's word upon the matter?'

'Stop it, stop it,' and Dobson wagged his finger at him. 'Dangerous talk, especially for a foreigner. Let's not fall out. Now, what about dinner?'

But Hadfield would not allow himself to be persuaded. He had spent the afternoon at the clinic in Peski, as he always chose to on Sundays, and he was too tired to think of anything more than the comfort of his own bed.

'I need to pace myself,' he said, rising to his feet. 'Lady Dufferin has returned to Petersburg and she's invited me to join an embassy party at the Yusupov tomorrow.'

'You're such a favourite with the ladies, old boy, especially those of – shall we say – maturer years . . .' replied Dobson with a mischievous smile.

'Dobson, are you jealous?'

'I haven't squeezed the hand of a pretty girl in months.'

'If it's any comfort, nor have I.'

'No comfort. You could have if you'd wanted to.'

Perhaps I could, yes, Hadfield thought as he let himself out of the building and on to the snowy street. There had been two or three pretty young ladies who had caught his eye at parties, but he had felt no inclination to be more than amiable. His aunt teased him that when the ladies retreated after dinner he was often spoken of and always in favourable terms. One of the most eligible young men in Petersburg, she said. Well, at least on the English Embankment. And it was quite true that his reputation was growing with his practice and his credit at the bank.

The wind had dropped a little but it was snowing harder than ever, large soft flakes falling thickly, an unhealthy yellow in the light of the street lamps. It was only a short walk to the Nevsky Prospekt, his boots crunching on the virgin snow, and the freezing air roused him from the torpor he had been in danger of sinking into in front of Dobson's fire. There was something magical about the city in the first hours of a heavy snowfall, before the cabs cut rough ridges of ice in the streets and the gutters and pavements were awash with filthy meltwater. Clean and strangely peaceful, but for the Sunday chiming of old Russia. On an impulse, he decided to visit the Kotomin House for a glass of Glühwein, and climbing to the second floor was shown to a table with a view of the frozen Moika. It had once been a favourite with the literati, and rich students, academics and cultivated professionals chose to patronise the restaurant for that very reason, but on this evening it was almost empty. He sat at the table sipping his wine and staring out of the window at the passers-by trudging heavy-footed along the embankment. There had been talk at the clinic of the attempt on the tsar's life, and some of the students whom he had recruited to help him there were impressed and openly expressed sympathy for The People's Will – rather too vociferously so. Hadfield kept his counsel. He was in no doubt that Anna, the Figners, Goldenberg and their friends were involved, but he had seen and heard nothing of them for months. He missed their camaraderie, their idealism, their sense of mission – precisely those things Dobson liked to dismiss as 'romantic tosh' – and sometimes he was conscious of feeling inexpressibly restless and disgusted with the bourgeois complacency of his life. But he took comfort and pride in his work, in the real and practical difference he made day after day to the lives of his patients. He had pushed Anna to the back of his mind, but when someone spoke of politics a memory of her – always frowning – would force its way to the front and make him smile. Sitting in the restaurant, staring out to the snow falling in a luminous carpet below, he felt a sudden, an annoying, an irrational longing to see her. After a few minutes, he ordered the bill and paid without finishing his glass of wine. The cold air would bring him to his senses.

But the same puzzling ache was with him through the evening: as he watched the maid light the fire and sipped the broth she had brought him from the kitchen below, and he was conscious of it still as he read a letter from his mother and sat at his bureau with his medical journal. It was as if the doubts he felt about his life and his purpose were crystallising about Anna like ice on metal. Too much introspection was unhealthy. Since childhood he had struggled to prevent his thoughts taking him to dark places.

The following morning, he walked to his surgery with a lighter heart. It was a cold clear day, the snow blinding in the yellow winter sunlight. Workers were clearing the pavements on either side of Line 7, shovelling the snow into dirty heaps in the gutter. The traders at the market hall had set out their stalls and were hawking their wares to women bundled in coats and scarves and valenki boots, shapeless and ageless but for their eyes. Hadfield had rented rooms for his practice from the German pharmacy at the corner of Line 7, opposite the pretty pink and white Cathedral of St Andrew. He was on excellent terms with the cathedral priests because he visited the parish orphanage free of charge, and they more than repaid this small service by praising his skill as a physician and his Christian generosity to their wealthier parishioners. He spent the morning dispensing advice and reassurance, pills and potions to a procession of women in furs who were for the most part in rude health, and to an elderly lawyer suffering from severe and persistent over-indulgence. At a little before one o'clock, a messenger delivered a note from Lady Dufferin asking him to call at the embassy to examine one of her children and inviting him to stay for afternoon tea. The Dufferins had just returned from a long visit to England and their estates in the north of Ireland. The ambassador had left almost at once for Berlin, where he was representing the government's case on the Ottoman question to Prince Bismarck. But the Countess of Dufferin was busy placing the new furniture she had brought from home and preparing for the first official reception to be held at the embassy since her husband's appointment to the imperial court.

Little Freddie Blackwood was suffering from nothing more than a head cold and a severe attack of boredom. A precocious four year old, he was bubbling over with curiosity to see the tsar and his Cossack guards and ride in a troika, but his anxious mother was refusing to release him from the embassy. Hadfield had taken his part: 'Perhaps a little air and a little excitement would do him no harm.' Since his visit to her bedside six months before – a journey Her Ladyship now recalled as an heroic life-saving dash across the city – his word as a physician went unquestioned at the embassy. The same could not be said for his judgement of pictures.

'Do you like this one?' she asked, as they were taking tea in the small drawing room. Two of the servants – one rather short, the other a little too doddery for the task – were holding a large landscape to the wall.

'French?' he asked uncertainly.

'After Poussin,' she replied, waving her hand at the servants. 'A little to the right please. Yes, that's perfect there.'

The picture hangers looked unsure what was expected of them.

'Oh, would you, Doctor?' said Lady Dufferin, exasperated.

Hadfield explained in Russian that Her Ladyship would like them to hang the picture precisely where they were holding it now.

'The Countess von Plehve and Madame von Pahlen were very taken with the painting. Quite as good as some of the pictures in the Hermitage, they said. And I showed them the French furniture we have brought here for the dining room,' she continued. 'Madame Pahlen says it is finer than the furniture at the French embassy and that the Grand Duke Vladimir has just purchased something very like it.'

Hadfield smiled and nodded politely. He had no particular views on Louis Quinze cabinets and chairs or on the French Rococo style in general. But to an accompaniment of banging step ladders and hammering, Lady Dufferin slipped seamlessly from furniture to politics. Hadfield wondered if that was why conversation was commonly described as a drawing-room art rather than a science.

'. . . and the Countess von Plehve said the imperial family was still shaken by the attack on the train. The police have been ordered to round up anyone suspected of sheltering or supporting these nihilists.'

'I thought they had already done that, Your Ladyship,' Hadfield replied.

'No, not there, to the right!' she shouted, rising from the sofa. 'Oh, will you tell them, Doctor?'

The picture hangers climbed down their ladders and reassembled them closer to the mantelpiece.

'. . . yes, well, it appears not,' Lady Dufferin said, picking up the thread of their conversation. 'But the ladies say one of the plotters is in custody, a Jew from Kiev called Silver. The most extraordinary thing: he was dragging a bag of dynamite along a station platform. Anyway, the police hope he will give them the names of the other conspirators.'

She paused again. 'That's it, that's it. There.' Then, settling her dress around her on to the sofa, the conversation moved just as seamlessly from politics to the sledging hills at the yacht club and the evening's expedition to the Yusupov.

But Hadfield's thoughts were with the little Jew called Silver and his dynamite. Silver or Gold? How many Jews from Kiev were there in the revolutionary movement? Poor Anna. He could remember the warmth as well as the exasperation in her voice when she spoke of him. Would she be safe? Perhaps she was in custody too? And would Goldenberg mention to his captors the English doctor who had once had the temerity to question the wisdom of killing a tsar?

'. . . Doctor?'

'I'm sorry, your Ladyship.'

'Please explain to them I want the McCulloch of the Highlands in the dining room . . .'

To Major Vladimir Barclay's mind the Jew looked anything but a desperate terrorist in his torn and dirty great coat. They had spoken only briefly; Goldenberg to spout a well rehearsed justification of the attack on 'the tyrant'. Barclay had ordered him to hold his tongue or he would teach him some manners.

Rising from his seat, he stepped over to the window – the station concourse was crowded with people – then back to the stove. The train was late, there was a gale blowing through the detention room, and Barclay's patience was wearing very thin.

'Fetch me some tea,' he barked at the corporal standing at the door.

He had been waiting at the Nikolayevsky for nearly three hours. Goldenberg was wedged between gendarmes on the seats opposite, and there were a dozen more outside. They were going to take no chances. Not only had he fought like a tiger at Elizavetgrad – it had taken six of the local gendarmes to subdue him – but he was the only one of the conspirators they were holding in custody.

Barclay had arrived in Moscow two days after the explosion and had seen the cottage and the remains of the tunnel the terrorists had dug to the railway embankment for himself. On his third day in the city, he had helped the local gendarmes arrest a well known radical at the university. After a little direct pressure, the student had admitted sheltering a revolutionary called Hartmann and his female companions in the hours after the explosion. One of the women was certainly Sophia Perovskaya. His description of the other – small, silent, a little sullen with strikingly blue eyes – had brought to Barclay's mind a mental picture of Anna Romanko. The student had accompanied the three of them to the Belorussky Station where Hartmann had purchased a ticket for Berlin. He was not certain, but he thought the women had taken a train to St Petersburg.

The corporal returned with some tea and the news that word was spreading through the station that one of the terrorists who had tried to kill the tsar was being held in the detention room. A hostile crowd was gathering at the foot of the stairs.

'Can I have some tea too?' It was Goldenberg.

Barclay glanced over the top of his glass at him contemptuously.

'Well?'

'If you don't shut up, you'll get more than tea. I'll hand you over to the mob.'

Goldenberg wrinkled his face disdainfully. 'You're not going to do that, Major. Not yet. I'm far too valuable.'

Damn the fellow, Barclay thought, he was right.

# 17

They spoke of it often, and always with deep sadness and a sense of injustice. To have prepared so thoroughly and to have come so close – it was a blow to the morale of all. One evening after their return to St Petersburg, Anna was preparing supper in a safe house on Nevsky. Conscious of a particularly long silence, she looked up to find Sophia Perovskaya standing at the sink, her hands in icy water, eyes fixed blankly on the wall.

'Sonechka,' Anna said, rising from the table, a knife still in her hand.

'It wasn't my fault, was it?'

'How could it be your fault?' Anna stepped over to the sink and put her arms about Sophia's waist, pressing herself against her small body. 'We only managed to get as far as we did because of you.'

'I'm sorry,' she said, turning in Anna's arms to face her. 'I'm fine, really. I know I must be strong.'

Anna reached for her hands, still rough and chapped from the work at the cottage, and very cold. 'You are the strongest among us.'

It was a little shocking. No one had seen Sophia falter. But weeks of nervous exhaustion, hard labour, the scheming, the lying and the fear of the gendarmes at the door had taken their toll on all of them. They sat side by side at the table and finished preparing supper – for the most part in silence – until they were joined by other comrades, Kviatokovsky, Morozov and Olga Liubatovich. No one spoke again of past failure that evening or of the plans for the future, but when they had eaten they laughed and joked and drank and sang together until late in the evening. Sophia Perovskaya's apartment was a cab journey away and she left at ten o'clock with Kviatkovsky, who lived close by. Anna was to spend the night in the little flat on Nevsky with the other two and return to her schoolhouse at Alexandrovskaya in the morning. She was anxious about her safety and would have preferred the life of an 'illegal' with her comrades in the city, but the executive committee had decided she should resume her teaching post in the village. 'The party needs people who can move freely, without fear of arrest,' Alexander Mikhailov had told her. The Director had assured him the Third Section was a long way from identifying her and she was 'clean'. Of course, there would be questions after so many months away, but Mikhailov had made her write regular bulletins on her mother's health to the local priest and had arranged for them to be sent from Kharkov.

It was the first night Anna had spent in the Nevsky flat and she was a little shocked to discover she was to sleep on a pallet in the kitchen while her comrades shared the only bed. Morozov and Liubatovich were dedicated revolutionaries with long police histories, but they had chosen to ignore the party's strictures against intimate relationships and had become lovers. She wondered at their audacity. It was Nikolai Morozov who had written the manifesto with its emphasis on personal sacrifice. Would he leave Olga if the executive committee required it of him? The opportunity to express deeper feelings, sexual love; she could not help but feel envious. She was alone on a hard mattress, the mice scratching at the skirting boards close to her head. It was more than two years since she had last seen her husband, Stepan – the marriage was over and she was glad of it. But after weeks of frantic activity preparing for the attack, the fear and the loneliness, the role of revolutionary ascetic seemed harder to play than it had before. Life might end tomorrow before she heard a man say, 'I love you,' and mean it. Shaken along endless miles of track, in daydreams and through restless nights, one man had whispered love to her and she had imagined what it would be to share a bed with him and feel his body pressed to hers. But this man was beyond her reach. Clever and different in many ways that frightened her, how could they love when he was not of the same mind? 'No. Not one of us,' she thought, 'not one of us.' Olga and Nikolai were fortunate to have found each other. But the comfort of others was no comfort to her and the longing for affection and closeness was still with her when she woke cold and stiff in the morning.

Anna had resolved to leave for the village straight after breakfast and had packed her few possessions before the others began to stir. Olga was the first to rise, a man's padded smoking jacket over her nightgown. She was a peculiarly masculine-looking woman with a full mouth, weak chin and heavy eyebrows that met above a Roman nose. Not at all handsome but formidably clever, and her comrades admired her independence of thought and strength of purpose. She was only twenty-five but after years of prison and internal exile, she had the air of someone older and more worldly wise.

Nodding to Anna, she reached for the cigarette case she had left on the kitchen table the night before and lit one with obvious pleasure. Only when she had drawn deeply upon it two or three times was she ready for conversation. Olga's appetite was already legendary, and once the small range was lit she set about frying eggs, the cigarette hanging loosely from her mouth. She was on the point of serving them when they were surprised by a quiet but urgent rapping at the door.

'Don't open it!' It was Morozov from the bedroom next door.

Seconds later he joined them, blinking myopically, his long hair tousled, spindly legs beneath his greatcoat.

'The revolver!' he hissed at Olga.

But before she could open the table drawer the knocking began again and this time they heard Sophia Perovskaya's high pitched voice. 'It's me. I need to speak to you.'

Anna opened the door at once and Sophia almost fell into the room. 'It's Kviatkovsky! The police are going to raid his apartment.' She had run up the stairs and was still gasping for breath, her eyes wide with alarm.

'How do you know?' asked Morozov.

'A note from Mikhailov . . . we must warn him! There are papers . . . but it may be too late. I can't go – Alexander can't go . . .'

'Here.' Anna pulled her towards a chair. 'I'll go now.'

'No,' said Morozov. 'It's too dangerous. I will ask Maria Oshanina to go. She's clean. The gendarmes have nothing on her.'

'I'm clean,' said Anna crossly. 'There's no time to waste.'

'Too much of a risk. You're a friend of Goldenberg's. And you know too much.'

'Anna's right. Someone must go now.' Olga was already moving towards the bedroom.

'But not you or Sophia. It's too dangerous,' said Morozov with alarm.

'No. It has to be Anna,' she shouted through the half open door. 'But I'm going to wait in the lane in case . . .' She did not need to finish the sentence. They knew what she meant.

A little after eight o'clock in the morning, Nevsky was bustling with traffic – workers on the way to the Admiralty yards and the factories on Vasilievsky, civil servants to the great ministries – and it was a while before they were able to hail a droshky. There was a biting wind from the north-east carrying with it a flurry of snow, and Olga put her arm about Anna to share the warmth of her body, pressing her close.

'If the police stop you tell them you are delivering a message from me to the dressmaker at Number 8,' she whispered. 'Nikolai and I have cover papers in the name of Khartsov.'

The driver dropped them at last at the corner of Zagorodny and Leshtukov Lane. It was a respectable part of town, popular with junior army officers and their families and doctors at the nearby hospital. Kviatkovsky was another of the gentleman revolutionaries and one of the most influential. The apartment he shared with Evgenia Figner was in a handsome yellow and white four-storey mansion in the middle of the lane. Anna knew the block well.

They hurried along Leshtukov in silence, arm in arm, their faces almost covered by their scarves. Mittened and muffled children were throwing snowballs at each other as they made their way to school. A dvornik was scraping snow from his yard into the street and an old lady, a black bundle in coat and shawl and hat, was inching unsteadily along the frozen pavement towards them with a shopping basket. There was no sign of gendarmes or the city police. A short distance from the mansion, Olga pulled Anna into an open yard: 'I'll wait here.' She leant forward and kissed her on the lips. 'Be careful, comrade.'

Kviatkovsky's grand apartment was on the third floor, with a fine gallery window over the street. Nothing appeared out of place. Anna turned under the carriage arch into the yard and walked with purpose towards the back entrance and the servant's staircase. Gazing up at the back of the block, she could see no sign of a parasol, the signal that was to be posted in a window when it was safe to visit. One foot lightly in front of the other, she began climbing the stairs, pausing after a few seconds to listen for voices or boots or the clatter of a rifle butt. At the door to the third-floor landing, she stopped and listened, but could hear only the faint trundle of a passing carriage in the street and the ferocious beating of her heart. It was no time for timidity; a deep breath, her small gloved hand firmly on the door knob, and she turned it quickly and stepped on to the landing. There was no one there. Kviatkovsky's door was closed and there was nothing out of the ordinary – muddy footprints on the tiled floor, scratches on the varnished door, a splintered frame – nothing to suggest there had been a struggle. Perhaps there was still time. With another deep breath she stepped forward and rang the bell. At once, the door jerked open to reveal a portly middle-aged man in the black uniform coat of the city police.

'Oh, I'm sorry,' she said, almost falling against the stair rail. 'Goodness, you made me jump. I was told the dressmaker lives here.'

'No, miss, the dressmaker lives in the apartment opposite.'

'Oh, how silly of me.'

'Sergeant Kirill Korovin, at your service.'

'I need the dressmaker,' said Anna, turning away.

'I am afraid my orders are to take anyone who calls at the apartment to the station and I always obey my orders. Why don't you come in?' He stood aside to let her into the apartment.

Every muscle in Anna's body was taut, her heart pounding, but she sought and held eye contact with the policeman, smiling sweetly.

'It's a mess in here,' he said, as she slipped past into the hall. The drawing-room door was ajar. It looked as if a bomb had gone off inside. The upholstery had been ripped out of the soft sofa and armchairs, the contents of the sideboard drawers were strewn all over the floor along with copies of a statement on the attack printed on the party's new press. They were to have been secretly posted around the city that night. Worse still, she could see copper drums, a roll of wire and a secure box that

172

was identical to the one they had used to store dynamite at the cottage in Preobrazhenskoe.

'Hey you, back in the kitchen!' the sergeant bellowed behind her, and turning, Anna saw the little face of the maid peeking round the door. The poor girl was petrified and bobbed back inside at once.

'In here, miss,' said the sergeant, pointing to Evgenia's room. Anna cleared more copies of the party's statement from the bed then perched at its edge, her hands held demurely in her lap.

'Sergeant – I really can't stay. I must go,' she said in a plaintive voice.

Korovin ignored her, turning his head to shout to one of his men: 'Haven't you finished in there?'

'My mistress is expecting me,' she whined. 'Please let me go. I promised I would only be an hour.'

But the policeman just looked at her coldly.

'Please. I don't want to be in trouble.' Taking out her handkerchief she began to snivel noisily into it.

'What a performance. Bravo,' said Korovin, clapping. 'You're wasting your breath, miss.'

Although Anna tried her best with desperate looks and tears, he was not to be moved. As soon as the constables had finished searching Kviatkovsky's bedroom, she was escorted from the apartment, the crunch of police boots at her back, echoing up and down the stairwell. She was afraid but calm and clear-sighted, absorbed in rehearsing the story she would spin at the station. Time. She needed to buy as much of it as she was able. Olga was waiting a short distance away, but would she notice?

The sergeant stepped forward at the bottom of the stairs to hold the front door open. 'After you, miss.'

The self-satisfied sneering in his voice made Anna furious. As he led her on to the pavement, she pretended to stumble and cried out in pain. Lifting her dress a little, she reached down to her ankle. 'I've twisted it.'

'Oh?' said Korovin, quite unconcerned. 'It's fortunate your carriage awaits you.' And he waved to the police driver parked a little way along the lane.

'Aren't you going to help me?' Anna burst into noisy tears.

'All right, all right,' he said. But by now she had worked herself into a pitiful frenzy, her body heaving with sobs, and it was all the embarrassed sergeant could do to prevent her collapsing to the snowy pavement.

Her little pantomime was beginning to attract the attention of the street.

'What are you doing to her?' a young man in an expensive coat called from the pavement opposite.

'Shame!' shouted a woman from a window above.

'Come on with that carriage,' bellowed Korovin. A moment later it drew up in front of the mansion. 'All right, all right, let me help you,' he said impatiently.

Anna limped forward, pausing at the step to glance furtively down the lane. Yes, Olga was watching. There was no mistaking that blue scarf and enormous old fur coat.

The district police station was on the second floor of a run-down building on Zagarodny. It was oppressively hot, the waiting room crowded, and Korovin was obliged to shout and shoulder his way through to the administration office. He left Anna on a chair in front of the chief clerk's desk and went in search of the station superintendent. A few minutes later, he was back and the scowl on his heavy face suggested he was very out of sorts: 'Name and address?'

'I'm going to be in so much trouble. Please let me go.' She buried her head in her hands.

'You're in trouble now,' the policeman barked. 'What's your name?'

'Anna Petrovna Kovalenko,' she muttered between her hands.

'And where are your papers?'

But Anna refused to say more. Threats, imprecations, promises, even a reassuring arm, nothing he tried would elicit another word from her. And the more he tried the more hysterical she seemed to become until he began to wonder at her sanity.

'You can cool down for an hour.' He grabbed her arm and dragged her roughly to her feet. 'Here, you, Rostislov,' he said, addressing a constable bent in conversation with the chief clerk. 'Take this one to Room 6.' And turning to Anna again, he said, 'An hour. If you don't give me your address and answer for yourself after that I can promise you now, you'll be spending the night in the Peter and Paul Fortress.'

It was a box room with a tiny barred window, furnished with only a wooden bench and a bucket. Anna pressed herself into a corner, her knees up to her chest, exhausted by the nervous tension of the last two hours. She knew she should rehearse her story, but she had neither the will nor the energy. Mikhailov had assured her she was clean but it was only a matter of time before they found a witness – perhaps the servant girl – who could tie her to Goldenberg or Soloviev or one of the others. She closed her eyes and groaned quietly into the crook of her arm: that it had come to this already. Her head was still buried there a few minutes later when she heard the rattle of the key in the lock. It was Constable Rostislov.

'It seems you don't have to remember where you live after all,' he said dryly. 'Follow me.'

He led her down a windowless corridor and into what looked like a secretariat, with clerks sitting at a block of desks in the centre of the room. At the opposite end, the sergeant was standing beside the only polished doors in the station.

'Still limping, then?'

175

Before she could reply, the door was opened by the super-intendent's gatekeeper who announced His Honour Ivan Andreievich Kuznetzov was now ready to see the prisoner.

The superintendent's office was like those occupied by middle-ranking policemen all over the empire, with its oppressively dark wallpaper, cheap burgundy drapes, filing cabinet, desk and undistinguished print of His Imperial Majesty. Kuznetzov was sitting beneath it, his grey head bent over his papers. Almost lost in a high-backed chair in front of his desk sat a woman, her dark hair drawn tightly into a bun. Anna could see no more than the top of her head but there was something in the shape of it and the way she held it that was familiar. The woman raised a hand to sweep a loose strand of hair behind her ear and Anna let out an involuntary gasp of pain.

'Go on – what's the matter with you?' It was Sergeant Korovin at her shoulder.

'Ah, it's you!' Olga Liubatovich twisted in the chair to look at her. Her eyes were almost lost beneath a heavy frown, her voice full of resentment. 'Did you deliver the note? What am I going to tell my husband, you foolish girl? Look at the trouble you've got us into.'

Clever, clever Olga. Burying her face in her hands, Anna began to sob pathetically, her small frame shaking with the effort.

'All right, all right,' said the superintendent irritably. 'Sit down.' He waved his hand to Korovin to indicate he should guide her to a chair.

'Now, can you tell me who this woman is?' he asked when she had settled in front of his desk.

'My mistress, Elizaveta Dmitrievna.'

'Look at me.'

Anna raised her eyes for just a second then looked away. He had a thin face and severe mouth, as if years in the police had ground him to a sharp point.

'Now tell me what business you had at a terrorist's apartment?'

'A message to the seamstress,' she snivelled.

'For goodness sake, stop behaving like a child!' the superintendant roared and he thumped his fist on the desk so hard some of his papers floated to the floor. 'Do you know who lives in that flat?'

'No.'

'And you,' he said turning to Olga, 'where do you live?'

Olga ignored him and turned to Anna again. 'My husband will be so cross! This is your fault,' she said. 'I've a mind to turn you out!'

Anna resumed her noisy sobbing. It was a more than respectable performance, but the superintendent had been in the service many years and was a difficult man to deflect. For an hour, he kept returning to the same questions: why had she visited the apartment? What was the message for the dressmaker? Where did she come from? He worried away at both of them, coaxing and bullying in turn.

'All right, we'll see,' he said at last, getting to his feet stiffly. 'Take them home, Sergeant. Examine their papers. Search the apartment from top to bottom and speak to the husband.'

As the two of them were bundled into a police barouche, Anna managed to lean across and whisper 'Thank you'. It was below freezing, the light was fading and the sky threatened more snow, but her spirits were lifting in the cold air after the stuffiness and anxiety of the station. A policeman sat on the box beside the driver, another two travelled on the footboard at the back, and behind them a dozen more in cabs. But once they were beneath the canopy, Olga reached across to give her hand a little squeeze: 'We have a chance.'

It was only a short drive to the building on Nevsky. Glancing up furtively, Anna could see the parasol was no longer posted in the window: the flat must have been cleared of incriminating papers and Morozov would have left too. A posse of policemen huffed and puffed up the stairs after them and gathered on the narrow landing at the top. For appearance's sake, Olga rang the bell, confident no one would answer. After a few seconds, she began rummaging in her bag for the keys, but before she could find them they heard footsteps in the hall and the sound of a heavy bolt drawn back. To Anna's dismay, the door opened to reveal a very startled-looking Nikolai Morozov: 'What on earth—'

Olga threw herself upon him, clutching him tightly. 'Darling, I'm so sorry. Please don't be angry. The police have arrested Anna. I had to go to the station, and now they won't let us go. Please don't be angry.'

'What?' Morozov had regained his composure at once. 'What's happened to you?'

Sergeant Korovin was ready with his own explanation: 'Your maid was arrested at the apartment of two people we suspect of blowing up the tsar's train in Moscow. We're going to have to search your flat.'

'Please do,' said Morozov, stepping back from the door.

'No. No. You first and your wife – and you,' Korovin said, pulling Anna roughly by the arm.

They sat on the edge of the bed in silence as the police turned the place upside down, ferreting through cupboards and drawers, moving the few small pieces of furniture, lifting rugs and loose boards, examining their clothes, stirring the ashes in the stove. After an hour they had turned up nothing in the least incriminating and Korovin had no choice but to call a halt to the search. Until their personal papers had been checked against police records they were under house arrest, he told them, and to be sure this order was obeyed he left two constables at the door.

'It will take them a while to check our identities,' said Morozov when it was safe to talk. 'But my papers were stolen from a merchant in Tula. He's bound to have reported the theft to the local police.'

'Why did you stay, Nikolai?' Olga asked him, leaning forward to stroke his hair. 'You should have gone.'

'Don't be silly.' He reached up to grab and hold her hand. 'Sophia helped me clear the flat. She's gone to warn the others. What's important now is getting out of here.'

There was a shimmering halo around the street lamps in the prospekt. Snow was falling again. It was after seven o'clock and a steady stream of workers was trudging home along the slush-covered pavements. To Anna's exhausted mind, they appeared blurred and dark at the edges like a badly taken daguerreotype. Gazing from the sitting-room window, she felt unaccountably empty, as if the stuffing had been ripped from her by one of the constables. Her companions were still at the table, whispering to each other, holding hands, drawing strength from their intimacy.

'All right, I think it's time.'

The two young policemen looked thoroughly miserable. It was only a few degrees above freezing on the stairs and for an hour they had been shifting stiffly from foot to foot, stamping and slapping their sides like awkward marionettes.

'My husband wants me to order some tea,' Olga said, as they turned to look at the two women. 'Maria Alexandrovna,' she shouted in a stentorian voice. 'Maria Alexandrovna!'

The landlady's name echoed down the stairs and a few seconds later a door opened on the landing below. A large woman in her fifties in a black scarf and ankle-length coat peered up at them. 'What's this racket?'

'Maria Alexandrovna, we would like some tea.'

Tea, she huffed. Tea – when the police had taken over her house! She kept a respectable house . . . Olga cut her short:

'Maria Alexandrovna – the samovar. Some tea, as soon as possible, please.'

A few minutes later Anna was allowed to visit the landlady's kitchen with one of the constables and returned with a large pot and glasses. They tidied the sitting room, clearing the floor, replacing the drawers, making it as homely as possible, and Morozov fed the little stove and placed some chairs before it.

'All right,' he whispered to the two women. 'This is our chance. Quick – in the kitchen and remember to take your boots off.'

A moment later, they heard the front door open and Morozov's silvery voice inviting the policemen to step inside for a glass of hot tea. 'It's so cold out here. Please join us. My wife is preparing a little food.'

The seconds ticked by, Anna's ear pressed to the kitchen door. Surely they were not going to refuse. She felt dizzy with the strain, bent double, and both of them in their heavy winter coats.

'Talk, we must talk normally,' Olga whispered at her shoulder.

But before Anna could think of something to say there was the sound of footsteps in the corridor.

'Sit by the stove,' they heard Morozov say. The sitting-room door clicked shut.

'Now!' Olga hissed.

'No. Wait until they've settled.'

Ten, twenty, thirty seconds, then Anna began to gently lift the latch on the door. One of the policemen was talking, there were footsteps – Morozov would be serving the tea – and now some laughter. Slowly, lightly, they shuffled along the corridor in their stockinged feet. Morozov had left the apartment door ajar. On the landing, they put on their boots then stood anxiously by, Olga gripping Anna's arm, the keys ready in her hand: she would have to be quick. After a tense few minutes they heard Morozov's voice. 'They're in the kitchen. I'll fetch them.' Perhaps one of the policemen said something or he heard them get to their feet, for a second later Morozov was thumping down the short corridor towards them. He almost fell through the door, grabbing the handle as he did so. It slammed shut behind him, but not before Anna heard the policemen cursing and stumbling after him. Olga was fumbling with the lock.

'For God's sake . . .' Morozov shouted. 'Have you done it?'

'Yes, yes! It's locked.'

Bang. A shoulder hit the door: 'Open it now! Open it!' Then another crash as the heel of a heavy boot struck the frame. 'Open it!'

Morozov gave Anna a shove: 'Come on. Let's go.' The shouting and the banging chased up and down the stairs, and on the landing below the landlady was at her door. 'What are you doing, you can't leave them . . .'

'In the name of the executive committee of The People's Will,' said Morozov, cutting across her, 'I warn you, Maria Alexandrovna, if you value your life you will leave them there. Do you understand me?'

He did not wait for an answer.

They thundered down the stairs and burst through the door at the back of the building into the snowy yard. Olga took Anna by the arm and they walked beneath the carriage arch and on to Nevsky.

'We'll go to the flat in the Izmailovsky district,' said Morozov. He stepped off the pavement to hail a passing cab. Seconds later its sleigh blades slithered to a stop. 'We'll all squeeze in somehow,' and he reached for Anna's hand to help her to a seat.

'No. I'll join you later,' she said.

Olga grabbed Anna by the shoulders and turned her quickly to look her in the eye. 'You must come with us!'

'There's something I have – I want to do,' she said, correcting herself.

'What?'

'It's my concern.'

'Everything we do is the party's concern.'

'You don't believe that, Olga. You and Nikolai . . .'

'I do,' she said, sharply.

'There isn't time to argue now. The police could be here any moment. You go. Go now. I'll see you later.'

'We must go,' said Morozov, pulling at Olga's elbow. 'Be careful, Anna. You're an "illegal" now.'

She did not wait to see the cab pull away but walked on quickly, turning off the prospekt into a side street. No money, no clothes but the ones she was wearing, no home, no papers and wanted by the police, and yet she still felt the exhilaration of freedom won at great risk. And a thought, a hope had planted itself almost unnoticed in the tense hours of that day. It had flashed through her mind at the police station and again when she was cowering in the kitchen, and as the cab pulled alongside them on the prospekt it had been quite impossible to ignore.

# 18

The front rolled westwards after midnight, leaving Peter still and fresh for a few precious hours beneath a blanket of virgin snow. It was as if the wind had swept the filth and stench of a million people from the city, plastering the fissures in its buildings white and filling its rutted streets, bathing all in the fairy tale light of the late November moon. Gazing back across the frozen Neva, Hadfield was struck again by its beauty and his great good fortune. What was life in London to this? He had spent the happiest of evenings with his cousin, Alexandra, and their friends from the embassy, careering at breakneck speed down the great ice slide that had been erected in the Field of Mars. Not content to leave it there, they had dined well then set out on an exhilarating troika ride, wrapped together in bearskin rugs, silver harness bells tinkling, the driver whooping wildly and cracking the whip to warn the careless that they stepped from the pavement at their peril. His head a little fusty with vodka, happy and excited still, Hadfield had delivered his cousin to the English Embankment in a cab, then set off for home on foot. By the time he reached the end of Line 7, he was beginning to regret his own impetuosity, conscious of the hour and his list at the surgery later that day. The snow had drifted a little against the wall of the House of Academics, forcing him from the pavement into the street. It was only two minutes' walk to his apartment, but for those minutes he was always on his guard, watchful, alive to the crunch of boots in the snow, careful to give doorways and courtyards a wide berth. Line 7 was quiet and badly lit and footpads had been known to make use of the winter darkness to set upon rich students reeling home along it after a good night out. His uncle had insisted he take a stout stick, and Hadfield made a point of changing his grip on its handle in case he had to wield it as a club. But the street was empty and he did not see or hear anything at all out of the ordinary. Disgusted with himself for his timidity, he stood on the step of Number 7 stamping and scraping the snow from his boots. It was after one o'clock and the dvornik would be sleeping or in a drunken stupor. Reaching into his coat pocket for his keys, he was turning towards the door when he caught a movement at the corner of his eye.

Something or someone had flitted into a doorway a little way up the street. Hadfield changed his grip on the stick again. He was still standing with the key in the lock between his fingers when the man stepped out of the doorway and began walking towards him. But it was not a man. It was a young woman who walked with upright carriage and a short purposeful stride. And he knew her at once: beneath the thick coat, the rabbit fur hat and scarf was Anna Petrovna Kovalenko. A frisson of excitement tingled down his spine. After weeks, months, out of the darkness as if in a dream or a fairy tale, why, what was it she wanted after all this time?

'Miss Kovalenko. What a surprise.'

She stepped up to him and his heart jumped a little. She had pulled her scarf over her mouth and nose but even in shadow her blue eyes were twinkling like ice and he could not help but smile at the little frown lines on her brow.

'Call me Anna. Are you well, Doctor?'

'Call me Frederick. What are you doing here? How long have you been waiting? You're shivering.' He turned the key in the lock. 'You must come in. I'll light a fire.'

'No, it's just that—'

'Are you in trouble?'

'No.'

There was a fine crust of snow on Anna's coat and hat and he could tell from the distance in her voice that she had been waiting some while and was chilled to the marrow.

'Look, you've come to see me. It's too cold to stand on the step,' and he stood aside to let her pass.

She stood in the middle of his drawing room dripping on the rug, teeth chattering, too cold and exhausted to remove her coat and hat. Once the gas lamps were lit, Hadfield busied himself with the fire, drawing an armchair close.

'I'm sorry,' she said.

'For what? Give me those wet things. Here.' He handed her his dressing gown, and placed some trousers, a warm jumper and blankets on the chair. 'Now is not the time to stand on ceremony. Go into my dressing room and change. I'll arrange for the maid to bring you hot water.'

Would she do as he asked, he wondered, as he made his way down the stairs to the maid's room? The poor girl had to be dragged from a deep sleep and it was some while before he could be sure she understood what was expected of her.

Anna had taken off her wet clothes and was wearing his dressing gown, curled in the armchair beneath a couple of blankets. She looked totally worn out, her head resting on her arm, her skin quite ashen.

'We'll have some tea, but first a glass of brandy.' He went over to the drinks tray and poured a little into two tumblers.

'It's been so long. Didn't you think of writing to say where you'd gone?' he asked, handing her the glass.

'Why should I? We're just comrades.'

She was staring into the flickering fire, careful to avoid his gaze. Hadfield flopped into the chair opposite, his legs crossed, glass balanced on his knee. 'Just comrades? Then why are you here?'

'I'll go, if you like,' she snapped and lifted her eyes in an unequivocal challenge.

'Of course you can't go.'

'I'll leave when I want.' Her voice was determined now and her bare feet slipped to the floor.

'Please stay. I . . . I've missed you.'

So it had slipped from him already. He could not help himself: how beautiful she looked in the yellow firelight, lost in his father's old silk dressing gown, strands of hair loose about her face and elegant neck. She gave him a sweet, accepting but weary smile then lifted the brandy to her lips, hiding her blush behind the twinkling glass.

'I'll light another fire to dry your dress,' he said, anxious all of a sudden to be busy.

'I'll do it.'

'I'm a doctor,' he said, reading the concern in her voice. 'I'm used to women's clothes – and bodies.'

And he saw with some satisfaction that he had made her blush again.

Later, they sat in silence drinking cups of sweet tea and Hadfield watched her struggling to keep awake in the warmth of the fire, too exhausted to answer questions, close, he thought, to an emotional edge. After half an hour or so, she lost her battle, drifting into sleep, her small hand gripping the tea glass. Gently, he lifted her fingers from it and, placing it on the tray, settled back in his chair to watch her, rising from time to time to prod at the fire. There were many questions he wanted to ask but for now he was content just to sit with her. He had found her again, or, to be truthful, she had found him.

When the English long case in the hall struck three, he crouched down beside her and shook her shoulder gently. She whimpered and woke with a start.

'What is it?'

'Nothing important, it's just I think you should go to bed. There's a guest room.'

'No. No, thank you,' she said, her eyes half shut. 'I'm fine here by the fire.' And barely conscious of what she was doing, she reached up to brush his cheek lightly with the tips of her fingers. He caught her hand, held it then lifted it to his lips. Her eyes were closed now but she smiled and made no effort to withdraw it. 'There's something I want to tell you.'

'In the morning. You must go to bed.'

'It's been two years since I saw my husband,' she said sleepily. Her eyes were still closed. 'He never loved me. He treated me badly.'

'So you left him,' he said, squeezing her hand.

'No. He left me. But I would never go back. Never.' Her eyes flickered open long enough for him to glimpse her pain. Pulling her hand free, she placed it palm up on the arm of the chair and settled her head on to it again.

'Do you still love him?'

'I never loved him.'

When Hadfield woke, there were only glowing embers in the fire and the chair was empty but for the red silk dressing gown. He called her name, but she did not reply. He searched the flat but she had gone. On the mantelpiece among the gracious printed invitations from gentlemen and ladies to dinners and parties and balls was a note on a scrap of paper: *Meet me in the main reading room at the Imperial Library at 4.30. Anna.*

The dynamite had been moved the day before but a drum of detonation wire was still sitting in the middle of the polished mahogany table. Collegiate Councillor Dobrshinsky ran his fingers across its top. There was a fresh scratch in the varnish that must have been made by a careless policeman.

'Where were his papers found?' he asked, turning to look at Agent Kletochnikov at the door.

'In the drawer of the desk by the window, Your Honour. They've been sent to your office.'

'And Kviatkovsky's companion?'

Kletochnikov took a step into the room to balance his file on the edge of a side table: 'Evgenia Figner. She's not an illegal, but her sister Vera is wanted by the police, and another sister – Lydia Figner – is serving a sentence in the east.'

Dobrshinsky nodded. 'And the three who escaped?'

'Liubatovich and Morozov were living together at 124 Nevsky Prospekt. They rented the place with stolen papers. The other woman's papers are in the name of Anna Kovalenko.'

'Kovalenko?' the special investigator asked sharply. 'Do you have a description?'

Kletochnikov lifted the file to peer at the page: 'Small, dark brown hair, heavy brow, blue eyes – the police sergeant described them as light blue – he said she was quite pretty . . .'

Dobrshinsky closed his eyes for a moment and sighed with exasperation.

'Your Honour?' Kletochnikov was blinking anxiously at the collegiate councillor, his right hand holding the rim of his glasses.

'I want you to telegraph all the details you have on this Kovalenko woman to Kharkov at once.'

'Kharkov?'

'Yes. Kharkov. And Kletochnikov . . .'

'Your Honour?'

'Circulate this description to the police stations in the city again, but this time describe her as Anna Petrovna Kovalenko, sometimes known as Romanko.'

When the agent had gone, Dobrshinsky began examining the revolutionary's books, pulling open drawers and cupboard doors in the desultory hope of finding something the police had over-looked or discarded as unimportant. Then, feeling a little dizzy, he stepped over to the window and sank into the chair before Kviatkovsky's open desk. The leaf of the bureau was down and covered in roughly printed propaganda sheets. Without thought, he leant forward and swept the leaflets to the floor with his forearm. Buried beneath them was a small soft leather sketchbook. He picked it up and began turning the pages. Someone – perhaps Evgenia Figner – had drawn a number of fine pencil portraits of serious young men and women. One of the sketches was of Alexander Mikhailov. On another page, the profile of a young woman with a high forehead and small girlish features who closely resembled the section's photograph of Sophia Perovskaya. He put the sketchbook down and, half rising, reached into the pigeon holes of the bureau. A pen, a pack of playing cards, some clips and in a manila envelope he found three seals. Lifting them to the light he could see they were engraved with the imperial eagle for official use.

He was still sitting at the desk a short time later, his fingers pressed to his lips in thought, when Major Vladimir Barclay knocked at the drawing-room door. Kletochnikov was standing at his shoulder.

'Have you heard?' Dobrshinsky turned to face him. 'They let three terrorists just waltz out of an apartment on Nevsky.'

Barclay nodded.

'See if any of the policemen who saw them can find a drawing of Kovalenko in this.' The special investigator held up the sketchbook. 'There are others in here too.'

'I thought the police had searched this apartment,' said Barclay, stepping forward to take it from him.

'So did I.'

He stared intently at Barclay for a moment then leant to his right so he could see beyond him to the door. 'Leave us, Kletochnikov, please,' he said.

The agent was taken aback. 'Your Honour?'

'Now.'

The door closed behind him and Dobrshinsky turned to pick up the seals.

'Recognise these?'

'They look like ours.'

'I think this one must have been particularly useful to them,' Dobrshinsky said, offering the gendarme officer the largest of the seals.

Barclay held it close to his eye. 'For authorising identity papers. But how on earth did they manage to lay their hands . . .'

'I think we should keep this between ourselves for now, Vladimir Alexandrovich,' said Dobrshinsky, cutting across him. 'Tighten security, but say nothing. We don't want to frighten their informer. We want to catch him.'

# 19

The Imperial Library on Nevsky was a peculiar choice for a rendezvous, but quite how much so was only apparent to Hadfield when he peered through the doors of the reading room for the first time. Beneath the vaulted ceiling, a sea of heads bent as if in prayer to the goddess of learning; venerable academics poring over leather-bound tomes and their acolytes – students in the uniforms of the university, the engineering school and academies, and the populace too, many with no interest in study but grateful for the silence and the warmth. Once inside, he stood in front of an enormous gilt-framed picture of the tsar, casting about for a table that might offer a view of the traffic to and from the reading room. How could he possibly speak to Anna in here? The studious silence was broken only by shuffling feet, the flutter of pages and the occasional strangled cough.

He found a seat at the end of a row, opposite a man in his sixties with a full grey beard who smelt of pipe tobacco. He was huffing over the French language *Journal de St Petersbourg*, shaking his bald head in disgust, much to the undisguised irritation of his neighbours at the table. Taking his journal from his medical bag, Hadfield pushed it into the circle of light beneath the brass table lamp and settled back to wait. It was too cold to walk far but there was a pleasant confectioner's opposite the library that served hot chocolate and cake.

'They always blame the Jews.' The grey beard opposite had lowered his paper and was addressing Hadfield in a very audible whisper. 'Some ignorant muzhiks in Kiev are driving them from their homes. For God's sake, how can you blame Jews for the attack on the emperor?'

He was interrupted by his neighbour – a well-to-do student, judging from his clothes and the silver pince-nez on a ribbon he was twirling foppishly in his hand – who hissed at him and wagged a patronising forefinger.

'Don't shush me,' the old man replied indignantly, shaking his newspaper at the student. 'Show more respect!'

'This is a library.'

'I know that, you ignoramus. I come here every day.'

Heads turned and one of the library supervisors in the gallery above the main floor began to make his way to the stairs.

'Tell him to be quiet.'

'Tell me yourself!'

For some reason both men had begun appealing to Hadfield for support.

'Please, Your Honours.' The supervisor had scuttled over to restore order. 'Doctor Bloomberg, please.'

The exasperation in the supervisor's voice suggested the grey beard was well known to the library. The argument rumbled on until, with very ill grace, the student was persuaded to move to a seat some way from the old man. Annoyingly, the kerfuffle had drawn Hadfield's attention from the entrance long enough for Anna to have slipped into the reading room.

Pushing his chair away, he walked between the tables to the bookshelves that lined the walls beneath the gallery and, picking a book from the nearest – Rousseau in French – he stared over the top of it at the bent heads, confident he would recognise hers. To be certain, he shuffled along the bookcases to the far end of the hall: if Anna was there she would surely see him. She was a little late – but perhaps she had missed the train from Alexandrovskaya or did not have money for a cab. He returned to the table with his copy of Rousseau, pulled back the chair and was easing himself into it when he noticed someone had pinned a small square of paper to the cloth cover of his journal. It had clearly been ripped from the flyleaf of a library book. A note was scribbled in a small hand he did not recognise: *Anna is sorry but she cannot meet you.*

His first thought was that it had been left there by his eccentric neighbour. He stared at Bloomberg for a few seconds but the old man was too engrossed in his newspaper to notice. No one else at the table made eye contact or seemed in the least bit interested in him.

Hadfield folded the paper slowly and slipped it into his pocket. How typically ungracious, a peremptory one line note, and he flinched as he remembered her brutal put-down at their first meeting. No social grace, he thought as he scooped up his journal and bag. And intent on committing rude sacrilege, he pushed his chair back roughly, the legs screeching on the polished floor in protest.

He was poor company that evening. Dobson ascribed his moodiness to fatigue and lectured him sternly about the hours he was keeping at the hospital. But the anger of the library did not last long, only the disappointment and a growing sense of anxiety for her safety. She had been too tired to answer questions, but a late night visit, mysterious notes, a rendezvous in a public library; it did not take much to imagine what it might mean in the wake of Goldenberg's arrest. Were the police looking for her? Lying awake in bed, his father's old dressing gown draped over a chair close by, he wondered if he was already entangled in a web he could not see. He had taken risks out of conviction, yes, but also from a spirit of adventure, and for . . . for love? What was it that he felt for her? It was more than the pull of her body. He recognised a certain insecurity in her, quick to anger and take offence, but purpose and energy too, and above all he felt a common feeling he could not explain. There was still time to row back. He need do nothing but forget.

Forget. But how to treat a patient who will not accept a cure? There was his father's gown and he could see her in it now, a small frown on her brow even as she slept, her feet tucked beneath her, the steady rise and fall of her breast.

He caught the train from the Warsaw Station at nine o'clock the next morning and arrived in the village forty minutes later. It was a cold clear day and still, the yellow winter sun streaming through a pall of wood smoke. Some peasant women had set up simple plank tables in front of the station and were selling pickled vegetables, and candles and rabbit-skin gloves. Yes, of course they knew the schoolhouse – left off the main street and immediately on your right. No, they had not seen Anna Petrovna that day nor did they know if she was at home. She had been away visiting her mother, perhaps she was still.

Smoke was spiralling from the chimney of the house and a shadow passed across the window of the main room. Perhaps Anna had visitors, for there was more than one set of footprints in the snow before the front door. Hadfield stood at the gate for a moment and then knocked and waited stiffly on the step, hat in hand, rehearsing his first lines. To his surprise the door was opened not by Anna, but by a burly middle-aged man in a frock coat. Later, he would wonder at his own naivety.

'Excuse me – isn't this Miss Kovalenko's house?'

'It is, yes. And who wishes to see her?'

It was a reasonable question and asked with an amiable smile but there was something in the timbre of the man's voice that put Hadfield on his mettle. His posture too, for although he was dressed like a bank clerk, he was slouching like a policeman. And he must have read something of the sort in Hadfield's expression because the smile fell from his face at once. 'Major Vladimir Barclay of the Gendarme Corps. Come inside, would you?' He stepped back to let Hadfield pass.

'Is something wrong, Major?'

'We'll see. Mister?'

'Doctor Hadfield.'

'You're a foreigner?'

'No more than you, I think, Major Barclay.'

The policeman coloured a little: 'I am a Russian.'

What foul luck, Hadfield thought, as he stepped into the little living room. The gendarmes could only have arrived a few hours before him, for they were still busy searching the place. Two of them were ferreting through drawers, turning over pots and pans, dragging blankets from the bed, and a velvet couch – the only comfortable piece of furniture in the room – had been slashed, spilling horsehair on to the floor.

'Sit down,' said Barclay, pointing to a corner of the couch. 'As you can see, we're as anxious to speak to Miss Kovalenko as you.'

The major righted a kitchen chair and dragged it closer. 'Papers, Doctor, please.'

'I don't have my passport with me. What would you like to know?'

'You can begin by telling me who you are and where you live.'

Hadfield gave his address and spoke of his work, conscious that the policeman was following him intently, the tone of his voice, his expression, every small gesture. How peculiar then that he felt none of the anxiety he had felt waiting for Anna on the step.

'How long have you known Miss Kovalenko?'

'A few months only. She used to help at a clinic I run in Peski. That's why I'm here,' he said.

'Oh?'

'Yes. She's been away. But she's a very capable nurse and I was hoping to persuade her to come back to us.'

'Ah. I see.' The policeman scrutinised his face carefully, his bushy eyebrows meeting in a frown. 'You're smiling, Doctor.'

'Am I?'

'Please, share the joke.'

'Oh, just that it occurred to me you may have missed your calling, Major. You have an excellent bedside manner.'

'I haven't missed my calling, Doctor,' said Barclay coolly. 'I am an excellent policeman.'

'I don't doubt it,' Hadfield replied. 'But I would be grateful if you would have the courtesy to explain what on earth is going on here.'

'When did you last see Miss Kovalenko?'

'Three months ago. But I refuse to say another word until you tell me why you're in her house.'

'Then I will arrest you and take you to a station for questioning.'

It was quite apparent from the steel in the policeman's voice that he was in earnest. Hadfield could feel the colour rising in his face. Once inside it would be impossible to disguise his involvement with the sort of people his family and patients considered undesirable and dangerous.

'Well?' Barclay asked.

'Well, I will explain to my friend, the chief prosecutor, when he visits me in your cells that I was happy to answer your questions but you were unwilling to offer me the common courtesy of an explanation.'

'You know the Count von Plehve?'

'Yes. He's a friend of my uncle's.'

'And your uncle is . . . ?'

'General Glen.'

Barclay pursed his lips thoughtfully. There was a cool intelligence in his manner that suggested he would not be intimidated by names. But no policeman in Russia would be foolish enough to ignore rank or connections entirely.

'Of course you're right, Doctor,' he said at last. 'Would you like some tea?' Turning, he shouted over his shoulder to one of the gendarmes.

Coat pulled tightly about him, a glass of tea burning his fingers, Hadfield sat on the torn couch and listened to the major speak of the woman he had knelt beside and whose hand he had kissed only a short time before. Anna Petrovna Kovalenko, also known by her married name of Romanko, a member of the terrorist organisation The People's Will, suspected of involvement in an attempt on the emperor's life, a dedicated revolutionary who had only recently escaped from house arrest. The policeman's eyes never left his face.

'Believe me Major, I had no idea,' he said. 'She seemed a good-hearted woman . . .'

There were more questions. Hadfield answered them without difficulty. Yes, he promised to inform the police if Anna Petrovna visited the clinic or tried to make contact with him, and yes, of course he would be happy to identify her. No, he had not met her friends, nor had she spoken of them, but the major could be sure he would do anything he could to help bring a terrorist to justice.

The major was grateful. The major was prepared to let him go. 'I hope we meet again, Doctor,' he said, offering his hand.

And Hadfield was conscious as he walked from the house that he had just played the first moves in a subtle and deliberate game. Not even the laziest policeman in an empire that was not short of them would leave it there. And Barclay was no ordinary officer. He was working for the Third Section, and he would use its network to pick at every piece of Hadfield's story. By this evening one of the clerks at Fontanka 16 would have written his name at the top of a new file with special reference to the terrorist Anna Kovalenko.

The driver was cursing, his horses blown by the time the carriage slid to a halt before the steps of the House of Preliminary Detention. Barclay dumped the bearskin on the seat beside him and hoisted his stiff body on to the pavement. It had been quite as unpleasant as he anticipated, shaken and jolted for two hours. But there was no time to waste, not since the attempt on the tsar's train, not since the bungled arrest of some of those responsible. The mantra was 'results now, results now'. The Third Section could not afford to fail again.

'Major Vladimir Barclay for the special investigator, His Honour Anton Frankzevich Dobrshinsky.'

He handed his identity papers to the greasy clerk in reception, who scrutinised them carefully although he had seen Barclay many times.

'Hurry up, man, hurry up.' He was in no mood for pettyfogging bureaucracy. It was a wonder anything was ever achieved in the empire. When it really counted, the system proved itself anything but careful. A warder led him across the vast exercise yard, the snow packed hard by the boots of the prisoners, to a door in the corner of the east wing. 'Abandon hope all ye who enter here,' he muttered to himself as he stepped through the door once again. Who would have predicted that hell would rattle like an empty bin? The clatter of boots along the iron galleries, the clanking of the heating pipes and the tap, tap, tap of the prisoners in solitary, desperate for human contact even if it meant spelling it out with a spoon. A constant soulless echo that Barclay felt sure would threaten his sanity if he had to endure it for more than a few hours at a time. But then the inmates' sanity was surely in doubt in the first place – and none more so in Barclay's judgement than the Jew, Goldenberg. Perhaps that was why Dobrshinsky was spending so much of his time trying to befriend him. A special case, he had said, cryptically.

The special investigator had received word of Barclay's arrival and was waiting for him on the landing outside the interrogation room. 'I can see you have news for me,' he said, as Barclay approached. 'That's good.'

'I've come straight from the Kovalenko woman's house. A matter of some urgency, Your Honour. A delicate matter.'

Dobrshinsky led the way to the warder's office at the end of the wing. But for the cheap furniture and an engraving of the tsar, it resembled one of the prison's larger cells, the walls painted dark grey, the floor of black asphalt with only a small double casement window on to the world. As they entered, the occupants jumped to their feet, one of the clerks knocking his chair over in his haste.

'Leave us, please. You,' Dobrshinsky pointed to the unfortunate clerk, 'bring us some tea.'

As soon as the door closed behind them, the special investigator turned his sharp little eyes to Barclay like a fox sizing up his supper. 'Well? A delicate matter, you say?'

'Yes. Yes it is. But first, Your Honour was quite right. Anna Kovalenko does meet the description of the woman seen leaving the square after the attempt on the emperor's life in March. The police in Kharkov have confirmed that her married name is Romanko. Her poor dupe of a husband is a village merchant – he used to be a policeman – of course he knows nothing about her activities.'

'He should have taken better care of her, shouldn't he?' Dobrshinsky said sardonically. 'Check the file, but I think you'll find she meets the description of the woman seen leaving the Volkonsky house with Alexander Mikhailov too. A busy little bee. And if you remember, Kovalenko was one of the names on the list our informer left at the Neva Hotel.' His face wrinkled in an uncomfortable frown. 'Damn the city police for their incompetence. But you said there was a delicate matter?'

Barclay began to describe his meeting with the English doctor and the substance of their conversation. 'I would have brought him in for questioning but he seems to be very well connected.'

'Oh?'

'His Excellency the financial controller is his uncle and he says he's a friend of Count von Plehve's.'

At the mention of the count's name, a little smile began to play on Dobrshinsky's lips: 'Well, well! Who has the chief prosecutor been consorting with?'

A knock at the door and the clerk shuffled into the office with a tray and two glasses of strong black tea.

'And what was your impression of this Dr Hadfield?' Dobrshinsky asked when the clerk had gone.

'Perfect Russian. Confident, relaxed, dressed like a . . .' Barclay paused.

'Well?'

'Like a radical – well, like a rich student or a Frenchman. The thing is, he seemed a little too relaxed. He didn't seem very surprised to find me in Kovalenko's house.'

'I see.' Dobrshinsky lifted the glass of tea to his lips and blew on it distractedly, before lowering it back to the table without taking a sip. 'So is he our spy?'

'Your Honour?'

'I think the count was hoping he could put our troubles at the door of a foreign power.'

'Do you want me to have him arrested?'

'No. No. What would the count say? Aren't they friends? The doctor may be telling the truth. Perhaps he's just an English Samaritan. We need to make some discreet inquiries.' The special investigator sat in silence for a moment, a thoughtful frown creasing his brow, then pushed his chair from the table and rose abruptly to his feet. 'I can't keep Grigory waiting. Walk with me.'

They stepped out on to the wing, ambling slowly past the heavy iron doors, behind each a prisoner in a grey box five small steps long and three small steps wide.

'I will ask Goldenberg about our Englishman,' Dobrshinsky

said. 'He will refuse to answer but his face may betray something.' He paused and turned to Barclay. 'You're probably wondering why it's worth persevering?'

Barclay thought for a moment. 'There are many ways of obtaining information from a prisoner in a place like this, Your Honour,' he said. He was no stranger to the 'direct' approach.

'No. No martyrs. He'll have his day in court. And our little Jew is very impressionable. He thinks he'll be beaten, so it's important to break his expectation. He'll prove valuable in time.'

They walked on until they reached the interrogation cell. Peering through the eye in the door, Barclay could see Goldenberg fidgeting at the iron table, pulling at his wispy beard, a sorry sight in his prison greys. It would not be difficult. Give me two burly warders and an hour with him, he thought.

'Tell Kletochnikov to send me what he can find on our English doctor,' said Dobrshinsky at his back. 'I'll speak to Count von Plehve. Oh, and see if the name Hadfield jogs Madame Volkonskaya's memory.'

The special investigator nodded to the warder at the door who stepped forward with the key. As it swung open, Barclay saw the prisoner rise respectfully from his stool with a broad smile on his face. A cunning fox, he thought admiringly: if anyone was going to lure the Jew into an indiscretion it would be His Honour Anton Frankzevich Dobrshinsky.

# 20

Her note found him in the middle of a consultation with a patient exhibiting symptoms of scarlet fever. Gathered about the bed were a dozen students and the matron in charge of Barrack Ward 1 at the Nikolaevsky.

'This rash,' and Hadfield pointed to the old man's naked torso, 'is characteristic of the condition. Usually accompanied by abdominal pain, vomiting, a sore throat and swollen tongue. Show me your tongue.'

The patient offered his large strawberry tongue to the students. As they shuffled closer to examine the inflamed papillae, Hadfield felt someone jog his elbow. His assistant, Anton Pavel, was standing at the edge of the circle, clutching a grubby envelope. 'This was left by a babushka at the hospital entrance. She insisted I deliver it to you in person.'

Hadfield glanced at the handwriting then slipped it into his pocket.

The eyes of all in the room turned to him again.

'In the case of a fever like this, it is important to keep the patient's temperature under control,' he said with a wry smile that must have puzzled his students. 'Sponging the surface of the body with tepid or cold water should do it, or wet packing a sheet, but sometimes ice bags are needed.'

Later, he sat in the small study he shared with two other doctors, his boots on the desk, the little envelope between his fingers. Two anxious weeks had passed since their meeting and his visit to her house in Alexandrovskaya. He had expected his uncle to summon him to the English Embankment or the police to insist on questioning him further, but life had gone on as always, his daily routine punctuated by winter festivities, sledging and skating and a particularly hectic round of parties.

The ambassador and his wife had invited him to accompany them on a bear hunt, no doubt to ensure the comfort of medical advice at all times. He had slept in a village hay loft with 'the boys' from the embassy. The third secretary, Lord Frederick Hamilton, had bagged a she-bear. By some miracle, and to the consternation of the shooting party, her cubs managed to escape. Hadfield had blasted away with the rest but was secretly relieved he missed everything he aimed at.

He was impatient to hear from Anna but it had never occurred to him that she would not contact him when she was able. Her note was to the point, as always: he was to be before the Church of St Boris and St Gleb at nine o'clock. He had arranged to spend the evening with Dobson and 'the boys' from the embassy. Dumping his feet from the table, he picked up a piece of the hospital's headed paper and began composing his excuse.

He left the hospital at half past seven, in time to take a cab home and change into warmer, less conspicuous clothes. And as he dressed, he was conscious of a disturbing excitement, and of the need for extreme caution. He was to meet a woman implicated in a plot to kill the tsar, her name and description known by now to every police station and gendarmerie in the empire. From the wardrobe he took his old student coat and Swiss walking boots, and a peaked cap, every inch the petty bourgeois.

The dvornik gave him an uncharacteristically cheery 'Good evening' and tipped his hat as they passed at the door. Was he a police informer? The suspicion flitted through Hadfield's mind even before the door had shut behind him. He dismissed it: he must be calm and watchful, yes, but too much suspicion – there lay the road to madness. He took a droshky to the

Nikolaevsky Station, then walked a short way before hailing another, instructing its driver to drop him on the Nevskaya Embankment. Judging it wise not to arrive before the appointed time, he stood in the freezing darkness, gazing blankly across the river to the cathedral on the opposite bank, his stomach tight with nerves. At exactly nine o'clock he made his way to the front of the church. The gangly boy with the red hair who had met him on his first day at the clinic was waiting in the discreet shadow beneath the scaffolding, shivering in a thin serge jacket and factory cap, a scarf tied about his ears.

'Vasili, isn't it?'

He nodded and, turning without a word, set off down one of the icy paths that chequered the square. Hadfield followed at his heels, passing along dimly lit streets and alleys and across open yards, walking in tense silence. They stepped below a ramshackle gallery and climbed a wooden stair to a door on the first landing. Vasili opened it and led him into a draughty room lit by flickering candles. It seemed to be home to four, perhaps five, families. A baby was crying somewhere and the room reeked of cabbage and stale sweat. They walked across the naked boards to a door at the far end and on into another room almost identical to the first. An old man with a long grey beard and rheumy eyes reeled drunkenly towards him but Vasili had him by the sleeve, drawing him across the room and on to a staircase. He rattled down it, paused at the open entrance and looked left and right along the street before crossing quickly to a door on the opposite side.

He knocked sharply, stamping impatiently and blowing on his fingers. The door was opened by an old lady in a shapeless bundle of shawls and blankets, her brown wrinkled face tightly framed by a scarf. She said something to Vasili in a low voice then stepped back to let them pass into the dark hall. But the boy shook his head and turned quickly away, breaking into a heavy-footed trot along the street. Hadfield followed the old woman down the dark hall and slowly up two flights of stairs to a door on the right of the landing. Opening it, she led him through another series of interconnecting rooms with families living cheek by jowl, huddled about a table or a smoking stove. He felt as if he was in a peculiarly Russian dream, required to wander from room to dark corridor to room in search of Anna. Finally, the old lady swept back a curtain and he saw her sitting at a table with her head resting on her arms. Roused by the rattle of the curtain, she rose quickly with a smile:

'You came.'

'Yes.' His voice sounded hoarse.

'I'm glad.'

She was wearing a white blouse and navy blue skirt, a woollen shawl pulled tightly about her shoulders and upper arms.

'You had no trouble on the way?'

'No. No difficulty.'

They stood in awkward silence. He was conscious of the old lady beside him and of others within earshot, a shadow across a curtain, a whispered conversation, suppressed laughter.

'Would you like some tea?'

'Yes. Please.'

Anna spoke to the babushka in Ukrainian and she hobbled to the corner of the room and pulled back a drape. He caught a glimpse of two girls bent self-consciously over their sewing before the drape fell back into place.

'Is it safe for you here?'

Her eyes twinkled in the candlelight: 'As safe as it is anywhere.'

'You must go away. I can help you.'

'Let's not talk of it.'

'Switzerland . . .'

'Please.' Her dark eyebrows were knotted in a frown.

What was she thinking? Hadfield tried to catch and hold her gaze but it flicked to his face and away. She would not look him in the eye. The old lady came back with the tea, placed it on the table between them then left.

'I'm sorry I couldn't meet you at the library.'

'Why do you want to see me?'

She glanced up at him reproachfully. It was enough for him to find some courage. Still she refused to look him in the eye, but she smiled as he reached a trembling hand to her face. He heard her breath quicken as he caressed her hair, his hand slipping to the nape of her neck. She took his other hand and squeezed it gently. Then she reached up to remove an ebony clip and shook her hair loose over her shoulders. She lifted her face, her eyes half closed, her lips parted, and he kissed her. Breathless, they broke apart. He folded his arms around her slight shoulders. She was scented like an evening rose.

'Anna, I want you to . . .'

'Shhhh.' She lifted a finger to his lips. Then she picked the candle from the table and, taking his hand, led him across the room to an open doorway.

It was no more than a cubicle, a flimsy partition from the rest of the room with a single mattress on the floor and a stool. She bent to place the candle on the stool and he put his arms about her, even as she rose and turned to face him. They kissed, harder this time, and when they separated he could not help a groan of longing and joy and fullness. But again she pressed her forefinger to his lips: 'Shhhh. They will hear.'

Then she turned her back on him and began to undress. Conscious that he was watching her, she leant across to the stool and blew out the candle: 'Please.'

There was a quiet intensity to their lovemaking. He knew Anna was no innocent but he was surprised by her confidence and sensuality. Her lips and hands roamed freely and firmly about his body and, as she stooped to kiss him, the intoxicating scent of her hair fell about his face. He was lost inside her, consumed, without reason, conscious of nothing but the fierce heat of her body and her hands on his chest urging him on until she came with a breathless whimper.

Later, he could not sleep. He lay with her small frame against his, her white shoulders just visible above the blanket, the dull weight of her head on his arm. He listened to the calm rhythm of her breathing, rising and falling like waves on a distant shore. He felt a stillness in her arms he had never felt before. He felt a tenderness he had never felt for anyone before. And he tried to push thoughts of morning away.

They made love again. He was careless they were without the dignity of privacy, losing himself in her once more. But he was conscious there was something of her that was separate, elusive, a part of her she did not want to surrender. Perhaps that was why he had to tell her he loved her. She smiled and leant forward to kiss him and stroke his face.

They talked in whispers, her breath on his cheek. She was living in the city with her comrades, she said, but she would not say where. She was not afraid of what would happen, their work was too important: Russia must change, it would change. He told her of his visit to Alexandrovskaya. She was cross with him, the deep frown returning to her brow.

'Why did you go?'

He reassured her that he had said nothing and the police knew nothing. 'Don't you trust me?'

'Don't be silly.'


A little before sunrise, Anna told him he should go. He picked up his clothes from the floor and dressed, then bent to kiss her, naked still beneath the rough blankets. And he could not help lying beside her again.

'Will you come away with me?'

Her face was grey with exhaustion in the first light of morning. She smiled but did not open her eyes.

'When will I see you again?'

'I will contact you.'

'Can I contact you?'

'No. It isn't safe.' She opened her ice-blue eyes and fixed him with a determined look: 'Promise me you won't try?'

'I promise.'

And she leant forward to kiss him, her fingers brushing his cheek. 'Now you must go.'

The boy Vasili was waiting to lead him to the stairs and into the street. They walked in silence. This is not me, he said to himself, not me. I am not here. He could feel her warmth still, smell his sex upon her skin, hear the words she whispered to him, see the comfort of her smile. But then Vasili spoke to him and held out his hand for money. And suddenly he was tied to the morning, to the here and now, to the empty square before him, to the shell of St Boris and St Gleb's, left to find his own way back.

# 21

'Did I mention the lodger downstairs, Alexander Dmitrievich? The milliner? A spy. I'm sure of it.'

Mikhailov nodded indulgently. 'Yes, you did speak of her. We must all be careful, my dear fellow, especially when our cause is close to success. Now sit here beside me and tell me the news from the ministry.'

But Councillor Ivan Tarakanov was too agitated to sit for even a second, pacing his drawing room as if he was intent on wearing a hole in his expensive Persian rug.

'I don't know how you can talk of success. The papers are full of the arrest of Kviatkovsky.'

'Yes. A great pity,' said Mikhailov, running a hand through his hair in exasperation. 'But The People's Will has not been idle. You will see.'

'Yes, but I . . .'

There was a sharp knock at the door, and the old man began prancing with anxiety and self-pity.

'Calm yourself, calm yourself,' said Mikhailov, rising from the divan. 'It's our friend.'

'No – you must hide! Please,' Tarakanov stammered. 'It may be the police.'

Mikhailov shrugged. 'Yes, of course.' But as soon as the councillor left the room he settled back on the couch and reached across the table for the glass of claret his host had reluctantly poured for him. A moment later, Tarakanov was back with the new arrival at his heels.

'You're safe and you're here.' Mikhailov lifted his glass

209

in salute. 'Comrade Councillor – this is my friend, the Director.'

'It's almost nine o'clock!' said Tarakanov. 'We were expecting you sooner.'

'I'm sure our comrade would enjoy a glass of your excellent wine,' said Mikhailov with an easy smile. 'Then you must excuse us. We have urgent business.'

Tarakanov bit his lip and looked on the point of voicing resentment at being eased out of his drawing room. With the confidence of a man who is used to being obeyed, Mikhailov lifted his chin.

'Is there something wrong, Ivan Fedorovich?'

'You don't understand the risks I'm taking,' said Tarakanov sullenly.

Mikhailov smiled. 'And I'm grateful for your efforts on behalf of the party. So – just a few minutes, if you please?'

They waited until the door closed behind him and they could hear the squeak of his shoes on the polished parquet in the hall. Mikhailov slid impatiently to the edge of the divan. 'Well, do they know?'

'Not yet. They have some papers,' said the Director, pulling at his beard.

'What papers?'

'A rough plan of the palace, with markings.'

'They don't suspect?'

'I don't think so. The special investigator spends most of his time at the "Preliminary" with the prisoners.'

'Has anyone given anything away?'

'No. No.' Rising to his feet, the Director began to shuffle restlessly about the room with his wine glass, picking up small objects, peering at the councillor's pictures. He looked tired and distracted, Mikhailov thought, the loneliness, the strain of living with the enemy, the constant fear of discovery, was obviously taking its toll.

'How did the police find Kviatkovsky's flat?'

'Evgenia Figner,' replied the Director, bending to look at a small silver icon that was hanging beside the mantelpiece. 'The city police arrested a student with copies of the party's manifesto and she told them she had been given them by Evgenia.' Evgenia had given her real name, he explained. A foolish mistake. All the police needed to do was check it against their register of addresses.

'That was careless,' said Mikhailov. 'It almost led to the arrest of Olga and Anna too.'

'Yes. Anna.'

'Is there something wrong?'

The Director settled on the divan beside him, his knee bouncing nervously, turning the empty wine glass in his hand. 'Do you know of an Englishman called Hadfield?'

'Yes.'

'Is he a member of the party?'

'No.'

'The special investigator thinks he may be. I've just written his name on a new file. He made the mistake of visiting Anna's house. Major Barclay questioned him but let him go.'

'Oh?'

'And he may know the Volkonskaya woman too.'

Mikhailov reached over to the wine bottle and poured the Director a little more. 'Are they going to question him again?'

'I don't know. Perhaps. Do you trust him?'

'No.'

'Do you trust her?'

'Anna? Of course. But there is madness in love.'

'Love?'

'Nothing. A foolish thought,' said Mikhailov irritably.

'I must go,' said the Director, and throwing his head back he gulped down the claret. 'What a waste.'

'Post a note at the flat in Troitsky Lane when you have more.'

The Director nodded, pushing his spectacles up his nose. At the door he turned to Mikhailov again. 'How long now, Alexander?' There was an unmistakable weariness in his voice.

'Five weeks, my friend. Have courage. We'll be ready in five weeks.'

# 22

For all its dangers, Anna's new life in the city as an illegal was more fulfilled than the one she had known in the village. To her neighbours at 11 Podolskaya Street, she was the house maid Elizaveta Terenteva, who had moved from Kiev to live and work for her cousin and her lodgers. Under this guise she helped her comrades with a printing press they had brought piece by piece to the apartment. They could only use it when they were sure no one could hear its thump and squeak. More often than not they were obliged to ink the type and print by hand, pressing the paper down with a brush. The work was tedious and slow but Anna took pleasure in the lively companionship of the other women, the sharp humour of Olga Liubatovich and the warmth and sensitivity of a new comrade – Praskovia Ivanovskaia. Nikolai Morozov lived in the apartment as a 'lodger' too but he was too grand for inky fingers and spent most of the day shaping and reshaping the party's programme for power. 'So this is your new society is it?' Olga teased. 'Where the women still do all the work?'

At three o'clock each day, they would sit together for soup and a meat course and talk of small things. If the conversation turned to policy, Anna would listen but play no part. Her comrades did not ask her about the night she had spent away from the apartment and she did not speak of Hadfield. But Olga had drawn her aside to remind her pointedly they were 'illegals' and if the police caught one they would probably catch all. It was a heated exchange, Anna demanding to know what she was being accused of, her friend refusing to say. The atmosphere in the apartment was poisonous, until Praskovia lost patience with both of them and insisted on reconciliation 'for the sake of the revolution'.

Two days later, Alexander Mikhailov came to see her and it was apparent as soon as he stepped across the threshold that he was out of sorts. She noticed the same chilliness in his manner she had met on the night she rejected his advances. After examining the first copies of the new leaflet without enthusiasm, he turned to her.

'I have a job for you.' He corrected himself: 'The executive committee has a job for you.'

'Of course. I'm an agent of the executive committee.'

Olga looked uncomfortable. 'I'll make some tea,' she said, a note of forced bonhomie in her voice.

'It's a pick-up from Nikolaevsky Station. You'll need to take two men from the new workers' section. Their details are here.' Mikhailov handed Anna a piece of paper. 'Meet the 7.30 from Moscow in two days time. 18 December.'

'What am I picking up?'

'You don't need to know that,' he replied sharply. 'The delivery address is on the paper – Vasilievsky Island – the 11th Line. I'm sure you won't have any difficulty finding it.'

Anna frowned, the colour rising in her face. 'Is there something you want to say to me?'

'If you mean the doctor, that is a matter for the executive committee, not me.'

'It isn't anyone's concern.'

Mikhailov stared at her for a moment and she returned his gaze without flinching.

'Do you deny you've seen him?'

'No. Why should I? We agreed he would be useful.'

Mikhailov laughed unpleasantly: 'I see.'

'This is none of your business,' she said.

'But it is a matter for the executive committee. When you've delivered the cases come to my apartment.'

'Why?'

'To answer to the committee.'

A torn yellow copy of The People's Will's programme lay in the middle of the iron table between them like sacred text. Collegiate Councillor Dobrshinsky was as familiar with its words as the prisoner with the tousled red hair and intense gaze opposite him. He had studied it carefully and spent many hours listening to Goldenberg speak of the 'new order' it would help to shape, of freedom, democracy, an end to the old autocracy. He was speaking of it now, almost gabbling, leaning across the table with his hands together.

'. . . if the government – the tsar – decides to yield to the people then I know the party will give up its violence . . .'

Dobrshinsky was always conscious of the peculiar intimacy of their exchanges across the narrow table, within the four grey walls of the cell at 'the Preliminary'.

Goldenberg began speaking again, of a free vote, free speech, freedom of the press, freedom for labour to organise, things he had spoken of many times already. But the impression the special investigator had formed was of a man who knew nothing of freedom and would always be a prisoner of his past.

When he had finished, Dobrshinsky said quietly: 'You and I want many of the same things, and there are people close to the emperor who wish to introduce reforms. But there will be no progress until there is an end to violence.'

'Who wants reform?' Goldenberg asked.

'Senior figures, ministers, but they cannot be seen to give in to terrorism. You do see that, don't you?'

Goldenberg frowned and was on the point of replying, but the special investigator leant forward and raised his hand to stop him. 'You can play an important part, Grigory Davidovich, you can help your comrades and the people. It will take vision and courage but you can end the violence. You can help save Russia.'

Goldenberg sucked his teeth sceptically. 'Why should I trust you?'

'Because we have more in common than you think,' said Dobrshinsky, leaning forward earnestly. 'We are both from Kiev – my family came from Poland, so we are outsiders, but educated men. You must see – terrorism will only make the lot of the people harder, believe me, it is killing hope of reform. Russia needs progressive people like your comrades to help shape the future.'

'The party cannot lay down its arms until the tsar has made it known he will establish an elected assembly,' Goldenberg replied mechanically. 'Only then can I help you.'

Dobrshinsky stared at him impassively for a moment then, placing his fingers on the manifesto, drew it slowly back across the table. 'A pity. Without leadership, nothing will change,' and he rose to his feet.

'But there is more we can speak of,' said Goldenberg. 'I may be able to help you interpret the programme.'

'You've done that. I understand you perfectly,' replied the collegiate councillor. 'What I propose . . . but it is perhaps too much to ask of one man.'

'But you will speak to me again?' Goldenberg's voice sounded a little shrill.

'It is a matter of trust, Grigory Davidovich. Of course, I don't blame you. I'm only sorry I can't persuade you to trust me because you are one of the few people who can change things for the better.' Dobrshinsky turned to rap at the door.

'But we must talk again, Anton Frankzevich,' said Goldenberg, rising from his stool. 'There are things – there is more we should speak of . . .'

The cell door opened and a guard stepped into view.

'It is possible to find a way . . .'

'You think so?' Dobrshinsky asked. In a moment the door would clang shut behind him and Goldenberg would be alone in his cell again.

'We must talk soon,' said Goldenberg, 'please. For the good of the country.' He was standing at the table still, an anxious hand to his face.

Dobrshinsky smiled at him: 'We will.'

The comrades from the workers' section were waiting for Anna at a coffee shop close to the station. Alexei and Pavel were in their early twenties, labourers at a textiles plant on Vasilievsky, and this was their first assignment for the party. They were on edge.

'The courier will meet us at the guards' van. I'll sign for the trunks then we take a carriage to the Haymarket, and that's where you leave me. There shouldn't be a problem if the courier's papers are in order,' Anna said with a confident smile. 'If we're stopped, remember you're being paid to help Miss Terenteva with her cases. Leave the rest to me.'

The station concourse at the Nikolaevsky was bustling with travellers. If they were quick and efficient they would pass unnoticed in the crowd. There were gendarmes at the entrances to the station and on the platforms but they were more occupied with travellers than those who were there to meet them. The 7.30 from Moscow arrived ten minutes late in a hissing cloud of soot and steam, snow thick on the carriage roofs, the windows opaque with ice. Within seconds the platform was heaving with the gentlemen and ladies of first class, junior officers and chief clerks from second, peasants and porters and screaming children, a ragged tide of humanity surging into the station, relieved to be at the end of their journey. Head bent a little, Anna pushed forward towards the guard's van, her companions at her back, anxious to make the contact, pick up the bags and leave before the platform was empty.

A harassed-looking guard was trying to organise the unloading of the larger pieces from the van, an impatient ring of porters and uniformed flunkies shuffling towards him. Where could he be? She was to look for a young man in the uniform of the engineering school. She was about to press forward into the tightening circle when someone jogged her elbow.

'Elizaveta?' He was a tall man with a thin face, neatly trimmed beard and spectacles, smartly dressed in a navy blue cap and velvet cloak that was fastened at the neck with a gold clasp.

'Konstantin, at your service.' He held out his hand with a relieved smile.

'Have you got the bags?' she asked brusquely. 'No? Well, we haven't any time to waste.'

Anna watched with exasperation as the student and workers edged towards the guards' van. Next time she would use the station porters like everyone else. Not only were they less conspicuous, but for a few kopeks more they were prepared to use their elbows. Most of the passengers had picked up their luggage and left by the time the trunks were delivered to her feet.

'Thank you, Konstantin. Now go, leave us at once.'

'Is that all?' he asked, a little hurt.

'Yes. Go or people will ask what a rich student is doing in the company of a maid and two workers.' She turned her back on him and began walking towards the concourse. She could hear Alexei and Pavel lumbering along the platform behind her.

She waited for them to catch up at the platform gate: 'Keep moving across the station, whatever you do. Only stop if I tell you to, is that clear? If a gendarme wants to speak to us, leave it to me.'

Pavel nodded. Alexei was biting his lip. She gave his arm a reassuring pat. 'It will be all right, you'll see. Just look as if you know what you're doing.'

And on to the station concourse she led them, weaving her way through the crowd, alive to every movement, every suggestion of danger. She could see gendarmes at the entrance to the ticket office and the platform gates but it was the ones she could not see that concerned her most, the plain-clothes policemen, the informers and agents of the Third Section.

'Hey, watch out!' she heard someone shout, and she turned quickly. Alexei had driven the corner of his heavy trunk against a man's leg. The civil servant – to judge from his uniform – was bent double, rubbing his shin. Instead of muttering an apology and moving smartly on, Alexei had put the trunk down and was watching him with a guilty face.

'Hey, you!' Anna shouted. 'What are you doing with my bags? I've a cab outside and it's costing me money.'

'Look what the oaf has done,' the injured man complained.

'That can't be helped,' she replied, turning to the exit again. Two gendarmes were standing together beneath the arch, watching the traffic to and from the station. It was very unlikely that they would let workers with large trunks pass without question. She would have to distract them and hope her comrades had the sense to do what she had told them to do.

Anna scuttled towards the gendarmes: 'That man there, that man there,' she said breathlessly, pointing to the unfortunate civil servant. 'He's wanted by the police.'

The gendarmes looked at her as if she were mad or drunk or both.

'He's wanted by the police, I tell you!'

'Who are you?' the older of the two asked. 'What's he supposed to have done?'

'Quick – before he gets away!' Anna said, wringing her hands. 'Look, he's going, he's leaving!'

The civil servant had obligingly chosen that moment to limp towards a platform entrance.

'Who are you?' the older gendarme asked again.

'He's got a gun! I've seen it. He's a terrorist! Oh, why won't you believe me?' Anna began rocking back and forth, her head in her hands. 'For goodness sake, are you going to stand here and let him get away!'

The gendarmes exchanged glances.

'You'd better be right,' muttered the younger man. 'Don't move from this spot.'

Anna watched for a few seconds as the gendarmes forced their way through the crowd, cannoning into travellers, tripping over pieces of luggage, then she slipped into the stream of people leaving the station. The workers were waiting for her at the cab rank with the trunks.

'Quick – into a droshky,' Anna commanded. 'And you, Pavel – take another. Better we travel separately. 7 Spassky, off the Haymarket.'

She was a good liar. A skill, she thought, as she sat in the droshky, her heart still beating frantically, a performance learnt in childhood when fear of upsetting her father would drive her to many simple deceits.

At the Haymarket she took possession of the trunks and took another cab to the island. The door of the safe house was opened by a pale man in his twenties with languid blue eyes and a dark beard and hair that fell in a severe fringe across his forehead.

'A delivery for a friend.'

'Anna Kovalenko? I'm Nikolai Kibalchich.'

'Good. Is there anyone who can help you?'

Anna paid the cab driver while Kibalchich and a comrade she did not recognise carried the trunks into the ground floor apartment.

'Through here,' Kibalchich shouted from the main room.

He had already lifted the trunk on to a table and was fiddling with the locks. The room was long and narrow and furnished like a laboratory, with work benches, glass beakers and flasks, coils of wire, clamps, tongs, implements she could not name of all shapes and sizes. Kibalchich was the party's explosives expert but she had no idea the executive committee had its own small factory.

'It's all here,' he said, turning to her with a broad smile, eyes bright with excitement. 'By my calculation we need 320 pounds, but 360 would be better. We're at least forty pounds short at the moment.'

'I haven't the faintest idea what you're talking about,' she said.

'The attempt on the palace, of course. Our man has 280 pounds in place but we need more.'

'Yes, of course,' she said with a little laugh, the colour rising to her face. No one had told her. Another attempt was to be made on the tsar's life and no one had told her. Mikhailov had kept her in the dark.

'But will he be able to smuggle it into the palace in time?'

Kibalchich shrugged: 'In time for what? As long as it's there and no one finds it, but that isn't my concern.'

'No. Of course not.'

The cab dropped her before the Anichkov Bridge and, after taking care no one was following her, she turned into Troitsky Lane and walked quickly along it until she reached Mikhailov's mansion. It was a little before one o'clock when she rang the bell and was shown up to the second floor by the dvornik.

'Did you manage the delivery?' Mikhailov asked as the apartment door closed behind her.

'The dynamite, you mean?' she said tartly. 'Yes.'

The drawing room was crowded with familiar faces – Sophia Perovskaya and Andrei Zhelyabov, the son of the house serf from the Crimea, her flatmate Nikolai Morozov and others.

'Annushka, come and sit beside me,' said Sophia, drawing her by the hand to the settee. 'We've been speaking of you.'

'Oh?'

'Yes. Alexander was reminding us how easily you move unnoticed about the city.'

Anna did not reply. A tense silence fell on the room and faces turned to Mikhailov, but he seemed content to sit, his eyes half closed, hands clasped about his knee, as if enjoying the discomfort of his comrades.

'Alexander is concerned about your friendship with this English doctor,' Sophia said at last. 'Can he be trusted?'

'We've promised to put the party and the revolution first,' Morozov added from the table. 'It's about renouncing one's egotism for the sake of the Russian people. That is our supreme task.'

Anna looked at him with disgust. 'I'll take no lessons from you on sacrifices,' she replied. 'I don't think you've given up anything.'

'There is no need to be personal,' said Sophia.

'What is this if it is not personal? The committee is questioning my loyalty to the revolution.'

'No one is questioning your loyalty, Anna,' said Mikhailov. 'No one could question your loyalty, only the wisdom of becoming involved with an Englishman.'

'But we agreed he would be useful. You agreed,' she replied angrily. This was naked jealousy and she had to bite her lip to stop herself saying so.

'Yes, but the police have questioned him . . .'

'And he told them nothing.'

'They will question him again. The Third Section has a file on him.'

'It has a file on you and on me and on you and you and you,' Anna said, pointing to them all in turn. 'He'll be of service to the revolution. I know it.'

'Are you sure your personal feelings are not getting in the way?' said Morozov.

Anna snorted with frustration then barked a word in Ukrainian that no one in the room understood. Her cheeks were burning, her hands shaking. None of them would meet her eye. It was the son of the serf, Andrei Zhelyabov, a handsome bear of a man, who spoke at last.

'We must trust our comrade's judgement. She has earned that trust.'

Anna turned to him with a grateful smile. He understood her, he was of the people too, but they must all be told. 'You know me and you must know my loyalty is to the party,' and her voice trembled a little with emotion. 'I will do my duty to the people. The English doctor is my . . . my friend, and he can help us. I trust him. Vera Figner trusts him.'

Sophia Perovskaya reached for her hand and gave it a little squeeze.

'You understand how careful we must be,' said Mikhailov. 'Sooner or later they will have your doctor followed.'

'I will tell him.'

'Is there anything else?' Mikhailov glanced about the room at the other members of the executive committee. 'Then Anna can go.'

'There is something else,' said Anna, irritated to be dismissed as if she were a flunkey. 'I want to know why no one has told me there were plans for another attempt on the emperor's life.'

'The fewer people who know the better,' Mikhailov replied, his eyes fixed upon her.

'Well, I know now. So – what are you going to do? Have me killed and dumped in a street too?'

For a few seconds the silence was broken only by the awkward shuffling of feet and the creak of furniture.

'What do you know?' Mikhailov asked at last.

'We are smuggling explosives into the palace.'

'Careless of Nikolai,' Mikhailov said with a shake of the head.

'I want to tell Anna,' said Zhelyabov, leaning forward to look Mikhailov in the eye. 'She should know.'

Mikhailov shrugged and turned to Anna. 'We've had a member of the party inside the Winter Palace since October. He's a carpenter, and for weeks now he's been smuggling dynamite into one of the cellars.'

Only small quantities could be taken at a time because he was obliged to hide the explosives in his boots and the lining of his coat, but the police patrols knew him and trusted him and he had managed to build up a supply of almost 300 pounds. 'He sleeps in the cellar with the other workmen,' said Zhelyabov, picking up the narrative. 'He used to hide the explosives in his pillow but the fumes were too much for him so now he keeps the stuff in a box with his clothes. The cellar's directly below the tsar's dining room, so when we have enough . . . boom!' and Zhelyabov flung his arms theatrically into the air.

'Satisfied?' asked Mikhailov.

'I will be when it's done,' Anna replied.

'No one must know,' Mikhailov said, looking at her intently with his small brown eyes. 'They found drawings of the palace in Kviatkovsky's apartment. They've searched the cellar more than once since.'

Anna stiffened again, struggling to control her temper. Mikhailov's pointed 'no one' meant 'someone', someone in particular.

'Surprised?' Zhelyabov asked, as if to draw the sting from Mikhailov's words. She was surprised and excited and Zhelyabov must have seen it in her face. 'To kill the tsar in his own palace will show the people that the party has a long arm,' he added.

'But when?'

'Soon. Very soon. We're almost there. The new year will be a new dawn for the Russian people.'

# 23

Two Christmas days had passed and one new year before Frederick Hadfield received word from her again. For a time he could not enjoy an idle moment without being tormented by the tune from Mozart's aria *Amore un ladroncello*, and he would hum it as he dressed, in the droshky to the hospital and even on the wards. Love, the thief of time and of liberty that chains the soul, and he would hold his head and curse under his breath for an incurable romantic. He had celebrated a Protestant Christmas at his uncle's gloomy table, then thirteen days later an Orthodox one. The festive season had not been without cheer. There had been a succession of extravagant parties and balls and he had escorted his cousin to a glittering affair at the Nobles' Club, where the heir to the throne was the principal guest of honour. And he was to welcome the Russian New Year with the Glen family at the mansion of their neighbour, the immensely wealthy banker, Baron von Stieglitz. The general was insisting on a carriage to collect his nephew at nine o'clock. He was not to be late.

Frederick was dressing for the Stieglitz Ball when the dvornik knocked at his door. Anna's note – as peremptory as before – proposed a meeting at precisely the same time. It was the height of bad manners, of course, and he risked causing the sort of offence that could damage his position in embankment society irreparably, but he felt only joy at the prospect of seeing her. In the end he wrote simply that he was suffering from a fever. It did indeed feel close to the truth – and who was going to argue with his diagnosis?

By nine o'clock he was waiting before the west front of St Boris and St Gleb's. It was snowing hard and he was grateful for his old student coat and hat. New Year's Eve, it was below freezing, and instead of sipping champagne in the baron's opulent drawing room he was stamping his feet in an empty square in one of the poorest parts of town.

'What is so funny?'

'Where did you spring from?' Walking quickly towards her, he held her tightly before slipping the scarf down from her nose and mouth to give her a long, tender kiss, her lips soft and warm. Then he took off his gloves and held her face in his hands. 'It seems so long.'

'Three weeks.'

'So you've been counting too?'

She smiled weakly, pushing him gently away. 'Come on – this is no place to celebrate the new year. We're going to a party.'

She led him through the streets by the arm. From time to time they could hear the sound of happy and drunken voices through the thin glass of the poorer houses, and rough carousing from the basement taverns. They said very little to each other, he was content holding her little hand tightly, turning sometimes to catch her eye, a prickle of excitement just walking at her side. He was disappointed when they stopped at the corner of a street and she announced they were almost there. Lifting her chin, her eyes searching his face, she asked in a quiet voice: 'Do you love me, Frederick?'

'Yes,' he said, and he bent to kiss her once more.

She put her hands against his chest and held him at bay. 'So I can trust you?'

'Of course you can.'

'Then you must be careful what you say to my . . .' she

hesitated for a moment '. . . to my friends. They must know they can trust you too.'

Her 'friends'. He felt a flutter of alarm.

'Well?' she asked sharply, her brows knotted together in that peculiar frown of hers.

'They can trust me.'

'Good.'

But he felt ill at ease as he followed her down the street and into the yard of a mansion block. The servants' entrance was unlocked and she led him quickly up the back stairs. On the third landing she turned before a door to give him a reassuring smile, then knocked sharply twice. After a few seconds it was opened by a broad, handsome man with a full beard, unruly hair and warm brown eyes.

'So this is your doctor,' he said to Anna with a robust chuckle. 'My name is Zhelyabov, Andrei Ivanovich at your service.'

'He is not my doctor!' said Anna, blushing hotly.

Zhelyabov chuckled again and placed an affectionate arm about her shoulders: 'Come in and let me take your coats.'

The living room was heaving with people, flushed with alcohol and good humour, draped over the furniture and sitting on cushions. In the centre was a round table and upon it a large tureen. A group of men and women were busy preparing some sort of punch with rum and wine and sugar and spices. No one seemed surprised to see Hadfield.

'The punch is ready,' an earnest-looking man in his twenties shouted from the table. 'Out with the candles.' A hush fell on the room and everyone crowded round the punch bowl. Anna touched Hadfield's arm: 'Come on.'

Zhelyabov struck a match and put it to the punch and a flame began to dance about the bowl. The earnest fellow who had called the room to order pulled out his dagger and laid it across the bowl. Zhelyabov did the same, and then another man and another, as if enacting a pagan blood ritual, gold and red shimmering on their blades. Then one of the men began to hum a lively folk tune.

'It's a song from the Ukraine,' Anna whispered, her eyes shining with pleasure.

The candles were lit again and the strong rum punch served to all.

'Here.' A petite young woman soberly dressed in black offered him a glass. 'Dr Hadfield, isn't it?'

'Yes.' He seemed to tower over her.

'My name is Sophia Perovskaya. I'm glad to make your acquaintance.'

So, this was the daughter of the former governor general of the city. She was rather plain, with an oval face and high forehead. There was a girlish innocence in her expression that was difficult to reconcile with her reputation. He had heard her name spoken at the best parties, invariably with a disapproving and incredulous shake of the head.

'Anna says you love our country and that you're a socialist,' Sophia said, her blue eyes wide, her gaze uncomfortably intense.

'Yes, yes, I am.'

'Let us hope Russia changes for the better in the year to come.'

'Yes.'

'Perhaps you will play a part in that transformation.'

He gave a slight nod, hoping this would satisfy her. One of the comrades called for music to general approval, and for a while Hadfield was spared awkward questions by some hearty folk-singing. At midnight there were kisses and they drank to freedom for the homeland. The earnest young man who had been the first to place his dagger over the punch – his name was Nikolai Morozov – predicted the new year would bring an end to 'slavery'. Then, from the edge of the circle, the man Hadfield knew as 'Alexander' spoke. He must have slipped into the apartment just before midnight because he was wearing his heavy black overcoat, wet with melting snowflakes.

'To Alexander Soloviev. To our comrades in prison, to "The People's Will" and to our revolution.'

As Hadfield raised his glass with the rest, he could sense Alexander's sharp little eyes upon him, and he made a point of holding his gaze. He was heavier than Hadfield remembered him, his fine frock coat stretched tightly across his chest, that rarest of men, a plump revolutionary. He saluted Hadfield very deliberately with his glass before someone plucked at his sleeve and he was obliged to look away.

The new year ticked on into the early hours. Anna showed no inclination to leave. 'No doubt you believe it your duty to be with your comrades even to the end of a party?' Hadfield risked teasing her. Anna gave a little frown, but the corners of her mouth twitched as she struggled to suppress a smile. A woman called Olga suggested a séance and a large sheet of paper was conjured up from somewhere, the letters of the alphabet written around its edge.

'No one believes in this superstitious nonsense, do they?' he whispered to Anna.

'I do,' she said crossly.

'But I thought you were an atheist.'

'I am.'

'But you believe in this?'

'I don't know. Yes, a little.'

They took their places at the table, a saucer upside down on the paper, and by the light of a flickering candle they tried to summon the spirit of Tsar Nicholas.

'We must ask him how his son will die,' Olga whispered.

'Why do we want to spoil our new year by inviting an old tyrant to join us?' asked Zhelyabov.

Olga hissed at him to be quiet. 'How will Alexander meet his death? How will the tsar meet his death?' she intoned.

The saucer began to move, dragging Hadfield's forefinger across the table. The whole thing seemed not only ridiculous but in very poor taste, and he was grateful for the anonymity of darkness. For ten minutes the saucer glided meaninglessly about the table as if struggling to find a common will and then it moved to 'P' and 'O' and the letter 'I' in front of Hadfield, then to 'S' and to 'O' again, and finally 'N'. POISON.

'But that's impossible!' said Olga.

Hadfield could not help smiling: how very 'old Russia'.

'It's ridiculous,' said someone else. No one at the table believed the tsar would die from poisoning because it was not a weapon the executive committee of The People's Will would ever approve.

Zhelyabov tried to laugh it off: 'What can we expect from such nonsense?' But it seemed to Hadfield that instead of raising spirits the séance had only succeeded in dampening them.

'It's almost three o'clock. We must leave,' Alexander said from the darkness beyond the table. 'But first – the *Marseillaise*.'

'Do you know the words, Doctor?' asked Sophia Perovskaya.

Yes, Hadfield knew the words well and he joined with the singing, softly and cautiously, lest the neighbours heard their call to arms. But he was conscious of Anna silent beside him, shifting uncomfortably, the revolutionary from the village who did not know the words to a socialist anthem but believed spirits could be summoned to a drunken table. And he felt a warm surge of love for her difference and reached for her hand.

They left the party in pairs and threes to avoid the unwelcome attention of the street superintendent, and at last he was alone with her. As soon as he could he pulled her into the shadow of a yard and bent to kiss her tenderly. 'Happy New Year, my darling'.

'Am I your darling?'

'How can you doubt it?'

They spent the rest of the night wrapped in each other's

arms on the mattress in the old Ukrainian woman's cell. There had been other women in Switzerland and London but none that had touched him like Anna. She was always with him, every minute, every second, at the core of his being. It troubled him that he could not understand why it was so. There was a darkness in her, fragility, confusion, a stubbornness beyond reason. What was it she felt for him? She did not say, and he wondered if she knew. She was capable of slipping from submissiveness to defiance and intemperate anger in little more than the blink of an eye. And yet there was a femininity and subtle intelligence there, too, that was deeply attractive. Lying beside her, the early sun dropping down the wall opposite, Hadfield knew that for better or worse their fates were bound together – and that this new year marked a new phase in his life.

# 1880

Yes, it's a sin for revolutionaries to start a family. Men and women both must stand alone, like soldiers under a hail of bullets. But in your youth, you somehow forget that revolutionaries' lives are measured not in years, but in days and hours.

**Olga Liubatovich,**
**Member of The People's Will**

You can call [terror] the heroic method but it is also the most practical . . . if you keep on with it unceasingly. Occasional individual attacks may alarm the public, but they do not effectively demoralise an administration. You must make attack after attack uninterruptedly and relentlessly against one fixed and prearranged target.

**Andrei Zhelyabov,**
**Member of the executive committee of**
**The People's Will**

# 24

'. . . The Minister of Justice has agreed to an amnesty for your comrades.'

The little man with the wispy red hair and goatee beard nodded his head calmly, but beneath the table his hands were wrestling anxiously with a pencil. He was dressed in prison greys several sizes too large, his head and shoulders hunched forward as if cowering from an invisible presence. Perhaps it was the ghost of his irascible father – he had spoken of him often to Dobrshinsky in the course of their conversations – or the rough Jew-hating neighbours of his childhood in Kiev. Perhaps he was bent by guilt and the long shadow of Alexander Mikhailov, or by exhaustion, his senses blunted after days in the interrogation room, coaxed and cajoled, his illusions stripped from him one by one.

'And I have your word,' Goldenberg said at last. 'I have your word they will be safe? If even one hair on the head of a comrade is hurt, I'll never forgive myself.'

'You know I respect your cause. I admire your courage. We trust each other. Here . . .' The chief investigator picked up the vodka bottle on the table between them and poured a little into two small glasses. 'To reconciliation. To reform. To a new year for Russia and an end to confusion,' he said, raising his own in salute. Then, turning to the clerk at the table in the corner of the interrogation room, 'The last few sentences.'

The young clerk ran his forefinger along the page of his open log book: '. . . *discussed my idea for the assassination of the emperor with Alexander Mikhailov and others* . . .'

'A group of us met and we—'

'Who?'

'Mikhailov, a Pole called Kobilianski, Kviatkovsky, Zunderlich, Soloviev . . .'

'Anna Kovalenko?'

'Yes. I wanted to do it and the Pole volunteered too, but Mikhailov said the tsar should be killed by a Russian – not a Pole or a Jew. So Alexander Soloviev agreed to do it and I helped him prepare.'

Dobrshinsky gave a little nod.

'But I wouldn't have missed,' said Goldenberg with sudden passion.

'And Anna Kovalenko – she was there with Soloviev in the square?'

Goldenberg licked his lips, then, lifting his right hand to them, began biting at his thumb nail. So vain, so weak, so anxious for praise and attention, Dobrshinsky wondered how a clever man like Mikhailov had made such a mistake.

'I must know the truth to bring this to an end as we agreed,' he said quietly, leaning forward at the table in an effort to hold eye contact with the prisoner.

'Anna was there to report on what happened, that's all,' said Goldenberg reluctantly.

'And Bronstein, how did you discover . . . ?'

'The informer? I don't know. That was Mikhailov. Mikhailov knows everything. He has his own sources. A man he calls the Director who he says guides him.'

'And this man works for the police?'

Goldenberg shrugged: 'I don't know, but Mikhailov seems to know a lot about the police and the Third Section.'

Before Dobrshinsky could shape the next question there was

an insistent knock at the door and a prison clerk entered unbidden bearing a note from the chief prosecutor.

Count Vyacheslav von Plehve had squeezed his ample frame behind the untidy desk in the assistant governor's office. 'This is in strict confidence, but I wanted you to know at once,' he said, indicating with a wave of his plump hand that Dobrshinsky should take the chair opposite. 'There are to be sweeping changes, a new Supreme Security Commission, and heads are to roll. I think it is certain General Drenteln will be replaced at the Third Section.' The chief prosecutor placed his elbows on the desk, his fingers at his lips, a courtroom silence.

His news did not elicit a flicker of a response. Dobrshinsky resented being summoned from an interrogation to hear rumours of a new council, gossip about who was rising up the empire's greasy pole and who was falling. His orders were to keep His Majesty alive. Service politics was a distraction.

The count may have had a sense of what he was thinking because he began to wriggle uncomfortably behind the desk.

'The investigation,' he said at last. 'Are you any closer to arresting the leaders of this nihilist party?'

'We have Kviatkovsky.'

'Kviatkovsky?'

'We took the plans for the Winter Palace from his flat,' said Dobrshinsky.

'The police have found nothing. They've searched the palace from top to bottom a dozen times, and all the neighbouring buildings,' said von Plehve brusquely. 'Every morning they check to see if any of the stones in the square have been lifted and they search the servants. If you've fresh evidence they will be overjoyed to hear it.'

'The People's Will may have called off the attack when they discovered we had Kviatkovsky in custody.'

Pushing his chair back sharply, the chief prosecutor rose and walked over to the tiled stove in the corner of the room and bent to the heat. 'Anton Frankzevich, we need to demonstrate we are making progress to the chairman of the new Supreme Security Commission when he is appointed.' He paused again, then said with quiet emphasis, 'It's important we make a good impression. Your future will depend upon it. Ah, you smile, but it's true.'

'I can say with confidence we are making progress,' said Dobrshinsky.

'What sort of progress? The Jew?'

'I have persuaded him terror is slowing the pace of reform. That the emperor wants to introduce a democratic assembly and freedom of the press but he can't be seen to bow to terror.'

'And you think he believes you?' asked the count.

'Yes.'

'Is he mad or simple?'

'He thinks I'm a liberal and I can be trusted to tell the truth.' Dobrshinsky paused, a thoughtful frown on his face. 'He wants to believe he can play a role in shaping Russia. I'm trying to convince him that his part is in persuading his comrades to stop, that this is the only way to bring about reform. Oh, and I have assured him none of them will be harmed.'

'So he's a simpleton.'

'Lonely, naive, weak, vain . . .'

'So when can we look forward to . . .'

'Arrests? I have names, descriptions, and we can tease more from him – more names and, I hope, some addresses. But these things take time,' said Dobrshinsky. 'We have a little way to go.'

'Good, good, but not too much time,' said the count with a resigned nod of the head. 'Keep me informed. Now, if you will excuse me, I am expected at the ministry.'

The chief prosecutor had grasped the door handle and

was on the point of stepping out when Dobrshinsky spoke again.

'There is one thing more. Your friend, the English doctor, Dr Hadfield . . .'

The count interrupted him crossly. 'He's no more than an acquaintance. I met him at the British embassy. He made a very poor impression on me.'

'Quite so, quite so,' said Dobrshinsky. 'Goldenberg remembers him well. He was at the woman Volkonskaya's.'

'I see. So do you think he's a spy?' Von Plehve seemed excited by the possibility.

'I can't be sure. He lied to my officer. I've had him followed and he's given my men the slip once or twice.'

'Do as you see fit, but we don't want a diplomatic incident with the British.'

For a time, Dobrshinsky remained in the assistant governor's bare office, reflecting in a haze of cigarette smoke. What was it von Plehve had said? 'Your future will depend upon making progress'. It had been impossible not to smile. No one was more adept at claiming credit and reapportioning blame than the chief prosecutor. A Supreme Security Commission would ask questions the count would have to answer, so it was important for him to be able to pass the responsibility for failure on to others. Vanity, ambition, fear came in so many guises. What was there of substance to distinguish the chief prosecutor in his immaculate ministry uniform from the helpless Jew in his prison greys? Goldenberg was naive, vain, despicable, but at least he believed in something. Dobrshinsky was almost sorry for him. He leant forward to grind his cigarette into an ashtray, a spiral of smoke still curling before him like a temple offering. Really, was stupidity the worst crime?

Taking headed paper from the pile on the desk and the pen from the silver stand, he wrote a short note, slipped it into an envelope and addressed it in a careful hand: *Dr Frederick Hadfield, The Nikolaevsky Hospital.*

'See this is delivered at once,' he said, dropping the letter in front of the assistant governor's clerk as he left the office. It was time he met this English spy.

# 25

The first time Anna asked Hadfield for money he gave it without question. The second time, she told him she needed a little for clothes.

'Of course, darling,' he said, running his hand over her smooth skin and leaning forward to kiss her forehead. 'How much?'

The third time he refused to give more. They were lying together on the old mattress, the diffuse light of a Sunday morning in January creeping into the makeshift bedroom, their conversation conducted in whispers lest they wake the old lady and her granddaughters.

'You're still wearing the same clothes,' he said.

Anna was lying on her back staring at the ceiling, but even in the dim light he saw her face stiffen to a scowl.

'Why are you wearing the same clothes?'

Ignoring his question, she gathered the sheet to her shoulder and turned to lie on her side with her back towards him. And at once he felt a pang of regret. How could he refuse her? It was money, nothing more. He reached out to stroke her hair. 'Of course I'll give you money. You don't need to lie to me.'

She turned sharply to look at him, the sheet sliding from her chest. 'What do you mean?'

'Don't tell me you want money for clothes. Don't tell me anything.'

She blushed a little and her face softened. 'No. I won't.' And she leant forward to kiss him tenderly, her fingers resting on his cheek.

But Anna did not ask for more money. She asked him to pay the party in kind. On the first occasion, he arrived home late one evening to a note urging him to 'come at once' to the Ekaterininsky Embankment. A 'friend' was in great need of medical care. The dvornik's brain was too fuddled with alcohol to be sure when the note had been delivered.

It was close to midnight when the droshky dropped him in front of a smart terracotta-coloured mansion near the Voznesensky Bridge. To his surprise, the door was opened by a young footman in a blue and gold uniform.

'Doctor Hadfield – I've been asked to call.' He gave the flunky his card. A moment later, he was being shown up the stairs to the first floor and into an elegant drawing room. Anna was standing before a large pier glass between the windows with Sophia Perovskaya.

'Why has it taken you so long?'

He was irritated by her proprietary manner. 'I came as soon as I received your note.'

'Thank goodness you've come,' said Sophia with more grace, holding out her hands to greet him.

'The midwife is with her but there are complications,' said Anna, her face tense with anxiety.

'Who is this woman?'

'Does it matter? She needs your help.'

The young woman had been struggling for more than fourteen hours and was in great distress. The midwife had done what she could but the baby was breech.

'This woman should be in hospital! Why have you waited so long?'

'She can't go to hospital, she'd be arrested,' said Sophia. 'They would question her – if she's feeling weak she will give too much away . . .'

Sophia's face was milky white and she flinched as the woman screamed in pain.

'You're prepared to take the risk of losing mother or baby, or both?' Hadfield asked incredulously.

'Can't you do anything for her here?'

'I may have to perform a Caesarean. Pray to God I don't,' he said, rolling up his shirt sleeves.

Two hours later the baby was born, his exhausted mother weeping tears of relief and pain and gratitude. He had to cut her, but he was able to deliver the boy without an operation. Nineteen-year-old Tatiana was strong. 'Congratulations,' he said, sweeping damp hair from her face. She was lying in a nest of pillows, her baby pressed naked against her breast. The midwife was hovering on the opposite side of the bed with a swaddling sheet. There was a knock at the door and it opened a few inches.

'Can we come in?' Anna's voice trembled a little with emotion.

'For a moment. She needs to rest.'

Anna and Sophia tiptoed across the room as if frightened of what they would find.

'Dark eyes like his father,' said Tatiana when they were at her bedside. She bent to kiss his little head. 'Would you like to hold him, Sophia?'

'I would like to,' said Anna, and she lifted him with the confidence of one used to holding babies. She held him close, her cheek brushing his head, and when she looked up again Hadfield saw that her eyes were wet with tears.

'I will come back tomorrow,' he said, as they left the room.

'It would be best if you came late in the evening,' Sophia replied. 'This house belongs to a friend of the party but we don't want to draw attention to our presence.'

'Is Tatiana safe here?'

'For now, yes.'

'And the father?'

'He's in the "Preliminary" awaiting trial. He was caught distributing copies of the party's paper at the university. He may not see his baby before the revolution.' Sophia seemed detached, as if speaking of the everyday, a tram ride into the city, shopping at the market.

'A terrible price to pay.'

'But his son will live in a better world.'

That night Hadfield persuaded Anna to return to his apartment and they made love without the inhibitions of others close by. There was an additional strange intensity to their lovemaking, as if the birth of the baby had left its emotional stamp on both of them.

'I saw you wipe away a tear,' he whispered, his cheek against hers, their naked bodies together.

She did not reply.

'It will be so hard for her,' he said.

'She should have been more careful.'

'Careful?' he asked, edging from her a little to look at her face.

'Revolutionaries shouldn't have children.'

'Ah yes, revolutionaries can't be happy. I forgot.'

'Don't be sarcastic. It's cruel, a sin to have children when we could lose our freedom or our lives at any time.'

'All this talk of martyrdom and sin,' he said, leaning forward to kiss her lips. 'I thought you were no longer a believer.'

'Don't tease me. Go to sleep. I don't want to talk about it.' She turned abruptly from him.

But he could not sleep. Curled about her, her skin warm to his, his mind restless, he felt sad. If it was foolish for a revolutionary to have a family, was it foolish to risk love and tenderness too? What were her feelings for him? He pressed closer, trying to empty his mind of all but the happiness he felt lying at her side.

A few days later his surgery assistant brought him another note from 'a friend of Anna's'.

'The messenger says it's urgent and that he'll wait for a reply,' his assistant said apologetically.

The note was in a scruffy hand and badly spelt: an emergency, a 'comrade' badly hurt, 'come at once'. A friend of Anna's? He cursed quietly under his breath: what on earth was she thinking? He would not become the party's physician of choice. The messenger was standing, cap in hand, at the waiting-room door. It was evident from his manner and dress that he was a worker at one of the factories or shipyards on the island.

'Your Honour, it's only a short walk. We must hurry.'

Instructing his assistant to rearrange appointments, Hadfield grabbed his coat and medical bag and followed the man from the surgery. At the end of Line 7, they turned on to one of the island's arteries, bustling with horse trams and cabs and traders at their stalls, stamping their feet, blowing into frozen hands. Hadfield did his best to make conversation but his guide was tongue-tied, incapable of more than a 'yes' or 'no' to simple questions. They slithered along the icy pavement for five minutes, turning left at Line 11 and walking on until they reached the door of a run-down three-storey house at the far end of the street. His guide gave two sharp knocks, paused for a few seconds then gave two more. The door was opened with an impatient jerk by a dishevelled man in his twenties who was plainly suffering from shock, for his face was drained of colour, his pupils abnormally dilated.

'Thank goodness – come . . . come in . . . come in,' he stammered. 'It's poor Valentin – this way, please.'

Hadfield followed him along a short corridor and into a ground-floor apartment.

'We wouldn't have brought you here but Anna . . .'

'Is she here?'

'No, no.'

'Where's the patient?' Hadfield snapped.

'In here, please.' He held the door open.

The injured man was sitting on a damp mattress with his back to the wall, a bundle of bloody rags round his right hand. There was a deathly pallor to his face and he had clearly lost a lot of blood because his shirt was stained red, and there were dark patches on his woollen waistcoat and trousers.

'Valentin, I've brought a doctor.'

The injured man nodded weakly but did not open his eyes. The room was furnished with nothing more than the mattress and a simple wooden chair.

'You, what's your name?' Hadfield turned to the first man.

'Kibalchich, Nikolai Ivanovich, at your service.'

'Well, Nikolai Ivanovich, I need water, towels, soap, and quickly.'

While he was away, Hadfield began gently peeling the rags from the injured man's hand. It was a severe trauma injury, ragged tissue, ragged bone, three fingers gone, forefinger and thumb reduced to bloody stumps.

'How did you do this?'

'A piece of machinery, Doctor,' said Kibalchich from the door. He was holding an enamel bowl, a towel draped over his shoulder.

The loose skin round the wound was blackened and in places red raw. Hadfield could smell burnt flesh and the injured man's hair and eyebrows were singed, his shirt sleeve too. 'A piece of machinery that burns?'

Kibalchich licked his lips uncertainly and looked away.

'I'll do what I can, but you know he should be in hospital?'

'Is there anything else you need?' Kibalchich asked, kneeling beside him with the bowl.

'You must help me, I need to give him an anaesthetic.' Hadfield took out a bottle and sprinkled some drops on to a gauze pad: 'That should be enough.' It was hard to judge the correct dose.

'Ether?'

'Yes. I can see you're interested in chemistry,' said Hadfield, giving a nod to the injured man's hand. The irony in his voice was not lost on Kibalchich.

It took almost an hour to clean the wound, to cut away the dead flesh, tidy, stitch and dress.

'He's in pain still,' said Kibalchich, as the patient groaned long and loud.

'He'll be in pain when he comes round. I'll give you some morphine, but you must take him to a hospital.'

'Your hospital?'

Hadfield frowned: 'It would be better to take him somewhere else. The Nikolaevsky's a military hospital.'

'I'll speak to Alexander Mikhailov.'

'If you can't find somewhere, contact me – but discreetly. The wound needs to be checked and dressed regularly. Now I must wash.'

Kibalchich left the room to fetch clean water. Getting to his feet, Hadfield stretched on tiptoes to the ceiling, blood flowing back into his stiff limbs. There were patients waiting to see him, he was to be at the hospital in two hours and he had no intention of lingering in the apartment. The less he knew of their chemistry experiments the better.

He stepped out of the room into the gloomy corridor. 'Hey, Nikolai?' Where was his water? He walked down the corridor and opened the first door he came to.

He stood with his hand on the knob, staring in amazement at the workbenches with their flasks and clamps and Bunsen burners. There was a confusion of broken glass and laboratory instruments on the bench furthest from the door and a large black smoke shadow on the wall. Valentin had lost his fingers in an explosion. If he took the trouble to look he would find them on or below the bench.

'As you can see – the party's laboratory.'

Alexander Mikhailov was standing in the hall at the end of

the corridor, with Kibalchich at his shoulder. His voice was calm, even relaxed, but Hadfield felt a prickle of perspiration creep over his skin as he turned to face him.

'The scene of Valentin's unfortunate accident?'

'Yes. A mercury fulminate. Nikolai,' Mikhailov addressed his companion, 'the doctor is still waiting to wash his hands.'

Kibalchich stepped forward too quickly, sloshing water along the corridor.

'Put it in the laboratory,' said Mikhailov, slipping out of his black coat. 'We have nothing to hide now, the doctor knows our business.'

As he stood at the workbench soaping his hands and forearms, Hadfield was conscious of Mikhailov's lazy-lidded eyes watching him intently.

'You're the only person to set foot in this room who isn't a party member,' he said, leaning forward to offer a towel. 'Quite an honour.'

'An honour I could do without,' replied Hadfield shortly.

'Important work is done here.'

'I don't doubt it.'

'And now you've played your part.'

Hadfield frowned, dropping the towel on the bench: 'I've done no more than I would for any man.'

'Ah, yes, your obligation as a doctor. But I'm sure we can count on your discretion too,' Mikhailov paused for a second, his lips twitching with amusement, 'comrade.'

Hadfield looked at him impassively, refusing to be drawn. Kibalchich stepped forward with his jacket and coat:

'Thank you, Doctor, thank you.'

'Remember, Nikolai – take your friend to a hospital.'

They followed him to the door of the apartment. Kibalchich was drawing the bolts back when Mikhailov caught his arm.

'A moment,' he said, turning to Hadfield again: 'We owe you thanks too for helping Anna with the informer.'

'What informer? I don't know what you mean.' Then it came to him with a little shiver of disgust. 'The drunk at the clinic? You murdered him!'

'No,' said Mikhailov coolly. 'He was executed by an agent of the executive committee.' He paused again to be sure he held Hadfield's eye. 'The party has a long arm, Doctor.'

He dropped his hand and nodded to Kibalchich to open the door. But Hadfield did not move. For three, four, five seconds, he stared at Mikhailov, making no effort to hide his distaste. Then he turned away and walked out of the apartment and out of the house.

As he walked he could feel the man's shadow at his back, or was it his subtle poison? What was he being drawn into? Every day new threads were binding him tighter to The People's Will, small favours, small deceptions, the fine silk of intrigue woven into a web he would not feel until he was trapped, without independent thought, and with no hope of escape. It must stop.

'Do you trust him?'

'He seems to be a good doctor.'

'That wasn't what I meant.'

'I know,' said Mikhailov with a small smile. 'Of course I don't trust him.' He was standing in the makeshift laboratory gazing at the instruments shattered by the charge. 'He's a sentimental liberal,' he said, picking up a spatula from the workbench and rolling it thoughtfully between his thumb and forefinger. 'But Anna has him wrapped round her little finger.'

'Oh?' There was a puzzled look on Kibalchich's face. He was an unworldly sort of revolutionary, first and foremost a scientist, his true passion not politics but rocketry, but the party was fortunate to have such an accomplished explosives engineer.

'I suppose she's an attractive woman,' he ventured after a little thought.

'Yes, she's an attractive woman,' said Mikhailov tersely. 'But we must consider your work. The date has been fixed'

He was interrupted by a low moan of pain from the bedroom. The ether had worn off at last. The injured man groaned again and in a dry sticky voice called: 'Nikolai, I'm going to be sick.' A few seconds later they heard Valentin retching and whimpering with discomfort.

'You need more help,' said Mikhailov. 'We have four days and we need all the explosive we can manage.'

Kibalchich nodded slowly. 'Will the cellar be empty long enough to connect the charge?'

'Our friend has invited the workmen he shares with to celebrate his engagement at a tavern nearby.'

'He has a fiancée?'

'No, no, my friend,' said Mikhailov, slapping him on the back good-humouredly. 'At six o'clock he'll tell them he's going to fetch his fiancée, but he'll go to the cellar and light the fuse.' He stroked his beard thoughtfully for a moment. 'We'll have a fiancée close by in case things go wrong.'

But nothing could be allowed to go wrong. It was the perfect opportunity. The tsar, his sons, the entire imperial family gathered about a table to eat off fine china and drink from crystal twinkling in the candlelight, and below them – three hundred pounds of dynamite. The People's Will be done.

# 26

For once Anna had arranged to meet him in person and in a public place, trusting to darkness and the inclement weather. It was snowing heavy soft flakes she could reach up to and catch in her open hand. Beyond the cemetery railings, the tombs of the great, the dome and towers of the Alexander Nevsky Monastery were merely indistinct shadows on a billowing sheet of snow. She pulled her scarf tighter about her nose and mouth and stepped out of the light to rest her back against the railings. It was almost eight o'clock. It would be too dangerous for her to wait for more than a few minutes, but not since his first visit to the clinic almost a year ago had he been late for a meeting. Sure enough, the droshky slithered up to the cemetery gates before the monastery clock began to chime the hour.

Hadfield jumped down and kissed her on both cheeks. Then pulling off a glove, he gently wiped the flakes from her eyebrows with his thumb. 'I thought skating and then dinner?'

'Let's just eat.'

'Fine. Hey, Vanka – Baskov Street.'

The driver – a bear of a man in his thick furs – nodded sullenly, showed the whip to his horse, and a moment later they were gliding along Nevsky. Hadfield reached for her hand and gave it an affectionate squeeze. 'I've missed you.'

'But we only saw each other two days ago.'

'Yes. But I missed you.' He was a little aggrieved. 'Haven't you missed me?'

She laughed and shook her hand free, pulling the fur rug to her chin: 'It's going to snow like this for days.'

The restaurant was a simple whitewashed cellar a short distance from the Preobrazhensky barracks, and a number of the regiment's officers were drinking and bantering noisily at its tables.

'Are you comfortable here?' Hadfield whispered as he helped her with her coat.

'Yes, this is all right.'

They were shown, at his insistence, to a discreet table in a corner where Anna sat with her back to the rest of the restaurant. The waiter took their order and brought a bottle of rustic wine Hadfield declared to be undrinkable.

'We must have something better,' he said, clicking his fingers for service. He was on edge, fiddling with his napkin, the cutlery, the stem of his glass, smoothing his hair with the palm of his hand.

'What is it?' she asked, leaning forward.

He looked up and, catching her eye, gave her a weak smile. 'I have acquired two new patients.'

'What do you mean?'

'Your . . .' he paused to let a waiter sweep past, 'your comrades called upon me again. The unfortunate Valentin has injured his hand in an explosion.'

'Is he all right?' she asked mechanically; she barely knew the man.

'He'll have to learn to write with his left. But,' he looked at her sternly, 'I don't want you or your Alexander Mikhailov or any of your other "friends" to think they can call on my services.'

'What do you mean? Isn't it your job to help the sick?'

'Yes. But I don't want to be drawn into your conspiracies. The explosives laboratory, the informer murdered at the clinic . . .'

'Executed.'

'So you knew about that.'

'Keep your voice down!' she hissed. 'This is not the place to talk.'

'No one can hear us.' He tried to reach across the table for her hand but she drew it away.

'You're afraid,' she said contemptuously.

'No. That's not true. I don't believe killing anyone will change things for the better in this country. And—'

He stopped abruptly as the waiter approached with their Shchi and bread. As the soup was served, Anna was conscious of him trying to make eye contact and of his foot reaching for hers beneath the table. But she was boiling inside. Did he think so little of her? She had taken a solemn pledge to dedicate her life to the people. After a few seconds she picked up her spoon then banged it down again: 'I must go.'

'Why?'

'I must go.'

'Not until you explain why. I'm not going to let you just run away.'

'I can't explain.'

'Try.'

'Because our struggle means more to me than you do.'

There, she had said it. Why had he pushed her? He flushed as if slapped in the face, took a deep breath and lifted his eyes to the ceiling for a moment. Then, drawing the napkin from his lap, he screwed it into a tight ball and dumped it on the table. 'You don't have to choose,' he said at last. 'Look, you're right, we can't talk here.' And he waved the waiter across.

But it was still snowing hard outside and Anna could tell from his expression that he was no more enthusiastic than she was about the prospect of wandering the streets.

'Come to my apartment,' he said.

'I don't think that's a good idea.'

They did not speak and the silence was broken only by the steady crunch of their footsteps in the snow. Anna gazed with envy into the bright halls of the mansions they passed and at the chinks of light between their drawing-room curtains, the tantalising suggestion of warmth and refuge from the street. Why had it become a battle? She knew she was being unreasonable and she was sorry, but her feelings frightened her.

As luck would have it, there was a droshky waiting at the district gendarmerie.

'Stay here, I'll call him over,' said Hadfield.

'You take it. I can't afford it anyway.'

'For God's sake!' he said, exasperated. 'If it makes you happy, we can both use him.'

'Where shall I tell the driver to take you?' he asked when they were sitting in the cab. She hesitated, reluctant to commit herself, and Hadfield took her silence for lack of trust.

'I don't mean your address, just where you want to be left,' he said irritably.

'No, no, I wasn't trying to – oh, anywhere. The Tsarskoe Selo Station,' she said, flustered.

He leant forward to give instructions to the driver, but before he could speak, she clutched his hand and gave it a tight squeeze. And he turned to look at her with a smile.

'Well? Where to?' the driver demanded bad-temperedly.

'The Church of St Boris and St Gleb.'

Later, as they lay together on the mattress, his knee between her thighs, his chest warm to hers, rising and falling almost together, she wondered how she would find the strength to turn him away when the time came. Was it a mistake to have shared this intimacy, to have sought and accepted love? She watched him dozing, his auburn hair tousled about his face.

He stirred, opened his eyes and, after gazing into hers for a few seconds, he leant forward to kiss her tenderly. 'There's something I must tell you,' he whispered.

'Please. Let's just be happy.'

He smiled and raised his hand to her brow, smoothing away the deep crease between her eyes with his thumb.

'Do you remember in the restaurant that I said I had two new patients? I must tell you of the other one.'

A letter had been delivered to the hospital from a man called Dobrshinsky who wanted to consult him on a medical matter and requested a visit at home.

'I was suspicious and contacted my newspaper friend, Dobson. It seems this man is a special investigator at the Third Section.'

'Why didn't you tell me sooner?' Anna exclaimed, raising herself to her elbow.

He rolled on his back and looked up at her with a wry smile. 'We didn't get further than Patient Number One, if you remember. And what difference does it make?'

'What difference? He'll ask you about me and the party,' she said crossly.

'Yes. And I'll lie.' He tried to pull her down but she wriggled free.

'What will you say?'

The story he told to Major Barclay of their meeting at the clinic, he said, his respect for her work as a nurse and his shock when he heard she was a terrorist. 'Please stop worrying. I'm a respectable member of the medical bourgeoisie. The cream of Russian society is happy to place its life in my hands.'

'I don't think you should go. He could arrest you.' She was tense, but tried to smile.

'He wouldn't invite me to his home if he was going to do that.' He paused and reached up for her again: 'Come here.'

And this time she let him pull her down. And he kissed her, tenderly at first and then more fiercely, his hands kneading her back and buttocks until, breathless with excitement, he entered her again. And when they had both reached a climax and lay still in each others arms, he whispered, 'I love you.'

'You will be careful, won't you?' she said.

He did not reply.

# 27

For all Hadfield's confidence the night before, he was full of apprehension as he was shown up the stairs to the special investigator's apartment. Collegiate Councillor Dobrshinsky's well-groomed valet took his hat and coat – carefully brushing the ice crystals from the collar – then led him from the hall into the study and informed him that His Honour would be with him shortly. Hadfield tried to ease his nerves by peering at the books that lined the walls from almost floor to ceiling. It was a catholic selection that included volumes he was sure the censor considered unsuitable. Conscious that his choice might interest the investigator, he deliberately pulled an anodyne history of the Empress Catherine from the shelf and was pleased when he found a reference to his great-grandfather, the first General Glen.

'Do you enjoy reading, Doctor? I'm sorry, I surprised you.'

Hadfield turned quickly to find his new patient at the door. 'You did, sir. I read a good deal.'

Dobrshinsky closed the door quietly and stepped into the body of the room. 'What are you reading?'

Hadfield told him, mentioning his great-grandfather.

'Ah, yes,' said Dobrshinsky with an amused smile. 'And how is General Glen?'

'Are you acquainted with my uncle?'

'I have had the honour of being introduced, yes.'

'He's well, thank you.' Hadfield inclined his head. 'Now,' he said, 'how may I be of assistance, Mr Dobrshinsky?'

'Anton Frankzevich, please,' said Dobrshinsky. 'My man will

bring us some coffee.' Lifting his tailcoat, he eased himself carefully into one of the leather library chairs in front of the desk, indicating with a casual wave that Hadfield should take the one opposite. He was immaculately dressed in a dark brown suit and black tie, his hands beautifully manicured, but his face was thin and there were dark rings about his eyes, his skin an unhealthy grey. Hadfield wondered if he was a little anaemic or taking strong medicine because his pupils seemed abnormally small.

'May I ask who recommended me to you?'

The special investigator did not answer at first but gave him a cool, appraising look, small dark brown eyes fixed on his face. If he was hoping to intimidate he was doing very well. Hadfield bent down to his medical bag and began searching inside it for a journal.

'Surely you can guess, Doctor,' said Dobrshinsky at last. 'You told one of my colleagues that you were a friend of the chief prosecutor's.'

'One of your colleagues?'

'Major Barclay.'

'I see. You're a policeman. I think I may have mentioned Count von Plehve's name, yes,' Hadfield said, rising from the bag with his journal. 'Now perhaps you can tell me what you think the problem may be – your symptoms?'

'The problem?' Dobrshinsky gave a little laugh and, with a dismissive sweep of his right hand, brushed a fleck of dust from the knee of his trousers. 'Please excuse me, Doctor, but the problem is not really with my health but with yours.'

'Oh?'

'It seems you've been keeping dangerous company.'

'You mean Anna Petrovna?' Hadfield interrupted. 'I explained to Major Barclay: she was an able nurse and I know nothing more about her than that. Naturally I was shocked to hear she was wanted by the police.'

'Quite so. Quite so. But you didn't mention to Major Barclay that you attended an illegal gathering, that there were a number of terrorists wanted by the police there, one of them the Kovalenko woman.'

Hadfield leant forward. 'I've never knowingly been in the company of terrorists. I'm a doctor . . .'

'We all need doctors, don't we?' Dobrshinsky replied with an amused smile.

'You don't seem to need me,' said Hadfield haughtily, 'but I have patients who do.' He bent again to his medical bag as if preparing to leave.

'Aren't you ready to help our investigation, Doctor?'

'I can't see how I can.'

'Do you know Madame Volkonskaya?'

'Yes.'

'Then you will remember her political salon.'

'I do remember a rather disagreeable afternoon at her home,' Hadfield said calmly. And he described briefly the gathering and the discussion, but without mentioning the names of those who were there.

'So you admit there was talk of the attempt made on His Majesty's life?'

Hadfield gave a short laugh. 'There was talk of that in every home in the city.'

'Do you think of yourself as a Russian?'

'I think so, yes.'

'And a loyal subject?'

'Yes,' he lied.

There was not a flicker of emotion – anger, disbelief, disappointment – in the investigator's face. He was a patient man – that much was apparent – but Hadfield detected something else, a certain distance in his manner he could not entirely explain.

'Would you inform the police if you knew someone was trying to kill His Majesty?

'Yes.'

'Who spoke up for the assassin?'

'A small Jewish fellow called Goldenberg. Red hair. Voluble.'

'He remembers you too.'

'I should hope so. We argued about the attempt to murder His Majesty.'

'But you didn't see fit to inform the police?'

'I thought he was a hothead but essentially harmless.'

The investigator clucked sceptically: 'Goldenberg is a murderer.' He clearly did not believe a word of Hadfield's story, and for another half-hour he snapped question after question at him, dismissing his man servant with a wave when he dared to interrupt with the coffee. Did the doctor expect him to believe he had not seen Anna at the salon? What about the meeting at the opera? Questions, questions. Hadfield batted them back with either an angry denial or a sad, incredulous shake of the head: 'Are you going to accept my word or the lies of a murderer?' he asked eventually.

'Don't you think a murderer capable of the truth?'

'An interesting question to debate at length, Anton Frank-zevich, but you have spent an hour trying to prove I am a terrorist, so there really isn't time.'

'Simple questions, that's all, Doctor,' Dobrshinsky said, his thin lips twitching with amusement.

'If you're not going to arrest me for having had the misfortune to accept an invitation to the wrong sort of party then you must excuse me,' Hadfield replied. 'You see, I generally charge for my time.' He paused. 'But perhaps you would like me to examine you? You don't look well.' He bent again to his medical bag. There was nothing more likely to distract and worry a man than a doctor's professional concern.

'That isn't necessary. I'm in good health,' said Dobrshinsky irritably.

'As you wish,' said Hadfield, easing himself out of the low library chair.

The special investigator rose, too, carefully smoothing the creases from his tailcoat. What a peculiar fellow, Hadfield thought, fastidious, with a lawyer's eye for detail but – what else? He had a certain louche quality.

'Have you read Mr Dostoevsky's *The Devils*?' Dobrshinsky asked. His smile was disingenuous.

'No,' Hadfield lied again.

'You must.' Dobrshinsky walked over to the bookcase to the right of the fireplace and took out two volumes.

'But I can buy my own copy.'

'No, I insist. You can return it. I think you'll find it illuminating. In particular, the ease with which clever people can be tricked by the unscrupulous acting in the name of principle.'

In the street outside, an image began to form in the back of Hadfield's mind.

At first it was diffuse, like sunlight through a morning mist. By the time he had hailed a cab, it had sharpened into the recollection of an evening in Zurich in the company of a young man with a pallor and distance very like the collegiate councillor's. As the evening had progressed the student had become agitated and his thin body had begun to shake uncontrollably.

Hadfield's exclamation so alarmed the driver he brought his cab to a halt.

'Is something wrong, Your Honour?'

Of course, he had treated cases since; Dobrshinsky clearly exhibited some of the symptoms. If he was a betting man he would have placed money on his diagnosis – the tsar's special investigator was addicted to opium.

# 28

'It's ready.'

'It's ready?'

'Didn't I say so,' Khalturin snapped at her.

'Then what do we do now?' Anna asked, turning to the figure at her side.

'We wait.' Andrei Zhelyabov's voice shook a little with excitement. He took a deep breath to steady himself. 'You may have to go back with Stepan to the tavern. His friends are expecting his fiancée.'

After weeks of living on his nerves Stepan Khalturin was unable to keep still for a second, treading the snow about them into a hard crust. Anna could not see his face. Both men had pulled their hats low over their eyes and Khalturin was muffled in a black woollen scarf. They had met close to the workman's entrance to the Winter Palace and she had watched as they hurried across the square towards her, their heads bent low against the driving snow. It had barely stopped in three days, shaping a new monochrome cityscape with peaks of snow and ice rising from the rivers and canals, the streets unfamiliar, the smallest journey a trial.

'How long?' Anna asked.

'Five minutes at most,' said Khalturin, his voice strained and unhappy.

'Did anyone see you in there?' Zhelyabov asked, resting a large gloved hand on the carpenter's shoulder.

'There was one man looking for some tools. The rest are in the tavern waiting for me.'

'Calm yourself, my friend, calm yourself,' and Zhelyabov placed his arm about his shoulders. 'We have only a few minutes to wait and then we'll be away.'

They stood in restless silence in the shadows beneath the arch in the General Staff Building, fidgeting with hats and gloves, glancing every few seconds at Zhelyabov's pocket watch. Ministry officials and soldiers scurried past in search of shelter or a cab to take them home. Anna watched the fuzzy glow from the lighted palace windows and tried to imagine the scene in the dining room; the footmen gliding about the table with wine and silver serving dishes, the flutter of excitement at the door as the butler whispered sharp instructions to the servants – perhaps there was someone to taste the emperor's food for poison. She blinked, then looked away as another image flitted through her mind – the eruption from below, splintering mirrors and the crystal chandelier, tiny stabbing pieces of glass whirling in a dusty vortex. Would there be children at the tsar's table? She shuddered at the thought. Taking it for nervousness or the cold, Zhelyabov gave her forearm a reassuring squeeze.

'Any minute now, Anna, then we will—'

But before he could finish his sentence there was a sharp orange flash and the palace plunged into darkness. A throaty rumble like thunder split the heavy white silence, rolling across the square towards them.

'Oh God,' Khalturin muttered. 'Oh God.'

Seconds only, then silence again. They could see nothing but the silhouette of the building through the snow falling steadily, a soft blanket over all.

'We must leave now,' said Zhelyabov, turning quickly from the palace.

But Anna could not move. She watched, transfixed, as soldiers poured into the square from the barracks buildings close by and began to form a cordon about the commandant's entrance.

'Come on!' Zhelyabov tugged at her arm: 'Come on.'

They walked towards the Nevsky, not daring to glance back again. Police and soldiers hurried past. In the distance they could hear the clanging of fire bells.

'You've done it, my friend, you've done it!' Zhelyabov whispered to the carpenter. 'I congratulate you.'

But Khalturin's face was rigid, his eyes fixed on a point directly ahead. Anna could see he was close to collapse.

'Think what people will say!' Zhelyabov continued. 'We have struck at the evil heart of this empire – believe me, my friends, we have shaken the world today.'

What reply could she give her comrade but a polite nod and a smile? If it was a blow for liberty and justice, why did she feel so very sad?

The tsarevich was still at the door of the main guard room when Anton Dobrshinsky arrived twenty minutes after the explosion. The heir to the throne looked like a wraith in the candlelight, his uniform, his face and beard grey with dust.

'Appalling,' he muttered, and taking Dobrshinsky for a medical man, urged him with trembling voice to do what he could for the wounded.

The air was thick with choking smoke and dust and the sulphurous smell of dynamite.

'More light – at once!' Dobrshinsky shouted to no one in particular.

It was evident from the coughing and heart-wrenching groans – someone was screaming uncontrollably – that the guard room was full of injured and dying men. As his eyes adjusted to the darkness, he could see that the force of the explosion had blown a huge hole in the floor, tossing granite paving slabs to the sides of the room. Chunks of plaster and rubble had collapsed into the cellar below.

Behind him he heard General Gourko, the governor of the city, coaxing the tsarevich to leave for 'the good of the empire'. 'Your Highness, there is nothing you can do here.'

A troop of firemen arrived with a doctor and began to pick their way through the ruins of the room. By the light of their torches, Dobrshinsky could see figures trapped in the debris – to judge from their dusty uniforms soldiers of the Finland Regiment. Among the smoking mounds of stone and plaster, arms and legs, the ragged white remains of those blown apart in the explosion. And on the walls, black stains where they had left their bloody shadows.

'More light, for God's sake!' barked the governor. 'Is that you, Dobrshinsky?'

'Yes, Your Excellency,' he said.

'A damn mess. A little more dynamite and they would have wiped out the imperial family. This granite floor . . .' the general prodded a broken slab with the toe of his boot, 'saved them – this and a little discourtesy. You know the Yellow Dining Room is directly above us?'

'No, Your Excellency.'

The hero of the battle of Plovdiv looked uncommonly fierce in the flickering torchlight: 'What on earth are you chaps at the Third Section doing? This is a disgrace.'

'Regrettably, I'm not responsible for security within these walls, Your Excellency,' the special investigator replied coolly.

'If you'd caught these madmen they wouldn't have been able to carry out an attack,' replied the general, pulling distractedly at his large moustache. He turned back to the chaos of the room, bellowing orders to the rescue party, anger and frustration ringing in his voice. Judging there was nothing to be discovered in the rubble while the wounded were the first concern, Dobrshinsky made his way up the dark marble staircase to the first floor and into the dining room. One of the gas chandeliers was still burning and he could see by its light that the blast had blown open the windows, the draught drawing in flurries of snow and stirring the smoke that hung in a sulphurous yellow layer about the room. The carpets and furniture were covered in dust, and fissures had opened up in the plaster ceiling and walls. China and crystal had been shaken from the table and lay in sad splinters about the floor, but he noticed that none of the chairs had been pulled away, which suggested no one had taken their place for dinner. General Gourko was right: the terrorists had hoped to wipe out the tsar and his immediate family. The bomb must have been planted in the cellar with a timing mechanism, something like a Thomas device. Perhaps a soldier – or more likely a workman – but how had he managed to smuggle so much explosive into the palace undetected? It was fiendishly clever. If anyone was still foolish enough to underestimate the audacity and skill of these people after the train bomb, this would serve as a rude awakening.

'Can I help Your Excellency?'

A young footman, his uniform and hair thick with dust, had slipped into the room with the silent discretion of the better sort of servant. In answer to Dobrshinsky's question, he confirmed the tsar had not sat for dinner at the appointed hour but had been kept waiting by Prince Alexander of Hesse who had been late arriving at the palace. This impropriety on his brother-in-law's part had probably saved the lives of the emperor and his family.

There would be questions, changes, Dobrshinsky thought as he made his way carefully down the dark stairs. Those who gave thanks to God for saving their emperor were unlikely to ascribe the failure in security to his hand too. There would be many – like General Gourko – who would account the Third Section responsible. The clamour for vengeance and arrests would be deafening.

266

A crowd was gathering beyond the cordon in the square, and some simple souls were singing a hymn of praise to the Virgin, standing in the driving snow with their heads bent in thanks for the deliverance of their tsar. Were these the people the terrorists were acting in the name of? Dobrshinsky wondered. Mikhailov, Figner, Perovskaya – what did they know of the will of the people? He elbowed his way roughly through the cordon and walked quickly across the square to where his carriage was waiting in front of the General Staff Building. The driver was shivering on the box, nipping surreptitiously at a bottle of vodka wrapped in brown paper.

'The House of Preliminary Detention, and quick about it,' Dobrshinsky barked.

He would not leave the Jew's cell until he'd squeezed every last drop of advantage from him. Every last drop.

The wounded began arriving at the Nikolaevsky in the hour after the explosion. Sixty casualties, soldiers and palace servants, severed limbs and broken bones, severe blast burns and shock. Frederick Hadfield assisted as a colleague operated on one of the soldiers – no more than nineteen years of age – his chest crushed by falling masonry, his right leg attached by only a white sliver of bone. His chances of survival were slim: a tall fair-haired Finnish soldier who would die because he had the misfortune to be on duty at that hour. Had The People's Will given him a thought? Hadfield wondered. No one was sure how many men had died in the guard room or how many would die of their wounds in the days to come. And yet not a hair of the tsar's head had been harmed in the attack. On the hospital wards the wounded could hear the city's bells rejoicing at his escape. For most of the evening, Hadfield was too busy to give it more than a passing thought, but there were moments – restraining a man with agonising burns over most of his body, and at the bedside of the young Finnish soldier – when he found himself trembling with anger and guilt.

At a little before eleven, the superintendent of the hospital visited the ward where most of the injured were being treated with General Gourko. In a stentorian voice he informed them they would be receiving a royal visitor within the hour and no one was to leave the hospital.

'The tsar or tsarevich,' one of Hadfield's colleagues whispered. 'The governor wouldn't be here for anyone else.'

The corridors echoed with shouted orders as guards were posted on the neighbouring wards and at the entrances to the hospital wing. The beds were given fresh covers, porters arrived to scrub the floor, clean uniforms were issued to the nurses and the doctors straightened their ties and brushed their tailcoats. Hadfield could sense the excitement of those wounded men who were conscious enough to be aware of the preparations. What would Anna say if she could see them refusing pain relief or a sleeping draught lest they miss an opportunity to greet their tsar?

A short time later, the regular beat of military steps and the presentation of arms signalled the arrival of the royal entourage. Hadfield stood to attention as the superintendent had bidden them to do for the Emperor of All the Russias. And then the man Anna and her comrades called a tyrant, the despot, the divine villain, stood before them tired and bent, his face drawn and an unhealthy yellow. He cut a lonely figure in the doorway with his staff a respectful step behind, and for a moment he seemed uncertain what he should do. Collecting himself, he turned to speak to the hospital superintendent, then walked with him to the bed of the nearest wounded soldier. After a few minutes he moved on, stopping and talking to each man in turn, regardless of whether they were capable of replying, pressing a small olive wood cross into their hands. And as he moved closer, Hadfield found even his own heart beating a little faster, caught up in the reverence of the room, the mystery of monarchy.

'Your Majesty, may I present Dr Frederick Hadfield?' said the superintendent. 'The nephew of His Excellency, General Glen.'

The emperor acknowledged Hadfield's bow with a weak smile and said in French: 'Can you understand such a thing, Doctor?'

'No, Your Majesty.'

The emperor stared at him for a moment and Hadfield was struck by the softness, melancholy perhaps, in his large brown eyes. Then he turned to the Finnish soldier in the bed beside him. 'Poor fellow. Is he badly injured? Please give him this when he recovers consciousness.' He took one of the crosses from the superintendent and placed it on the cover.

'Your Majesty,' Hadfield said with another bow.

The tsar moved on, passing from bed to bed until he stood at the door again. After exchanging a few words with General Gourko, he glanced wearily to the ward for the last time before he turned to leave. Hadfield picked the little wooden cross from the bedcover and placed it on the soldier's pillow. The young man's face was livid and stiff, his body heaving then falling back, air rasping in his throat as he fought for breath. Badly injured? He would never know his emperor had stood at his bedside. By the morning he would be gone.

It was almost two o'clock in the morning when Hadfield left the hospital, and for the first time in days the night was still and clear, the sky frosted with stars. He stood for a few minutes at the entrance, grateful for the sharp air in his lungs and its prickle on his face. He could hear the muffled drumming of hooves in the street, shouted orders and the jingle of cavalry harnesses. The police and army had secured the city's main thoroughfares in a show of strength, just as they had done after the first attempt on the tsar a year ago. The journey home would be painfully slow, with questions to answer at half a dozen checkpoints. But he had no mind to go there anyway. He wanted to walk quickly, hard exercise to free his mind from a confusing fog of thoughts and feelings. Walk, walk away from the hospital and wounded soldiers, the tsar and those who sought to kill him, walk and keep walking.

He was not sure how he found his way to Malaya Italyanskaya Street or quite what drove him there at that late hour, but he was relieved to see the lights still burning in George Dobson's study. They had seen very little of each other in recent weeks. Hadfield had spent most of his evenings either in Anna's company or more usually waiting to hear from her. His friend was in love too – or infatuated – with a 'graceful creature' called Natalya, a dancer with the Mariinsky Company. Was she with him now? Hadfield was too empty and tired to feel anything but indifferent to the embarrassment he might cause.

Fortunately, Dobson was writing his account of the attack on the palace. He stood at the door in his shirt sleeves, a cigar smoking between inky fingers.

'Goodness gracious, Hadfield, you've heard the news!'

'Yes. May I come in?'

For a moment, he stared at Hadfield distractedly, his eyes glittering with excitement, lost perhaps in a half-written line. Then, 'My dear fellow, of course,' and he stepped aside to let him pass. 'What on earth are you doing here at this hour?'

'Working late.'

'Ah.'

Dobson ushered him through to the study, sweeping papers from a chair and reaching for a bottle of claret that he confessed he had almost emptied already. Words began to tumble tipsily from him. The tsar almost murdered in his own palace – all of

Europe would be talking of it in the morning: 'Escaped by the skin of his teeth, old boy. The skin of his teeth. The tsarevich too. And dozens of guards killed.'

'A dozen. But many more injured.'

'Oh? What do you know? By Jove, you've come to give me more of the story,' he said, slipping behind his desk and picking up a pen. 'Good of you. Is this from your uncle?'

'The wounded were brought to the Nikolaevsky.'

'With what sort of injuries?'

Hadfield told him what he wanted to know, of the deaths and the wounded and of the tsar's visit.

'He looked ill, you say? Who wouldn't? He's not even safe in his own home,' said Dobson. 'Uneasy lies the head that wears a crown.'

'Isn't that how it should be?'

'Please, Frederick, don't attempt to explain or condone this.' Dobson laid down his pen and leant forward to fix Hadfield with a disapproving look. 'You know they found the body of a student on the Neva yesterday, his throat cut, almost covered in snow. The terrorists said he was an informer and executed him in the name of the people. Tsar, student, soldier – no one who stands in the way of these Jacobins is safe. Don't be sentimental. They're murderers.'

'I am not going to defend that sort of terror,' replied Hadfield.

'What puzzles me is how on earth they managed to get away with it.' Dobson shook his head in disbelief. 'My contact told me the police raided one of their apartments two months ago and found a plan of the palace and dynamite. It's criminal negligence. A drop more?'

Rising from his chair, he crossed the room to a glass-fronted bookcase from which he took another bottle of wine. It was open and Dobson pulled the cork with his teeth.

'He says he's met you, by the way.'

'Who?'

'My contact in the Gendarme Corps.' Dobson stepped forward and leant over Hadfield to pour a little more wine into his glass. 'His name's Barclay. He's well connected.'

Hadfield must have jumped a little because his glass clinked against the neck of the bottle.

'Careful,' said Dobson, grabbing his hand to steady the glass. 'Yes, Barclay said he ran into you by chance in a village. One of these nihilist women was teaching at the school.'

He collapsed into the armchair opposite and stretched his legs towards the embers of the dying fire. For the most part, their conversation had been good-natured and bantering, but Hadfield could sense the atmosphere was subtly changing. Of course it was late, Dobson was tired, impatient for his bed, but there was something else; a different note, an almost imperceptible shift in tone, a slyness, as if Hadfield was no longer just a friend but a subject too. Dobson's bonhomie was of the practised kind, the easy familiarity of the skilful correspondent. He could sense the journalist scrutinising him surreptitiously over the rim of his glass.

'They didn't catch her.'

'Who?'

'I believe her name was Anna, Anna something. I have a note. Barclay says she worked at a clinic for the poor in Peski.'

Hadfield caught his eye and stared at him belligerently, daring him to say more. But Dobson ignored him and, rising to his feet, picked up the poker and began to stir the fire.

'Yes, George, I did know her. She worked at the clinic. And, yes, I did visit her house. Barclay clearly told you as much.'

Dobson did not reply but kept prodding the ashes. The little of his face Hadfield could see betrayed no emotion. For a few seconds the silence was broken only by the lazy ticking of a clock and the rattle of the poker against the grate. Then, with a casualness that sounded forced even to his own ears, Hadfield said, 'Anna Petrovna was a very capable nurse.'

Dobson held his hand for a moment, the poker hovering above the grate, then he began playing with the glowing splinters once more. Hadfield watched him, embarrassed by his clumsy deception. It was so much harder to tell a half truth to a friend than a bare-faced lie to a policeman. All the more so when he was aching to be completely frank.

With nothing more in the fire to reduce, Dobson lifted the poker on to the stand and slumped back in his chair. But almost at once he sprang forward again, hands together, forearms on his broad knees, an intense frown on his face.

'Look, Frederick. I don't know if you're involved in something you shouldn't be, something illegal . . .' He paused for a few seconds to allow for a denial, but Hadfield offered none. 'As a friend, I'm telling you – cut all contact with these people, with the clinic, with her, if she is the only one you know. To do anything else would be madness. After the attack on the palace – well, I don't need to tell you. Frederick, are you listening to me?'

'Yes.'

'Are you?' The correspondent was squirming at the edge of his chair, his eyes bright and fixed on Hadfield's face. 'You know your uncle will not lift a finger to help you?'

Hadfield felt weeks of anxiety and doubt rising inside him, a barely suppressed torrent of feelings. He wanted to tell Dobson everything. He wanted to say he loved her with a whole-hearted passion that left him powerless to pursue any other course. Feeble-minded, shameful, yes, but, but . . . 'She was an excellent nurse.'

Dobson looked at him scornfully, his lips pursed as if sucking something sour, then he leant back abruptly in his chair in a gesture of resignation. They sat in uncomfortable silence for a while, avoiding eye contact, Dobson spinning the stem of his glass on the arm of the chair.

'Sleep,' he said at last, rising quickly to douse the lights. 'You know your way to the other bedroom.'

273

'Yes. Thank you, George,' Hadfield said with quiet emphasis, 'for everything.'

Dobson turned to look at him with a warm smile. Then, with a small shrug of the shoulders, 'Remember what I've said, Frederick – that will be thanks enough.'

# 29

It was the distant but unmistakable crack of a gunshot. Anna shuffled closer to the window and gazed furtively into the street below. Gendarmes were scurrying for the cover of doorways and yards. Someone was shouting. She stepped back for a moment to collect her thoughts, breathing deeply to calm herself. She had come within a hair's breadth of being caught inside a security cordon but the police had taken her for a passerby and directed her away. Entering the back of a building in the neighbouring street, she had found a stairwell with a view over the Sapernaya and had watched with rising panic as the gendarmes took up positions. It was a little after six o'clock in the morning and her comrades would have been in their beds. There had been shouts, a hollow thumping, someone inside the flat had smashed windows – the glass showering into the snowy street below – and then smoke had begun pouring from the sitting room. Her comrades must have barred the door and were burning their identity papers and the forged travel passes Anna was to have collected that very morning.

Crack. Another shot. Then another, and more shouting. Anna knew it was her duty now to leave and warn the rest of the party, but her step faltered as the crash of rifle fire reverberated in the street. The gendarmes were now firing through the door of the flat.

It was still dark, the streets almost empty, more so than was customary at that hour. A mad collective fear gripped the city, rumours of attacks to come – bombs in stations and cathedrals and galleries – and the authorities were encouraging people to stay at home. It was harder to move freely, with police and soldiers patrolling the prospekts and at every major junction. She had lost the anonymity of the crowd. Anxious to avoid the main thoroughfares, Anna hurried along alleys and through open yards, pausing every few minutes to check no one was following her. By the time she reached Troitsky Lane it was after seven o'clock and the city was beginning to stir. Stopping a little short of the mansion, she turned into an open doorway and waited in the shadows. Only when she was satisfied she was still alone did she step up to the house, and – after glancing up to find a parasol in Mikhailov's window – she tugged the doorbell.

The gaslights were burning low in his drawing room and the maid had lit the fire. Even at that hour, Mikhailov was immaculately dressed in a dark suit and burgundy tie. He listened to Anna without emotion, his face expressing not a flicker of surprise or regret. All of them had felt downcast since the tsar's escape – all of them but Mikhailov – even this calamity he had taken in his stride. Every day that had passed since had brought worse news, of supporters arrested, a small press seized, safe apartments raided. But nothing seemed to ruffle Mikhailov's smooth feathers.

'That's the fifth address in four days,' he said, rising to his feet. 'I thought we'd dealt with the problem.'

Anna stiffened a little. 'You mean you executed the wrong man?'

'Of course not,' he replied, his lips twitching a little in a sardonic smile. 'Would you like something to drink?'

He walked to the corner of the room and began busying himself with the samovar. 'It's strange we've had no warning from the Director. I think it's time I spoke to him, don't you?' He poured a little hot water into his silver pot then spooned in some tea. 'These raids have damaged the party. We won't be able to make another attempt for a while. Some sugar?'

'No thank you.'

Mikhailov walked over to where she was sitting, the glass of tea almost lost in his large hand. He stood in front of her, square and solid like a country squire, gazing thoughtfully into the fire: 'The tsar has appointed Loris-Melikov as minister of the interior in charge of security. He's a wily old Armenian bird. Things will be harder. We're going to have to plan more thoroughly. We've been taking too many risks.'

He placed the glass on a small table beside Anna and turned back to the samovar. 'Too many risks.'

His words made her uncomfortable. Was he trying to suggest Frederick was a risk? Life lived in the shadows meant every word was to be doubted, every action a conspiracy, one had to be ever vigilant, ever watchful. Spies, informers, curious neighbours, frightened comrades – it was hard to prevent suspicion creeping like a cancer into every corner of your life.

'You were careful, weren't you?' Mikhailov had stepped over to the window and was gazing into the lane.

'Yes. Of course,' she replied hotly. 'Is something wrong?'

'Perhaps.' He took a step away and began peering round the drape.

'What is it?'

'I wonder who Viktor has befriended.'

'Your dvornik?'

'Yes.' For a few seconds more he stood glancing up and down Troitsky and across at the mansion block opposite. Anna was on the point of rising to join him at the window when he turned abruptly to her: 'Grab your coat.'

'What is it?'

'Do as I say.' Reaching over to the desk drawer, he removed a revolver and slipped rounds and some powder in his jacket pocket. Then he stepped over to the drape again and carefully lifted the dainty pink parasol from the window. 'Ready?'

'What about your papers?'

He drew a small leather case from beneath the desk. 'Here,' he said, slapping the revolver against it. 'I am always prepared for unwelcome visitors.' He took his heavy black coat and a high hat from the hall and led Anna out on to the landing. 'It may be nothing,' he said in a low voice as they walked swiftly down the stairs, 'but I think I've seen Viktor's new friend before. Round-shouldered, hand constantly at his mouth, he looks like one of the agents who followed me from the Haymarket a few months ago. Best not to take chances.'

At the bottom of the stairs, Mikhailov paused at a window over-looking the yard, then beckoned Anna to follow him into the servants' corridor. But instead of leading her to the rear entrance, he took a key from his pocket and opened the dvornik's door.

'What if he brings the gendarmes?'

'He won't bring them here. He doesn't know I have a key.'

The room was a windowless box, the only furniture a low bed, a rough plank table and chairs. On the wall above the bed a small dark icon of Virgin and Child, and a number of prayer cards, one bearing the face of the tsar. Snatching up a rag from the table, Mikhailov wiped one of the rustic chairs and sat down. 'This place stinks of cabbage.'

They sat in silence for half an hour, Mikhailov with his eyes closed, arms folded complacently across his chest; Anna fidget-ing anxiously in a chair by the stove. At last they heard the dvornik coughing like a sick horse as he shuffled along the corridor. Rising quickly from the table with a lightness of step surprising in such a large man, Mikhailov took a position to the left of the door. A moment later, the rattle of the key in the lock and it swung open to reveal Viktor in his padded winter kaftan and fur hat.

'What . . .' His jaw dropped at the sight of Anna beside his stove.

'Come in and close the door,' she hissed at him. 'I've a message for you.'

The old man pulled a face, his little eyes almost disappearing beneath his brow, in two minds whether to do as he was bidden. Then, judging himself a match for a petite young woman, he took a step inside.

'Hello, my friend . . .' said Mikhailov, placing a heavy hand on his shoulder. The dvornik flinched as if from a blow, and his face creased with fear: 'Alexander Dmitrievich . . .'

'The same. Now, Viktor . . .' Mikhailov turned the old man's bent shoulders firmly about so they were facing each other. 'Who was that ugly fellow you were speaking to in the lane?'

'He was . . . he was very interested in you, Your Honour,' the dvornik stammered. 'He said you were a—' The sentence died in his throat.

'Does he have friends with him?'

'I saw one, Your Honour. He said more . . .'

'. . . are coming?'

'Yes, Your Honour.'

'Then we have no time to waste,' said Mikhailov, turning to address Anna. Pulling the revolver from his coat pocket, he broke it open. 'You're going to stay here in your room, Viktor, aren't you?' Snap. The cylinder clicked back into place. The dvornik nodded vigorously, his eyes fixed on the gun, his right hand pulling anxiously at his beard. 'You won't disappoint me?' Mikhailov asked quietly, and he placed a firm hand on the old man's shoulder again.

'No, Your Honour. No.'

'Good fellow. And you haven't seen us, have you?'

'No, Your Honour.'


The yard was empty and there was only one set of footprints in the snow.

'You must leave first. Keep walking, whatever happens. Do you understand?' There was an iciness in Mikhailov's voice, in his heavy-lidded eyes, a subtle change that left her in no doubt as to his intention.

'Yes. I understand.'

'Go then,' he said, and stepped away from the door.

She walked quickly, her gaze fixed on the wicket in the old carriage gate, silently repeating a small prayer – 'Please God there is no one, please God' – a tight knot of fear in her stomach. Crisp fresh snow beneath her feet, her breath a little short, yes, please God it would end well. But there was someone. A shadow at the gate. Caught by the morning sun streaming through cracks in the planking. He must have heard her footsteps and was ready. Her only hope was that he would take her for a maid. She pulled her scarf a little higher and, with her heart in her mouth, stepped through the wicket into the lane. She was aware of him only feet from her but turned the opposite way. Before she had gone more than a few steps he was at her heels.

'Hey, miss.' He spoke with rough authority like an army sergeant. 'Stop there.'

But Anna ignored him and walked briskly on as Mikhailov had instructed her to do. She began to pray again: frantic, inarticulate, a jumble of feelings and words.

'Stop!' He clutched at her sleeve, then her shoulder. 'Now!'

She pulled away but he held her and she was forced to turn, his face close, a beard streaked with grey, and beneath his navy blue cap, rheumy brown eyes. Older than his voice.

'Let go of me! Who are you? Help, someone!' She tried to turn from him.

'Police.'

Out of the corner of her eye she saw him pull a revolver from his pocket.

'Stop. Now.' He rammed the barrel into her side. As she crumpled in pain, he grabbed her shoulder again, dragging her to the wall: 'Bitch.'

Furious, she lashed out, striking him in the throat.

'Bitch.' Instead of trying to turn her, he pushed her face to the wall, forcing his body against hers. And she whimpered in pain. He was breaking her neck.

'Stop fighting, bitch.'

She could smell his stale tobacco breath, his body hard against hers. And then the crack of the revolver. For two, three seconds, she was deaf and blind and she sank to her knees. His body lay in the snow beside her, a plume of blood about his shattered head, mouth open, the eyes of a fish, and her face wet with his blood. She was shaking uncontrollably, gasping, but Mikhailov was dragging her to her feet, pulling her away.

'Oh, God. I knew . . .'

'There is no God. Now come on or they'll take us,' he said and shook her. 'There's a place a few streets from here.'


Experience taught it was best at such times to lay low, but for once Mikhailov felt obliged to ignore good practice. At dusk he went in search of the Director. He smiled at the relief on Irena Dmitrievna Dubrovina's face as she let him quietly out of her apartment. She had been reluctant to take him into her home. It was impossible, too dangerous, she had told him. Not only was it possible, it was imperative, he had replied, and quickly too before the police caught them on her doorstep. Poor Madame Dubrovina. She had almost collapsed when she heard from a neighbour that an agent had been shot in broad daylight a few streets away. She had dismissed the servants, drawn the blinds and taken to her bed chamber. But that had suited them well enough. Anna had bathed then soaked the blood from her coat, and now she was sleeping in a fine French bed with thick cotton sheets, a fire in the grate. What had come over her in the street? Mikhailov was surprised by her weakness. It was something new. Was her resolve weakening?

Mikhailov pondered this question for some while. It troubled him as he slid to and fro on the seat of the badly driven droshky, and it was still troubling him when its grumpy driver deposited him at last in a snowy street close to the Director's flat.

The Director rented his rooms in a large house divided and sub-divided many times, home to tradespeople, the better sort of prostitute and civil servants of the lowest class. In such a place it was easy for a stranger to climb dark stairs unmarked by the occupants. Nikolai lived alone on the fourth floor, between a tailor and a junior bank clerk.

Mikhailov was quite sure he would be alone. It was impossible for a man in his delicate position to be anything but alone. 'I've been expecting you,' the Director muttered, and he stepped away from the door to let him pass.

'I don't like coming here. It's not safe,' Mikhailov replied.

He sat on the edge of the Director's narrow bed and watched him pour a glass of black tea from the chipped pot on the table. His hand was trembling, his eyes bloodshot. The tiny bed-sitting room was thick with dust, the windows almost opaque, and there were dirty plates on the table. Newspapers and books were roughly piled on the floor against one wall, leaving space for no more than the low bed, two wooden chairs, the table and an unemptied chamber pot.

'Doesn't the maid clean for you?'

The Director shook his head: 'It's too risky, especially now. They suspect, you know.'

'You?'

'They know they've got an informer in the police or the Third Section.'

'How can you be sure?'

The Director pulled a face, then pushed his little round glasses up his nose with a grubby index finger. 'Dobrshinsky isn't prepared to trust anyone outside his inner circle. He won't tell us anything. There's a poisonous atmosphere at headquarters.'

'What are you doing?'

'I'm just doing as I'm told and keeping my head down.' He got to his feet a little unsteadily. 'I need a drink,' he said and walked round the table and out of the room, returning a minute later with a small bottle of vodka and two cloudy glasses.

'Drink?'

Mikhailov shook his head. 'There have been five raids in as many days. There was an agent at my apartment . . .'

'Was it you who killed him?'

'Who's helping them? Is it one of our prisoners?'

'Weren't you listening?' the Director asked tetchily. 'I don't know. One of the prisoners may have been broken, of course. Dobrshinsky is handling everything personally. Nothing is committed to paper.'

'And you don't have any idea who he's spoken to?'

'The only person I know for sure he's spoken to is the English doctor,' the Director said with a dismissive wave. He sat down opposite Mikhailov and poured himself a glass of vodka: 'But what can he tell them?'

Mikhailov frowned. 'When?'

'About two weeks ago. He visited Dobrshinsky's home. That's all I know. There's no report of their conversation – at least, if there is, I haven't seen it.'

Mikhailov leant forward a little, his large hands clasped together, his eyes glittering in the candlelight. 'I think perhaps I will have that drink, my friend.'

The Director poured vodka for them both. 'Perhaps they're using the Englishman as a channel,' said the Director quietly, turning his glass on the table. 'I suppose you've considered that?'

'Yes.'

The bottom of the glass tick-ticked like a broken clock as he turned it slowly against the chipped wood. A drunk was shouting incoherently in the room above; the crash of a chair and, a moment later, the light beat of a woman's shoes on the stairs.

'What will you do?'

'What will I do?' Mikhailov fixed the Director with a cold stare: 'Whatever needs to be done. Don't I always?'

# 30

Frederick Hadfield was in his carpet slippers and dressing gown when the dvornik knocked at his door with the note. His heart leapt with joy and relief. For all the lateness of the hour, the regret, the shame he had felt since the explosion at the palace, he was desperate to be with her. But he took no pleasure in the necessary deception; it was no longer an adventure. Since the interview with Dobrshinsky he was sure he was under surveillance, and he presumed the dvornik had been instructed to report on the hours he kept and on his visitors. Dressed as a doctor and with medical bag and coat he made his way noisily down the steps to the front door. Sure enough Sergei the dvornik was there to greet him with an obsequious bow.

'Is everything all right, Your Honour?' He pushed his fleshy face, flushed with drink, towards Hadfield's.

'Acute myocardial infarction,' said Hadfield. 'A serious case.'

The dvornik looked at him blankly. 'Does Your Honour wish me to summon a cab?'

But it was an emergency, no time to waste. Hadfield brushed past him and into the snowy street.

The city's clocks were striking midnight at St Boris and St Gleb's, and half past the hour by the time he reached the rooming house door. The old Ukrainian lady greeted him with a warm wrinkled smile. The rest of the building was sleeping. Anna was curled beneath a thick feather bedspread he had not seen before. He knelt beside her and swept a strand of hair from her face. She looked tired and there was an angry graze high on her right cheek. He took off his clothes and lay on the mattress beside her. And she turned to him with her eyes closed, lifting her chin, an invitation to kiss her full on the lips.

'You were so long,' she whispered sleepily.

'What happened to you? You must let me look at your cheek.'

She smiled. 'My personal physician.' And she pressed closer, sharing her warmth, her head upon his arm, his thigh raised between her legs. 'Things are so difficult, I wasn't sure you'd come,' she said.

'Yes.'

'What did you tell that man Dobrshinsky?'

'No more than we agreed.'

'Good.' She leant forward to kiss him, plucking playfully at his bottom lip with her lips. Then she said, 'But you must be even more careful. They won't leave you alone.'

'I know. He knew much more than I expected. Your friend Goldenberg has changed sides.'

'That's not true!' she said sharply, pulling her head away to look him in the eye.

'I'm sorry. It is true.'

'Did Dobrshinsky say so? How can you be sure?'

'I'm sure.' And he told her of his conversation with the special investigator. She listened with a deep frown of concentration, propped on an elbow, her eyes an intense darker blue in the candlelight.

'But that only proves he told them about you,' she said. 'He must have thought they wouldn't hurt you.'

Hadfield raised his eyebrows sceptically. She fell back on the pillow beside him, a hard expression on her face.

'Don't shoot the messenger,' he said, reaching up to stroke her hair.

'What?'

'Nothing.'

'It explains everything.'

'Does it?'

'I must tell the others. I should go.'

'For God's sake!' he exclaimed. 'I've only just got here.'

'Shsh. Someone will hear you.'

Their faces were inches apart, her chest rising and falling against his chest, his leg pressing her pelvis, and yet, and yet, it was as if they were drifting away from each other, the confused feelings of the last days creeping between them.

'I spoke to the tsar,' he said.

'What?'

'He visited the hospital after the explosion. I helped treat some of the wounded.'

She closed her eyes, her face stiff, even hostile.

'I helped to remove the leg of a young Finnish soldier, but he died in the night.'

'Please, Frederick, don't.'

'Why not? Is it so hard?'

'I'm going.'

'As you wish.'

But she made no attempt to rise, and he did not relax his hold upon her.

'Come away with me. Leave this madness,' he whispered, pulling her closer, his cheek to hers. She winced with pain.

'Is that such an awful thought?'

'No. No. It was my cheek.'

'Then say yes.'

'I can't, Frederick. You know I can't, I can't . . .'

'Then what do you want from me?' he asked coldly. 'This? Is this all I am permitted to share? A damp mattress?' Anna did not reply, and after a few seconds he pulled away a little to study her expression: 'Well?'

Still the stubborn, passive silence. A darkness in which resentment, unhappiness, despair might breathe.

'Do you love me?' He wanted to shake her.

Her face stiffened with anger and she opened her eyes and stared at him: 'Yes.'

'Why was it so hard to say? Then let's leave this country.'

'No. I have a duty to my friends and my people. A higher duty.'

'A higher duty?' He laughed bitterly. 'Some might call it a passion for martyrdom.'

'Be quiet,' she hissed.

'What about those soldiers at the palace – my young Finnish soldier, or the student they found murdered on the ice? What about those people?'

'Keep your voice down!' She gave him an angry shove. 'You should go.'

'What sort of country will you build with your terror? A place where anyone who stands in your way is judged to be an enemy of the people?'

'Shut up.' She pulled away so no part of her was touching him, but he shuffled closer again, reaching out for her shoulder.

'We can be our own country.'

'Go!' She pushed at his chest.

'What's more important?'

'I'm going, then.' She began to rise, pulling the bed clothes with her to cover her nakedness. He could see she was lost in an angry mist and quite beyond reason. She did not want to look at him. She would not listen to him.

'Don't be silly. I'll go,' he said.

'Don't patronise me.'

'I'll go,' and he got to his feet and began to dress. She had put on her underwear and was struggling in the corner of the tiny room with her dress, determined to stand as far from him as possible. It was comical, and he fought a mad urge to laugh. Look at us, he thought, just look at us.

'I don't think we should see each other again,' she whispered, her back still to him.

'Is that what you want?'

'It is what I want.'

They finished dressing in cold silence. When he was ready Anna picked up the candle and snuffed it out with her fingers.

'That simple?' he asked.

'You leave first.'

'You know I love you,' he said.

'I'm sorry, Frederick, but this is best for you.'

'Don't tell me what's best for me,' he said bitterly, and he stepped across to the entrance and tugged the curtain aside. He glanced over his shoulder at her. 'You know how to find me, Anna.' And the curtain fell back silently behind him.


Anna walked until her chest ached, faster, faster, stumbling in the dark, sliding, almost falling. She walked in a mist, the city streets opaque and confusing, and yet by five o'clock she had found her way back to Podolskaya Street in time to become Elizaveta the Ukrainian maid once more. Hollow, heavy-footed, she climbed to the second floor and let herself into the apartment. The bedroom she shared with Praskovia was at the end of the hall, but to avoid waking her and the questions that would follow she decided to spend what was left of the night on the couch. Staggering like a drunk with the effort, she removed her boots and shuffled slowly down the hall to the small drawing room. The door was a few inches ajar. She gave it a gentle push and stepped inside. The shutters and drapes were closed, the room as black as a coalhole, and she was obliged to use the wall and furniture to grope her way towards the couch. She was on the point of collapsing exhausted on to it when she heard a light scuffing noise and with a shudder of fear she realised there was someone in the room. She could feel him there at the shuttered windows. She began to edge away, every muscle tense, poised to run. Then a blinding yellow flash. He had struck a match.

'You,' she said, trembling with rage.

Alexander Mikhailov lifted the flame to a candle and, rising from his chair, walked over to the stove to light another, the light playing across his face.

'Did I startle you?'

'You wanted to.'

He stared at her, inscrutable like a cat, a face that kept secrets. The room was cold and he was still in his coat and scarf.

'What are you doing here at this hour?' she asked, dropping on to the couch. 'Did you see the Director?'

He stepped over to the door and closed it quietly: 'Yes.'

'And what did he say to you?'

'Have you been with your Englishman?' he asked, settling into the chair opposite.

'That's none of your business,' she snapped.

'Have you been with him?'

She stared at him defiantly, refusing to answer. 'I'm tired. I need to sleep,' she said at last.

His insolent smile made her blush with embarrassment and anger.

'I want to sleep,' she said again and she began to shuffle round, preparing to lift her legs on to the couch.

'Is he still useful?' Mikhailov asked. 'You said he was useful.'

'Yes, yes, he's useful,' she said angrily.

'Keep your voice down . . .'

'The help he gave Valentin – and tonight he told me Grigory had broken and was giving them information. So, yes, he's useful.'

'Goldenberg? How does your doctor know?'

Anna hesitated. 'From the special investigator.'

'Dobrshinsky?'

'Yes.'

'When did he speak to Dobrshinsky?'

'Two weeks ago.'

'And did you know he was speaking to Dobrshinsky?'

'Yes. But I trust him.'

'You trust him?' Mikhailov gave a short laugh: 'You're blind.' He leant forward, his podgy hands together like a judge before a court. 'Your doctor met the special investigator at his home.'

'Why ask if you know? Please, can we talk of this later?'

'What did your doctor tell Dobrshinky?'

'What?' He had pushed her too hard and her fragile temper snapped: 'Everything, everything,' she shouted, jumping to her feet to stand shaking with anger before him. 'Everything. Satisfied?'

He stared at her, the colour rising to his cheeks. 'Sit down and be quiet. What did he tell Dobrsinsky?'

She was too tired to fight him. 'Nothing. He said nothing.'

'You've taken too many risks,' Mikhailov said. 'You've forgotten your loyalty to the party.'

Oh, that's your verdict, is it, Comrade Mikhailov, she thought with disgust.

'It must stop. No one is more important than the party. That is the promise we made each other.'

'It has stopped,' she said quietly. 'I've told him I can't meet him again.'

'Or have any contact?'

'Didn't I say so?' Did he want her to write it in blood? She wanted to cry, to scream, to tear at his smug face with her nails, but she was not going to let him see how hurt she felt.

'We must all make sacrifices,' Mikhailov said, rising to his feet. 'You are a good comrade, Anna.'

She said nothing but watched him cross to the door, turning to glance back at her before he slipped from the room.


Praskovia Ivanovskaia found her later that morning curled on the couch.

'You look ill. You must go to bed at once,' she said, blinking myopically at Anna. And she did go to bed. She lay beneath the covers in her clothes, listening to her comrades about the apartment, the thump of the press, conversation and companionable laughter. She tried not to think of Frederick, but snatches of their conversation kept forcing their way into her thoughts and she buried her head in the bedclothes, her eyes tight shut. 'Is that what you want?' he asked her again and again, and she groaned silently.

She rose at midday and joined the others. They must have been talking about her because the air of gaiety was forced, as if they were trying a little too hard to lift her spirits. At two o'clock there was a knock on the apartment door. Printing stopped at once, a cover was thrown over the press, type and papers were cleared away and the sitting-room door was locked. Anna was sent to receive their visitor. She was surprised to find Sophia Perovskaya on the doorstep. Party members were discouraged from visiting the little print works unless their business was approved by the committee. Anna led her friend into the kitchen and introduced her to the others and they made tea and spoke for a while of the arrests, of foreign newspaper reports and the fear of more attacks that still gripped the city. But Sophia Perovskaya was uneasy, her tiny hands turning in her lap or playing with her glass. The others must have sensed it too because the conversation began to peter out, the awkward silences to lengthen, and there was something close to a collective sigh of relief when she turned to Anna at last and announced that she had come with a message from the executive committee.

'We met this morning, Annushka,' she said, when the others had gone.

'Oh? And did you volunteer or were you instructed to deliver its message?' asked Anna acerbically, her eyes fixed on her friend's face.

'The committee thought it best if I spoke to you,' she replied, reddening a little. 'It would like you to take Stepan Khalturin to Kiev. His nerves are lacerated since the explosion. He's close to a breakdown. After all those weeks at the palace he thinks he's failed us. He can't be trusted.'

'Ha!' Anna exclaimed with an angry wave. 'So the committee wants both of us out of the way.'

'No, Annushka, no.' Sophia leant forward for her hand but Anna refused to give it.

'Don't pretend this has nothing to do with Frederick.'

'Alexander has explained. He thinks it will be easier—'

'For whom?'

'For you. Someone must go with Khalturin,' said Sophia firmly. 'It is the decision of the executive committee.'

'I give him up and now the party wants to punish me,' Anna replied, her voice strained and unhappy. And this time she did not resist when Sophia picked up her hand and gave it a gentle squeeze.

'You're a true comrade, Annushka. There is no one I trust more. It will only be for a few weeks.' And, rising from her chair, she came to stand beside Anna, an arm around her shoulders.

'He loves me, you know.' Anna began to cry, her tears pattering on to the rough table.

'Shshhhh, Annushka.'

But Anna could not control herself any longer. Her small frame shaking, she leant forward to place her head on the table and wept.

# 31

It was an excellent disguise. He looked every inch the gauche impoverished student of the sort to be seen on the streets of the island every day. A good student, but a very poor police informer. Hadfield had spotted him lurking in the yard opposite when he left his apartment in the morning, and he was conscious of being followed to his surgery and then to the Nikolaevsky later that day. And the poor fellow was standing opposite the hospital entrance in the evening, ludicrously conspicuous beneath a street lamp, stamping his feet, slapping his sides, frozen to the marrow. His dogged persistence deserved recognition. Taking a professional card from his medical bag, Hadfield scribbled the name of a restaurant on the Nevsky Prospekt on the back and tipped a hospital porter to present it to him with his compliments.

George Dobson was in the best of humours, delicately executing a conversational *pas de deux* over dinner that led them from the politics of terror to the theatre – 'quite as senseless and brutal' – and to a paeon of praise for 'his lovely' dancer, Natalya. He had arranged to meet her after the performance at the Mariinsky and was anxious not to keep her waiting, unapologetically glancing at his pocket watch every few minutes. 'She is so upset if I'm late. Hope you don't mind, old fellow.'

For once the correspondent's acute powers of observation deserted him and he did not register that Hadfield was out of sorts and drinking heavily. By the time they rose from the table, he was the worse for wear for wine and Dobson was obliged to take his arm and lead him from the restaurant. Hadfield was too befuddled to notice if his police shadow was waiting on Nevsky and quite past caring. He took a cab as far as the English Embankment, then crossed the river by a well worn path over the ice. The freezing air helped clear the claret fumes but not the thoughts of her that filled every idle minute of his day.

It was a little after eleven o'clock when he reached the pier below Line 7 and climbed unsteadily to the embankment. At the top of the steps, he slipped and almost fell back, grasping the wall, his heart racing. Bloody fool. A broken neck wouldn't help. He took a deep breath and walked on, anxious to reach home and bring the day to a close, head bent, concentrating hard on an imaginary line. For once he did not take the precaution of walking in the middle of the street, and after a few paces he was startled by a man who stepped sharply from the darkness of a doorway into his path. Sober in an instant, his body tensed in readiness to fight. Then he recognised the slight figure of his police shadow and he laughed with relief.

'You!' How absurd. 'Dobrshinsky won't thank you for frightening me to death, my friend.'

The informer took a step closer. He had a thin face, serious, clean-shaven, with large brown eyes, his long hair swept back from his forehead. He was dressed in what may once have been a student uniform.

In the seconds it took to look him up and down Hadfield recognised he had made a foolish mistake.

'In the name of the executive committee of The People's Will, you are . . . you—' The student's voice shook uncontrollably with fear. He was fumbling in his coat pocket. A knife? A gun? Hadfield threw himself forward, driving the student to the ground, punching his face with his right hand, pinning his arm to his side with his left. The young revolutionary cried out in pain as his head struck the icy pavement. And Hadfield grabbed at his hair, swinging his head and banging it down hard again.

'You hopeless bastard!' he snarled through gritted teeth, enjoying the power, the excuse to punch, hurt, make the man cry out in pain. 'You hopeless, feeble little bastard.' And he struck him in the face again and felt his nose fracture.

'Does she know?' he shouted, his voice husky with rage. The student began to whimper. 'Shut up, you coward. Does she know?'

But his words were lost as a wave of incandescent pain broke behind his eyes and washed through his body. He must have crashed sideways on to the pavement because, as the pain began to recede, he saw the student lying curled in a ball at his side. Then someone kicked him in the chest and for a second his heart skipped a beat. Voices – two, three men, working men.

'Go on. Finish it.'

Rolling away, Hadfield tried to rise but was thrown back by a crushing blow, a fist like a hammer. One of them aimed another kick at him and in desperation he grabbed the man's boot, trying to drag him down.

Fight. Fight. Don't die. But one of the others kicked him in the back and he let go, gasping for air. Don't die. Don't. It beat in his mind through the pain. And with the strength of fear he began to rise again, clutching at someone's legs, head bent against their fists. They want to crush me. Blow after blow, his head, his sides. They are going to murder me. I'm going to die on the pavement outside the House of Academics. The will of the people. No fear, no pain now, only the jarring of his body and a struggle for breath at the edge of consciousness. And he began to float with Anna, with her playful smile and blue, so blue eyes. But a moment later she was lost to a dazzling light. And then the light was lost to darkness.

'Is he dead?'

'As dead as it is possible to be, Your Honour.'

'Let me see.'

The heavy iron door opened with a squeak and the warder stepped inside with his lamp, the circle of light creeping up the back wall of the cell. Grigory Goldenberg was hanging from the bars of the little window, his head twisted to one side, his tongue lolling thick and blue from his mouth, wispy red hair plastered across his forehead. His eyes had rolled upwards in his last moments, as if he was beseeching his god. He looked like a badly made marionette.

The party's little puppet, Collegiate Councillor Dobrshinsky thought with distaste, a dangerous enthusiast with a craving for active service and an inflated sense of his importance. It had taken time, but he had been able to turn him to good effect. A list of over a hundred names, descriptions, addresses and pages and pages of evidence. Yes, the little fanatic had done him a very good turn. Drenteln had gone but Dobrshinsky stayed, and the new man in charge of the Third Section had given his investigation fresh impetus.

'When?' he asked, turning to the warder.

'No more than two hours ago, Your Honour.'

'Does anyone know why?'

'He heard of the arrests from one of the other prisoners. He said he'd been tricked. Guilt, Your Honour. Guilt.'

Dobrshinsky took a step closer. Goldenberg's life had been choked from him. Only great despair and a supreme act of courage could have driven him to it. A prison towel torn into strips to make a rope, dangling from the bars, his hands loose at his side, his feet only inches from the floor.

'Cut him down and clean up the cell,' Dobrshinsky said, turning his back on the corpse. 'It could have waited until the morning.'

But it was not the end of the collegiate councillor's day. Just as his carriage was drawing to a halt in front of his home, the porter came scuttling down the steps to greet him with a note.

'I was to deliver it as soon as you returned, Your Honour,' he wheezed asthmatically. 'I've been waiting these last two hours.'

'Before I've had a chance to step from my carriage and take off my hat and coat?'

Dobrshinsky pulled off his gloves and, with a hand that seemed to tremble a little, he took the letter and broke the seal. He read it, then sat back in the carriage for a moment, his eyes closed, pinching the bridge of his nose.

'You did the right thing,' he said at last, and he took a few kopeks from his pocket and dropped them into the porter's hand: 'For your trouble.'


Major Vladimir Barclay was waiting for him in the office of the assistant superintendent of the Nikolaevsky, dozing at the stove, an empty glass of tea balanced precariously on the arm of his chair. Dobrshinsky took the precaution of removing it before he shook him gently by the shoulder.

'Anton Frankzevich, Your Honour,' he said, rising blearily to his feet.

'Where is our doctor?'

'His Excellency General Glen was here, and the first secretary from the British embassy,' said Barclay, doing up the buttons of his jacket.

The assistant superintendent had informed him Hadfield was suffering from a severe head injury, broken ribs, bruising to the chest and back and broken fingers. The head injury was causing particular concern.

'And where is the general?' asked Dobrshinsky.

'He's gone home, spitting fire, and says he'll be back in the morning.' Barclay grimaced at the thought. 'He's going to speak to His Excellency, Count Loris-Melikov, and to His

Majesty too. He's convinced the terrorists want to murder him and his family. He's insisting on a police guard. He seems to blame us.'

The special investigator smiled at the aggrieved note in his voice. 'My dear Barclay, surely you didn't expect anything else?'

'Some gratitude, Your Honour. They would have stuck his nephew like a pig if our fellow hadn't stepped in to save him. I tried to tell His Excellency—'

'Tell me.'

Agent Sudeikin of the Third Section had been following the doctor since the explosion at the palace but had lost him that night on the Nevsky Prospekt.

'Not for the first time,' Dobrshinsky observed dryly.

Sudeikin had noticed that a student was following the doctor too but he had not had the wit to associate him with The People's Will.

'And to be fair to Sudeikin, he doesn't look the sort of fellow they would trust with this sort of task,' said Barclay. But the student had three burly factory workers with him who were more than capable of kicking a man to death. Agent Sudeikin had come upon them as they were preparing for the *coup de grâce*, and had fired his revolver, wounding one in the arm and driving all but the student away.

'The doctor gave the fellow such a beating he was not in a fit state to run. He's in a cell at the Preliminary. He hasn't said more than that he's an agent of The People's Will.' Barclay chuckled: 'Looks as if he's been kicked by a horse.'

Dobrshinsky frowned thoughtfully, his head bent a little, staring at nothing in particular.

'It's puzzling,' Barclay offered. 'I was sure he was one of them.'

'Yes,' said Dobrshinsky, turning his sharp little eyes upon his colleague again. 'He was one of them and he was one of us. He's a lucky man.'

'Lucky indeed – they almost finished him off.'

'No, no, Barclay, I don't mean that,' the investigator replied with a sardonic smile. 'My dear fellow, he's lucky because who would dare to arrest him now?'

# 32

The pianoforte was in a drawing room on the floor above but the door was ajar and the deliberate melody of the prelude was ringing on the marble stairs and in the hall. Anton Dobrshinsky stood and listened with pleasure and surprise, for a highly accomplished performance of Chopin was not what he expected to hear in the count's house.

'The fellow from the Conservatory. My wife's invited some guests for a musical soirée.' Von Plehve had come to stand beside him at the foot of the stairs. 'Do you think he's good?'

'He plays beautifully.'

'I'm glad you think so. Her Highness Princess Dolgorukaya will be here, and the British ambassador and his wife.' Von Plehve touched Dobrshinsky's elbow and led him across the hall into his study.

Yellow evening light was pouring through the windows overlooking the Moika, shifting in the swirling smoke from the fire and softening the cold gilt edges of the room. It was expensively but unimaginatively decorated with delicate but uncomfortable furniture and dark Flemish pictures with Old Testament themes.

'I want you to see this before my man delivers it,' said von Plehve, picking up a letter. 'Please,' and he indicated with a casual wave that Dobrshinsky should take the library chair in front of his desk. The letter was marked 'Strictly Confidential' and carried that day's date.

To the Chairman of the Supreme Security Commission,
His Excellency, General Count Loris-Melikov

Your Excellency,

I have the honour to report that I visited this
morning The Earl of Dufferin, the British Ambassador,
and spoke with him for nearly an hour. In the course of
our meeting, the ambassador asked his military attaché,
Colonel Gonne, to join us. I inquired after the health of
the English doctor, Frederick Hadfield, and was assured
he was making good progress. As Your Excellency will
no doubt be aware, Dr Hadfield is recuperating from his
injuries at the home of his uncle, General Glen.

Turning to the matter of Hadfield's contacts with the
terrorists, in particular the woman, Romanko, Lord
Dufferin wished to repeat his confidence in the doctor's
innocence. He also asked me to reassure Your Excellency
that the British government was not involved in a
conspiracy to undermine His Majesty or the Russian
government, and would do all it could to prevent and
condemn terrorist violence. The military attaché, Colonel
Gonne, has spoken to the correspondent of The Times
newspaper in the city. It is the opinion of Mr George
Dobson that the doctor is nothing worse than a liberal.
He described the doctor as a little naïve, and raised the
possibility that he had become infatuated with the
Romanko woman while he was working beside her at a
clinic for the poor.

It seems unlikely the doctor offered any material
assistance to the terrorists and in view of their attempt
to murder him there can be no question of his
maintaining any further contact. Mr Dobson has
undertaken to keep Colonel Gonne informed of the
doctor's state of mind and movements. It is the firmly

*held view of Lord Dufferin that the doctor should be*
*allowed to continue with his work and that an attempt*
*to bring a case against him based on the flimsiest of*
*evidence would damage relations between our two*
*countries. Furthermore, it would be the cause of some*
*consternation in diplomatic and expatriate circles in the*
*city.*

*Your Excellency may wish to consider the doctor's*
*family connection and close association with a number*
*of influential people. I believe His Majesty met the*
*doctor when he was visiting the survivors of the*
*explosion at the palace and has sent him a message*
*expressing his sympathy and appreciation.*

*To conclude, I emphasised to Lord Dufferin the*
*unofficial nature of my representations and was assured*
*by him that our conversation would go no further. It*
*was agreed in the circumstances that it would be in*
*everyone's interests if the political nature of the assault*
*on Dr Hadfield were suppressed and newspapers*
*encouraged to report that he was set upon by common*
*thieves. As Your Excellency observed, 'This is a small*
*cloud that might be left to pass.'*

*I have the honour to be, with the highest respect,*
*Your Excellency's humble and obedient servant,*
*Count Vyacheslav Konstantinovich von Plehve*

Dobrshinsky looked up from the letter and caught the count's
eye.

'It was a delicate business, as you can imagine, but I pride
myself that no one could have managed it with more finesse,' said
von Plehve. 'You can question the Englishman again, of course.'

'I have, already. He had nothing more to say,' Dobrshinsky
replied.

'I hope the terrorists have beaten some sense into him.' The chief prosecutor reached across the desk to offer Dobrshinsky the cigarette box. 'No?' The count took one himself, rubbed it gently between his fingers then lit it, drawing in the sharp smoke with pleasure. 'His Excellency, Count Loris-Melikov, is satisfied that we are making some progress at last, thanks to the Jew's testimony.'

Dobrshinsky frowned and lifted an unsteady hand to his temple. 'We've made arrests but most of the members of their executive committee are still at liberty.'

'But not for long, Anton Frankzevich, I'm sure, not for long. I've told His Excellency that you have them in your sights,' said von Plehve.

Dobrshinsky did not reply but gazed impassively across the desk at him. Was there a more unscrupulous cultivator of connections and influence than the chief prosecutor? he wondered.

'I didn't mention your fear that the terrorists have a well placed informer in the Third Section,' von Plehve said, shifting uncomfortably in his chair. 'I judged it something His Excellency does not need to be troubled with. I am confident you will find him soon.'

Dobrshinsky continued to stare at him, watching as he picked up his pen and put it down again then ground his cigarette into a brass ashtray.

'Well?' von Plehve said, irritably.

'I can offer little hope of detecting the informer at present.'

'Didn't Goldenberg give you clues? What about the other prisoners?'

'The little I have been able to tease from them adds nothing to our understanding. Goldenberg was able to help a little.' Dobrshinsky paused and closed his eyes for a second, pressing two fingers against his temple again. 'No. You see, I think there is only one man who knows the identity of the informer and that is Alexander Mikhailov.'

The chief prosecutor grunted crossly. 'Well, can't you find some way to trap the informer?' he asked.

'We're looking into possibilities. Major Barclay is monitoring the activities of some of our agents,' said Dobrshinsky, choosing his words carefully. Then, after a moment's thought, 'But Mikhailov is the key.'

'I see.' Von Plehve returned his gaze for a moment then rose abruptly to his feet to indicate the interview was over. But he paused at the study door with his chubby hand on the knob. 'You speak a little Polish, Anton Frankzevich, don't you?'

'A little, yes.'

'Are you familiar with the proverb, *Nieznajomość prawa szkodzi*? Ignorance is no sort of excuse. No? Actually, I think it is a peculiarly Russian sentiment.' An easy little smile was playing on the count's lips. 'It pays for those of us in the tsar's service to bear this proverb in mind at all times. I will inform His Excellency of your confidence that the investigation is progressing well.'

A footman helped Dobrshinsky into his coat and handed him his hat. A carriage was waiting on the street to take him to Fontanka 16 but he lingered in the count's hall with an amused expression on his face. The pianist was still rehearsing for the soirée but he was now playing with seditious passion Chopin's 'Revolutionary Etude'.

# 33

The weeks Anna Kovalenko was to have spent in Kiev became months. The empress passed away, the emperor married again and the trees in the Tavrichesky were autumn oak brown, the birch and larch a rich yellow, by the time she was summoned to the capital once more. They had been lonely months, but months of activity. Student meetings, factory committees, speaking to the party's programme, and always only one step ahead of the authorities. While she had been away The People's Will had changed almost beyond recognition. Many old comrades had gone, arrested on information supplied by Goldenberg. In confusion and fear the party had become lethargic, its time and funds spent replacing those awaiting trial in the House of Preliminary Detention. The revolution seemed no closer than it had ever been and the death sentence against the tsar no more than an idle threat. Comrades with experience and fire like Anna and Vera Figner had been summoned back to the capital.

The printing family had abandoned the apartment on Podolskaya, after a neighbour began to grumble of strange banging and shunting noises, and rented rooms at the less salubrious end of the same street, close to the open sewer that was the Obvodny Canal, a stone's throw from the gasworks.

Praskovia Ivanovskaia was in charge of the press now and there were new faces and new rules: no one to write or receive letters, no contact with other party members, no meetings, no social gatherings. 'Things are so bad, Anna, dear. Alexander Mikhailov is trying to prevent more losses.'

The executive committee was fortunate in Praskovia, for she obeyed without question. She was the daughter of a village priest and there was something of the religious ascetic in her manner and appearance. She had a plain face with dark hair that she dragged off her forehead and tied in a tight bun, short-sighted, with spectacles on a chain, a large mouth that turned down a little at the corners. Although she was only twenty-seven years old she dressed in black like a widow twenty years older. No one was prepared to sacrifice more for the party, and she was baffled when others did not show the same stubborn loyalty.

'Olga has left Russia with Morozov,' she told Anna when they were alone together in the apartment for the first time. 'They're living in Switzerland as if they were man and wife.' She paused and leant forward to stare at Anna. 'What is it? Why are you smiling?'

'Olga used to say nothing should come before the party.'

'And Morozov used to talk about the revolutionary spirit, the need to give up selfish love.'

'Perhaps Olga can't help herself,' Anna replied quietly.

'But it's selfish. We pledged our love to the people and the party . . .' Praskovia hesitated, but could not check the resentment that had been building inside her for months. 'Things are not what they were, Anna. No one cares. Look at Sophia and Gesia Gelfman too. We used to be brothers and sisters . . . it's sapping the will of the party.' She closed her eyes and shook her head crossly: 'It's wrong.'

'You don't mean Sophia Perovskaya?'

'Yes. Our Sophia. She's sharing an apartment – a bed – a few streets from here with that bear Zhelyabov.'

Sophia Perovskaya. Anna's friend Sophia. Sophia, the perfect revolutionary. The Sophia who instructed her to leave Petersburg because she was too intimately involved with a man. They had all been so quick to preach, and she had wounded someone she cared for very deeply. If she had asked them why it was so very different for her they would simply have said he was 'not one of us'. And she would have been forced to admit they were right. She tried not to think of him because looking back could serve no purpose. In her months of exile she had come to a quiet acceptance that she would be ruled by the party in all things for the good of the people.

It was Anna who found the cheese shop on the Malaya Sadovaya. A respectable address that would meet the party's needs perfectly. The other premises in the street were occupied by smart residential blocks, prosperous merchants and the better sort of taverns. It was on the corner with Italyanskaya Street, only a few yards from the blue and white Petrine building where the chief prosecutor's clerks prepared cases for trial.

On a blustery autumn afternoon, a sharp northeasterly chasing leaves along the street, she visited the building with Andrei Zhelyabov, rousing the dvornik from post-prandial slumber. A basement with a shopfront and counter, a living room and vaulted cellar, clean, a little damp, annual rent twelve hundred roubles. Subject, of course, to the usual police checks.

They made their report at a secure apartment on Voznesensky Prospekt the following morning. The sitting room was cramped and stiflingly hot and most of the executive committee was forced to sit on the floor. Alexander Mikhailov presided in one of the chairs. He nodded curtly at Anna but offered no sort of welcome. He had put on weight, the buttons of his waistcoat under strain, his beard not full enough to disguise the roll of flesh beneath his chin.

Vera Figner called to her, 'Annushka,' weaving across the room with her arms outstretched in welcome. And a moment later Sophia Perovskaya was at her side, reaching up to kiss her cheek.

'I've missed you, Annushka. So much has happened while you were away.'

'Yes. I've heard a little.'

Sophia noticed her smile of amusement and blushed. 'We're very happy,' she said, glancing over to Zhelyabov.

'And I'm happy for you, Sonechka,' Anna replied.

'Are you?'

'Of course.'

Sophia leant confidentially close: 'I'm not sure everyone feels the same way.'

She was on the point of saying more when Mikhailov clapped his hands and called the room to order. Zhelyabov was the first to speak, his back against the wall, gesturing animatedly, a powerful passionate figure: 'We're all agreed on this new campaign, I know. And we're agreed that our best opportunity will be when the emperor is returning from the Sunday parade.' Stepping to the table, he picked up a simple hand-drawn map of the city and held it up for them all to see. 'The escort usually leaves the Mikhailovsky Manège and travels down Malaya Sadovaya, turning right on to Nevsky. But it can return to the palace along the Ekaterininsky Canal too. We will never know which way it's going to go. If we want to make sure we must use grenades.'

A bombing party would move into position as soon as it knew the route, he explained; three bombers at intervals in case the first grenades failed to explode or missed the target: 'There is one drawback . . .'

'. . . the bomber doesn't stand a very good chance of escape,' Sophia said, completing his thought. He nodded slowly, a reflective frown on his face.

'And who do you propose would lead this bombing party?' Mikhailov asked quietly.

'Me,' said Zhelyabov with a shrug of his broad shoulders. 'I can't ask anyone else to do it.'

An uncomfortable silence settled on the room. Zhelyabov began rolling the map as if no debate were necessary. Sophia stared at him, her small round face stiff and impassive, but her hands turning in her lap. It was Mikhailov who spoke next.

'I think we should consider the other option.' He turned to Anna. 'You've found a shop that might meet our requirements?'

She described the basement in the Malaya Sadovaya to them, venturing the opinion that it would be a simple task to drive a gallery beneath the street. Zhelyabov voiced objections, and it was only after an hour of heated wrangling that they reached agreement.

'So we must try both,' said Mikhailov. 'If we manage to detonate the mine there'll be no need for the bombing party, but with both we can be sure.'

The dvornik was sympathetic, and a picket had been posted in the street, but the committee had met for longer than was wise. Presuming the business to be over, its members began rising stiffly from the floor, stretching aching limbs, brushing dust from their skirts and trousers.

'I'm sorry, but there's one thing more.' There was an ominous note in Mikhailov's voice. 'I have been told the prosecutor is going to demand the death sentence.'

No one spoke. No one moved. It was as if Mikhailov had thrown open the windows and a bitter wind had sucked the warmth from the room. Anna turned to Vera Figner and was shocked to find her close to tears, her hand trembling at her mouth.

'Who are they going to condemn?' Anna asked tentatively.

'The city is alive with it, Annushka,' Sophia replied. 'They've arranged a show trial – Alexander Kviatkovsky, Evgenia and some of the others.'

'They will try to make an example of Kviatkovsky, and perhaps Presnyakov too,' Mikhailov added. 'They found the plan of the palace in Kviatkovsky's apartment.'

A man Anna did not recognise but from his bearing took to be a junior army officer demanded they attempt a rescue. No one bothered to reply. She took a step towards Vera and tried to put an arm about her shoulders.

Vera shook herself free. 'No. It's all right, really,' but she looked cross, almost hostile, angry that anyone should witness a moment of weakness.

After the meeting broke up, Anna took her friend aside. 'Evgenia will be all right, Verochka. They won't execute a woman.'

'What?' she asked irritably, the colour rising to her cheeks. 'You don't understand, Anna. It's not my sister . . .' She opened her mouth as if ready to say more then she closed it firmly and turned with a scowl to hide her pain.

# 34

They told Hadfield not to go. His aunt was concerned it would be too much for him and both Dobson and Colonel Gonne of the embassy were of the view it would be foolish to be seen in court.

'You will only remind the terrorists of your existence. They might make another attempt on your life,' Dobson had told him.

'In court?'

The correspondent had hesitated before suggesting quietly that it would be wise not to show too great an interest in their fate. But Hadfield went anyway.

The gendarmes had thrown a tight cordon round the building on Liteiny Prospekt and were permitting only those with a pass from the Ministry of Justice to enter. Hadfield had twisted Dobson's arm to arrange one for him, and they had gone together on the third day of the trial. It was a grey morning in late October, with the bitter promise of winter in the air, and both he and Dobson were grateful for the warmth and light of the crowded courtroom. Spare, whitewashed and panelled in dark oak, it was an almost perfect square with three floor-to-ceiling windows before which the judges were seated at a low table. To their left, the prisoners' dock, to their right, distinguished guests of the court and the gentlemen of the press, and the public were in a gallery of seats opposite. A full-length portrait of the emperor hung in one corner beneath burgundy and gold drapes. The prisoners – sixteen in number – were brought in under guard, and gendarmes in spiked helmets were posted at either end of the dock and at all the doors of the court. The prisoners were dressed smartly in academic black, but their faces were a sickly prison grey, starved of light and nourishment.

Evgenia Figner glanced over to the public gallery from time to time, but although she must have seen him, she was too clever to show it. She sat at the front of the dock with a look of cool defiance that reminded him of Vera, her features thinner and finer than the last time he had seen her, dark hair tidily arranged in a chignon. The defendants were accused of writing and distributing inflammatory propaganda, and Alexander Kviatkovsky and two other men faced the more serious charge of plotting the explosion at the Winter Palace.

'All sixteen will be convicted,' Dobson had told him. Apart from Goldenberg's testimony, read by a clerk with the lugubrious voice of an undertaker, there was plenty of supporting evidence – dynamite, a plan of the palace, false papers and the party's pamphlets – presented to the court on a table before the judges. At best the defence attorneys were lacklustre, at worse incompetent, as if tacitly acknowledging it to be an open and shut case. From time to time there was mention of those still at liberty – Mikhailov, Zhelyabov, Perovskaya and a woman called Anna Kovalenko.

'Did you see Special Investigator Dobrshinsky?' Dobson asked when the court adjourned at lunchtime. 'He kept glancing over at us. He's sitting over there, to the right of the judges.'

'No doubt a satisfied man.'

'Not until he's got the lot of them.'

'He'll never manage that, George,' Hadfield replied with a weak smile, 'not until Russia changes. Have you read the latest reports of famine in the south?'

Dobson's face crumpled into a pained expression. 'You may be right but really, is it sensible to say so here?'

When the proceedings resumed, Hadfield looked and found the special investigator seated beneath his imperial master, his face as drawn and grey as the prisoners'. He was careful to avoid catching his eye. The afternoon began with a fiery speech from Alexander Kviatkovsky justifying the party's 'red terror' as the only course open to those who believed in democracy and socialism. He was from a good family, he spoke well, and Hadfield was stirred by his passion and conviction but struck too by the futile waste of a young man who would almost certainly lose his life on the scaffold. As for the others, they would be sentenced to penal servitude for life for talking and writing of democracy, calling for the overthrow of a despot. Their heads would be shaven, they would be marched from the St Peter and St Paul Fortress to the station, and from there to Kara in the frozen east. And in time, he knew, this would happen to Anna too.

'All rise.'

The tinkle of a hand bell signalled the end of the court day. The judges were escorted from the room followed by the accused, almost lost within a phalanx of sky-blue uniforms. As the last was leaving, the special investigator slipped between chairs and walked across the courtroom towards him.

'I'm glad you've recovered from your injuries in time to see justice done, Doctor.'

Hadfield acknowledged him with a curt nod.

'Mr Dobson.' Dobrshinsky offered the correspondent his hand. 'I hope you're taking precautions,' he said, turning to Hadfield again. 'I can't rule out the possibility of another attempt on your life.'

'I'm careful,' Hadfield replied quietly.

'A terrible shock, really. You heard, I'm sure: the student was sentenced to twenty years. We're still searching for his accomplices.' Dobrshinsky paused then added, 'and Anna Kovalenko, of course.'

Hadfield leant forward a little to peer at him with scientific interest, a frown of concentration between his eyes.

'You'll be relieved to learn that our sources suggest she is in Kiev,' said Dobrshinsky. 'You may be safe for a little longer.'

Hadfield was careful to let nothing in his expression suggest this jibe had found its mark. His eyes did not flicker from the special investigator's face. Two seconds, three, four. Dobson cleared his throat nervously to break the silence.

'Are you quite well, Doctor?' Dobrshinsky did not attempt to disguise his irritation. Hadfield stared intently at him for a few seconds more, lifting his fingers to his lips as if wrestling with a particularly vexing problem. Then he turned abruptly to Dobson: 'George, you must excuse us. There is something I have to discuss with the collegiate councillor in confidence.'

The correspondent was quite taken aback, but after a moment's hesitation he nodded and took a few steps towards the door. The courtroom was empty but for the clerks gliding across the polished floor, tidying testimony and evidence from the tables.

'Well, Doctor?' Dobrshinsky asked when they were out of earshot. 'How can I help you?'

'Collegiate Councillor, it is a question of what I can do for you.'

'Oh?' Dobrshinsky raised his eyebrows quizzically. 'Do you have information that might be of use to our investigation?'

'No, no,' Hadfield said with a brusque shake of the head. 'In a professional capacity – as a doctor. You see, I have some experience of treating men with your problem – insomnia, stomach pain, a certain weakness of the body, loss of breath – it is a most pernicious habit.'

Dobrshinsky's face tightened in an angry frown, the colour rising for once to his sallow cheeks. After a few cold seconds, he said: 'I can't imagine what you're referring to, Doctor.' He leant a little closer and Hadfield could smell the sickly sweetness of his breath and feel it against his cheek. 'Are you trying to blackmail me?'

'To treat you.'

There was an intensely hostile gleam in the special investigator's eye. 'Be careful, Doctor. The days are shorter. You may not be fortunate enough to escape a second time.' He brushed past Hadfield and – ignoring Dobson – stalked out of the courtroom.

Society had twittered with the story of the handsome young English doctor beaten to within an inch of his life by terrorists. So fearless, so determined to bring His Majesty's enemies to justice, an innocent victim who had treated the wounded after the explosion at the palace. General Glen had given a party to celebrate his recovery, anointing him beneath the martial portrait of his great-grandfather, reading a message of sympathy and gratitude from the emperor. His aunt had tried to persuade him to move from the island to a larger apartment – 'You can afford it. Everyone wants to claim you as their physician.' And yes, he had found himself in the enviable position of having to turn patients away. But he refused to consider a change of address. If anything, he spent more evenings at home, and he had invested a little money in pictures and some furniture to stamp something of himself on the apartment. There were still society engagements on the embankment and at the embassy, evenings with Dobson and at the houses of rich patients, but more often than not he preferred his own company.

It was late one evening and he was sitting in his shirt sleeves before the fire with a book as usual when there was a knock at the door. The dvornik always thumped with the fleshy part of his fist and this was a lighter hand. To be sure, he picked up the small revolver his uncle had given him after the attack and held it to his side.

'Who is it?'

'An old friend from Zurich,' came the muffled reply.

'Come in then, old friend.' He opened the door and kissed Vera Figner warmly on both cheeks.

'Who else were you expecting?' she asked, pointedly looking down at the gun.

'I thought you would know.'

Vera frowned and reached out to rest her small hand lightly on his sleeve: 'What are you talking about, Frederick?'

They were still standing in his hall, Vera in her hat and dark grey cloak. 'I'm sorry. Come and sit beside the fire,' he said, and he led her into the drawing room and helped her from her things.

'Did Sergei the dvornik see you? It's not safe for you here.'

But Vera had been watching the house for some time and had waited until Sergei had stumbled off in the direction of the tavern on Bolshoy Prospekt.

'You look thinner, Frederick,' she said, examining him with a clinical eye. 'How long has it been? More than a year, and so much has happened in that time.'

So she knew nothing of the attempt on his life. He was relieved. 'What has happened, Vera? We are still waiting for your revolution.'

She gave him a disdainful pitying look of the kind that only one full of perfect certainty is capable of giving. 'I don't want to argue with you, Frederick,' she said, 'especially when you've been so kind. Was it difficult to get tickets for the trial? I knew you would manage it.'

'A little. Your note was a surprise after such a long time,' he said with a wry smile.

'I want you to tell me what you saw, what you heard: Evgenia – how is she?' Vera's tone was clipped and matter-of-fact, as if the fate of her sister was no more important than the day's grocery order.

Hadfield studied her for a moment then rose without speaking and stepped over to the drinks tray. 'Can I pour you something?'

She nodded.

He poured a little brandy into two glasses, placed one on the table at her side and returned to his chair with his own.

'Well?' she asked impatiently.

'Evgenia looked a little grey but defiant, of course.'

'And the others?'

For half an hour he answered her questions, describing the proceedings and the evidence in the smallest detail. And he told her of Alexander Kviatkovsky's passionate words denouncing tsarist tyranny and his determined justification of terror as the only course open to the people. As he spoke her expression began to soften, a small affectionate smile, a twinkle of pride, and soon all the questions were of Kviatkovsky. And when he had told her all he could, she sat back in her chair with a heartfelt sigh.

'He means a lot to you?'

'Yes.'

They sat in silence for a while, Vera avoiding his gaze, turning her glass on the arm of the chair. She looked lovely in the firelight, calm, even a little severe, and his heart went out to her because he could sense her quiet pain.

'Is Anna safe?' He had to ask the question.

She looked up in surprise. 'Anna Kovalenko?'

'Didn't you know we were close?'

'No. I didn't. How peculiar.'

'How so, peculiar?'

She hesitated, searching carefully for her words. 'You're very different. Anna is so committed to our cause – and you're from such different families . . .'

He smiled sardonically. 'The provincial aristocrat speaks, and I thought you were of the people now.'

Vera flushed angrily. 'She is a good comrade. You're very different, that's all I was trying to say.'

'And you have no idea if she knew of the attempt to murder me?'

Vera frowned and leant forward, her small hands clasped tightly together. 'You should explain now, Frederick. Who tried to kill you?'

'The People's Will.'

'Don't be ridiculous,' she said with a cross shake of her head. 'This is some sort of delusion.'

'Oh, Vera,' said Hadfield with a mirthless laugh. 'I've suffered from delusions, but sadly this is not one of them.' And he explained to her what had happened. 'The student was taken. He told his interrogator I was to be executed as an informer.'

Vera listened with a pensive frown, perched at the edge of her chair, her gaze bent to the floor. Suddenly, snatching at her skirt, she rose abruptly from the chair. 'I must go. Where's my coat?'

He stared at her, confused by the cold determination in her face, then he stood up slowly and took a step towards her.

'I shouldn't have come here.' Her face and neck were pink, her shoulders twitching a little with barely repressed anger: 'The party will have had its reasons.'

'No, Vera. Weren't you listening?' He was struggling to control his temper. 'Your comrades tried to murder me.'

'There is always a reason,' she said. 'You were an enemy of the people and that is enough.'

'Weren't you listening to me? Where is the woman who used to make up her own mind?' He was trembling with fury now.

'If you don't give me my coat, I'll leave without it,' she said with icy resolution. He stared at her for a few seconds – she would not look him in the eye – then he said, 'I must check the stairs and the street first.'

They did not speak again until he had shown her safely from the house. But at the bottom of the street, close to where he had been set upon, she turned to him with a softer expression and, after a little hesitation, she said: 'I don't think she would have known, Frederick. Really, I don't think Anna would have known.'

# 35

They were the wrong couple to run the cheese shop. Bog-danovich looked the part all right, with his broad face and spade-shaped beard, the colour of a burnished samovar, but he knew nothing of commerce. The executive committee had chosen Yakimova for the role of shopkeeper's wife because of her 'democratic' manner. She had the face of a badly nourished factory girl and an accent that marked her as someone from the Vyatka province. But 'Bashka' – as she was known to all – knew even less about running a business.

It had been open a week when Anna Kovalenko visited it for the first time, and they had already begun work on the tunnel. The Malaya Sadovaya was a busy little thoroughfare with civil servants passing to the justice building at the end of the street, shoppers and crowded taverns. The men working on the tunnel began long after closing and they left before dawn to avoid arousing the suspicion of the neighbouring tradespeople. But Anna went during business hours, her basket of tools covered by a neat little cloth. The shop was empty but for Bashka, who was arranging her cheeses on the counter.

'And how is your husband, Madame Kobozev?' Anna asked, placing the basket on the floor and sliding it beneath the counter with her foot.

'Not as attentive as I would like,' said Bashka, and she burst into an infectiously earthy laugh.

'That's because he's a gentleman – far too good for you.'

'And don't you think women like us have something to teach a gentleman,' said Bashka with a wink and a mischievous chuckle.

'You mean about the rights of working women?'

Bashka chuckled again: 'My rights are very important to me.'

'And your business too, I hope?'

Bashka's face crumpled in a troubled frown: 'Not so good. Spirits are low. I've told them it must spur us on.'

The party was still reeling from the news that Kviatokovsky and Presnyakov would be hanged, and the rest had been sentenced to a lifetime of labour in the east.

Bashka bent low to pick up the basket: 'Can you mind the shop? I'll be back in a minute.'

'Is that wise?' asked Anna. 'I might run off with your cheese.' She was only half in jest. It was not businesslike behaviour: 'What if a customer comes into the shop?'

'Shout. But no one will come in. The only visitors we get are the other merchants.'

She slipped through the door at the back to the cellar, where Bogdanovich was clearing earth from the new tunnel. Anna used the time to examine the shop front, checking the stock, lifting the lids of the barrels. Some of the cheese was hard and barely edible, and a merchant with so little stock would surely go out of business in weeks. If they did not run the place properly and turn in a profit, the other tradesmen would begin to talk.

'Here we are, miss,' Bashka said as she swung her broad hips through the door and up to the counter. 'Some smelly Roquefort for you. It's French.' And she handed the basket to Anna.

'And how much is your French cheese?' Anna asked.

'Whatever you want to give,' she replied with a smile.

Anna shook her head with disapproval: 'Is that what you say to all your customers? Not much of a capitalist, are you? Have you visited the other cheese merchants?'

'No, of course not,' said Bashka.

'Well, you must.' And Anna tried to explain why it was important to behave like proper bourgeois shopkeepers fretting over every kopek, but there was a distant look in Bashka's eyes.

'Vera Figner was here,' she said at last, 'pretending to sell me some Gorgonzola. She wanted to know about you and the Englishman.'

'What business is it of Vera's?' Anna snapped, her blue eyes dancing like sun on hard-packed ice. 'And what do you know of him anyway?'

Bashka hesitated, startled and a little frightened by the vehemence of her challenge: 'There was talk. Your comrades were concerned . . . no one blames you.'

'Blames me for what?'

'How were you to know he was an informer?' Bashka rocked defensively behind her counter.

'Informer? Don't be stupid, he's—' But Anna could not finish. A cold sickness gripped her. 'What has he done to him?'

'Are you all right? Look, sit here . . .' Bashka lifted the counter, dragging a stool to the front of the shop.

'What has he done?' Anna repeated.

'Who?' Bashka was standing in front of her with the stool, pink with embarrassment.

'Mikhailov. What has he done?' Anna reached for her, digging her nails into Bashka's shoulder. 'What? Tell me.'

'You're hurting me.'

But Anna was possessed by fear and a determination to know the truth and she began to shake her, pushing her hard against the counter.

'Please, Anna.' Bashka sank trembling to her knees. 'Please.'

Anna did not reply. Her shoes clicked sharply on the

stone-flagged floor, and a moment later the doorbell tinkled and the shop filled with the bustle of the street.

Alexander Mikhailov was not in the best of humours. He had finished his piece on the execution after midnight and delivered it to the press at a respectable hour of the morning. The police screw was tightening and, but for the urgency, he would not have risked visiting the apartment on Podolskaya Street by day. And so it was galling to find that Anna was not at home. The rest of the printing family were busy with the new edition of *The People's Will* but none of them could be trusted with what would be a most sensitive task. Anna would have been the ideal person to slip in and out of the photographer's shop. He waited at the apartment for a while, drinking too many glasses of cheap black tea, while he considered what to do. All the photographers had been warned by the gendarmes to be on the watch for anything that might be of use for illegal propaganda. A police spy had followed him to the little shop on the Zagorodny and would know he had asked for copies of portraits of Kviatkovsky and Presnyakov. But someone had to pick up the photographs. Copies to Hartmann in Paris, copies to their friends in Berlin and London – a copy to Karl Marx – and copies to all the newspapers in St Petersburg; they needed the pictures by this evening.

The sky was a dingy winter grey, and lazy wet snowflakes that melted as they fell were sweeping along the street. Mikhailov turned up his collar in the doorway then set off at a brisk place. It was lunch time and most of the people he passed were hurrying home in the opposite direction, their heads bent into the wind. At the junction with Malodestskoselsky Prospekt, the stallholders were gathered round a crackling yellow fire with no thought to business. A scantily clad girl, her thin face thick with cheap make-up, stepped on to the street from a doorway and gave him a cold and hungry look. He walked on, avoiding her eye. He would take a cab from the Zagorodny to Madame Dubrovina's comfortable home. Perhaps she could be of assistance. But as he was approaching the end of the street, he saw Anna's neat figure hurrying towards him, the plain burgundy scarf he had given her when they were still friends pulled tightly about her face. She appeared distracted, and had almost rushed past him when he spoke her name.

She stopped, startled, then her expression hardened with contempt. 'You. You – what have you done to him? Tell me.' She spat it at him with a fury he had not known in her before.

'What on earth . . .' For once he was lost for words.

'What have you done?'

'Keep your voice down,' he hissed at her. What was she doing berating him in the street? They would be arrested.

'Don't tell me to shut up. What did you do?' She pulled her scarf away from her face. 'Have you hurt him?' There was a wildness in her eyes.

'No.'

'Liar! What have you done?' She gave him a shove.

'For God's sake, Anna!'

Passers-by were looking at them. He would have to send her away again. She was a danger to the party. Reaching out for her arm, he said: 'Anna, please. I don't know what you've heard, but he's alive. Now can we go somewhere else? This is not the place.'

'Tell me, liar. Tell me now.'

'He was an informer. The executive committee needed to deal with him.' His voice was harsh, matter-of-fact.

'You murdered him.' She tried to slap his face but he caught her wrist and twisted her arm down and she let out a little gasp of pain.

'He's alive, didn't I say so?' he hissed at her. 'Control yourself. Remember the party. Remember your duty.'

'Let go of me, you bastard!' She began to scream: 'Help! Someone please help!'

He let her go: 'Please. He's alive . . . I did what I thought best for the party.'

This time she did manage to slap him with ringing force across the face. 'You did what was best for you.'

'You were blind to the risk you were taking,' he said, touching his cheek. 'The Director was sure he was—'

'Liar,' she said again. 'I will speak to the executive committee. I will tell them the truth. You are a liar.'

She stared at him for a few seconds with an expression of contempt, even hatred, on her face, then walked away in the opposite direction, looking neither left nor right, proudly upright. And Mikhailov walked on too, ignoring the dvornik who had been watching them from a doorway on the other side of the street and the old lady at the curtains of her apartment. He could feel the imprint of Anna's hand on his cheek and he was shaking with quiet rage.

He turned on to the Zagorodny Prospekt and began walking east towards the cab stand in front of the station. But when he reached it he decided to go a little further. His encounter with Anna had disturbed him more than he cared to admit, even to himself. Perhaps the exercise and the cool air would restore his equanimity. A regiment of horse was being put through its paces, kicking up the dirt of the parade ground where Alexander Soloviev had met his end on the scaffold. What had become of the Anna who had hurried from the square with news of their first attempt to execute the tsar? How could she think it was something personal? He was still pondering what he should do with her twenty minutes later, after walking almost the entire length of Zagorodny. Before him was the extravagant yellow and white bell tower of the

Church of Our Lady of Vladimir, and in its shadow the russet-coloured block where the photographer lived and rented his premises. Next to it a busy market was spilling on to the pavement, street traders in traditional belted coats with baskets from the country at their feet, a beardless youth in a tall hat pushing a handcart of rags, a vodka seller offering cheap spirit to a passing work gang. Mikhailov stepped off the pavement into a doorway, where he could observe the entrance to the photographer's studio. Zhelyabov and the others had urged him not to go near the place, but now he was here he could not pass it by. He lit a cigarette and leant against the wall to scrutinise with an expert eye the stallholders and their customers, searching for a furtive conversation, a tell-tale exchange of glances. He was surprised to find that his hand was still shaking. Surely he had always acted in the best interests of the party, even if it meant making difficult choices? He forced himself to put the matter out of his mind.

'Hey, you, want to earn some money?'

The street urchin looked at him suspiciously. He was about ten years old, thin, dressed in a ragged grey coat and battered calf-length boots, his head and hands bare.

'I saw you looking into the window of that pastry shop. This would be enough for something special with cream.' Reaching inside his coat, Mikhailov took twenty kopeks from his waistcoat pocket.

All the boy needed to do was to stand in front of the entrance opposite and look inside the photographer's shop. To collect the money he would have to describe anyone he could see and anything out of the ordinary. 'Make a good job of it and there might even be a little more.'

The boy was back ten minutes later with his grubby palm out. 'Just the old photographer. A woman went in and he took out a big book. He wrote in it and then she left. That's all,' he said with a shrug.

'How do you know he was the photographer?'

'Because I see him every day,' the boy said with a cheeky smile.

Mikhailov paid him the twenty, and ten kopeks more.

The old man was still at his ledger when Mikhailov stepped through the door, and did not look up until he dropped his kidskin gloves on the counter. He lifted his grey head and his expression changed in an instant from an easy trade smile to shock, then something close to abject terror. Before he was able to open his mouth, Mikhailov had turned on his heels and was making for the door. What a reckless fool he had been. He knew he had only seconds. Seconds. Walk out. Keep walking. Someone was moving at the window. He heard the clattering of boots behind him as men crowded into the front of the shop. As he reached for the handle and pulled the door, the bell tinkled cruelly.

'Haven't you forgotten these?'

It was not the photographer's crackly old voice but a policeman's. And there was another on the pavement outside. Mikhailov closed his eyes and exhaled slowly, his shoulders sagging a little.

'You're quite right. I did forget to collect my pictures,' he said, turning back to the shop. 'Fyodor Ivanovich Korvin at your service.'

A burly plain-clothes officer stepped from behind the counter with a gun in one hand and the photographs in the other.

'Major Vladimir Alexandrovich Barclay at yours.'

The doorbell tinkled again and Mikhailov was aware of gendarmes at his back. The plain-clothes agent gave a nod and someone seized him roughly from behind.

'Can I ask what grounds you have for this behaviour?' he asked indignantly.

A gendarme was unbuttoning his coat, checking his jacket pocket for a weapon and his papers.

'What grounds?' Barclay asked, taking a step towards him. 'What grounds? You are Mikhailov. I think that's enough, don't you?'

# 36

'Frederick. It's me.'

She was standing beneath the little silver birch at the entrance to the hospital, her mouth and nose hidden by a burgundy scarf. It was dark – eight o'clock – the ground white with frost, and she was shivering.

'Frederick, can we talk?'

He stood on the path, his eyes fixed on her, patients brushing past his shoulder.

'Yes, all right.' He was surprised by how calm he felt.

She came to stand beside him and she looked up at him, her eyes as blue as he remembered them, even in the gaslight. She tried to take his arm but he shook it free. 'Nurses walk a few steps behind. It will arouse less suspicion.'

He led her to the carriage entrance and, with a friendly word to the guards at the gate, on into the hospital grounds, passing along the perimeter railings, turning right between Blocks 5 and 6.

They did not speak until they reached the neat little garden in the lee of the boiler house wall and could see before them the lighted windows of what was once Department 10.

Anna waited at the door of the second hut while he visited the porter's room and ordered the old man on to the ward. It was oppressively stuffy inside, the stove too large for such a small space, sparsely furnished and lit by a single smoky lamp. The porter had left his supper of bread and pickled herring on the table. Anna took off her coat and scarf and he could see she had made an effort with her appearance. Her dark brown hair was neatly arranged in a plaited crown in the traditional Ukrainian way and she was even wearing a little make-up. Dragging a chair from the table, she placed it facing him with her back turned to the window. They sat in awkward silence for a few seconds.

At last Anna said, 'Well, how are you?'

'As you see.' His hands swept down his body. 'But I'm careful not to present your comrades with another opportunity to finish me off.'

She stared at him solemnly, her eyes large in the dim light, her hands clasped tightly in her lap. 'I knew nothing. I wasn't in the city.'

'Oh?'

'You know that's true,' she said, leaning forward earnestly.

He said nothing, but gave her a sceptical look. He wanted her to feel guilty. He wanted her to apologise. Nothing of it:

'Stop it,' she said crossly, and her eyes were blazing. 'I would never have permitted it, and you know it.'

He could not stop himself from smiling because she was just as he remembered her, so quick to take offence, and like many who have difficulty with words, ready to attack at the first opportunity. 'You keep bad company,' he said.

She looked down at her hands. 'Will you tell me what happened to you?' she asked in a low voice.

He described the attempt on his life to her and the weeks he had spent recovering in hospital and at his uncle's house. 'And so I am above suspicion now – well, almost. I suppose I have your Mikhailov to thank for exonerating me in the eyes of the police.'

'He is not "my Mikhailov".' She paused for a moment, her face working as she struggled to control some strong emotion: 'He's been arrested.'

331

'Arrested?'

'Yes.'

'Are you sorry?'

'Of course I am,' she said indignantly. 'He was a good comrade. It's a terrible blow to the party.'

A caustic remark was on the tip of Hadfield's tongue but he managed to keep it locked behind his teeth.

'I must go,' she said, rising abruptly from her chair. 'Things are difficult. People are frightened. They're executing Kviatkovsky and Presnyakov at the fortress tomorrow.'

Hadfield picked up her old brown woollen coat – it smelt of the kitchen, something a little sharp – and helped her into it.

'I wanted to be sure you knew,' she said, turning back to him. And she smiled at him at last, her full lower lip trembling a little. How could she smile at him like that after so many months?

'Are we going to meet again?' he asked.

She gave him another, a broader smile. 'Of course.'

He bent to kiss her, but she held a finger to his lips: 'Not here against the window. I'll send word.'

They stepped into the corridor to find the porter waiting at the door, resentful he had been put out of his room at supper time. Hadfield reached into his pocket for a rouble. 'The lady's honour, you understand.'

He nodded and pinched it from his hand ungraciously.

At the hospital entrance, Hadfield summoned a droshky from the rank and helped her up the step. 'Where are you going?'

She leant forward to speak to the driver, huge in his padded blue coat and furs: 'How much to the Anichkov Bridge?'

'The usual,' he growled. 'From here – 20 kopeks.'

'Ten.'

She turned to reach out her hand to Hadfield's face and then the cab was gone.

Even before it turned out of sight, Hadfield had summoned

another. He did not stop to think what purpose it would serve until he was rumbling along the Slonovaya Street, drops of rain driving into his face, but he knew he could not bear to let her out of his sight so soon. He was too late. There was no sign of her on the Anichkov. She had probably changed cabs as a precaution. He paid his driver and walked across the bridge with half a mind to treat himself to a supper at the Europe Hotel. It was raining quite hard now, pattering on to the felt of his top hat, and he quickened his pace, crossing Nevsky at the Ekaterininsky Garden.

Stopping before a brightly lit restaurant, he lifted his coat collar and was rearranging his scarf when he saw the reflection of a familiar face in the window. The man was striding along the wet pavement towards him, and although Hadfield could not remember his name he knew he recognised him – and that he had seen him in Anna's company. A big fellow, in his late twenties, with a full brown beard and dressed as a worker in a short coat and peaked factory cap. Hadfield looked away, shifting his position a little so he could follow the man's retreating back. The name sprang to his mind the moment he turned left into the Malaya Sadovaya and disappeared from view. Zhelyabov. Was it a coincidence or was he meeting Anna? Intrigued, Hadfield walked back to the corner, then on into the lane, but Zhelyabov had vanished. The legs of a drunk were protruding from a doorway close by and he could see a couple of bedraggled prostitutes sheltering beneath a carriage arch, but the rain and chill had driven everyone else from the pavement. There were popular taverns on both sides of the lane and he strolled to the bottom, peering through their lighted windows, searching for Zhelyabov among the flushed faces of civil servants and shopkeepers, peasants and prostitutes, but he was nowhere to be seen. Wet and cross with himself for chasing trouble aimlessly about the city, he gave up the idea of visiting the Europe and took a cab home.

The following day Anna sent a message to the hospital asking Hadfield to meet her in the usual place. He found his own way to the lane in Peski, nameless still, dark, rubbish-filled, the rickety wooden homes of the poor clinging to the stone buildings like fungus. The old Ukrainian woman greeted him with a deferential nod and a sly 'you again' smile. And she led him up the stairs to her corner – everything as he had remembered it to be. Anna did not want to talk but kissed him hungrily, pushing him away, drawing him back with her eyes closed, and they made love on the damp mattress and on the floor, her finger at his lips, always in control. And after, he held her, small in his arms, and whispered words of love in English that she did not understand but which made her smile. They did not speak of politics, the past or the future, grateful only for this moment. Then at eleven o'clock she told him she had to leave. He knew better than to ask why. They walked arm in arm through Peski to the cab rank in front of the Nikolaevsky Station. At Anna's suggestion they shared a droshky, but only as far as the Ekaterininsky Garden. There she kissed him tenderly and promised there would be more time together, perhaps a weekend, at least a day. The driver whipped his horse on and, craning his neck over the folded canopy, Hadfield watched her cross Nevsky in the direction of the Malaya Sadovaya. He sat back in his seat. It was none of his business. Better not to know.

He did not hear from Anna for a few days. He spent his hours of leisure in the company of embassy folk, and there was a rowdy evening at an exotic club with some of the younger doctors at the hospital. His feelings seemed to oscillate alarmingly from quiet contentment to a state of jittery excitement that he characterised to himself as a type of neurosis. What if something happened to her? What if she changed her mind about him again? What if . . . ? At one of these fevered times, he found himself drawn to the place he had seen her last: the Malaya Sadovaya. It was a late morning in the middle of

November and the first heavy snow of winter was falling on the city. Wrapped warmly in his coat, his scarf pulled over his face, he took a cab to the end of Nevsky and walked the rest of the way. The taverns on the Malaya Sadovaya were doing good trade even at that hour, its shops with their fine meats and wines and cheeses drawing servants from the best house-holds and even gentlemen of quality. He took a table in a hostelry with a view of the lane and ordered bread and a glass of glühwein, which he sipped without pleasure for half an hour, watching the passers-by with no real expectation of seeing her.

He was relieved to leave the noise and darkness and smoke behind and step into the cold air once more. Opposite the tavern was the vintner's where Dobson bought most of his wine. With a little time to spare, Hadfield visited the shop and was tempted by the silver-tongued sommelier into spending a preposterous sum on a bottle of vintage champagne. 'To cele-brate,' he would tell Anna, although he knew she would frown and complain of the waste. How strange, he thought, I don't even know her birthday. The merchant below the vintner was taking delivery of new stock from a covered wagon, staggering under its weight as he felt his way down the slippery steps to his basement shop. It was parked too close to the vintner's door, the horse stamping and snorting restlessly in the shafts, and Hadfield was obliged to squeeze round to the back of the wagon. The merchant had returned for more and was trying – to the amusement of the old carter – to lift three heavy truckles of cheese at once.

'Hey – give me a hand there,' he grumbled.

But the carter laughed and shook his head: 'Get on with it, can't you see this gentleman is trying to pass?'

The merchant edged towards the basement steps again, but slipped, and the topmost cheese crashed to the pavement.

'Are you going to try and flog that now?' the carter observed with a sneer. 'I'll give you ten kopeks for it.'

The merchant glared at him and slid the remaining truckles back on to the cart.

'Well?' the old man asked. 'What about it?'

'Get lost. It wouldn't have happened if you'd lent a hand.'

Hadfield studied the cack-handed merchant carefully as he scooped ragged chunks of the broken cheese from the snow. The aroma was ripe and strong. Almost everything in his life reminded him of Anna in one way or another, but he could have sworn there had been a hint of it on her coat at the hospital.

# 37

The first time Barclay's agents noticed the man glancing up at the apartment they dismissed it as of no importance. Tavricheskaya was a busy thoroughfare in the evening, with many well-to-do merchants and professional people living in the new mansion blocks that were springing up in the district. The drawing-room lights were burning invitingly, a parasol in the window, and anyone wishing to visit Alexander Mikhailov would assume it was safe to do so. But the man in the official-looking coat sipped at the apartment like a secret drinker, careful not to break his stride for even a second.

Ten agents from Moscow had moved into Mikhailov's apartment, and another on the floor above, two days after his arrest. Their presence was known only to a few, their orders simple: watch, wait, listen and arrest anyone – Major Barclay had placed particular emphasis on that – anyone who called at Number 15/8. Only Mikhailov knew the informer's identity for sure, and he was keeping his mouth firmly shut.

'He won't be coaxed or bullied into an indiscretion – he's too clever,' Collegiate Councillor Dobrshinsky had observed after the first interrogation, 'he's no Goldenberg.' They had no choice but to wait for the Director to break cover.

The dvornik knew to keep his mouth shut and stay away, and in the week they had been there only a maid and a shoeshine had knocked at the door. So there was a flurry of excitement in the two apartments when the man in the service coat returned the following evening and lingered against the railings of the gardens opposite. Tall but stooped, slightly built, he was wearing a fur hat and most of his face was covered by a black scarf.

He bent to fiddle with his laces, glancing up at the apartment as he did so. After a minute he rose, stepped off the pavement into the road, hesitated, then walked quickly away.

'He'll be back,' Agent Marusin observed when Barclay visited him later in the evening. 'I'd wager he's your man.'

'But you couldn't see his face?'

'He was careful about that. The only thing ...' Marusin paused, 'now that I think of it, he was wearing spectacles.'

'You're sure of that?'

Yes. Marusin was quite sure. And on reflection he thought the fellow may have needed thicker lenses because he had peered at the apartment then bent very low over his boots, craning forward as some very short-sighted people do.

Barclay stiffened, his mouth set firm and the hard little lines about his eyes narrowed, but he refused to been drawn into speaking his mind.

He returned in the middle of the following day, slipping into the yard through a building in the parallel street and making his way into the mansion block by the tradesman's entrance. He had disguised himself as a labourer with a peaked cap pulled low over his face.

The apartment had been turned upside down by the Moscow agents, and the drawing-room floor was littered with broken furniture, books and propaganda leaflets. Sweeping more from a chaise longue, Barclay lay back with his eyes closed to wait for dusk, and was asleep in minutes. It was almost nine o'clock when he was woken by angry voices. Marusin and his colleagues were playing Skat for kopeks. One of them had accumulated a tidy sum and to the annoyance of the rest was preparing to leave the game.

'I didn't bring you here for this,' Barclay barked at them, cross with himself too. 'Shut up and put the cards away.'

The apartment was cold, the agents hungry, and it was plain the spirits of all but the lucky card sharp were low. Marusin reported no sign of their man.

'All right then, ask the landlady for food and send the dvornik up to light the fire.' Barclay picked up his coat in readiness to leave. 'I don't think you'll see our man now, but keep the noise down. Clear?'

The wind buffeted him as he stepped into the dark yard, drops of ice pricking his face, and in the lee of the buildings opposite he paused to adjust his scarf. His modest apartment was only a few streets away in the Smolny district. Mikhailov had been a neighbour. Hands wedged in the pockets of his short coat, he walked on with eyes bent to the icy pavement, his thoughts of home and the sharp words his wife would have for him when she saw him dressed as a common labourer. But he had gone only a few hundred yards when he heard someone shout and, looking back, he saw one of the Moscow agents running down the lane towards him. The wind whipped his words away but the urgency in his voice was clear enough. Barclay stood and waited, his fingers round the butt of the revolver in his coat pocket.

'We've got him, sir,' the man panted, his head bent over his knees. 'He arrived as soon as you'd left. Tried to get his gun out but Agent Marusin caught him a good blow.'

Barclay hurried back along the lane and into the mansion block, taking the stairs two at a time. An agent was at the apartment door and he brushed past two more in the corridor.

'He's in the bedroom, sir.' It was Marusin.

'Has he said anything?' Barclay asked, struggling to catch his breath.

'Only that he's one of ours and we should let him go. He refuses to give us a name.'

Barclay stood in the hall for a minute, breathing deeply, his hand on the door knob. Then, with his face set hard, he turned it and stepped inside.

Agent Nikolai Kletochnikov was sitting on the bed with his back to the wall, a bloody handkerchief clasped to his nose, his broken spectacles on the bedspread beside him. He lifted anxious eyes to Barclay's face for a second then looked away.

'I thought it might be you,' said Barclay, and to his intense annoyance there was a tremor in his voice. 'You left me for dead in the student Popov's apartment. I knew you were a coward, now I know you're worse.'

Kletochnikov looked up at him again, and this time Barclay read defiance and something close to hatred in his face.

'A traitor? My loyalty is to the people and to my real comrades,' he said quietly.

Only the collegiate councillor's strictures to avoid unnecessary violence held Barclay's hand. Oh, how dearly I want to see this creature brought down, he thought. I want to grind my boot in his face. 'Get him out of here,' he barked.

'Where to?' Agent Marusin inquired.

'Fontanka 16, of course.' Barclay's eyes were fixed on Kletochnikov's long white face. 'Everyone is anxious to meet the Director. But keep your hands off him – for now.'

Dobrshinsky tired of asking questions and receiving no answer and moved Mikhailov to the Peter and Paul. It was the nineteenth of November. Mikhailov did not know the date until he arrived beneath its white arch: a year to the day since the attack on the tsar's train. Inside the curtain wall the low scaffold where Kviatkovsky was executed for his part in the plot was thick with snow, ropes still hanging from the beam. Beyond Peter's cathedral, the grim face of the fortress proper and the gate to the prison. They led him in chains between a row of soldiers into a guardhouse, and from there across a small courtyard to the ravelin in the outer wall.

Rags for binding his legs, a filthy grey and brown smock,

peasant shoes and an unlined sheepskin coat saturated with the stale sweat of many.

The penance cell was lit by a shaft of light from a small barred window high in the wall, the stone floor covered in rubbish and fetid straw, the only furniture a narrow plank bed with a wafer thin mattress and a toilet bucket.

An old soldier from the time of Tsar Nicholas was posted at his door, pledged to guard him at all hours. The gendarmes called him 'Uncle Vishka', a filthy white-haired rat of a man who, after two decades within the ravelin's walls, was sick and bitter and malignant. His bloodshot eye hovered at the spy hole in the door for hours and he spoke only abuse to the prisoners. He would thrust his grubby hands through a window like a wicket in the iron door twice a day with a glass of tea, dry bread or a little weak soup that tasted of nothing and was often tainted by the guards.

The stench in the cell was overpowering, and Mikhailov's hair and beard were soon crawling with lice. But it was the oppressive silence that troubled him most. Once he heard screaming from the corridor and hammered on the door until Uncle Vishka spoke to him: 'They're thrashing some money out of a newcomer.'

'What?'

'Everyone has to pay,' the old soldier said carelessly. 'You gentlemen politicals get off lightly.'

His escape was to the past, conversations, people, whirling Anna about the dancefloor – he thought of her often – and summers on his father's estate. He took an unholy delight too in imagining the death of the tyrant, the revolution, a popular uprising that would set the prisoners free. But hope was inseparable from fear. There were times in the winter chill at night when he knew despair and he would pray to the Russian god he did not believe in for a quick release.

At first, he had been flattered by the attention of the

authorities, the procession of visitors to his cell at the Preliminary – senior policemen and soldiers, government ministers – who had learned of his importance to the party from the testimony of Goldenberg. Collegiate Counsellor Dobrshinsky had spent many hours trying to break him with threats and promises and even the offer of a pardon if he turned state evidence. He had expected and enjoyed resisting these blandishments. But he had been surprised and irritated by the particular interest the special investigator had shown in the English doctor. Why had the party tried to kill him? Was he a member of The People's Will? What help were they receiving from the British? Money? Explosives? Mikhailov had refused to answer all but the last of these, for he was a socialist patriot and would never have accepted assistance from a foreign power. What a trouble the Englishman had been to him. Would he have stepped inside the photographer's shop if Anna had not charged him so vehemently with acting only in his own interests?

By a wicked irony it was the doctor who brought him some relief from the cell and the ravelin at Christmas. It was late afternoon, to judge from the grey rectangle of sky, and in the corridor the confused echo of boots and a jangle of keys. The iron door opened and the warder stepped inside, his nose pinched between thumb and forefinger: 'You stink like a Tatar. What's your visitor going to think?'

For the five minutes it took to walk under escort to the Commandant's House he felt drunk with the hope his mother or sister was waiting to see him, or a comrade in disguise. The crunch of boots in the snow, the tolling of a barracks bell, a troika sliding towards the Peter Gate, clean air sharp in his chest, the sights, sounds, taste of the life he used to live.

But it was Major Vladimir Barclay who was warming his hands at the stove. With a weak smile and a casual wave, he indicated that Mikhailov should take a chair. For once, the major was in the blue and red of the corps, campaign medals on his broad chest and the Order of St Vladimir at his throat. To Mikhailov's mind he did not cut an impressive figure, rather foreign with his round beardless face, crafty eyes and thin brown hair.

'You look awful,' the policeman observed coolly. 'I'll speak to the warder. A bath and a shave. After all, you are a gentleman, aren't you? Tea?'

Mikhailov nodded.

'But you've lost a little weight; that's a good thing.'

The tea tasted as it should taste and Mikhailov sat at the table with a glass cupped in his hands, grateful for that small kindness. It was a warm panelled room with an eighteenth-century chandelier, fine walnut chairs and a stove of pretty blue and white Dutch tiles. It made Mikhailov feel dirtier and even a little ashamed, and that made him irritable.

'Well, what do you want?'

'Collegiate Counsellor Dobrshinsky has asked me to speak to you again,' said Barclay. 'The ravelin is no place for a gentleman. He said to me: "See if Alexander Dmitrievich is ready to help us a little, now he's had time to reflect upon his future".'

Mikhailov watched impassively as the policeman leant across the table and poured more tea into his glass.

'We know your little comrades are plotting another attempt on the emperor's life.'

'Oh?'

'You people can't take a shit without us knowing about it.'

Mikhailov looked at him disdainfully. 'Then I can't possibly be of service to you.'

'But you can.' The policeman leant forward again, his big hands clasped together, warm smile, eyebrows arched. 'How? When? Where?'

'I really have nothing to say.' Mikhailov wondered that the

special investigator had trusted this task to a man with the intellect of a common soldier.

'A porter has reported seeing your comrade Anna Kovalenko again.'

'Oh?'

'Yes, she was visiting the Englishman at the Nikolaevsky,' said Barclay, with a knowing voice.

Mikhailov felt the colour rising in his face. The policeman had swung wildly and caught him a glancing blow. He was not going to show it. Placing his palms flat on the table, he almost shut his eyes, as inscrutable as a plaster saint.

'If your comrades kill the emperor another will take his place, but if you don't help us you will die in a damp hole forgotten by everyone.'

'Right-minded people must give themselves to this struggle.'

'The gentleman peasant,' said Barclay with a cynical smile. 'Collegiate Counsellor Dobrshinsky was sure you wouldn't listen to reason. That's why he sent me, of course.' He sat up slowly, dragging his fists back across the table then rising to his feet.

'Do you recognise this one?' he asked, pointing to the red enamel decoration at his throat.

'The Order of St Vladimir.'

'I call it my Mikhailov medal,' Barclay said with a broad grin. 'I have you to thank for it.' Then, turning to the door, he shouted: 'Sergeant, I've finished with him.'

And again to Mikhailov: 'Oh, I forgot to mention. A comrade of yours is here too. Nikolai Kletochnikov.'

'I've never heard of the fellow.'

'What was it you called him, "your Director"? He hadn't heard from you for a while so he paid you a visit. He was at a loss without you. Resentful that you'd kept him from the rest of the party. Of course, he didn't know we'd picked you up already. A couple of his Moscow comrades were waiting for him – they were a little rough.'

344

'I don't know what you're talking about.'

'No? Well, if you change your mind – and you might – speak to your guards.'

Mikhailov could hear their heavy tread on the polished boards behind him, and a moment later the warder of the ravelin was at his side with handcuffs.

'Is the prisoner moving, sir?' he asked.

'Yes. To the Secret House. A chance for a little more reflection,' replied Barclay.

It was the final test for enemies of the state, a damp unheated solitary block below the level of the river, where prisoners were left to rot in medieval darkness.

Mikhailov gazed at him with unflinching contempt. 'You must know the tsar will die.' His voice was cool, matter-of-fact, full of certainty. 'It must be. It is the will of the people.'

# 1881

Alexander II must die ... the near future will show whether it is for me or another to strike the final blow. But he will die and with him we shall die, his enemies and executioners ... fate has allotted me an early death. I shall not see one day, not one hour of our triumph. But I believe that by my death I am doing all that I have in my power to do ...

**Farewell letter of Ignatei Grinevitski,
member of The People's Will, 1 March 1881**

# 38

Polite society celebrated Christmas as it always did in St Petersburg, with extravagant piety and glittering pomp. A score of expensively embossed invitations on Hadfield's mantelpiece presented a daily challenge to the maid. In the bright gilded rooms of the rich, the season was much as it had been the previous year and for many more before. And yet there was something subtly different too, like a reflection in a mirror warped just a little by age, an uncomfortable distortion of the settled order. The authorities were demonstrating unusual efficiency. Hundreds of arrests, executions *pour encourager*, and it was almost a year since the explosion at the palace had rocked the foundations of the empire. Expensive drawing-room opinion on the English Embankment was that this was so much to the good but, like the frozen Neva they could see from their windows, a troubling and irreversible current was flowing beneath the surface. And there was a general reluctance to talk of the future, even at gatherings where serious conversation was not deemed to be a breach of good manners.

Hadfield noticed another, more particular change in the embankment's opinion. Some of those who had been solicitous and most anxious to be his friend were beginning to avoid him. And while there were the invitations from the usual people – Baron Stieglitz, Count Shuvalov, the Baird and Gascoigne families – he was aware of a new stiffness in their smiles. At first he wondered if this was to do with his uncle's fall from grace. Villagers were close to starvation in many parts of the south and the government was without the means to alleviate their suffering. Blame was falling squarely on General Glen's shoulders as the controller of the empire's finances. But if Hadfield was tarnished a little by this association, it was nothing to the stain caused by the rumour of his 'unfortunate' affair. Snatches of conversation, an oblique warning from Dobson, and his cousin Alexandra's angry inarticulate tears one evening left him in little doubt that his private life was a matter of public speculation. Von Plehve or Dobrshinsky or someone acting under their orders must have set tongues wagging with a cleverly indiscreet remark. A hostess might welcome a handsome radical doctor into her drawing room to prove her liberal mind, but there was no social advantage to be won from someone who had conducted a relationship with a terrorist, a married woman to boot. The embankment felt aggrieved when it recalled the sympathy it had lavished upon him. So, although there were invitations still – he was a member of the Glen family, after all – no tears were shed when he made his excuses.

Hadfield was surprised by how little it bothered him. He had always felt himself to be an outsider, revelled in his secret difference, and yet he had enjoyed the privileges of family and his connections too. But when Anna had returned to him he had accepted her without hesitation. He did not share her faith in The People's Will, he rejected the morality and efficacy of terror, but he no longer felt comfortable with the easy assumptions of most of his class, nodding at balls and parties and dinners when the privileged spoke of the futility of hoping for democracy in Russia.

He saw very little of Anna at Christmas – a few snatched hours – and he spent the last day of the old year with his family. The first day of the new one arrived with champagne and dancing, the rustle of silk, gay uniforms whirling across a polished floor, familiar, happy faces. But Hadfield felt only the dull ache of separation. Later at home he sat with his journal on his knee and tried to write of his hopes, but mostly of his fears for the coming year, his sense of life on the cusp. But his befuddled mind could not conjure the words necessary to bring order to his feelings. He was still awake after *une nuit blanche* as the church bells rang out across the city the following morning.

In the first weeks of January Hadfield realised he was being followed once again. Tall – a little too tall to pass entirely un-noticed by someone on his guard – early thirties, neatly trimmed brown beard, plainly but well dressed, his shadow moved on a crowded street with the ease of one trained to the task. And there were others at night and skulking outside his home in the morning. His shadow was with him when he visited the British embassy to treat one of the secretaries who had wrenched his knee. The ambassador's wife no longer included Hadfield's name on her guest list for dinner. Fortunately, his professional judgement was still valued and he remained the embassy doctor in all but name. Lord Dufferin's secretary – an Anglo-Irishman called Kennedy – had fallen badly on the frozen Neva and his friends had been obliged to carry him back to the embassy on a hand cart.

Hadfield found him with a large glass of brandy in the ambas-sador's outer office. It was soon apparent from his ill-tempered muttering that his pride had taken as sharp a knock as his knee.

'Some cheeky wee buggers pelted me with snow while I was lying there helpless on the cart,' he explained in surprisingly broad Ulster Scots.

Hadfield gave him a mild analgesic and instructed him to rest for a few days.

'By the way, Doctor, Colonel Gonne was hoping you would spare some time to see him before you leave,' Kennedy informed him.

'A professional matter?'

Kennedy did not know.

351

The military attaché's rooms were in the gloomy west wing of the embassy but with a fine and fitting view over the Field of Mars. Hadfield had met the colonel for the first time at his uncle's house and twice more since, and he had formed the impression of a steely and ambitious character. A handsome man in his late forties, with red hair and whiskers, there was a glint in his eye that suggested he might be quick to take offence. 'Thank you for finding the time to see me, Doctor,' he said, indicating Hadfield should take the chair in front of his desk. 'I'll come straight to the point. Lord Dufferin has asked me to raise a delicate matter with you.'

'Oh?' said Hadfield in a carefully neutral tone. Most of the 'delicate' matters soldiers wished to discuss with a doctor belonged under the general heading of 'the wages of sin'.

Gonne frowned. 'Delicate and serious.' He rose to stand at the window behind his desk, almost a silhouette against the parade ground. 'Perhaps you know the emperor reviews the guards regiments at the riding school on Sundays.'

Hadfield nodded. 'The Mikhailovsky Manège.'

'Last Sunday Lord Dufferin was present at the parade with some of the other ambassadors. Count von Plehve of the Justice Ministry was in the gallery too – are you listening, Doctor?'

'I'm sorry, please – it's nothing . . .' and Hadfield indicated with a light wave of the hand that the colonel should continue.

'The count made some pointed remarks about you.'

'What sort of remarks?'

'He mentioned a woman, a terrorist – the Kovalenko woman – someone you used to . . . meet . . .' The colonel was trying to be delicate.

'I have not seen Miss Kovalenko for some time.' Hadfield's thoughts were racing and he was struggling to appear calm.

'I'm sure I don't need to remind you that any suggestion of a British involvement with these people will embarrass Her Majesty's government.'

'No. You don't need to remind me,' said Hadfield. 'As I informed the authorities, I met Miss Kovalenko at a clinic. She proved a capable nurse.'

'Yes. Yes. Well, I am sure a doctor is required to meet all sorts of people . . .' Gonne trailed off without conviction.

'Then if there is nothing else, Colonel, perhaps you'll excuse me?'

Colonel Gonne nodded curtly and stepped away from the window with the intention of escorting Hadfield from the room. But his sleeve caught a photograph at the edge of the desk and it fell to the floor with a splintering crash.

'Damn. Clumsy. I'm sorry, Doctor, I'm forgetting myself,' he said, bending to pick up the picture. 'My daughter.' He turned it over to show Hadfield the shattered face.

'It's only the glass . . . she's pretty.'

'Yes, well . . .' Colonel Gonne put the picture back on the table and walked over to the door. He was on the point of opening it when he turned suddenly to speak to Hadfield once more. 'Pretty girls . . . a word to the wise, Doctor. Take care. The secret police have spies everywhere.' He paused to make eye contact: 'You may not be as fortunate a second time.'

The police spy was waiting at the ice-bound pier outside the embassy, where the ferry left for the islands in spring. Hadfield did not give him a second glance. He could think of nothing but the parade at the manège, his mind swirling with the implications. That it should take a casual word from a British soldier who knew very little of the city. The  emperor would pass the cheese shop on the Malaya Sadovaya before or after the parade. What were they planning? There was no need to rent a shop if they were going to shoot the tsar and they had rented basement premises. Why? They were driving a gallery into the street. A mine. They were going to kill the tsar with a mine. He leaned back against the wall of the embassy, a cold sweat on his skin like a sickness. A mine. He was sure of it. And how many soldiers like the young Finn he had treated after the palace explosion would die this time? Head bent, fingers pressing hard on his forehead, he let out a long anguished groan.

# 39

Collegiate Councillor Dobrshinsky picked up the surveillance log and, balancing it on his knee, began to turn its pages, marking passages in pencil before transferring them to the notebook on the desk in front of him. It was after nine o'clock at night but Fontanka 16 was still bustling with agents and clerks, and through the open door he could hear the incessant chatter of the Baudot receiver with telegrams from gendarmeries all over the empire. The terrorists were summoning trusted supporters to the capital. It was gratifying in a way, because arrests in the city must have left them in a parlous state, but it was clear they were planning another attempt on the emperor's life. Barclay had extracted this piece of intelligence with a relish quite ungentlemanly from the traitor Kletochnikov. But he had not been able to supply the when and the wherefore. For now, they were obliged to rely on surveillance and informers in the hope that the fresh faces from the provinces would be careless and let something slip.

*Sunday 21 February 1881*
*Dr Hadfield left his apartment at 12.30 a.m. He took a*
*cab to the Nevsky Prospekt then walked down the*
*Malaya Sadovaya and joined the crowd waiting for His*
*Majesty. At a little before 2.00 p.m. the emperor left the*
*manège with his escort to return to the palace. Hadfield*
*watched him pass then walked to 24 Malaya Italyanskaya*
*Street. An apartment in this house is occupied by an*
*English newspaper correspondent . . .*

Why was a well-to-do doctor with distinctly liberal if not republican views waiting in a frozen street on Sunday for a glimpse of the emperor? The special investigator had been concerned about security at the Sunday parade for a number of weeks, and the guard about the royal carriage had been doubled on his recommendation.

Dobrshinsky picked up a little hand bell from the desk and rang for the clerk in the outer office. 'Ask Agent Fedorov to step into my office, would you?'

'Did you organise a search of the buildings around the manège?' Dobrshinsky asked when Fedorov appeared.

'Yes, Your Honour, and in Italyanskaya Street.'

'The canal embankment?'

'No.'

'The Malaya Sadovaya?'

The agent shook his head.

'See to it then, as soon as possible.'

Dobrshinsky dismissed him and returned to the surveillance log on his knee. The Englishman had done nothing else of interest in the days since, and had made no effort to lose his police shadows although he was clearly aware of their presence. He turned to the previous day's report.

*Sunday 21 February 1881*
*The suspect Trigoni was followed to Number 17 2nd*
*Rota Izmailovsky District. He was seen leaving with a*
*blonde woman with a big forehead. A police agent*
*followed the girl but she eluded him on the Nevsky*
*Prospekt. The suspect Trigoni returned to his furnished*
*lodgings at 66 Nevsky Prospekt at 10.00 p.m. and did*
*not leave it again that day.*

The station in Odessa had warned them that Mikhail Trigoni had arrived in the city. He was another of the party's gentleman revolutionaries, the son of a general, with a weakness for expensive clothes that made him easy to follow. In his testimony, Goldenberg had referred to him by his English nickname of 'My Lord'.

Dropping the log on his desk, Dobrshinsky rose stiffly, fastidiously brushing the creases from his frock coat. This simple activity left him a little breathless, his heart beating faster than was comfortable. He was spending too many evenings at Fontanka 16 without the benefit of a *soporifique*. It was easier to think at home alone, easier to rest.

'Are today's reports ready?' he snapped at the clerk as he walked through his outer office.

'No, Your Honour.'

'Why not?'

Barclay was at the blackboard in the main inquiry room talking to an undercover agent. Drygin was one of the section's best, older than the rest, shrewder, with instinctive guile. He was still disguised as a country bumpkin in a dirty padded kaftan, his grey beard and hair unkempt. Something in his restless movement suggested he had news of importance.

'Your Honour?' Barclay had seen him at the door. 'We have a fresh report.'

The collegiate councillor stepped over to join him at the board where the latest intelligence on the chief suspects was chalked alongside their photographs. Dobrshinsky had taken the idea of a rogue's gallery from a French crime journal and it was proving a useful tool.

'Drygin was following our friend Trigoni,' said Barclay, pointing to a fuzzy photograph of a young man in a student's uniform.

'Yes, Your Honour. A busy chap today. Really put me to the test.'

Drygin picked up his notebook and turned slowly to the correct page: 'The subject left his apartment late this morning

– a long breakfast in bed, perhaps – then he walked along the Nevsky to a cheese shop on the Malaya Sadovaya. It is run by a couple called Kobozev. The shopkeeper is from somewhere near Voronezh—'

'The superintendent of the block says his papers are in order . . .' Barclay interrupted.

'The subject left at approximately midday and strolled over to the public library on the Bolshaya Sadovaya where he met a young woman – small, about twenty-five, brown coat, brown hair, quite pretty—'

'Anna Kovalenko?' asked Dobrshinsky.

Drygin shrugged. 'She gave him a note. They were together five minutes at the most. Then I followed Trigoni to a restaurant on Nevsky where he had lunch. At about 2.30 p.m. he took a droshky to the Nikolaevsky Hospital. He gave the note to a porter, with instructions that it should be delivered at once. The porter delivered it to me first. It was addressed to a Dr Hadfield, just a couple of lines – *I'm sorry it's been so long. Tomorrow 22.00. With my love.*'

'Good,' said Dobrshinsky. 'Then I want four of our best men with him tomorrow, and someone in the hospital. And no mistakes this time.'

The old man gave a respectful little bow then shuffled off in search of sustenance.

'I want that cheese shop searched, Vladimir Alexandrovich,' Dobrshinsky said when he had gone.

'Yes, Your Honour.'

'And I want you to take charge of Kovalenko. She's the one we want, but if we find them together we can bring him to trial too. Now,' Dobrshinsky turned back to the rogue's gallery, 'do you remember the names on the list we found in the hotel room on the Nevsky?'

'Bronstein's list? I think so: Mikhailov, Kovalenko, Morozov, Presnyakov, Goldenberg and Kviatkovsky.'

'All of them are dead or in prison except for Anna Kovalenko. Even this one,' and Dobrshinsky tapped his finger on the face of Nikolai Morozov. 'The gendarmes arrested him at the border last week. He was trying to cross into Russia on false papers.'

Barclay watched the special investigator, his chin in his hand, his little brown eyes flitting from photograph to photograph. He was greyer, thinner, wearier than when they had met over the body of the Jew in that dingy hotel room. The last two years had certainly taken their toll.

'His Majesty's still with us, of course,' said Dobrshinsky. 'For that we can be thankful. But are we any closer to winning? It isn't possible, is it?'

'It is possible to arrest the bitch Kovalenko,' Barclay replied. 'And there will be satisfaction in that after all this time.'

# 40

A nna could not take her eyes off the jar. It was sitting on the kitchen table in front of her, the size of a small amphora of wine but with all the nitro-glycerine they needed to send the tsar and his entourage to a better place. In a few minutes one of the men would collect it and pass it with great care along a human chain to the end of the gallery. Then it would be packed between sandbags to direct the charge into the street above. The enterprise had almost come to grief more than once. The police had inspected the premises and questioned the shopkeeper and his wife, then one of the tunnellers cut a sewer pipe and flooded the cellar with effluent. The stench lingered in the shop for days.

In those fraught weeks Anna had felt too unwell to be of real service to her comrades. She had tried to hide her sickness but her room-mate had seen her more than once with her head bent over a bowl. And although she prevailed on Praskovia to say nothing, some of the others had noticed how pale she looked and that the slightest thing would bring her close to tears. No one was used to seeing Anna Kovalenko close to tears.

'You're suffering from nervous exhaustion,' they told her. 'You must rest.'

Exhaustion, yes, because they were all tired of standing at the edge. More arrests, the constant fear of informers and discovery, and security was not what it had been when Mikhailov was there to instruct them all.

'You have to say goodbye to it.' Andrei Zhelyabov had come into the room and was standing at her shoulder. His face and beard were flecked with clay, and it was caked on his shirt and trousers.

'Goodbye?' She did not understand.

'Now don't frown at me,' he said with an amused smile. 'I mean the jar. You were staring at it as if you were hoping to summon a genie.'

'Wouldn't that be wonderful,' she said with feeling. 'Then our problems would be over.'

'Can you instruct a genie to kill someone, I wonder.'

'We could magic him away.'

He pulled a chair from the table and sat beside her, placing his large mud-stained hand on top of hers: 'Are you all right?'

'I . . . yes . . .' But at the warmth of his hand, his affectionate look – the easy informality of the village – Anna's chin began to tremble and she had to fight the wild uncontrollable tide of emotion welling inside her. After a few seconds she was able to say in a strong voice: 'Yes, fine. Really.'

Zhelyabov gave a heartfelt sigh: 'You know, when this is done, I will escape. Go south. Rest. Spend the summer there. You should do the same.'

'Will Sophia go with you?'

'I hope so, yes. And you should take your English doctor.'

Anna bit her bottom lip hard in an effort to hold the tide again: 'Can it happen? Vera Figner will call it selfish.'

'Yes. And perhaps Sophia too. But two years of hiding, looking over our shoulders, plotting . . . there is something terrible about being a terrorist. It dominates your mind so much that it affects your freedom of judgement.' He gave her hand a squeeze. 'But it will happen. You'll see.'

Zhelyabov carried the bottle through to the tunnel entrance. The charge was packed in place and a firing line run along the length of the gallery. It would be ready for the next Sunday parade. They sealed up the wall with a board of painted plaster and rolled the cheese barrels back into place. The lookout in the street gave a knock at the window – the coast was clear – and alone or in pairs they left the shop, Anna with Zhelyabov. On the Nevsky he took her hand and bent to kiss her cold cheek: 'Goodbye, Anna. Be careful. Remember our promise. Summer in the south.'

She watched him walk away, collar up against the biting wind, hat pulled low, the son of the serf with his princess, prepared to break all society's codes. Would Frederick feel the same?

The droshky took her to the Nikolaevsky Station and from there she walked on by a maze of small streets, stopping at corners and in doorways to be sure there was no one dogging her steps. The freezing air and the need for vigilance helped settle her nerves a little. The old lady had heard her footsteps on the stairs and was waiting on the landing to embrace her warmly.

'Just as well you arrived when you did or I'd have taken him for myself,' she whispered in Ukrainian, her body rocking with barely suppressed laughter. She led Anna into the room by the hand like a village bride.

Frederick was sitting at the table, playing with the wax at the base of a candle. He rose at once with a broad smile of relief and pleasure: 'Thank God. Why has it been so long?'

She stood at the door in her old brown coat and hat, waiting for him to draw her into his arms.

'I've missed you more than you can imagine,' he said, taking the hat from her and stroking her hair.

'I'm sorry. Things have been difficult . . .'

She could say no more, she was beaten, her voice strangled with emotion, the strain of the secret suddenly too much. And before he was able to kiss her, even with the old woman in the room, she burst into tears, burying her head in his shoulder.

'Darling, darling,' he whispered, kissing her hair, holding her tight. 'Shush, darling.'

He tried to wipe her tears, kiss her tears, but she did not want him to see her face. She was ashamed of her weakness.

'What is it?' he asked. 'Tell me.'

'No.'

'Tell me.'

She was not ready to tell him. Not yet. 'Things are difficult. But I'm all right.'

He tried to lift her chin and this time she let him, and he kissed her wet cheeks and eyelids and then her lips. Drawing her to the table, he made her sit beside him, her hands small between his hands.

'You look tired, have you been sleeping properly?'

No, she was not sleeping, and she admitted she had been feeling unwell.

'Then you must let me examine you,' he said. 'Your personal physician, remember?'

'Later.'

They sat gazing at each other in silence. He was trying to offer an encouraging smile, but there was something intense in his expression that unsettled her. 'Anna, you know I love you,' he said, and he lifted her hand to his lips. 'I love you very much.'

'Yes.'

'Don't be cross with me, but I know you're . . .'

'Oh, God.' And her heart beat faster, her chin quivering as she fought the urge to dissolve into tears again. 'I'm sorry, Frederick.'

He was clearly taken aback. 'Perhaps we're talking at cross purposes,' he said gently. 'What is it you think I know?'

She examined his face, his soft hazel eyes, a little smile of encouragement playing on his lips: 'No, you speak.'

The smile disappeared at once and he took a deep breath and sighed, as if bracing himself for what he clearly thought would be a difficult conversation.

'The cheese shop on the Malaya Sadovaya. I know, that is, I've guessed what you are doing . . .'

She felt a fleeting sense of relief. 'How do you know?' she asked. 'You've told no one?'

'No. But now I know, it has to stop.'

She must have been gaping at him in amazement because he could not help a small smile. 'Please, Anna, understand, I can't let this happen. I don't want to betray anyone but I won't have any part in the killing of innocent people.'

'What are you talking about?' And she flushed hot with anger, tearing her hands from his. 'Frederick, you're talking nonsense. It's a shop.'

'Tell me you're not trying to kill the tsar.'

'That's the party's business, not yours,' she said, her voice trembling with fury.

He reached for her hand again but she would not give it to him: 'What do you want me to do, Frederick? Tell my comrades my lover is threatening to betray them to the police. I thought you loved me.'

'Please try and understand, I can't let it happen. I won't be party to murder.'

'It will be the end for us, I won't see you again,' she said, her body rigid, her face white, fists clenched tightly beneath the table.

'I would never betray you,' he said, 'but I won't be party to murder.'

'But knowing of the shop doesn't make you party to murder. And it's not murder. He's a tyrant.'

'And those who will be travelling with him?'

'Stop it, Frederick,' she said, almost pleading with him. 'Stop it. Please, please stop it.'

He was at a loss to know what he could say to placate her, conscious too, perhaps, that he was in danger of taking an irrevocable step.

'Stop it, Frederick,' she said again. 'Don't. I thought you wanted me.'

'You know I do.'

'Then what are you thinking?'

The curtain rattled urgently and the old woman was standing in the doorway hugging herself, breathless, quite terrified.

'What is it?' Anna snapped at her in Ukrainian.

'They're in the street . . .' she stammered.

'Calm yourself. How many?'

'Many.'

'What is it?' Hadfield asked, touching her arm.

'The police.'

He moved towards the window, but before he could reach it they heard the thump of a fist at the door below and someone shaking the handle, then the echo of voices and steps on the stairs. The old woman began to whimper with fear.

'You must go.' Hadfield was pulling at her arm. 'Go, Anna. Leave here. Go now.'

'You must come too. You can't be found here.'

There was the sound of splintering wood.

'No,' he said, 'I'll be fine. I'll do what I can. Go.'

'Frederick, I'm going to have a baby.'

He stood gazing in astonishment at her.

She reached for his hand and held it to her face and for a moment he bent to rest his forehead against hers.

'Now go,' and he snatched his hand free and turned to the door. And then she ran. Racing through partitioned rooms, sweeping curtains aside, pushing past anyone who stepped in her way, until she found the other stairs. Down and then on into the darkness.

# 41

Anna made her way to the flat on the Voznesensky. Vera Figner let her in without comment and led her by the hand to the couch, where she lay in the early hours rolling the same questions through her mind until the worst was all she was able to believe. Then, at nine o'clock the following morning, they had news that the gendarmes had visited the cheese shop again and she knew he had failed her. But she could not speak of it to her comrades. She lay curled beneath a blanket while Vera gave instructions to the scouts. She was frightened as she had never been before. Please God she was wrong.

An hour later they received word that Zhelyabov was missing. He had arranged to meet Nikolai Kibalchich and the four bomb-throwers, but they had waited for an hour and were still waiting,

'Are you strong enough to go to them?' asked Vera.

Kibalchich had found abandoned workings close to the river at the northern edge of Vasilievsky. The ground was frozen hard enough to keep the market gardeners from their plots, and the vast wooded cemetery lay between them and the island's lines. They would be safe there from prying eyes and Anna would patrol the edge of the gravel pit to be sure. A fine mist was rising from the land, the weak sun shaping it into layers, the sky luminescent, a diffuse light, the towers of the city churches lost on the soft horizon. The winter silence was broken only by the distant cawing of the rooks in the cemetery treetops and from time to time the voices of her comrades as they practised in the pit with their dummy grenades.

Kibalchich called to her, his eyes shining like a schoolboy's: 'We're going to try one with a charge.' It was heavy, the size of a large grapefruit, and the worker – she was not to know his name – threw it with both hands. It detonated on the frozen ground with a sharp yellow flash and a fizzle like a damp firework.

'Well, it works. That's a comfort,' said Kibalchich cheerfully, 'but they'll have to be close to be sure of killing him.'

When the bombers had learnt all they could of trajectory and blast radius they left to ready themselves as best they could for the following morning. Kibalchich took a droshky back with Anna to the Voznesensky apartment. Two sharp knocks followed by two more, the tinkle of the lock, the drawing back of bolts and Vera stood there with doubt and even a little fear written in her face.

'They've taken Andrei Zhelyabov. Last night.'

The door closed behind them and they stood in the small hall.

'Does Sophia know?'

'Yes. She'll be here soon.'

Poor Perovskaya. She loved him deeply. Everyone would share her grief, hug her, speak to her with sympathy, but there will be no word for me, Anna thought.

'Can we go ahead without him? Is there word from the shop?'

'No. I don't know . . . oh, Anna, what is happening?'

There was still no report from the Malaya Sadovaya when the executive committee gathered at three o'clock. Long faces, frustrated, frightened, and so many comrades missing. This time there were chairs in Vera's little sitting room for all. There was no comfort they could give Sophia and she was impatient with those who tried, but she accepted Anna's hands and offered in return a weak smile. Her face was white and strained, and appeared even more so in her simple black dress. But there was no mistaking her composure, and she was the first to speak.

'There is no turning back. Whatever happens we must act tomorrow.' She paused to look about the room, defying any of them to challenge her: 'The mine must be laid and the bombs primed by morning.'

'What if they've discovered the tunnel?' asked Figner.

'We still have the grenades. And we must act for the people. Do we act?' Sophia asked quietly. 'Vera, do we act?'

'Yes. We act.'

'It's suicide. The police will be everywhere.' It was the young naval lieutenant, Sukhanov. He was sitting at the edge of his seat, his hands pressed over his ears in a gesture of incredulity. 'The grenades are not properly made. The gendarmes are in the shop . . . suicide.'

Sophia Perovskaya gave him a steely look: 'Do we act?'

'What will be left of the party after this?'

'Do we act?'

'I don't know,' he said with a shake of his head. 'We must hear from the shop before we can decide.'

Sophia Perovskaya stared at him coldly for a moment, then turned to Anna: 'Annushka, do we act?'

Dead comrades, comrades in prison, the isolation, fear, so much sacrifice in the two years they had been fighting. Zhelyabov would never feel the warm southern sun on his shoulders again. There was no longer a choice.

'Annushka?' Sophia asked, again.

'Yes. We shall act . . .'

'Will you help us, Doctor?'

'If I can.'

'Then where will we find Anna Kovalenko?'

'I don't know.'

'But you would tell me if you did know?'

Hadfield did not reply but folded his arms across his chest and stared impassively at the special investigator. They were sitting on either side of an iron table in the House of Preliminary Detention. The interrogation room was larger than his cell but with the same bleak grey walls and asphalt floor, lit by an unscreened gas flame. They had given him an ill-fitting prison uniform with trousers he was obliged to grasp like a village simpleton to prevent them falling to his ankles. The duty doctor had made a respectable job of cleaning and stitching the wound in his head, but a little blood was seeping through the bandage. It was not how he would choose to dress for an embassy soirée but there was little chance of his name appearing on the guest list for a while.

'Why did you visit the Sunday parade?'

'To see the emperor.'

'Were you helping your terrorist friends with information?'

'No.'

'Then why were you there?'

'To see the emperor.'

Dobrshinsky sighed with exasperation: 'I don't think you understand how serious your situation is, Doctor. Consorting with a terrorist – the old Ukrainian woman has told me of your meetings – resisting His Majesty's servants in the line of duty . . .'

'He wasn't in uniform.'

'Doctor, that's quite insulting.' Dobrshinsky leant forward

earnestly, elbows on the table: 'You're an intelligent fellow – if misguided – you know Anna Petrovna and her comrades are going to make another attempt on the emperor's life. Isn't that why you went to see the Sunday parade?'

Hadfield did not reply.

'Do you think killing the emperor will solve anything in this country? '

'No,' said Hadfield emphatically. 'I'm opposed to terror, whether it's directed at or by the state.'

'Said with creditable frankness. But then you must help me prevent another outrage.' Dobrshinsky paused to let him answer, and when none was forthcoming: 'Didn't you make a promise to preserve life?'

'You asked me if I would help you if I could and I said "Yes – if I could".'

'You're not telling me what you know,' said Dobrshinsky. 'Is she worth the disgrace and imprisonment? What about your principles?'

'If I could, I would help you.'

'A facile mantra. You think you're trapped, but you have a choice. You're a doctor, a gentleman, a man of reason – please use it.'

Dobrshinsky paused again, his little brown eyes watching Hadfield intently, perhaps hoping for a flicker of weakness – of sense. But there was nothing Hadfield could say. He could own that he used to be a man of reason and even some principle, he could admit to his confusion, to terrible doubt, he could say he had not made a decision to pursue this course, that it was a feeling, a compulsion he was in thrall to. Would a man who struggled with an irresistible impulse of his own understand a little of this?

'No one knows you're here,' Dobrshinsky continued. 'Help me and you will walk free. You can return to your patients and to society. If you don't help me you'll be sent to trial and then to a convict settlement, a disgrace to your family and your country.'

'This is my country.'

'Then serve her.'

'If I could, I would help you,' Hadfield repeated.

'We will catch Kovalenko and the rest, Figner, Perovskaya. We've arrested Zhelyabov. You have a choice . . .' Dobrshinsky paused, then, almost as an afterthought, added: 'Perhaps I should arrange for you to speak with your uncle?'

'As you wish,' said Hadfield with exaggerated composure.

Dobrshinsky's thin lips twitched a little with amusement: 'Of course that would have unfortunate consequences. You understand the choice you must make. I urge you to think on your future and the right course.' He pulled a gold timepiece from his waistcoat pocket: 'Four o'clock. I'll return in a few hours.'

Rising stiffly from the table, he smoothed the creases from his frock coat with great care and turned to the door. He knocked sharply then turned once more: 'Did you read those volumes of Mr Dostoevsky's I lent you, Doctor? There's a line, I can't remember it precisely but it is something like, "Do not underestimate how powerful a single man may be." That power is given to you now. Choose wisely.'

### THE PEOPLE'S WILL APARTMENT
### 25 VOZNESENSKY PROSPEKT

They were saved by a cat. Yakimova had left as soon as she was able and hurried to the flat on the Voznesensky. The gendarmes had arrived at the cheese shop with a surveyor of buildings.

'Not just any old surveyor. He was a general,' Bashka reported.

They had searched all three rooms but were most interested in the cellar. The general kicked at the pile of coke they had placed in front of the gallery entrance but did not ask for it to be moved. Nor had the gendarmes taken the trouble to look under the shopkeeper's bed and in the barrels where they would have found the earth from the gallery. The general had been on the point of asking for one to be opened when Bashka's cat had bounded down the steps into the cellar and rubbed against his shiny boots.

'He bent to stroke her and I began rattling on about her history, and that was enough to distract him,' Bashka said with a throaty chuckle. They were now on the best of terms with the gendarmes. It was the first piece of good fortune they had enjoyed in weeks.

By eight o'clock the mine was charged for firing and the rendezvous set for the bomb-throwers. Nikolai Kibalchich would work through the night to ready the grenades. There were six of them left at the flat on the Voznesensky, cutting the kerosene cans for the shell of the grenades, bending and twisting the metal with fire tongs in the grate and casting weights on the kitchen table. Anna Kovalenko and the other women knew nothing of explosives, but fetched and carried and measured and mixed as they were bidden. The living-room floor was covered in shards of metal, the apartment full of stinging acrid smoke. They spoke little and only of the tasks they needed to perform. At eleven o'clock Sophia Perovskaya left them to rest as best she could before the morning.

'You must go too, Annushka,' Vera Figner said a short time later. 'You're exhausted. You should be fresh for tomorrow.'

But Anna could not sleep. She lay on the bed in her stained dress, conscious of Sophia restless beside her and the noise of the bomb-makers in the sitting room. With nothing to distract her tired mind, she became a prisoner of her thoughts again. Where was Frederick?

'Are you awake, Annushka?'

'Yes.'

Sophia turned to face her and reached up to touch her cheek.

'He didn't betray us, Sonechka,' she said, trying to hold back her tears.

'Who, Annushka? Are you crying?' She brushed the moisture from Anna's cheek with the back of her hand, then leant forward to kiss her brow.

'Your English doctor,' she said. 'You love him.'

Anna did not answer. She was ashamed to speak of him when her friend's thoughts must be with Zhelyabov.

'Are you afraid, Sonechka?' she asked at last.

'Only that we may fail again.'

And Anna could see in the splinter of light from the open door the implacable resolve in her white face.

# 42

The pavement was slippery and the bombs were too delicate to risk carrying far. Anna found a cab just beyond the frozen Fontanka, its driver snoozing in his furs, hat pulled down over his eyes and ears. Sophia was waiting for her beneath the carriage arch of the block, the bombs in her arms like a baby. As the cab slid along rutted streets, she nursed them in her lap for fear a jolt would cause one or more to explode. It was early, a little after eight, a cold clear day, the snowy pavements Sunday quiet, church bells calling believers to prayer.

The four members of the bombing party were already at the apartment in the Telezhnaya.

'But where is Andrei?' they asked. Andrei Zhelyabov was their mentor and talisman. But Andrei was not going to come. A petite woman with her bombs in a stout paper bag had taken his place. Was it possible without him?

Yes, it was possible, Sophia told them with quiet assurance. The executive committee of The People's Will had decided that the attempt would be made that day. There could be no turning away. They sat in silence, fidgeting with their tea glasses, hands, buttons, avoiding her gaze, too frightened to speak but too frightened to break the circle. Anna stood watching at the window, her mouth dry, her chest tight.

Sophia Perovskaya unfolded a pencil map of the streets and marked with neat little crosses the positions she had chosen for the bombers. If the emperor took his customary route to the parade he would pass the cheese shop on the Malaya Sadovaya. If the mine did not kill him the bombers would be able to make sure. If he came by the other route – the Ekaterininsky Canal – then they would catch him on his journey back to the palace.

'If you see me at the corner of the Malaya Sadovaya with a handkerchief in my hand,' she said, 'that is the signal to take up new positions along the canal. Is that clear? Good. Comrades, courage. Today is a day of hope for the people.'

They found a café close by and ordered coffee and cakes. The bag with the bombs sat on the bench beside them.

'And me, Sonechka? What must I do?' Anna asked, when there seemed nothing more to discuss.

Sophia placed a tiny hand on top of hers. 'You must go back to the apartment on Voznesensky and wait for us.'

Anna was aghast. How could her friend suggest such a thing?

'I knew you would be upset but it is the will of the executive committee.'

'You mean it is your will.'

'Annushka. It is important someone is there . . .'

'Vera will be there. Please Sophia, I must . . .' Again Anna was struggling to control her tears. She pulled her hand free, clenching her fists in frustration. I have become so weak, she thought.

'Shhhh, Annushka.' Sophia's face softened and she reached for Anna's hand. 'There are things you must do, your future . . .' She hesitated.

'But you will need a lookout . . .'

'No, Anna,' she said firmly. 'No. It is the will of the executive committee. And that's an end to the matter.'

They paid and left the café and on the street they kissed and held each other for a moment.

'Wish me luck, Annushka.'

Anna kissed her cold cheek again and stood watching her comrade's diminutive figure until it was lost among the passers-by.

12.45 P.M.

THE WINTER PALACE

The tsar had risen at half past eight and his valet reported him to be in high good humour. He had taken a turn about the Winter Palace gardens with his children and, after divine worship, he ate a light breakfast. At ten o'clock he received His Excellency Count Loris-Melikov in his study and listened with satisfaction to his account of the arrest of the notorious terrorist Zhelyabov.

'It's a feather in all our caps, Anton Frankzevich,' the chief prosecutor reported. 'I've spoken to His Excellency and he sends his compliments to you and Major Barclay.'

To communicate this courtesy, Count von Plehve made a gracious little bow to his two companions.

Dobrshinsky returned it with a small smile. 'Please pass on my thanks to His Excellency.'

They were standing in the courtyard of the palace in the midst of great activity as the royal grooms prepared the emperor's covered coach for the review at the manège. The stones rang to the restless clopping of the horses, the Cossacks gathered in a cloud of vapour beneath the carriage arch.

'And did His Excellency represent our views to His Majesty?' asked Dobrshinsky.

'His Majesty is determined to take the parade,' von Plehve

376

replied, raising his shoulders a little in a gesture of resignation. 'The imperial chamberlain asked him to reconsider, but he will hear none of it.'

'Folly.' Dobrshinsky slapped his cane against his boots in exasperation.

'He has acceded to your request for an additional escort,' said von Plehve, almost apologetically. 'Major Barclay will travel in the police sleigh.'

'And the route?'

'That is for His Majesty to decide, but our concerns were made known to him. We can only hope he was listening.'

'Amen to that,' said Barclay, crossing himself vigorously.

Yes, it was time to fall back on prayer, Dobrshinsky reflected, what more could they do?

There were gendarmes outside the manège, and his own people were posted among the crowd, but it was impossible to guard against reckless hate.

'Health to Your Majesty!'

The soldiers in the covered entrance shouted their customary greeting and a moment later Tsar Alexander II stepped into the courtyard with the captain of his guard a few steps behind. He stopped to adjust the clasp of his cloak, blinking in the winter sunshine. A word to his coachman, then he stepped inside and a moment later the royal cortège pulled away, the Cossacks with swords drawn in front and on the flanks, the police bringing up the rear in two small sleighs.

'A fine thing, I'm sure, to have your police escort travelling behind you,' muttered Dobrshinsky.

'Well, take a little comfort,' the chief prosecutor observed tartly, his gaze fixed on the coach as it trundled through the echoing arch into the street. 'His Majesty has just instructed his coachman to take him over the Pevchesky Bridge.'

'Yes, there is comfort in that,' Dobrshinsky replied. So he

had listened to that much advice. The tsar would follow the route along the Ekaterininsky Canal to the parade. 'Perhaps it will be enough to keep him alive.'

Anna did not obey the executive committee but waited near the manège for the crump of the mine. She felt sick with anxiety and a little faint and had to turn away to find support against a wall. Perhaps it was the baby, too. Then, at a little after one o'clock, the crowd began to twitter with excitement and she heard horses at a fast trot and the rumble of a coach. She caught only a glimpse of him at the window, his large eyes turned towards her, a soft expression, whiskers and moustache greyer than in the paintings that hung in every public building. People about her were cheering and crossing themselves like pilgrims at the tomb of a saint. I could have tossed the bomb beneath his coach, she thought. And yet, although she wanted him to die she knew she no longer had the strength or will to be his executioner. She could picture her comrade Frolenko in the cheese shop clasping the wires in his workman's hands, poised to make the connection that would not only kill the tsar but bring part of the building down on top of himself.

'Hurrah!'

Through the tall windows of the manège, she could hear the cheers of the Life Guards as they welcomed the sovereign, and then a military band struck up a quick march as the battalions trooped their colours. A mounted gendarme was pressing the spectators back quite unnecessarily and an old woman cried out in pain as his horse stepped on her foot. Some of the men began to remonstrate with him but the gendarme was too drunk with self-regard to care. Anna was suddenly conscious that she was shivering with apprehension and the cold. Why was she

378

waiting? There was nothing she could do. Without a task, she risked recognition and arrest for nothing.

She turned her back on the manège and the insistent rattle of the Life Guards' drums with half a mind to do what she had been instructed to do. A contingent of mounted gendarmes passed at a slow canter on to the gates of the Mikhailovsky Palace. The city police were already clearing the public from the pavement close by and, peering through the huge wrought-iron railings, she could see the grand duchess's flunkies scraping ice from the carriageway that swept up to the palace entrance. As she watched them bent double over their spades, she cursed herself for a dull-witted simpleton. They were preparing for the emperor, and if it was his intention to visit his cousin at the Mikhailovsky he would return to his own palace along the canal embankment. The mine in the Malaya Sadovaya was quite useless. Would Sophia guess?

Without wasting another second deliberating, she set off across Mikhailovsky Square in the direction of the cheese shop. But before she had gone more than a hundred yards she saw one of the bombers struggling through the crowd towards her. He had a shock of blond hair and an earnest clean-shaven face, and in his arms he was carrying a white paper bag the size of a large box of chocolates. If someone jogged his elbow a dozen or more passers-by would be blown to pieces. He noticed her only as their paths crossed, and gave her an anxious little smile. Sophia must have given her signal, because he was walking purposefully towards the canal. After a few seconds, Anna turned to follow him.

The royal cortège would turn right on to the Ekaterininsky Embankment, with the frozen canal on one side and the imposing wall of the Mikhailovsky Palace garden on the other. On the opposite bank, the imperial stables and the yellow and pink mansions of the more impecunious members of the nobility, divided and sub-divided into apartments. The bombers would have only two minutes, three at the most, before the tsar turned to cross the canal for the Winter Palace.

To avoid compromising her comrades, Anna walked in the opposite direction in the hope of crossing to the other side before the royal party reached the embankment.

There were very few people on the street at that hour. She passed a boy with a large basket of meat, and she was forced from the narrow pavement by two men carrying a couch. The service at the Kazan Cathedral had just finished and some of the worshippers were making their way home along the embankment. Snow had been swept from the street into grey heaps on the frozen canal, and four small boys were chipping away at chunks of ice then racing them across its surface. Their laughter sharpened Anna's anxiety and she wanted to shout to them to go home. They should not witness a bloody act of violence.

She was still a long way from the bridge on the Nevsky when she heard the muffled beat of horses' hooves on hard-packed snow. A middle-aged couple walking towards her – petty bourgeois, to judge by their dress – stepped into the road to peer along the embankment. And as she turned to look too, Cossack outriders – six, or was it seven, of them – cantered into view, followed a few seconds later by the royal coach, the sun glinting on its polished black paint-work. She grabbed the canal railings to steady herself, her heart racing, her shoulders lifting involuntarily in anticipation. But the coach was rattling on at a stiff pace, a lively ride over the frozen cobbles, the two police sleighs trailing a few yards behind. Something had gone wrong. She was too far away to see the bombers or Sophia on the other side of the canal but the coach had passed the first position and was gathering speed, the driver whipping his horses on towards the bridge.

'God Bless His Majesty!' she heard someone say behind her.

And she could see a young woman waving from the pavement as the coach swept by. Surely the coach had passed the second position too.

'It's over,' she said out loud, and at once nervous tension began draining from her.

'What's over?' she heard someone say.

She was on the point of turning to see who when the bomb exploded into a sheet of yellow flame.

**2.20 P.M.**

**THE EKATERININSKY CANAL**

Young, short, blond, a black coat, the bomb in a white package above his head. Major Vladimir Barclay knew with sickening certainty the second before he hurled it in front of the advancing coach that he was a terrorist. There was a flash and a deafening crash, and the coach was engulfed by a billowing cloud of acrid white smoke. Barclay's sleigh slewed towards the canal, the driver struggling to control the horses.

'Stop them, man,' he shouted. 'For God's sake, the emperor . . .'

He saw Colonel Dvorzhitsky jump from the other sleigh and run into the smoke. A moment later Barclay was running too. The imperial coach had pulled up a hundred yards further on, its back splintered by the blast. Pounding heavily in his stiff uniform towards it, a long forgotten prayer from childhood slipped into his thoughts: 'Oh God, defend us against the assaults of the enemy . . . Oh God, deliver me from my trouble and misery . . .'

Out of the corner of his eye he saw a group of Cossacks forcing the bomber to his knees. The others had dismounted and were gathered about the coach and, as Barclay reached them, someone wrenched open the door.

'Help me,' and reaching for the arm offered to him, the

tsar stepped from the shattered coach like Lazarus from his tomb.

'Thank God, I'm not wounded.' His voice was empty with shock. He looked round at the anxious faces, his large brown eyes wide, unblinking, then crossed himself twice, and Barclay offered his own prayer of thanks for what was surely a miracle.

'There may be others,' Barclay heard himself say, gasping still for breath.

Colonel Dvorzhitsky must have had the same thought because he stepped forward without hesitation. 'There may be more of them, Your Majesty.'

The emperor stared at him blankly for a few seconds then gazed along the embankment to where a grey pall of smoke hung over the blast site. 'I want to see,' he said, and he took a few uncertain steps towards the canal, grasping the heavy iron rail at its edge for support.

Barclay had seen the same distant look in the eyes of men on the battlefield. In such a state, even an emperor was incapable of thinking clearly. 'You must tell His Majesty, sir.'

But the colonel gave him a look as if to say: 'Who can tell a tsar?'

The emperor's cavalry boots slipped on the icy cobblestones and Barclay sprang forward to hold him by the elbow. The sound of the explosion had reverberated through a Sunday quiet city and the concerned and merely curious were scrambling across the frozen canal and up on to the embankment. The escort was trying to screen the emperor with its horses. One of the Cossacks had been killed outright, his mount still twitching in a pool of blood in the centre of the road. A passer-by had collapsed in a ball at the edge of the pavement, his clothes tattered, his face covered in blood, and against the palace wall on the opposite side of the road, the broken body of a boy of ten or eleven, the raw meat he had been carrying in his basket scattered in a macabre arc around him. The bomber was standing close to the blast site in the custody of four soldiers.

The tsar approached him unsteadily, dragging his left leg, and with a trembling hand pointed to the dying boy. 'You see, I'm all right, thank God, but look, look at your handiwork . . .'

'Do not thank God yet,' the terrorist replied defiantly.

'This is madness,' Barclay muttered, and he touched the colonel's arm: 'For God's sake speak to His Majesty, sir.' Then he addressed the emperor himself.

'Your Majesty, there is a sleigh close by. Please, Your Majesty, it isn't safe.'

The tsar turned slowly to look at him, and Barclay was struck by the sadness and bewilderment in his eyes. 'First, I want to go a little closer.'

A squadron of cavalry had turned on to the embankment from the manège and began to take up positions about the emperor. But mounted, the guards could play no part. Their horses were shifting restlessly at the edge of a large circle while the crowd of onlookers gathered on the pavement near the emperor with no one to hold them in check.

Barclay could barely contain his anger. But what could he do? There were senior officers there, it was their duty to reason with His Majesty.

'I want to see the site of the explosion,' the emperor insisted, and he began walking towards the small crater in the middle of the road. He had taken no more than a few steps when a young man at the canal fence swung round to face him and, lifting his arms above his head, hurled a bomb at his feet. A scorching rush of air and Barclay was knocked to the ground, his face stinging, blinded for a second and completely deaf. And there were others on the cobblestones beside him. Through the dense smoke he could see an officer with white epaulets – was it Dvorzhitsky? – rising unsteadily. His ears were ringing but after a few seconds the sound of someone screaming reached him as if from far away, then a plaintive cry for help. With a supreme effort he picked himself up and stumbled forward through the smoke. Dvorzhitsky was kneeling over the tsar. His back was against the granite base of the canal fence, he was bare-headed, his coat in tatters like a beggar's, his face covered in blood. One of his eyes was closed, the other empty of expression. His legs had been shattered by the blast, the right one hanging by strips of flesh, and blood was pumping from his severed arteries. And as the smoke cleared Barclay could see a score of dead and wounded about him, some crawling, some standing, the snow stained with plumes of blood. Among the fragments of clothing, the hats and swords, were severed limbs and pieces of torn flesh. Close to the tsar, his face unrecognisable, lay the man responsible for the carnage. If not yet dead, he was very close to it.

'I'm cold, Dvorzhitsky, cold,' the emperor said, his voice weak and flat. The colonel was swaying over his sovereign, close to collapse and in no fit state to issue orders. And to Barclay's dismay, a crowd of onlookers and guards was stepping through the wounded to gather about the tsar, their hats in their hands.

Couldn't they see their emperor was dying? Struggling to control the grief and guilt welling inside him, Barclay shouted: 'Get back! Get out of the way! You – a blanket for His Majesty. We're going to carry him to the sleigh.'

But before they could lift him, the Grand Duke Mikhail Nikolayevich appeared as if from nowhere, his guards forcing their way through the crowd. He fell to his knees and reached out gently with a white gloved hand to touch his brother's face. And the tsar whispered something Barclay did not catch, but a moment later the order was given to lift him into a sleigh and drive with all speed for the palace.

'The hospital – we must stop the bleeding!' But no one was listening to Barclay. 'Your Highness, the hospital . . .'

One of the Grand Duke's officers pulled at his sleeve: 'It's the emperor's wish.'

No one was going to question the word of the Autocrat of All the Russias.

Barclay watched in a daze as the sleigh sped along the embankment towards the Konyushenny Bridge and passed from his view. There were no more miracles. They had killed the tsar. And standing there in the street, surrounded by the wounded and the dead, tattered pieces of uniform, a broken sword, he shed silent helpless tears for his emperor and for Russia and for himself.

3.30 P.M.

THE NEVSKY PROSPEKT — SADOVAYA — VOZNESENSKY

At half past three in the afternoon the double-headed eagle of the House of Romanov was lowered at the Winter Palace. As word spread through the city, people began to gather in the streets to listen to the rumours and to weep or pray. There was talk of a palace coup, a royalist plot, and of Russia's foreign enemies, but most were sure the 'nihilists' were to blame.

'Do you know what they've done to our tsar?' an old lady asked Anna, wiping her eyes with her mittens. 'They say he was helping the wounded from the first bomb when they killed him.'

'He was the liberator,' said a merchant in a fine fur-lined coat. 'Why would they kill the tsar who gave the serfs their freedom?'

Anna hurried on, the carnage filling her mind, walking across streets without care, her eyes flitting from face to face, the noise of passing traffic a confused and distant hum like the last of an echo. In the Haymarket, people were standing about the square in small groups, bewildered, unsure what to say to each other but drawn together for comfort. And at the Church of the Annunciation the priests were leading the faithful in an oath of allegiance to the new tsar. On the Voznesensky, a detachment of cavalry cantered past her with their swords drawn as if preparing to go into battle, even though the battle had already been lost.

There was a rolled newspaper in the window of the apartment. It was still secure. But for how long? They had taken the first bomber, perhaps the second too. They had taken Mikhailov and Kletochnikov and Zhelyabov. Could the party survive the death of the tsar, Anna wondered, as she climbed heavy-footed to the apartment. What they hoped would be the first step might become their last. She was greeted at the door by smiling faces, comrades without doubts, who kissed her and embraced her and wanted her to celebrate with them. Vera was weeping tears of joy and so were some of the others; Praskovia from her printing family, Frolenko and Bashka from the cheese shop, and the young naval lieutenant, Sukhanov.

'Annushka, you know? You saw? We've done it,' said Vera, taking her coat.

And they led her through to the sitting room where Praskovia performed a little jig about the floor: 'Dance with me. What is the matter? You're tired. Sit down. Have you seen Sophia?'

Vera sat with her on the couch and spoke breathlessly to them all of the heavy burden that had lifted from their shoulders. 'The tsar has atoned for the blood of our martyrs with his own blood. There will be a new Russia, a better future.'

'And the rest of Europe – Vienna, Berlin – we have lit a torch for freedom everywhere,' said Frolenko.

'Can't you sense the excitement of the people?' said Praskovia, wiping tears from her face. 'They cannot refuse us free elections now. And in time they must free our prisoners.'

Anna watched and listened to their talk of liberty and the future with a dull ache in her chest until she could stand no more of it and left the room. She curled up on the bed she had shared the night before with Sophia, hoping they would leave her alone. But, after a while, Vera came to find her: 'Annushka, help us celebrate. We have some wine.'

'No, Vera, please, I want to be alone.'

'But you must, we've done this together.'

'Yes. Together . . .' Anna could not contain herself any longer. 'But it's the end, Vera!' And she burst into tears.

'The end of what?'

But Anna would not say.

8.00 P.M.

## THE HOUSE OF PRELIMINARY DETENTION
### 25 SHPALERNAYA STREET

Hadfield had heard the first screams in the middle of the afternoon. They were followed by a frenzy of tapping on the heating pipes. By the evening he knew: the tsar was dead and the warders were going to punish the 'politicals'. Some prisoners shouted protests at the abuse of their comrades and banged on their cell doors with tin plates, but then they received a visit too. Hadfield lay on his bed trying to block the empty echo of the prison from his mind, the clatter of boots on the landing outside, the shouts, the screams, the grey soullessness of it all. Would they want to punish him too? He did not care. He had made his choice and kept what he knew hidden. He did not regret that choice, only that it had been necessary to make one. The tsar was not an evil man but as much a prisoner of family and circumstance as everyone else. He could picture him at the bedside of the Finnish soldier, his brown eyes full of pain and bewilderment. And others must have died with him too. What part had Anna played in those deaths? Was she safe? He wanted to hold her, to feel the warmth of her skin.

Heavy footsteps dragged him back to the here and now. Three men in boots, a conspiratorial murmur of voices on the landing, a jangle of keys. He sensed a hush on the wing like the stillness after a heavy snowfall. He was not surprised when they stopped at his door, but he was surprised when Major Vladimir Barclay stepped inside his cell. The man's face was red raw, his hair and eyebrows scorched, and there were dark patches of blood on his blue uniform jacket.

'You were there?'

'Yes . . .' Barclay's voice cracked a little. It was plain from his grim expression that he had not come to speak but to punish. Turning to the burly warders at his back, he gave a slight nod then stepped aside. The door slammed shut and they advanced towards Hadfield, one with a broad leather belt in his hand and the other with a cane.

Hadfield jumped to his feet. It occurred to him that he was about to enjoy the dubious distinction of being beaten by both sides.

The first man swung with the belt but Hadfield caught it with his left hand, yanking him forward and punching the side of his face with his right. He connected well. But the other warder had climbed on to the bed and began laying about him with the cane. Hadfield dived for his legs. His shins struck the metal bed frame but his arms closed about the warder's knees in a perfect tackle. He tumbled backwards heavily like a tree, turning a little in a desperate effort to break his fall with his arm. But Hadfield was left prostrate on the bed and the other warder was on top of him before he had a chance to rise.

It did not last long. They punched him in the face until he was still, his eyes swollen, his lip split, then they beat him across the back and buttocks with the cane. And when it was over Barclay came to stand above him for a moment.

'That is in case you manage to escape responsibility.' He spat on Hadfield. 'Now, physician, you can heal yourself.'

# 43

The following day the party posted a notice in the city.

> Alexander the Tyrant has been killed by us, Socialists. He
> did not listen to the people's tears. A tsar should be a good
> shepherd but Alexander II was a ravening wolf. The party
> has taken the first step, and under its guidance workers
> should rise to claim their freedom.

But there were no barricades or demonstrations in the streets,
no general rejoicing, no one heeded the call to revolution.
St Petersburg was subdued, even a little fearful, the churches
full of mourners and those seeking the comfort of the old
order. People with a living to make went about their business
as always.

At the apartment on the Voznesensky, members of the executive committee composed another manifesto, to be addressed
this time to the new tsar.

What were they thinking? Anna asked herself as she listened
to them argue over the party's demands. They were careless,
drunk with their own sense of importance. The first of the
bombers was in police custody. It was only a matter of time
before those who helped him were there too.

Her fears were well-founded: that night, just as the
committee's call for 'freedom' and 'reconciliation' was being
printed, 'the white terror' began in earnest. In the early hours,
the police broke down the doors of the apartment in Telezhnaya
Street. Comrade Sablin shot himself and Comrade Gelfman

was arrested. And later that morning a member of the bombing party was taken. On the 4th they raided the cheese shop. The party's chief propagandist, Comrade Tikhomirov, began wearing black and visiting churches to pray for the soul of the tsar.

On the night of the 6th there was a knock at the door of the apartment on the Voznesensky.

'Verochka, may I spend the night with you?' It was Sophia Perovskaya.

'How can you ask that?' Vera replied reproachfully.

Sophia looked exhausted, thinner, her face a distressing pallor, with dark rings about her blue eyes. No one had seen her since the death of the tsar. She had moved through the city from friend to friend, determined not to stay more than a night in one place.

'Sonechka, you have as much right as any of us,' said Anna, stepping forward to give her a hug.

But Sophia held her at arm's length: 'I have to ask. If they find me here they will hang you both too.'

'I will shoot if they come, whether you're here or not,' replied Vera, and she pointed to the revolver she kept beside her bed when she slept.

That night Anna lay close to her friend. She could sense Sophia's grief, the dark conviction that nothing would ever be the same, the time left counted in days. At a little before dawn, Sophia turned to her.

'Annushka, why didn't you tell me your doctor was in prison?'

'You have your own sorrow.'

Sophia gave a sad smile and reached down to squeeze Anna's hand.

The following morning, Sophia Perovskaya slipped away from the apartment without saying goodbye. Four days later she was arrested on the Nevsky Prospekt. Then Nikolai Kibalchich was betrayed by his landlady and his friend, Frolenko, was captured at his apartment too.

On the 19th they transferred the body of Alexander II to the Cathedral of St Peter and St Paul, the fortress's minute gun echoing along the Neva. The river was lined with tens of thousands of onlookers, many from the country, some to mourn, some only to enjoy the spectacle. And as the long cortège of soldiers and civil representatives left the palace the city's bells began to toll, their solemn note reaching into every home and even into the subterranean cells of the Secret House. For the first time in days Anna left the apartment seeking the anonymity of the crowded streets. She dressed in her old brown woollen coat, a little tight now, with Mikhailov's burgundy scarf pulled up over her face. To feel the sharp air in her chest, the crunch of snow underfoot, to find relief in exercise, the stiffness leaving her body, and put the gloom of the last days, the staleness of the apartment behind her. Perhaps it was the freedom she allowed herself in the fresh air to think again of a time when she might be with Frederick that caused her to lower her guard for once. Was it in the Haymarket or on the Nevsky Prospekt? She was never quite sure. But at some point she was seen and followed by a 'pea-green coat', as the party liked to call the police department's spies. He waited until she turned on to the Fontanka Embankment, then grabbed her roughly from behind. 'Thief, thief!' she screamed and managed to break free. She ran into a yard and to the back door of a mansion, but the dvornik had been roused by the commotion and met her on the stairs, driving her from the building. It was only a matter of seconds before they were upon her.

They drove her to Fontanka 16 and then to the studio of Alexandrovsky and Taube on the Nevsky for a police photograph. By the time she returned to the Third Section its corridors were crammed with agents and officials from the justice ministry loitering in the hope of catching a glimpse of another of the regicides. She was taken to the basement and locked in a cell with a guard to watch her at all times. The sergeant in charge of the prisoners refused to listen to her appeal for some privacy to go to the toilet. For an hour or so she sat at the edge of the bench with a dull pain in her chest, resigned to what she had long believed to be inevitable. She tried not to think of her baby. In the early evening a doctor – an elderly sober-suited German – came to examine her. Again the sergeant refused to remove the guard. She said nothing to the doctor of her pregnancy but after examining her for a few minutes, he placed his stethoscope on her belly. Then he lifted his round brown eyes to her face and gave her a knowing look.

He left without saying anything more than that she was in good health. A short time later the collegiate councillor called Dobrshinsky, whom she knew to be the special investigator, came to inform her that some dignitaries were waiting in his office to see her. He escorted her under guard up the broad marble stairs to the second floor. Then, with more gracious-ness than she expected, he introduced the two men who were sitting at his desk as the chief prosecutor, Count von Plehve, and General Sereda of the Gendarme Corps. A chair had been set for her in the middle of the room.

'Is it the jealousy of the peasant, Madame Romanko?' von Plehve asked contemptuously, as soon as she had settled. He was fidgeting restlessly with a pen, a high colour in his cheeks. 'Is that why you became a nihilist?'

She stared at him unmoved.

The count was needled by her refusal to reply. 'We have a witness that places you on the embankment – he spoke to you only minutes before His Majesty was murdered. It will hang you.'

Again Anna refused to be drawn.

'Your only hope of escaping the gallows is if you help us,' he barked, his elbows on the desk, hands clasped together in a large fist.

Anna noticed the suggestion of a frown on Dobrshinsky's face as if he disapproved of the count's bullying manner. Frederick had spoken of the special investigator with grudging admiration, describing him as a 'subtle Pole'.

But it was General Sereda who spoke next. 'You seem so small. So unassuming.' He was quiet and considerate in his address, like an avuncular old priest.

'Were you expecting someone with two heads?' she asked with a wry smile.

'Precious little brain for one,' said von Plehve, breaking in belligerently, 'but a great deal of unruly passion.'

The general ignored him. 'What did you hope to achieve? Do you know the tsar signed a draft law to introduce reforms only hours before he died?'

'There is nothing I want to say before my trial,' Anna said, determined not to be drawn into a political discussion.

'Why didn't you have children, Madame Romanko?'

'My name is Anna Kovalenko.'

'If you had had children this would never have happened to you,' the general said with a little shake of the head.

Anna could not help smiling at this strange observation. She sensed that, although the general was hopelessly misguided and old-fashioned, he meant well.

'Enough of this nonsense!' von Plehve blustered. 'Madame Romanko, you will go on trial alongside your comrades in the next few days. The outcome is a foregone conclusion unless you help us.'

Anna frowned but said nothing. What was the point?

'And what of your lover?' he continued, a mean little smile in his eyes. 'Your English doctor. Do you think of him? What a strange hold you have on his imagination. You can help him.'

She flushed a little but did not reply.

'It might be possible for him to go free.'

After a pause, she said: 'Frederick Hadfield has done nothing. He knows nothing.'

But the count was not satisfied and fired questions and threats at her for another ten minutes, working himself into a mighty rage. Finally, he gave up, issuing orders to the guard to take her back to her cell. She assumed that would be the last she would see of her interrogators until the morning. But two hours later she was woken from a light sleep and escorted back to the office to face the special investigator alone. He offered her something to eat and she accepted some tea.

'But you should eat to keep up your strength,' he said gently. 'Prison food is very insubstantial.'

But she was only interested in the tea. Dobrshinsky summoned a clerk from his outer office and gave him instructions, and a few minutes later he returned with a pot and glasses and also a little vodka.

'I hope you'll forgive the chief prosecutor's intemperate display, Anna Petrovna,' said Dobrshinsky, pouring her a glass and pushing it across his desk towards her. 'He does not understand that you and your comrades love Russia and her people as much as we do.'

So reasonable, so plausible, Anna thought; he is as wily as a fox.

'Ah, you smile,' he said. 'But I know your political programme as well as you, and there is much that you ask for that I would support – an elected assembly, freedom of speech and press – I share these aspirations too.' He leant across his desk, his small dark eyes not flickering from her face.

'The tsar is dead but where is your revolution? That is not the will of the people at all. They want change, yes, but not violence. Grigory Goldenberg understood this,' he added, 'that is why he was prepared to help me.'

'Poor Grigory was tricked by smooth words and he knew it,

and that's why he took his own life,' she said curtly. 'I won't make the same mistake.'

'It's over. The People's Will is finished. It died on the embankment with the tsar. Who of importance is left? Only Vera Figner.' He paused, his eyes scrutinising her face for any sign of weakness or emotion. 'And I am sorry to say Count von Plehve is right – your closest comrades will be executed – even Sophia Perovskaya.' He noticed her body tense.

'You thought she'd escape because she's a woman and an aristocrat?' Again he paused, staring at her intently for a few seconds more. Then he said: 'But you will not be executed. You will be saved by your baby. Yes, of course I know. Your unborn child is deemed by the law an innocent. But I know, too, what happens in such cases. Your baby will be taken from you when it's born and placed in an orphanage. It will grow up knowing nothing of its mother and father. A Class 14 clerk will give your baby a name and an institution will be responsible for its well-being. Have you visited a city orphanage? Can you imagine your child in such a place?'

Anna felt a sharp, breathless pain as if his white hands were squeezing her heart. She had presumed her baby would have followed her into exile.

'I think it's barbaric,' he added, 'but what I think counts for nothing. I want you to understand the choice you must make is not just for yourself but for your unborn child. What life can your child look forward to in an orphanage?'

She did not answer, her face rigid and white.

'It is a painful choice. Whatever happens, you will go to prison for life. It is possible, if you help me, that I may be able to arrange for your child to be given to your family, or even Dr Hadfield's. Then it would know of its mother and father and know love . . .'

It was as if he was talking to her from a great distance, the subtle sibilant hiss of the snake in the garden. What was she prepared to risk for her child? How could they threaten to separate a child from its mother? She wanted to release the pain, to scream, to throw her tea glass against the wall.

'. . . you must have time to think . . .' He was still speaking to her. 'It is a choice you make for your child. What is most important to you?'

# 44

For many days Hadfield saw only the warders and a doctor who stubbornly refused to say more than he deemed professionally necessary. The beating had left him with superficial injuries, but fearful the bruises would precipitate a scandal, the governor of the Preliminary had placed him under close medical supervision.

For half an hour each day, he shuffled in silence round the edge of the frozen exercise yard with the other inmates. He listened to messages painstakingly tapped on the pipes and memorised the names of 'politicals' from every corner of the empire and the distinctive chinking rhythm of their spoons. It was from one of these he learnt of Sophia Perovskaya's arrest.

'Is there word of Anna Kovalenko?' he tapped slowly on his own pipe. No one had news of her. But after that he asked the question every day.

It was the powerlessness he found most oppressive. His fate in the hands of others, and even the smallest details of his life determined without reference to him. Finally, in his third week of captivity, he received a visitor.

His Excellency General Glen was standing by the mantelpiece in the governor's office, resplendent in the Finance Ministry uniform, the gold and silver stars on his coat twinkling in the light of a lively fire. The governor was at his side but withdrew with a respectful nod of the head.

Hadfield stood in the middle of the rug, conscious of the sorry figure he cut in his prison greys, his hand clutching the top of his trousers. General Glen did not move from the fire, pity and contempt written in the lines of his face. Only when the door closed quietly behind the governor did he speak.

'What have they done to you?'

'This?' asked Hadfield, touching the yellow bruises on his cheek and about his eyes. 'It's not as bad as it appears.'

'Pity. Damn it, you deserve it.'

They stood gazing at each other in awkward silence. Hadfield wanted to say he was sorry but he was sure it would be like lighting a blue touchpaper.

But an apology was what the general was waiting to hear. 'What do you say for yourself, sir?'

'That I deeply regret the pain and the embarrassment I have caused you and my aunt after all the kindness you have shown me.'

'But why, sir? Why?' The muscles in the general's face were twitching as he fought to hold his anger in check. 'You've disappointed everyone. The ambassador, the British government . . . Lord Dufferin was obliged to assure the emperor that no one at the embassy had the slightest inkling you were involved with these people, this woman . . . and I have had to apologise to His Majesty. Lady Dufferin feels you betrayed her trust. We all do. Explain yourself, sir.'

Hadfield took a deep breath, as if collecting his thoughts, but there was nothing he wished to say. He could not speak of his feelings. There was no need. A ferocious diatribe burst from his uncle like warm champagne from a bottle: the disgrace his nephew had brought upon him, his aunt's pain and the disappointment of his cousin Alexandra. 'And your mother. Did you think of her? How could you allow yourself to be deceived by this Romanko woman?'

'Do you know if she is still—'

'Your mistress is not my concern.'

'Don't call her that.'

General Glen looked away for a few seconds, his face puce, hands balled, as if struggling to contain an urge to punch his nephew. 'My only concern is that we avoid a public trial,' he said at last. 'We're going to have to dress this up as an unfortunate affair of the heart, of course, a dangerous infatuation.'

'Of course.'

General Glen took a menacing step closer: 'Damn fool. I'm only doing this for your mother and your aunt's sake.'

'I'm sorry.'

'You have your aunt and cousin to thank for my presence here today.'

Hadfield nodded. 'Please give them my—'

'There is no reason to be optimistic,' said the general, cutting across him impatiently. 'The Ministry of Justice is pressing for trial and an exemplary sentence. You are fortunate Lord Dufferin is still willing to speak on your behalf as a British subject.'

'Yes. Thank you.'

'I don't want your thanks, sir. I want to see the back of you.' He stared at Hadfield for a moment, then walked over to the governor's desk and sat down. 'Who was responsible for those?' he asked, pointing at Hadfield's face.

'An officer of the Gendarme Corps.'

The general listened to a description of the attack with his head bent, turning the signet ring on his right hand distractedly, interrupting only once to check and make a note of Barclay's name.

'Not the behaviour of a proper gentleman,' he observed dryly when his nephew had finished. 'But he may have unwittingly done you a good turn. And this fellow Dobrshinsky?'

'I haven't seen him for two or three weeks.'

'Did he strike you? Is there anything I should know about his conduct?'

For a fleeting moment, an image of the special investigator's

399

pallid face, his small brown eyes and trembling hands, flitted through Hadfield's mind. He dismissed the thought at once.

'Nothing? Damn fellow,' said General Glen, rising from his chair. 'It was his job to prevent this whole sorry business.' There the interview ended, cold, businesslike, without affection and with the presumption their paths would not cross again.

Within a few days the emptiness of the prison filled his mind once more. The only relief came with the patient tapping of the pipes. More arrests, and there was to be a trial in the court building next to the prison. One of the warders was unable to contain his excitement.

'Tomorrow. They're here in the prison already. I've been to take a look at Zhelyabov. Is it true he was sleeping with the aristocrat?' But he knew nothing of a Kovalenko or a Romanko.

Hadfield heard his first word of Anna the following morning as the courtroom was beginning to fill. Clink, clink, clink. A frenzy of tapping and a bittersweet message for the doctor: 'Anna sends love.'

On his knees, spoon in hand: 'Where is Anna?'

He heard his question passed down the pipe by his neighbour. Half an hour later there was a reply: 'Here.'

Unable to contain his disappointment, he jumped to his feet, pacing, spinning in his tiny cell, struggling to hold in check an urge to shout, bellow, beat on the door. Oh God. What now? Trapped, helpless, there was nothing he could do but tell her he loved her too. Sinking back to his knees, he chinked it on the pipe, over, and over and over.

After that he fretted about Anna and their baby constantly, searching every few hours for an excuse to send her a message by the prison telegraph. But there was no reply. He lay for hours on his bed, churning the same fears over and over until he reached the pitch of misery beyond which only madness lay. Once he dreamt he passed invisible through his door on to the landing and was drawn by fairy tale light to her cell where, to his surprise, the ceiling seemed to dissolve into a starry night sky, and he bent beneath it to kiss her tenderly. But a door clanged shut on the landing below, resounding in the well and forcing him back to the complete darkness of his own cell.

The trial lasted only three days, the verdict never in doubt.

'Were you a friend of Sophia Perovskaya's, Doctor?' One of the younger warders asked at breakfast one morning.

'An acquaintance.'

'They say she's the only one who may escape. The emperor would have to confirm her sentence personally because she's nobility.'

But the new tsar was not inclined to show clemency. No exceptions would be made for sex or birth and the sentences were confirmed on all five of the regicides. The news travelled along the pipes to every corner of the prison and, when everyone knew, there was silence. Even the warders seemed to step more lightly on the iron stairs. In his mind's eye Hadfield could see Anna curled in misery, with thoughts of the ordeal her comrades must face, and his heart ached for her and with the fear that one day the same harsh justice might be meted out to her too. In desperation he sought the governor's permission to write to his uncle and to the embassy. He would acknowledge his unborn child and request it be given the protection any British subject was entitled to. For a day he heard nothing. Then he received word the governor was seeking guidance. And, on the eve of the executions, a visit at last.

'But who were you expecting, Doctor?' asked Dobrshinsky. He paused for a few seconds, his eyebrows raised in a quizzical expression: 'Your uncle again? You know, he has done you great service. Sit down, please.'

Hadfield did as he was bidden.

'First let me apologise for Major Barclay's behaviour. He was overwrought but that is not to excuse him. He was most ungentlemanly.'

'Yes.'

'I have just visited the condemned cells. You know the regicides are to be executed in the morning?' The special investigator's voice was reflective, his eyes fixed for a moment on the middle distance. There was the same sickly pallor in his cheeks, his skin drawn tighter across the bone.

'Have you tried to imagine how you would behave if you were the condemned man?' Again the curious cold tight-lipped smile. 'Or woman?'

'Is it possible to imagine?'

'You are fortunate you will not have to try. But your friend Anna Petrovna . . .' Dobrshinsky's voice tailed off suggestively. 'Of course, you know she is a prisoner here,' he added. 'Is it your child? I thought so.'

'Has she seen a doctor?' Hadfield asked, trying hard not to betray any emotion in his voice.

'Would you like to examine her yourself?'

'And the price for this act of humanity?'

Dobrshinsky winced and lifted a trembling hand to his temple as if to soothe a stab of pain.

'The old problem?'

The special investigator frowned and dropped his hand behind his back. 'I am quite well, thank you, Doctor. We are still in need of a little help – an address, two addresses actually. Vera Figner and the printing press.'

'And you want me to ask Anna? I took you for a more astute fellow.'

'You would need to tease it from her. Do you have any conception of what will happen to your baby if you don't?' And he explained that the infant would be taken from Anna and placed in a state orphanage with no name and no registered parents.

'But the baby is mine and I am a British subject!'

'I believe the state prosecutor will take the view that it is only possible to be certain of the baby's mother.'

Hadfield rose angrily to lean across the table. 'That is an ungentlemanly slur.'

'You have become involved in an ungentlemanly business, Doctor,' said Dobrshinsky coldly. 'Your own conduct is hardly above reproach. I can help Anna Petrovna, but only if you can offer me some assistance. Believe me, I have no wish to condemn a child to misery before it is born but my hands are tied. Reflect, Doctor, I beg you. We will talk again.'

Hadfield spent a long night brooding upon the collegiate councillor's words, grasping first the hope he was being bullied by an idle threat then slipping back into a pit of misery. In the early hours his thoughts turned to the vigil the condemned were keeping and he felt sure Anna would be watching through the night too. Close to dawn, he fell into an exhausted sleep, but was woken after only a short time by boots on the landing outside his cell. Before he could rise, the door opened and a warder stood before him, silhouetted against the gaslights on the wing: 'Wake up, Doctor, we've a surprise for you.'

His head still thick with sleep, they bundled him out of the cell and down the iron stairs to the visiting room. His own clothes had been laid out on the table, still dusty, the sleeve of his coat torn in the scuffle with the gendarmes. He was ordered to dress quickly, and as soon as he had he was escorted to a closed prison carriage.

'Where are you taking me?'

But they refused to answer.

It was early, perhaps seven o'clock, but to judge from the street noise, remarkably busy, and before long the carriage horses were obliged to slow to a fast walk. Above the rumble of the wheels he could hear the murmur of a great number of people, and he realised with a start that they were gathering for the executions. The driver began shouting for a passage, enlisting the support of the soldiers lining the route, but after only a few minutes they came to an abrupt and final halt. Even in the darkness, Hadfield was conscious of the huge crowd swelling round the carriage like the tide about a rock. The doors were flung open and for an instant he was blinded by spring sunshine. Curious faces turned towards him, excited whispers, and rising from the bench, his eyes were drawn across the sea of heads to the scaffold with five ropes hanging from its crossbeam. And as he gazed at it, he was gripped by the breathless fear he was to witness Anna's death.

'Why am I here?'

Again the gendarmes did not answer but pulled him roughly from the carriage and began leading him in a catatonic daze towards the platform. The parade ground had been churned by horses and the boots of thousands and, after a few steps, he stumbled, falling to one knee in a dirty puddle before being hauled back to his feet.

'Why am I here?' he asked again, making no effort to keep the desperation from his voice. 'Please tell me.'

The older of the two gendarmes – a sergeant with a bold cavalry moustache – gave an unpleasant barking laugh. 'Calm down. It's not your day.'

'Then why am I here?'

'Orders,' and that was all he would say.

He took in the scene as a series of disparate sounds and images only; green and gold uniforms, the cotton-wool sky and domes of the regimental cathedral, six black steps up to the platform, the humiliation posts with chains and manacles, and the red-bearded hangman with the five criminals who were to act as his assistants. In front of the foot guards about the platform was a seated area reserved for the privileged with tickets and police officials, and it was to here the gendarmes led him. A tall but slightly stooped figure in a German hat stepped forward to meet him. 'You are in good time, Doctor.'

Collegiate Councillor Dobrshinsky looked deathly pale in the sunshine and in his sombre black suit, as if he had crept from the cells of the Secret House.

'Why am I here?' Hadfield asked at once, his voice shaking with anxiety.

'To help you make up your mind.'

'So Anna is—'

'Not this time.'

Relief washed through his body and soul, leaving him reduced and trembling inside. Then, in its wake, a shameful euphoria.

The gendarmes escorted him to the rear of the enclosure to stand with the foot guards at his back. Dobrshinsky sat a short distance from him with a man in the dark green uniform jacket of the Justice Ministry.

'Fifty thousand people,' Hadfield heard the gendarme on his right say.

'Closer to a hundred,' replied the sergeant on his left. He was shifting his weight restlessly from foot to foot, pulling at the chain about Hadfield's wrists, clearly delighted to enjoy such a privileged view of the spectacle.

There was a rustle of excitement then a hush as the carriages carrying the priests and coffins rumbled up to the steps of the platform. In the distance Hadfield could hear the strains of the military band marching in front of the carts of the condemned. Closer, closer it came, a jaunty march tune so inappropriate and macabre it made him shudder.

A moment later the tumbrels rattled into view, the five terrorists strapped by the waist to an iron bar and mounted in chairs for all to see. They were dressed in black, with a placard about their necks that bore the single word 'Regicide'. In the second cart, Sophia Perovskaya's tiny frame was wedged between two of her comrades. And the savage relief Hadfield had felt was gone, forgotten, replaced by disgust and guilt that he was to witness their humiliation. Handcuffed, legs fettered, they were helped from the carts then up the steps to the platform where the executioner and his assistants chained them to the posts. The priests offered the condemned the cross to kiss and all of them accepted this small comfort. The tallest – Zhelyabov – was craning his neck about in an effort to speak to Sophia. And as Hadfield watched him straining at the post, he felt a knot like the executioner's noose tighten in his own throat. The waste. He closed his eyes and groaned: 'Anna, Anna, Anna.'

An official read the sentence in a voice almost no one could hear and the prisoners were unchained and allowed to exchange kisses. Then they were drawn forward to stand beneath the gallows. A white cowl with a broad slit in the neck for the rope was placed over each in turn. Five white figures on the black platform.

A rumble of muffled drums. At precisely 9.20 a.m. the executioner removed his coat. A small stand of three steps was slipped into place before the first prisoner. Blind and fettered, he was led step by step by step to the top. The rope was drawn tight about his neck.

'Oh, Anna, Anna.' Hadfield held his breath. He must watch for her sake. The executioner bent to draw away the steps. There was a sigh like a gust of wind from the crowd as the prisoner hung free, struggling then twitching as life was choked from him. Then it was the turn of the second man, but the drunken sot of a hangman made a mess of it and, after a minute, the victim crashed to the platform. The crowd roared with disgust – but surely this was the entertainment they had come to witness? The condemned man was led up the steps again, but the noose slipped and he fell a second time. The soldiers pressed at Hadfield's back as the crowd surged towards the platform. This time the prisoner could not lift himself and the hangman's assistants had to haul him up with the rope. And as they dragged him aloft, Sophia Perovskaya stood waiting in her white cowl. Hadfield's mind was blank with the horror of it all. He watched the executioner lead her up the steps, so small, her frame so fragile. And he pictured her at the new year party, her cool hand in his, earnest, demure, those piercing blue eyes through which she viewed her life as a crusade. There was a deathly hush as they slid the steps away and she swung free, jigging like a badly strung marionette. Hadfield clenched his teeth, his body stiff, willing it to be quick, holding his breath, his eyes fixed upon the twisting cowl. Oh, Anna, never.

At half past nine the drummers fell silent. Five white figures were hanging from the beam, the executioner resting on the platform rail below. Hadfield lifted a trembling hand to his brow. Every degrading inhumane detail of the scene would be seared into his memory for ever. He felt deep sadness but also an uneasy sense that something terrible and yet profound had taken place. The country was set on an inexorable course that could only end in more bloody violence. Not tomorrow or next month or next year but soon. As he watched them lower Perovskaya's limp body, he knew this was her apotheosis. She had trapped them all. Anna would never desert her legacy. Not now. Never.

'What a squalid spectacle.' It was the cool voice of the collegiate councillor at his shoulder. 'You must speak to her.'

'Is it necessary for me to stay here longer?' Hadfield asked flatly. The crowd was dispersing behind him, the rough coffins were being loaded on to carts, and some of the privileged ticket holders were negotiating with the hangman for lucky strands of rope.

'Will you speak to Anna Petrovna?'

'No.'

Dobrshinsky stared at him for a few seconds then gave a small nod of the head as if this was the answer he had been expecting. 'Then this is no longer a matter for me. I'm sorry.'

He was on the point of saying more but checked himself and turned to leave.

As Hadfield watched the hunched figure in black walk away slowly, he was reminded of the condemned who had climbed to the scaffold only a short while before. 'And what about the child?' he shouted. 'My child?'

The special investigator stopped and his head dropped wearily, as if considering whether it was worth the effort to answer. But he turned slowly again: 'Don't come back, Doctor.'

'What about the baby?'

'The baby?' Dobrshinsky shrugged. 'How would those who died today have put it – "a sacrifice for the greater good of all"?'

A moment later the collegiate councillor was lost from view in the crowd of soldiers and souvenir-hunters. The gendarmes led Hadfield towards the prison carriage. His mind was empty but he could feel a great weight pressing on his chest. It was not until he was sliding about the bench between the gendarmes that he remembered Dobrshinsky's 'Don't come back, Doctor'.

Surely they would not send him away? He hated the loneliness, the greyness of prison, the banging doors and clatter of heavy boots, but Anna was only stairs and corridors from him. They slept on the same iron bed, their cells were lit by the same dim gaslight, the black floor, the walls the same, everything the same, and in this he had found comfort and the will to endure. There was no liberty on the outside. He would be trapped in a darker place by fear and guilt and grief.

'I won't go,' he said in English.

'What?' The gendarme sergeant shook his head a little: 'Speak Russian. Better still, don't speak at all.'

And Hadfield did not speak again, even though his heart was sick.

\*

'Did the doctor witness the executions? Good. He leaves for Berlin tomorrow. It was in no one's interests for this to become a diplomatic affair with the British.' The green leather armchair groaned as Count Vyacheslav von Plehve eased his heavy frame to its edge. It was a little low, and from the other side of the desk he appeared to be resting his chin at its edge between the brass ink stand and some red files. 'You don't seem surprised, Anton Frankzevich,' he said, a note of irritation in his voice.

'I'm not,' replied Dobrshinsky.

'Your fellow Barclay didn't help matters, of course. No matter now. The doctor will be accompanied by the British military attaché. Of course, he's not to see the woman before he goes.'

'No.'

The count shifted at the edge of the chair as if in two minds whether to rise. If he was feeling uncomfortable, that was how it should be. Dobrshinsky had no intention of making his task easier.

'Of course it's galling we can't punish him properly,' said the chief prosecutor.

'Love, livelihood, family . . . he will lose all those things.'

'Not enough,' said von Plehve impatiently, 'withholding information, consorting with terrorists, and God knows what else he was doing for them.'

They gazed across the desk at each other, the count smoothing his large moustache with his thumb and forefinger. Dobrshinsky had barely set foot in his office at Fontanka 16 before the prosecutor arrived unannounced at his door. He was dressed in his ceremonial uniform and had come directly from a meeting with the tsar's chief minister, Loris-Melikov, that he described with the slippery understatement of the consummate politician as 'difficult'. Dobrshinsky was quite sure he knew why. He had been expecting a 'difficult' conversation for some while. Perhaps it was only coincidence but it struck him as a fitting one that von Plehve should choose the hour the tsar's murderers were to be laid in their unmarked graves. In the morning the English doctor would be gone too. It was like a *roman policier*, with the loose threads gathered in the final pages. And yet the story was not over. How could it be?

'Of course, everyone is very grateful to you, my dear Anton Frankzevich,' said the count, breaking the awkward silence at last. 'His Excellency Count Loris-Melikov was particularly anxious I should say so . . .' He paused to allow the special investigator to acknowledge this gracious compliment. But Dobrshinsky had no intention of offering him even a sliver of encouragement. Von Plehve cleared his throat a little nervously. 'We all recognise what a . . . a challenge it has been . . . how difficult . . .' Again he waited for Dobrshinsky to reply but he was not to be drawn.

Irritated by his watchful silence, the count levered himself from the creaking chair with the intention of putting more than the width of the desk between them. His boots squeaked a little comically on the polished parquet floor as he made his way to the windows. The embankment was busier than was customary at that hour, with servants and tradesmen chatting on the pavement opposite, too excited by the spectacle they had witnessed to settle to their usual chores. 'The new emperor wants firmer measures,' von Plehve said, turning back to the room. 'No accommodation with terror.' He was almost a silhouette against the window. 'There is to be a new secret department – the Okhrana – based here, at Fontanka 16.'

'Same task, new name?'

'And new methods. Ah, you smile . . .' said the count tartly. 'What can there be to smile about?'

'New methods?'

'This is a battle for the soul of Russia, Anton Frankzevich. And in such a battle the Okhrana will use all the weapons at its disposal.' The count spoke with the glibness of one who has learnt lines but is yet to fully comprehend their meaning. 'It will be more robust, the ends will justify the means . . .'

'An interesting perspective from a lawyer.'

'My dear Anton Frankzevich, I should not have to remind you that the terrorist does not acknowledge the rule of law . . . no, we need new methods . . .'

'And new people?'

'Yes.'

The French mantel clock filled the silence again, as it had unfailingly done for the two years the special investigator had occupied his post. At first it had nagged Dobrshinsky but now he found comfort in its inexorable ticking, and he had resolved to take it with him.

'It is His Excellency's view that it is important to restore confidence . . . the death of the tsar . . . the bomb at the palace . . . those who were unable to prevent these outrages are to be found other work.'

The light from the window seemed to flicker as von Plehve shifted awkwardly from foot to foot.

'His Excellency appreciates your contribution in bringing the terrorists to justice – The People's Will is broken,' he paused, then added pointedly, 'even if the Figner woman is still at liberty.'

'There will be others. After the grisly spectacle today, there will be more assassinations, more bombs.'

'Yes, there will be . . .' Von Plehve hesitated to consider his next words carefully. 'But ours is not to question . . . we are servants of a tsar. To consider moderate measures is useless when circumstances and the hour are set at extremes.'

Dobrshinsky nodded slowly then pushed his chair away and walked round his desk to join the chief prosecutor at the window. They were only an arm's length apart, the view on to the street between them.

'You look ill. You must rest,' said von Plehve with a soapy

pretence at concern. 'Of course your old post will be held for you at the Ministry of Justice.'

Dobrshinsky gazed out on to the Fontanka below, as he had done on his first day. The ice was melting at last and the dirty snow on its surface would soon be washed away. The sun was lost in a low grey Petersburg sky that seemed to leach colour from the mansions opposite.

'Will we live to see it?' he asked suddenly.

'You mean . . . ?' Von Plehve was alarmed by the directness of his question and the implied pessimism. 'I take you to mean a revolution? Speaking for myself, I feel sure I won't.'

Dobrshinsky was still standing at the window a few minutes later as the count climbed the steps into his carriage. A lawyer, a politician, the director of the new Okhrana – oh yes, Dobrshinsky was sure he was to be the first – von Plehve would act without scruple in defence of divinely inspired order. But he bore him no ill will. He felt no anger, and only a little regret. He felt relief that it was over and a hunger for his dark corner and *un état oubli*.

# 1882

A more perfect, stronger revolutionary organisation will take the place of the groups that are wiped out ... A terrible outburst, a bloody subversion, a violent revolutionary convulsion throughout all Russia, will complete the process of the overthrow of the old order ... And so Your Majesty, decide. Before you are two courses.

**Letter to Tsar Alexander III
from the executive committee of
The People's Will pleading for a
democratic assembly and freedom of speech**

# 45

The well-built young gentleman in the top hat and fur coat was too merry to notice that someone was keeping pace on the pavement opposite. After a convivial evening at a restaurant on the Nevsky Prospekt, he had elected to walk home in the hope cold air would clear the claret from his befuddled brain. At first his pursuer had followed at a discreet distance, but it had shortened when it became apparent from his rolling gait that the young gentleman was very much the worse for wear from drink. Turning into Malaya Italyanskaya Street, he slipped on a patch of ice and, with desperate flailing limbs, fought to stay on his feet. It made his pursuer smile. What would the readers of *The Times* of London make of such an undignified display? Fortunately, the new mansion block where Mr George Dobson rented his apartment was only a few yards further and these he was able to execute safely with tiny Japanese steps.

Dobson was snoozing in a chair beside the fire with a glass of strong black tea balanced on the arm when the bell rang. It was nearly midnight, he had discarded his jacket and boots, his head was beginning to ache and he was in no mood to welcome visitors. It rang again as he was smoothing his hair in front of the mirror. Muttering profanities under his breath, he hurried into the hall and drew back the locks. It was a woman of perhaps thirty in a heavy brown coat that had seen many winters and was far too big for her small frame. She was wearing a green scarf about her face and a traditional winter hat of rabbit fur. She was better dressed than most peasants, but only a little.

'Mr George Dobson?' she asked in Russian.

'Yes.'

'May I come in?'

'Who are you?'

A gloved finger to her lips, she whispered 'Inside'.

Her face was very thin and white, the skin a little loose over the bone. She had thick dark eyebrows, a broad nose and a small mouth with a full lower lip and a thin Cupid's bow upper. She was not beautiful but striking, and even in the darkness there was a pale brilliance to her blue eyes that startled him.

Flummoxed by her boldness, he stepped back into the hall. She followed him at once but waited until the door was closed and bolted before she spoke.

'My name is Anna Kovalenko,' she said, and she pulled off her gloves and held out her hand in a very English way.

'Hadfield's . . . But you're in prison.'

'No. I am standing in your hall.'

Dobson leant forward a little as if gaping at an unusual zoo animal. 'They let you go?'

'Of course not!' she said shortly. 'Can we talk somewhere else?' And without waiting for an invitation, she set off down the hall in search of the drawing room.

'What are you doing here?' he asked crossly as he followed her. 'Did anyone see you?'

'No one saw me.'

She took off her coat and hat and dropped them on his couch. Her hair was cut short and in the gaslight she looked thin and severe in a plain black dress.

'You should draw the curtains.'

'How can you be sure?'

'Mr Dobson, I have been a revolutionary for a number of years.'

He plodded to the window and closed the drapes while Anna cleared newspapers from an armchair by the fire. 'I expect you know why I've come here?'

'No,' he said, slumping into the chair opposite. 'And frankly I would rather you weren't here. How did you escape?'

'It's not important. At Krasnoyarsk on the way east – with the help of the party.'

'Is there still a party?'

She gave a small smile: 'The correspondent with all the questions. I haven't come to talk about the party.'

'What have you come to talk about?'

She turned to look at the fire as if to compose herself, its flickering shadows playing across her cheek and neck. And when she looked at him again there was a sadness in her eyes and in the weary lines of her face that spoke of loss and pain and desperation. He knew why she was there and she knew he knew.

'My comrades have been looking for her,' she said. 'But you will understand how difficult it is for friends of mine to make inquiries.'

'Yes. But what can I do?'

'You know people. The British embassy . . .'

He stared at her for a moment then, rising from his chair, made his way over to the samovar and began to spoon tea into a pot.

'It would be easy for a correspondent to visit these places without suspicion,' she said.

His back was to her and she did not see his wry smile.

'Is that all?' he asked, turning with the tea tray: 'Why me? There are Russian journalists. I don't know you.'

She coloured a little: 'You've heard of me.'

'Most of St Petersburg has heard of you. Here—' and he handed her a glass.

'Have you tried?' she asked tentatively.

Dobson did not reply but stood at the fireplace blowing the steam from his glass, his high pink forehead wrinkled in a thoughtful frown.

'He's your friend,' she added quietly.

'Can't you speak his name?'

She turned to look at the fire again, lifting a small hand to her face but not before he noticed her lip tremble.

'I want to find my daughter. Will you help me?'

'And Frederick feels the same.'

'I know he feels the same,' she said quietly. 'That's why I'm here. My friends tell me you visited the Rauchfus Hospital and the orphanage on the Moika Embankment.'

'Yes. I'm doing what I can to find the girl.'

'Sophia. That's her name,' she said sharply, turning to look at him again.

'The state has given her a name, Anna Petrovna, but we have no idea what.'

'We?'

'Frederick has other friends.'

Anna nodded. Her lips were pursed, an intense frown hovering between her eyes, as if battling to hold deep feelings in check.

'It is impertinent of me, but do you still have feelings for him?' Dobson asked.

She stiffened, her shoulders narrowing, her hands turning in her lap: 'He must forget me . . .'

Dobson took a sip of his tea, watching her over the top of the glass. Then lowering it back to the arm, he said, 'I've told him to forget you. You know you've ruined his reputation.'

If he was expecting her to demurely acquiesce he was very wrong.

'He made his own judgements. I tried to warn him. He knew I was . . . I will always be with the people. The struggle is not over. It is only a question of time.'

'Yes, well, I have no respect for murderers, no matter how they dress up their crime. You're only sitting here still because I'm still a friend of Frederick's – for all his misguided loyalties.'

'Then I'll leave.' She began to rise.

'Sit down.'

She stared at him for a moment, a gleam of resentment and barely disguised hostility in her eyes, then sank back to the edge of the chair.

'Frederick is besotted with you. Sophia and, yes, you, Anna Petrovna, are all that seem to matter to him.'

She turned her head from him again in an effort to disguise the emotion written deeply in her face. 'When did you last hear . . .' She could not finish her question.

'Today. We walked together. I've told him not to leave his rooms by day but the damn fool does what he likes.'

'You mean he's here?' Anna leant forward in astonishment, her arm outstretched as if to touch him, and a kaleidoscope of feelings from delight through concern to anger flitted across her face: 'Why is he here? Why?'

'Didn't you listen? He wants you and your child.'

'He must leave. Go back to Zurich. Tell him. Please.'

'Don't you think you should tell him?'

She hesitated, biting her lip anxiously: 'Will he want to see me? I will write to him.'

'Be my guest.'

She rose and made her way over to Dobson's desk, where she scribbled a note on a sheet of his writing paper. When she had finished, he helped her into her coat and led her back along the hall. She pulled her scarf over her nose and mouth, drawing his gaze up to her pale hypnotic eyes.

'And you will do what you can to help?'

'I am already. But you must not visit me here again.'

'Thank you.' She looked at him more softly.

419

He bid her farewell then watched her from his window as she hurried across the frozen street into the city's shadows.

The following morning Dobson woke in his clothes with a throbbing head and a wooden mouth. Rolling from his bed, he stepped over to the window and drew the curtain aside a little. There was a light covering of snow in the street and the civil servants and better sort of merchants who lived on Malaya Italyanskaya were hurrying to work in clouds of vapour. A smart blue carriage with the arms of a noble family was waiting at the door of the mansion opposite. He had no idea what a police spy would look like but drew some comfort from the absence of anyone hovering in a doorway. An hour later, he stepped on to the street in his oldest coat and walked as briskly as he dared to the cab rank outside the Mariinskaya Hospital, cursing in English under his breath: 'Damn the fellow.'

The principal focus of Dobson's displeasure was sitting at the window of an attic room in a seedy looking house in the Izmailovsky district. Hadfield's hair was shorter, his beard fuller, and he was wearing a pair of simple wire spectacles with round lenses that made him appear intensely serious. To his neighbours he was a Volga German in his late twenties called Karl Schmidt, who had been enterprising enough to move in search of a better living in the capital. He was careful, a little distant in a Lutheran sort of way, and but for a portly foreign gentleman he received no visitors. He took few meals and his landlady was never quite certain when he was at home. But on that bright November morning the maid found him at the window, a newspaper on his knee, staring through the dirty panes at the rooftops of the city. The room was cold and he was wearing several layers beneath a jacket and scarf. She cleared his dirty dishes and left him with some tea. On the stairs she passed his foreign friend, pink in the face and breathing heavily as he hauled himself up with the aid of the banister.

The door opened before the correspondent could knock.

'It's good exercise,' Hadfield observed in Russian, with a small smile of welcome.

The correspondent pushed past his friend with a stony face and began to shrug his coat from his shoulders.

'There's some tea,' said Hadfield, closing the door behind him.

'No thank you,' Dobson replied hoarsely, and he pulled a chair from the small wooden table and sat down.

'Did you hear anything from your police contact?'

'Please, a moment to collect myself.'

Hadfield poured some more tea and sat beside him, his hands cupped around the glass, his foot tapping on the wooden floor in an involuntary display of impatience. Three months had slipped by since his return to St Petersburg and he had still not traced his baby daughter. His former assistant at the hospital – Anton Pavel – had found rooms for him and had readily agreed to help in any way he was able. They had made discreet inquiries at almost all the city's hospitals and charitable institutions but they had not discovered any firm intelligence as to her whereabouts. The little girl – Hadfield did not know her name – might have been placed with a family or spirited away to an orphanage in the provinces. To be certain, they needed access to her mother's police file. The three of them had discussed the matter at length and it had been agreed at last that Dobson would risk approaching his source in the new Okhrana.

'Your baby's name is Sophia.' Dobson paused to give weight to this revelation, a small smile playing on his lips. 'But no, I have not found her.'

Hadfield looked away for a moment. 'It means so much to be able to call her by her name.'

Dobson waited until he had collected himself sufficiently to continue, then said: 'I've arranged to see your old friend Barclay tomorrow. He's rising up the table of ranks – a colonel now. Not as clever as Dobrshinsky but a little more ruthless, which is, no doubt, why he's still useful.'

'But if you haven't spoken to him yet, how do you know my daughter's name?'

'Because I've spoken to her mother.'

'You've spoken to Anna? She's here in the city?' This time Hadfield could not contain himself and he jumped up, his chair crashing to the floor, his right hand pressed to his forehead, the room too small to pace. He stood above Dobson with an expression of bewilderment then hope on his face. 'She escaped?'

'Evidently. For God's sake sit down and I'll tell you the little I know.'

He told Hadfield of Anna's visit the evening before, and that she was searching for their daughter with the help of friends – 'the few still at liberty' – but he did not mention her note.

'I sense she is still committed to the revolution,' he said disparagingly. 'I know you're infatuated with her – and she is good-looking enough, I grant you – but she doesn't seem to have—'

'To have? You may as well say it.'

'She hasn't changed, Frederick. She's a dangerous fanatic.'

Hadfield shook his head crossly. 'She is fighting for the freedom of the people. You've said yourself that things are even worse here . . .'

'Since her friends murdered the last tsar, yes.'

'It will be a long struggle.'

'Don't be their mouthpiece,' Dobson snapped.

'I'm not.'

They glared at each other for a few seconds, until Hadfield leant forward to touch his friend's arm: 'You've done so much. I'm grateful.'

The correspondent's face softened a little. 'As your friend, I

422

must tell you I think she is only capable of seeing her life and the world one way. You should have seen the certainty in her face. I tell you, Frederick, her mind runs on rails.'

'I love her,' said Hadfield simply. 'Please do not speak ill of her.' He rose again and walked over to the window. In the silence they could hear the sound of water slopping on the stone stairs and the grating of a mop bucket as the maid pushed it with her foot. And in the street below, a young man – a clerk perhaps – was moving out of the house opposite, loading the few sticks of furniture he possessed on to a cart.

'Did she speak of me?' Hadfield asked quietly.

'She gave me a note for you.' Dobson drew it from the breast pocket of his jacket. 'Here.'

Hadfield stared at his name written in her untidy hand on the envelope and he felt a surge of love and hope. He was in no hurry to open it for he knew Anna well enough to be sure her message would be short and to the point, even after a year and a half apart. But his friend was watching him and waiting, so he slit the envelope open with a table knife.

*8.00 p.m. At the church.*

Terse even by her standards, he thought, and offered the note to Dobson, who glanced at it then handed it back without a word.

When the correspondent had gone, Hadfield sat at the window waiting for the blue-grey hours to slip away. It snowed for a time in the afternoon, falling straight and wet, the temperature hovering just below freezing until dusk, when a frost began to form between the inner and outer panes. His thoughts were in constant motion, swirling as if carried on a wind to the future and back to the past then lifted up once again. Always her, always Anna and their daughter. He imagined them in his own reflection and in his breath on the glass, until his gaze slipped beyond to the darkness of the city. She had suffered so much. The humiliation of the birth at the prison, the distress of separation, trial and sentence – a lifetime of penal servitude in the east. Her comrades in Switzerland had told him the little they knew from correspondence and, desperate always for word of her, he had scoured the papers every day for news, even when the little there was brought only pain and guilt. Baby Sophia was a year old already. At dark moments he wondered if he would ever find her and he was frightened that if he lost her he would lose Anna too.

At seven o'clock the maid brought him some bread and broth from the kitchen but he had no appetite. A short time later he left the house, racing down the stairs, eager to be in the freezing air and on the move. Walking fast, almost running, slipping on the icy pavements, he made his way to the Obvodny Canal, factory workers trudging home with their heads bent against the first flurries of another snowfall. The dead hand of winter creeping across the city until the corruption of its canals and streets and palaces was locked beneath a glittering white surface. But what did he care? It was a long way to the church and he must not be late. Run. Run faster. Run. And as he ran, he thought of the little room with its single mattress, of her finger pressed gently to his lips, of the silence and the stillness, the infinite stillness. He would help her escape from the shadow of the last years. Together. Together with Sophia. He held this feeling like a prayer, allowing it to fill his mind and body as he ran, careless of the snow and the curious glances he was drawing from passers-by. On past the Alexander Nevsky Monastery and on to the embankment of the Neva. 'Hey, watch out there!' a cabbie shouted from his box as he weaved his way across the street to the riverside walk.

The scaffolding had gone and rising complete was the Church of St Boris and St Gleb. The Romanesque arch at the west front in pristine brick and stone and, crowning all, a lantern dome with figures of the apostles in its niches. The church built to commemorate the tsar's miraculous escape from an assassin's bullet had been finished at last, and yet empty and lifeless inside, it was of no more significance than a shattered colossus in a desert, boundless and bare. Hadfield stood panting at the bottom of the steps as a bell in one of the western towers chimed eight o'clock.

A market trader removes the planks from his makeshift stall in the square. In front of a pink warehouse opposite the church, night watchmen are gathering about a brazier. Workers from the textile mill and the brewery on the embankment trickle home, black and shapeless in their heavy coats. The gaslights seem softer and very yellow as the snow quickens and falls in thumbnail flakes. She is a little late but she will come. Small, upright, striding across the square, and he will drop from the steps to kiss her, squeezing her so tightly and perhaps she will release her pain and cry with happiness and new hope.

# HISTORICAL NOTE AND SOURCES

The plot and many of the characters in *To Kill a Tsar* are based on real people and events. The two years that pass in the book's pages mark the rise and fall of the first important revolutionary terrorist group of modern times, the Narodnaya Volya or The People's Will.

Terrorism is 'the threat of violence and the use of fear to coerce, persuade, and gain public attention' (*Report of the Task Force on Disorders and Terrorism*, Washington, DC, 1976). It is a form of armed propaganda in an age dominated by the mass media. We live at a time when terrorists can change the lives of millions, take countries to war, and command the respect and support of many by committing suicidal acts of violence. The seeds of this kind of ruthless direct action were sown in the second half of the nineteenth century in Imperial Russia. 'To attract the attention of the entire world, is that not in itself a victory?' the Russian revolutionary Georgi Plekhanov observed after the assassination of Alexander II.

Alexander's reign began in 1855 with a liberal reform that earned him the sobriquet of 'Tsar Liberator'. The emancipation of the serfs in 1861 freed twenty-three million peasants from a system of slavery that bound them to the land and deprived them of rights enjoyed by his other subjects. But the tsar's belief in his divine right to rule was unshakeable and attempts by nationalist and democratic movements to challenge it were ruthlessly suppressed across the empire. Minority languages such as Lithuanian, Ukrainian and Polish were restricted, newspapers, letters and literature were censored, trial by jury suspended and those who called for reform were imprisoned and exiled to Siberia. One of the characters in this story – Nikolai Kibalchich – spent almost three years in prison on a charge of lending a dangerous book to a peasant. A short time after his release he became a committed revolutionary and a member of The People's Will.

Most peasants were faithful subjects of the emperor but among the educated, in particular the young, there was active support for representative democracy and radical reform. The tsar's secret Third Section was formed with the support of the police and Corps of Gendarmes, to protect the autocracy from dissent. Its notorious headquarters was at Number 16 on the Fontanka Embankment.

After the explosion at the Winter Palace in 1880, Count Mikhail Loris-Melikov (1826–88) became minister of the interior. Within a few months of taking office he had organised the police into a new department and replaced the Third Section with a secret investigative body known as the Okhrana. One of the first directors of the new Police Department and the Okhrana was Count Vyacheslav von Plehve (1846–1904) who appears as a character in the pages of this book. In 1902 Von Plehve became minister of the interior but was assassinated by a revolutionary on the streets of St Petersburg two years later. Another figure in this book, Anton Frankzevich Dobrshinsky (1844–97), served as head of chancellery in the Ministry of Justice with special responsibility for the investigation of criminal affairs. Dobrshinsky was responsible for questioning members of The People's Will and earned a reputation as a formidable interrogator.

There had been active terrorist groups in the south of the Russian Empire and in the capital itself for a number of years before 1879. In 1866 a student called Dmitry Karakozov attempted to kill the tsar, and it was to mark his miraculous delivery from the hands of this assassin that the foundation stone was laid for the Church of St Boris and St Gleb. In 1869 the Russian nihilist Sergei Nechaev wrote a manifesto that was to prove influential in the thinking of many young radicals. In *The Catechism of a Revolutionary* he declared,

> The Revolutionist is a doomed man. He has no private interests, no affairs, sentiments, ties, property nor even a name of his own. His entire being is devoured by one purpose, one thought, one passion – the revolution. Heart and soul, not merely by word but by deed, he has severed every link with the social order and with the entire civilized world; with the laws, good manners, conventions, and morality of that world. He is its merciless enemy and continues to inhabit it with only one purpose – to destroy it.

Ten years after this catechism The People's Will insisted its members demonstrate the same single-minded commitment to the revolution. *To Kill a Tsar* opens with the first attempt on the life of the emperor by those who were instrumental in the formation of the group a short time afterwards, and it ends two years later with their imprisonment and execution. For those two years it managed, in the words of one of the tsar's ministers, 'to terrorise the entire administration' with a series of well-planned and executed attacks on the emperor. The first of these attempts, by Alexander Soloviev – the attempt to shoot the tsar in front of the Winter Palace in April 1879 – was much as I describe it in Chapter 1. The would-be assassin had plotted his attack with Alexander Mikhailov, Grigory Goldenberg and two other prominent revolutionaries who appear briefly as characters in *To Kill a Tsar*: Alexander Kviatkovsky and Nikolai Morozov. These men were to play important roles in the formation of The People's Will three months later. Among the first to join them in the new group were Andrei Zhelyabov, Sophia Perovskaya and Vera Figner.

The People's Will was never large; its chief instrument, the executive committee, was made up of only twenty members. Fewer than fifty people were actively involved in its day-to-day activities in the capital, with about five hundred more in the provinces. Another three to four thousand people were sympathisers who helped distribute the party's propaganda, and from time to time concealed illegals wanted by the police. One such was the government official known to the party as 'Bucephalus'. An account of his work as a concealer can be found in *Underground Russia: Revolutionary Profiles and Sketches from Life* by Sergei Kravchinski. The author was a friend of Alexander Mikhailov and a prominent revolutionary who, in 1878, stabbed to death a head of the Third Section in a St Petersburg street. Kravchinski fled to Britain where he wrote articles and books in support of his comrades in Russia. He was a useful source for the operational methods of the terrorists.

It was the contention of The People's Will that by 1879 peaceful protest had demonstrably failed and that change was only possible through direct terrorist action. The party was socialist, but democratic in character, committed to an elected assembly, freedom of speech and religious worship. Its programme called for a political revolution and terrorist activity designed to remove leading government figures, protect the party from spies, and inculcate a fighting spirit in its members. But from the first, its time and money were spent planning the assassination of the tsar. In the person of the emperor its members saw the embodiment of autocracy, antipathy to democracy and the oppression of ordinary people.

The membership of The People's Will was drawn from all classes of Russian society with the gentry and the educated especially well represented in its ranks, as too were women; Sophia Perovskaya and Vera Figner were particularly influential members of the group. One of their male comrades on the executive committee noted that 'the girls are fiercer than our men'. A number of the female recruits to The People's Will became involved in revolutionary politics while studying medicine in Switzerland. One such was Vera Figner, whose gripping account of her life, *Memoirs of a Revolutionist*, has been an important source for this story. Women like Figner and Perovskaya fell in love and had affairs with male comrades but not at the expense of their commitment to the party and revolution. 'A man who admitted putting me above the cause, even in a moment of passion,' the revolutionary Ekaterina Obukhova wrote to a friend in 1879, 'would destroy everything that connected us' (as quoted in Barbara Alpern Engel, *Mothers and Daughters: Women of the Intelligentsia in Nineteenth-Century Russia*). Vera Figner was not the only revolutionary to leave her husband because he did not share her political views.

More background on the revolutionaries of The People's Will and their world can be found on the website www.andrewwilliams.tv.

I drew on both primary sources and published histories for my account of the attempts on the Tsar's life and his final assassination. A number of the exchanges between the terrorists in the story are based on written records of the group's secret meetings left by those who were there. In her memoir Olga Liubatovich describes the party and séance that Frederick and Anna attend on New Year's Eve (*Five Sisters: Women Against the Tsar*, edited and translated by Barbara Alpern Engel and Clifford N. Rosenthal). I have drawn details of the printing press and descriptions of some of the leading terrorists from Praskovia Ivanovskaia's published account of her time in The People's Will. Both Figner and the revolutionary Katerina Breshkovskaia (in her memoir *Hidden Springs of the Russian Revolution*) left vivid accounts of interrogation and imprisonment in the House of Preliminary Detention and the St Peter and St Paul Fortress. I visited and photographed the streets and exteriors of the apartments in St Petersburg that were used by The People's Will between 1879 and 1881 as well as many of the other buildings mentioned in the story. Photographs, contemporary engravings and reports from British, French and Russian newspapers and periodicals were useful for descriptions of the terrorists, their attempts to kill the tsar, trials and executions. The newspapers were also able to provide more general information about life in the empire, the health of the tsar's subjects, winter sports and royal engagements. *The Times's* correspondent George Dobson was a particularly helpful source and an intelligent liberal commentator on the nihilists and the challenge they presented to imperial authority. Dobson was the newspaper's man in St Petersburg for more than twenty-five years, and only left the city with the Bolshevik revolution in 1917 after a short spell of imprisonment in the St Peter and St Paul Fortress.

For the background and upbringing of my heroine Anna, I drew inspiration from the early life of the formidable socialist revolutionary Elizaveta Kovalskaia. Kovalskaia's father was a landowner in what is now the eastern Ukraine, her mother one of his serfs. Anna is very conscious of the village and her roots, and like another important revolutionary figure, Vera Zasulich, is inspired by a Kondraty Ryleev poem celebrating a Ukrainian uprising. At the end of *To Kill a Tsar* Anna is obliged to give birth in prison as the revolutionary Geisa Gelfman was forced to do in September 1881. Gelfman's baby was taken from her, marked 'parents unknown', and sent to an orphanage. Gelfman died in prison six months later. Anna is able to escape from custody on her journey east into exile. Elizaveta Kovalskaia managed to do the same in February 1882 but was later apprehended. A number of terrorists were more successful. In July 1878 Olga Liubatovich escaped from western Siberia by pretending to commit suicide.

Most of the revolutionaries mentioned in *To Kill a Tsar* spent many years in prison. Both Alexander Mikhailov and his spy inside the Third Section, Nikolai Kletochnikov, died in the cells of the St Peter and St Paul Fortress in 1883. Stepan Khalturin, the carpenter responsible for the explosion at the Winter Palace, was arrested and executed in 1882. As recounted in this book, Grigory Goldenberg committed suicide in prison when he realised that his testimony had led to the arrest of many of his former comrades. In my story I endeavour to reflect the appalling anti-Semitism in Russian society at this time. Rumours that the Jews were involved in the assassination of Alexander II were used as an excuse to launch pogroms in Kiev, Odessa and Warsaw.

Andrei Zhelyabov, Sophia Perovskaya and Nikolai Kibalchich were executed with two of the bombers on 3 April 1881. After their execution the 'Venus of the revolution', Vera Figner, became the leader of The People's Will until her arrest in 1883. She was imprisoned in the St Peter and St Paul then the Schlüsselburg Fortresses and spent many years in solitary confinement. Finally released in 1905, she died in Moscow during the Second World War. Olga Liubatovich gave birth to a daughter in Switzerland whom she placed with foster parents. The baby died six months later while Olga was in Russia attempting to organise the escape from prison of her child's father, Nikolai Morozov. She was arrested in 1882 and banished without trial to eastern Siberia where she spent the next twenty years in exile.

In 1886 a young revolutionary called Alexander Illyich Ulyanov was inspired by the example of The People's Will to join a small group of terrorists. On 1 March 1887 – six years to the day after the death of Alexander II – Ulyanov and his comrades were arrested and charged with plotting to assassinate the new tsar. Two months later he was hanged at the Schlüsselburg Fortress where many of The People's Will terrorists were imprisoned. Ulyanov was the older brother of the man who was to lead the Russian Revolution in 1917: Vladimir Lenin.

The hero of my story, Frederick Hadfield, is from a British community that played an important part in the life of St

Petersburg and the empire. The British began to arrive in the city during the reign of its founder Peter the Great, and the first grand residential embankment built on the Neva came to be known as the English Embankment. Anglo-Russian trading dynasties established themselves here over the next two hundred years but there were prominent professionals too; in particular a number of medical men served the imperial court. Sir James Wylie (1768–1854) was the personal physician to three tsars and founded a hospital in St Petersburg. Another famous Scottish doctor at the court was Sir Alexander Crichton (1763–1856) who entered the service of Tsar Alexander I in 1803 as physician-in-ordinary, and six years later was appointed physician-general to the Russian medical department. Engineers and soldiers were also well represented in Anglo-Russian society. Hadfield's mother's family in *To Kill a Tsar* resembles the Griegs, who were prominent members of the British community for a hundred and fifty years. Admiral Sir Samuel Grieg was born in Scotland in 1736 and entered the service of the Russian navy. He was appointed the Empress Catherine's naval commander-in-chief in 1775. Admiral Grieg chose to marry a Scots woman, and like many Anglo-Russians sent his son Samuel to university in Britain. Three more generations of the family lived on the English Embankment and served the empire in both a military and civil capacity. General Samuel Grieg – the third to bear the name – was appointed the tsar's minister of finance in 1878, a post he held without distinction for two years.

The former British embassy in St Petersburg is now an academic institute, but some of the rooms remain, including its extraordinary White Ballroom. The British ambassador's wife, Lady Dufferin, kept a gossipy journal of her life in the city between 1879 and 1881, and I have drawn on this for much fine detail (Harriot Georgina Blackwood: *My Russian and Turkish Journals*). For the serious day-to-day business of the embassy I consulted the telegrams and ambassador's reports at the National Archive in London. *Diplomatic Reminiscences*, the memoirs of Lord Augustus Loftus, British ambassador to Russia (1871–9) were also a useful source. A third secretary, Lord Frederic Hamilton, wrote a lighthearted memoir of embassy life at this time, *The Days Before Yesterday*, in which he describes the theatricals he organised for Lord Dufferin. He was also a witness to the execution of the regicides. The Foreign Office Diplomatic List provided me with the names and backgrounds of key embassy staff including the military attaché, Lieutenant-Colonel Thomas Gonne. Gonne's daughter, Maud, was the English-born Irish revolutionary whom the poet William Butler Yeats loved recklessly, and who inspired some of his finest work including 'He Wishes for the Cloths of Heaven', the lines I quote at the beginning of this book.

For ordinary Russian life in St Petersburg, its geography and history, I consulted many written sources. Particularly useful for the geography of the city were *Baedeker's Russia 1914* and the online *Encyclopedia of St Petersburg* (www.encspb.ru/en). Although many of the city's buildings are much as they were in 1879, the Soviet era left its mark and some of the churches mentioned in the story have gone. St Boris and St Gleb's Church was closed in 1934 and demolished in 1975. The names of some streets and prominent buildings were changed after the revolution. I have used anglicised spellings of the 1880 Russian names for streets and all but a few well-known buildings and districts such as the Winter Palace and the Haymarket, which are rendered in English. Of course, nowhere is the colour of St Petersburg at this time captured better than in the pages of Dostoevsky. One of his neighbours in the apartment building where he lived on Kuznechny Lane in 1880 was an important member of The People's Will. Dates quoted are according to the Julian Calendar then in use in the Russian Empire.

\*

The historian Dr Sergei Podbolotov of the European University of St Petersburg was my guide to the city. I am grateful to him for his hospitality, good humour and the patience he showed in answering my many questions about nineteenth-century Russian customs and society. I discussed my idea for a book on The People's Will with my friend Kate Rea who also helped me with the initial research. I owe a great debt of gratitude to family and friends for their support and enthusiasm when for one reason or another mine began to falter. My agent, Julian Alexander, provided helpful advice on the story outline, so too my editor at John Murray, Kate Parkin, whose judgement and criticism were invaluable in helping me to shape the narrative. Caroline Westmore of Murrays eased its passage to publication. Responsibility for omissions – deliberate or not – and any mistakes there may be rests with me alone. I have taken liberties with the history but endeavoured to do justice to the spirit of the place and the times.

# Read more ...

## Andrew Williams

**THE INTERROGATOR**

**A war is fought on many fronts ...**

Spring, 1941. The armies of the Reich are masters of Europe. Britain stands alone while Hitler's submarines prey on the Atlantic convoys that are the country's only lifeline.

As the Blitz reduces Britain's cities to rubble and losses at sea mount, interrogator Lieutenant Douglas Lindsay becomes convinced Germany has broken British naval codes. But he's a lone voice, and his superiors don't trust him. In one last desperate throw of the dice, he sets a trap for his prize captive – the U-boat commander who sent his ship to its doom.

'A flair, grasp of detail and strong characterisation that reminds me of *Enigma*' *Daily Mail*

'One of the most gripping books I have read for some time' *The Times*

*Order your copy now by calling Bookpoint on 01235 827716 or visit your local bookshop quoting ISBN 978-0-7195-2381-6 www.johnmurray.co.uk*